36 Hours to Save the President

To Sue, with love and appreciation

PROLOGUE

A feeling of calm was beginning to descend over the White House. The Civil War had finally come to an end. Although Abraham Lincoln assuredly experienced a keen sense of relief in the knowledge that he no longer had to deal with the horrors of the war, the melancholy that was his constant companion since the death of his son, Willie, had not diminished. He also had to continually bolster his wife Mary's spirits whenever her thoughts turned to their dearly departed son.

However, all was not downcast within the Executive Mansion. With the winning of the war, Lincoln was now at the pinnacle of his power and popularity with the citizens of the North. There was not only the issuance of the Emancipation Proclamation, which he deemed his crowning achievement, but also the recent passage of the Thirteenth Amendment outlawing slavery throughout the land. Lincoln was so grateful and relieved that his hard work had led to its adoption, that he had taken the most unusual step of actually signing the amendment, something that was neither required nor customary. He could finally look forward to having the opportunity of being the president of all citizens of the United States.

His focus now turned to the people of the South and the monumental task of Reconstruction. The president wanted to assure the Southerners that he was worthy of their trust and that he intended to put into practice the words he had spoken at his second inauguration. It was his plan to exhibit no malice to the rebellious states and to welcome them back to the Union with charity so as to bind the nation's wounds and achieve a just and lasting peace.

The conclusion of the war also had a profound effect upon Mary Lincoln. She delighted in the fact that she could finally act as the type of White House hostess she had always envisioned. Now she could arrange for the lavish dinners and levees befitting her position, without fear of continued criticism from the newspapers that she was foolishly spending money on soirées while the boys on the battlefields went without blankets.

But most of all, Abraham and Mary could now look forward to spending their remaining years in peace and tranquility, including making plans for life after the presidency. They often spoke of travelling to California, Europe and the Holy Land and it appeared that they could now actually consider such plans.

However, neither could possibly imagine what lay in store for the president in just a few short days. The nefarious plot being hatched by John Wilkes Booth and his co-conspirators would be the death knell to the Lincolns' optimistic and longed-for goals. Now, only divine intervention or an inexplicable presence could alter the course of history and permit Abraham Lincoln to live through his second term.

AUNT ROSAMOND

It was Alex Linwood's fourteenth birthday. He had been looking forward to this day, as he always looked forward to birthdays. Best of all, it was his choice to decide where the family would go out for dinner that night. Did he crave Italian food, or was his heart set on a Mexican burrito? Or would it be more grown-up to suggest the local steakhouse?

This year his birthday dinner was going to be even more special than usual. His Great-Aunt Rosamond, whom he had heard of often but never met, was coming into town. Ever since he could remember, Alex had received a birthday card from her, always with a check enclosed: money that he was allowed to use for whatever he wanted. He had used the money in the past to buy comic books, baseball cards and his favorite *Mad* magazine. Alex wondered with anticipation what she might give him this time.

The morning began as most school days did. His mother, Beth, had come into his room to wake him and his 12-year-old brother, Jack, with whom he shared a room. And, as always, Jack jumped right out of bed, while Alex stayed put with the covers pulled up to his neck. He had always slept with the covers drawn up tightly against his chin, whether it was a cold winter night or a warm summer evening. Several minutes later, Beth entered the room again and pulled the covers down to his knees.

"Alex, we go through this every morning," she said with

mock consternation. "Get up now or you won't have time for breakfast!"

Alex grinned at her as he swung his feet out of bed and jumped onto the floor.

"Come here," said his mother, as she threw her arms around his shoulders and gave him a kiss on the cheek. "Happy birthday!"

"Oh, that's right," said Jack mockingly. "Today is your birthday. As if we didn't know. You've only been talking about it for the past week."

"Hurry up and get dressed and come down for breakfast," Beth called out as she made her way down to the kitchen. "I'm making your favorite—French toast."

"Did Dad leave for work already?" asked Alex, as he sat down to breakfast. His big sister Sally joined his brother and him at the table.

"Yes," replied Beth. "He had an early meeting, but he'll be home in time for your special dinner. And he will be bringing Aunt Rosamond with him. Have you decided where you want to go?"

"I want to go to Pasta di Roma and get angel hair pomodoro."

"What a surprise," said Sally, and they all laughed.

Alex and Jack grabbed their books and lunch and headed for the bus stop. The school bus soon arrived and they climbed aboard. Alex sat next to his friend Scott, while Jack proceeded to the rear where a group of his classmates was seated.

"Hey, Alex," said Scott. "Happy birthday! Did you get any of your gifts yet?"

"No, not until tonight. Plus, I may be getting something special. My great-aunt is coming for dinner and it will be really cool to finally meet her."

"You mean you've never met her before?"

"Nope. She lives almost across the country and is flying in to spend a week at our house. She's a lawyer." And then he added wistfully, "I wonder what she's going to bring me."

Before long, the bus pulled up to the school, the doors opened and one by one the children exited to make the trek across the athletic field to their classrooms.

Normally, Alex enjoyed being at school. He liked his teachers and, for the most part, did very well in his classes. He was not usually a clock-watcher, but this was not a normal day for him. Today each class seemed to last longer than the one before. At lunchtime, Alex sat with a group of friends at their usual table. Conversation centered on last night's TV shows and the upcoming baseball season. Alex was generally one of the more vocal participants, but today he simply ate his lunch in silence. No one really seemed to notice and that was fine with him. Soon the bell rang and it was off to PE.

Then, finally, sixth period came and all he had to endure was math class, where Mr. Morse was explaining some fine points in fractions. Several of his classmates had been called up to the blackboard to solve equations and he hoped that he would not be chosen today.

Alex looked again at the clock above the door: 2:45. All he had to do was lie low for another 15 minutes and the bell would release him from this interminable day. He turned his attention back to the students at the blackboard. Like everyone else, he was supposed to try to solve the written problems at his desk, but today he was just going through the motions.

He heard Mr. Morse tell the three students at the board that they had correctly solved the problems and could return to their seats. Three new equations appeared on the board and the teacher surveyed the class for the next three victims. "Not me, not me," thought Alex as hard as he could, but the teacher called out, "Next—Richard, Karen and Alex."

Oh, no! thought Alex, with a feeling of dread settling into the pit of his stomach. He rose slowly and made his way to the front of the classroom. Just as he was about to pick up the chalk, he heard the most wonderful sound imaginable: the 3 o'clock bell pealed loud and strong.

"OK students," said Mr. Morse, "That's it for today. I will see you all on Monday. Have a nice weekend."

Alex walked as fast as he could out of the classroom and to his locker. He threw his books in, grabbed his jacket and slammed the door shut. Turning quickly, he almost ran into Mrs. Lefferts, his guidance counselor. "Hey, slow down there Alex," she said with a mock stern face. "I know it's the weekend, but let's watch where we're going."

"Sorry, Mrs. Lefferts." Alex walked slowly toward the door, but once outside, he hurried as fast as he could to where the school buses were lined up. He climbed aboard quickly and then realized that he had rushed there for nothing. The bus still had to wait for the other students and, even though it was Friday, many of them were not nearly as anxious as he was.

Finally, after what seemed like forever, the bus was full and the driver eased away from the curb and into traffic.

After about thirty minutes, the bus came to Alex's stop. He, Jack and a few other students got off and Alex and Jack walked toward their house. As they got closer, they saw their father's car in the driveway.

"Hey," exclaimed Alex. "Dad is home early. I wonder if Aunt Rosamond is here, too."

The two boys ran up to the front porch, leapt up the steps and threw open the front door. "We're home," Alex called.

"I can see that," replied his father, Ralph. "Happy birthday, son."

"Thanks, Dad."

"Boys," Ralph said to Alex and Jack. "There is someone I want you to meet. This is your Great-Aunt Rosamond."

A medium-built woman with brown hair was seated upon the living room sofa. She wore black slacks, a white button-down blouse and a dark, waist-length jacket. She studied the boys with her deep brown eyes, but, as she rose to her feet, she smiled warmly. "Hello, boys. I have been anxiously waiting to meet both of you. Here, come and give me a hug."

The boys slowly walked to her and each was affectionately embraced. Although this was indeed the first time they had ever laid eyes upon Aunt Rosamond, there was something strangely familiar about her.

"Well," she said, looking at Alex. "Today is a very special day, isn't it? Happy birthday, dear."

"Thank you," replied Alex. "Did you bring me anything?"

Jack laughed. Ralph merely shook his head. "Alex!" said his mother in her stern, no-nonsense voice. "What kind of a thing is that to ask?" Turning to the older woman she said, "Oh, Aunt Rosamond, I am so sorry—and so embarrassed. Alex," she said in the most suggestive of voices possible, "don't you want to wait until we get back from dinner to see what Aunt Rosamond got for you? You can open your gift then."

"Aw, Mom!" This was the only response Alex could muster.

Turning to Beth, Aunt Rosamond said, "I don't mind giving Alex his gift now, if it's all right with you."

"Well, fine." Beth looked again at Alex. "But I think you owe Aunt Rosamond an apology."

Aunt Rosamond laughed gently. "No need to apologize. Nothing wrong with his being a little over-anxious. Alex, if you wait here a minute, I will be right back."

She disappeared into the guest bedroom and returned with a parcel wrapped in blue-and-white paper.

"Here you are, dear. I hope you will thoroughly enjoy this and perhaps even be inspired by it."

Alex was not sure what she meant and was very curious to see what was hidden by the wrapping paper.

"Read the card first," cautioned his mother.

He tore open the envelope and scanned the card as if to take in its words, although he did not fool anyone.

"Very nice," Alex said, as he unwrapped the gift.

It was a book. A book by Carl Sandburg, entitled, *Abraham Lincoln: The Prairie and War Years*. Inside, it was inscribed, "To Alex with love on his 14th birthday. Aunt Rosamond."

Just a book? His hopes of going to the store with cash in hand to buy whatever he wanted were dashed.

As Alex cradled the book and began thumbing through its 700 pages, he couldn't hide his disappointment. Aunt Rosamond seemed to sense his discontent. "Alex," his aunt said gently, "Mr. Lincoln was not only our greatest president, but one of the greatest Americans who ever lived. And Carl Sandburg is one of the best authors of all time. It is my hope that this book will encourage you to want to know more about Lincoln and come to admire him, as I do."

"Thank you, Aunt Rosamond," replied Alex, trying to muster as much sincerity as possible. "I will begin reading it this weekend."

Unbeknownst to Alex, this gift would be only the first of many books on Abraham Lincoln to find its way into his personal library.

Soon the family was assembled and they set out for the restaurant.

ALEX LINWOOD

Over the years, Alex Linwood developed an appreciation, even a fondness, for Abraham Lincoln. The book given to him by his Aunt Rosamond began a quest to learn as much as he could about the president. There was always a book on his bedside table and, more often than not, Abraham Lincoln was the subject.

Alex had read several books about Lincoln's political philosophies, but found these to be too dry for his taste. He much preferred stories about Lincoln's life, which also included discussions about Lincoln's political point of view.

At first, Alex enjoyed trips to the public library, but eventually he decided to build a collection of his own by browsing in local bookstores for paperbacks he could afford. Alex began his modest library with these soft-covered books, some of which he read several times.

He was interested in every facet of Lincoln's life, including what little was known of his childhood. New Salem, Illinois, the small rural village where he spent his formative years, held great fascination for Alex. In the books that covered this period, Alex learned about Lincoln's foray into the world of business as part-owner of a general store. He read with great interest about Lincoln's first trip down the Mississippi River to deliver goods to New Orleans, culminating in his initial exposure to the horrors of slavery. Having personally witnessed black men and women being transported in chains, and hearing their anguished cries at a slave auction, Lincoln developed a deep hatred for what was often referred to as that "peculiar institution." This trip began a lifelong desire to do what he could to put an end to slavery.

Alex admired Lincoln's continual quest for knowledge and the fact that he could often be found sitting under a tree, reading—or re-reading—one of his few precious tomes. His father, Thomas Lincoln, frowned upon this activity, being of the opinion that farming was the way his son should be spending his time. This however, did not dissuade Lincoln from reading at every possible opportunity.

There was an incident in Lincoln's early life that Alex found particularly interesting. During the Black Hawk War in 1832, Lincoln was one of many locals to volunteer for the Illinois militia. When the men were sworn in, the first order of business was the election of a company commander. Many of the men were friends of his from New Salem, and as a result, Lincoln was elected captain. He would later say that this was his most satisfying win, as it marked the only time in his political career that he was elected directly by the people.

One story in particular about Lincoln's experience in the Black Hawk War had always stuck with Alex. Although he and his men never saw any action, Lincoln was still required to put them through their daily drills. One day, the men were marching in formation, four abreast, when they came to a fence blocking their way. Lincoln saw that there was a narrow break in the fence, which would only allow them to pass through one at a time. The problem was that he had forgotten the command that would direct them to form a single-file line so they could march between the fence posts. Thinking quickly, he instructed his men to halt, issued an order that the Company was dismissed, and told them to immediately reassemble their ranks and fall in on the other side of the fence.

Alex learned that during his stint as postmaster in New Salem, Lincoln used to read all the newspapers delivered to the post office. This sparked his interest in politics, beginning at the local level in Sangamon County. While he lost the first race he entered, the second attempt proved much more successful. Lincoln won a seat in the Illinois House of Representatives. His love of politics would remain ingrained for the rest of his life.

Many books described how Lincoln decided to study the law and, upon moving to Springfield, pursued this goal by working in the law office of John Todd Stuart, cousin to Lincoln's future wife. After about a year of preparation, he was admitted to the Illinois State Bar.

As time went by, Alex's personal library of Lincoln books steadily grew. He also purchased several "coffee table" books, including one that featured photographs of Lincoln taken throughout his lifetime and another depicting reproductions of famous documents written in Lincoln's own hand. Alex enjoyed nothing more than repeatedly thumbing through these visually appealing volumes. There were also DVDs of programs that he saw on television, which he made a part of his Lincoln library.

Alex's friends were acutely aware of his interest in Lincoln, so much so that on his birthday, he often received cards with Lincoln's face gracing the cover. Then, for a milestone birthday, his wife, Sarah, hit upon a wonderful idea: a party with Lincoln as the main theme. The invitation was based upon the Gettysburg Address, the cake had a silhouette of Lincoln's profile on it and a special appearance was made by a Lincoln impersonator.

Alex also had some whimsical keepsakes including a bobblehead of Lincoln, adorned in his finest black suit and posed as though making a speech. There was also the box of Lincoln Band-Aids that Alex found in a novelty store, each individually wrapped bandage depicting a full-length caricature of the president; the box, sporting a portrait of Lincoln, contained the words, "I will heal your wound as I healed a nation."

Alex looked forward to emails from Barnes & Noble alerting him that a new Lincoln book had been published. With each new purchase, Sarah would tease him, reminding Alex that Lincoln dies at the end, with Alex's reply always being, "No, he can't. Not in this one too." But Sarah never did try to discourage him from building his Lincoln book collection because he enjoyed it so much.

As the years passed, Alex's interest in Mr. Lincoln never waned.

35 YEARS LATER

Alex Linwood walked up to the counter at Barnes & Noble with his latest purchase to add to his Lincoln library. He presented his member card and placed on the counter Doris Kearns Goodwin's *Team of Rivals*—his 81st book about the president. They ran the gamut from the well-known biographies of Mr. Lincoln by David Herbert Donald, Michael Burlingame, Harold Holzer and Ronald C. White, to oversized coffee table books such as, *Lincoln, Life Size*, by the Kunhardts: Philip, Peter and Peter, Jr., and *In Lincoln's Hand*, a compilations of Lincoln's own writings edited by Joshua Shenk. He also, of course, owned a copy of Roy Basler's *Complete Works of Abraham Lincoln*, which contained speeches and letters from his earliest days as an Illinois state legislator through his time as president.

His extensive collection also included books specific to the assassination, such as the seminal work *The Day Lincoln Was Shot* by Jim Bishop, *Manhunt* by James L. Swanson and *American Brutus: John Wilkes Booth and the Lincoln Conspiracies* by Michael W. Kauffman. One of the more interesting lesser-known works was one he went through quite often: *Lincoln Day by Day*, a chronology of virtually every day of Lincoln's life from birth to death, edited by Earl Schenck Miers and C. Percy Powell.

Alex often chuckled to himself, knowing that he had a long way to go to collect the over 15,000 books written about

Mr. Lincoln. In fact, the only person about whom more b\
have been written is Jesus Christ.

After paying for the book, Alex drove home. It was a beautiful fall day in Los Angeles and Alex went out to the patio to enjoy Ms. Goodwin's tale of Lincoln and his cabinet.

Alex and Sarah lived in a three-bedroom home in Sherman Oaks. They had been introduced by mutual friends and realized from the start that they had a great deal in common and wanted to get to know each other better. Now they had been happily married for 26 years, sharing—among many other things—a common interest in American history.

The couple had two children, both of whom were in college. Their older son, George, was a junior at Arizona State University and their younger son, Bradley, was a freshman at Berkeley. After being a stay-at-home mom for many years, Sarah had gone back to work as an Executive Assistant at a property management company.

Alex and his partner, Mark Raymond, had a successful dental practice in Encino. They had been in practice for over 20 years and were close friends as well as business associates. Each was almost excruciatingly aware of the other's interests outside of the office. Alex was smitten by golf and was part of a foursome that teed it up at a variety of courses almost every Saturday. Mark played on occasion, but did not share Alex's intense interest in the game. Mark was also keenly aware of Alex's fondness for Abraham Lincoln and happily tolerated such things as the painting "The Peacemakers" by George P.A. Healy that hung in the reception room.

In turn, Alex respected Mark's passion for fishing, a sport about which Alex knew next to nothing. Mark could not understand why being on a boat in the middle of a lake or several miles off the Santa Barbara coast, or wading hip-deep in a freshwater stream, held no fascination for Alex. Just as Alex listened to Mark describe the ones he caught as well as the ones that got away, Mark humored Alex when he described pulling off a shot that "even a pro would be proud of."

The one thing the partners did agree on was the need to allow each other vacation time to pursue their individual interests. While Mark had a few fishing excursions lined up, Alex was going to do something different in the coming year. He could not wait until the next day, when he would see Mark at the office and, over their daily lunch, tell him about the plans.

But first, he was going to sit down with Sarah and tell her what he wanted to do after years of contemplation. Sarah had been out running errands and when he heard her car pull into the driveway, he put down his book and went inside. She came in carrying two Macy's shopping bags.

"Hi, honey, how are you?" asked Sarah. "I did some major damage," she chuckled. "There are two more bags in the car. Could you get them for me?"

"Sure. Anything for me?" Alex asked his wife with the feigned anticipation of a child.

"You didn't ask for anything. But, I am still looking for that driver with a 10½-inch shaft that you want!" They both laughed: Alex had told her a couple of years ago that he wanted a new Callaway driver with a 10½-degree loft. Sarah, not a golfer, had mistakenly repeated that she would buy him a new driver with a 10½-inch shaft for his birthday and this malapropism became an inside joke.

Walking out to the Highlander parked in the driveway, Alex

took out a bag from one of his favorite stores, Designer Shoe Warehouse, and another from Sarah's favorite, Chico's. Alex had asked her so many times to say hello to Groucho and Harpo when she was in Chico's that she now basically ignored the pun.

He brought in the bags, set them down on a landing under the stairs, and told Sarah there was something that he wanted to talk to her about. "Let's go into the living room," he suggested. "We hardly ever sit in there."

"What's up? Everything okay?" asked Sarah as she took a seat on the couch.

"Of course," replied Alex settling into one of the wingback chairs opposite her. "What I want to talk to you about—well, there are two places that I really want to visit and they of course both deal with—"

"Lincoln." They uttered the word in unison. Sarah smiled, shook her head and rolled her eyes.

"Um, yeah," said Alex. "I want to go to Springfield, Illinois, to visit where Lincoln lived and worked and where he is buried. Then I want to take a second trip to Washington, D.C., to visit the Capitol, Ford's Theatre and the Lincoln Memorial. I was thinking of going to Springfield sometime in March and D.C. maybe in mid-April. Of course, I need to clear these dates with Mark."

"I think that's a great idea," Sarah said. "You have been talking long enough about going to both of those cities." After a slight pause, she continued. "Just one thing. I think you should go alone. I know I would find these places interesting, but I would not be as fascinated as you. And I can only imagine myself waiting for you while you spend an hour looking at things that might take me ten minutes."

"Are you sure?" asked Alex somewhat surprised. Then a new thought popped into his head. "You know, I actually kind of agree with you. You wouldn't mind if I went alone?"

"Not at all. These are places you have always wanted to go, and truthfully, I think you would enjoy your trip much more if it was just you."

"Thank you, dear." He leaned over and gave her a kiss. "After I talk to Mark tomorrow, I'll start making plans. Now, how about a glass of wine while we talk about where I can take you for dinner?"

On Monday morning, Alex got to the office just before 8 o'clock. He asked Sonya, the office manager, about the day's schedule.

"You have an eight-thirty with Mr. Thompson to put in his permanent crown and then Karen Simpson's two fillings at ten."

"That sounds fine," Alex replied, just as the door to the doctors' inner office opened and Mark walked in.

"Good morning, all," said Mark. His salutation was returned by Alex and Sonya. "What have I got scheduled this morning?"

"While you two go over that," said Alex, "I'm going to get the room ready for my first appointment. Oh, Mark, are you free for lunch twelve-thirtyish?"

"Sure, that should work. How about we just walk down the street to the deli?"

"Fine," said Alex as he left the room.

After the two men finished seeing their morning patients, they met at the door leading from the inner office to the reception room.

"Ready to go?" asked Mark.

"All set," replied Alex. They exited their fifth-floor suite and walked to the elevator. Mark pushed the call button and in less than a minute the bell tone sounded and the doors slid open. The car was filled with people. Mark and Alex entered and both turned to face the closing doors. Then all eyes within the car focused on the number displayed above the door. As it descended, Mark turned his head to look at Alex and in his expert, deadpan delivery, said: "Sir, I would appreciate it if you would keep your hands to yourself!"

Alex could feel his ears getting warm and was sure they turned red. Some of the people in the elevator chuckled, while others looked at them somewhat nervously. Alex, ordinarily quick with a comeback, was absolutely miffed and could not think of a thing to say. Then he thought it was best to say nothing at all and there was an awkward silence during the remainder of the ride.

When the doors opened, Alex could not get out of the car fast enough. After the two men took several steps toward the building exit, Alex finally had the opportunity to retort.

"You son of a bitch!" he said with a big smile. "What the hell was that?"

Mark good-naturedly slapped Alex on the back. "Someone recently did that to me, so I had to pay it forward. Now it's your turn to use it on some poor unsuspecting schmuck."

The two of them laughed and chatted amiably as they walked the three blocks to the deli. Once seated they each ordered iced tea and a salad.

"So," said Mark. "Do you have any vacation plans for next year?"

"I do," Alex replied, "and I wanted to clear dates with you.

This may sound strange, but I am planning on going to Springfield, Illinois, in a couple of months and then to Washington, D.C., in the spring."

"Hmm. Sounds like a couple of Lincoln-themed trips."

"Pretty astute of you."

"You don't have to be Sherlock Holmes to figure that one out. They're not exactly my cup of tea, but I can see how you would certainly find those places interesting."

"Yeah, there's quite a bit to see in both places."

"And Sarah wants to go with you?" asked Mark, a hint of sarcasm in his voice.

"No, actually, she is the one who suggested that I go by myself. She said I would have a better time doing it that way."

"Your wife is very smart—and very understanding. Just watch out for the payback," he added with a laugh.

"Don't I know it! So, how about you?"

"Well, I don't have a date set yet, but I'm planning on going to Alaska for some salmon fishing. Like your Lincoln trip, this is something I've always wanted to do." As Mark had been divorced from Margaret for nearly six years, he could plan his vacations freely, especially his fishing trips.

The server brought their salads and refilled their drinks and the two of them enjoyed each other's company as they ate. Once they finished and the plates were cleared, they took the check to the register and split it, as they always did. Then Alex said, "Back to the office. But we're taking separate elevators!"

Mark laughed and they walked the three blocks to their office building, chatting about the Dodgers' chances in the upcoming season.

SPRINGFIELD, ILLINOIS
PRESENT-DAY

FIRST DAY

A t 8:30 p.m., Alex Linwood exited the plane shortly after it taxied to a stop at the Abraham Lincoln Capital Airport in Springfield, Illinois. He was finally in Springfield to visit the historic locations associated with the twenty-four years, from 1837 to 1861, when Lincoln lived and practiced law in the capital of Illinois. After entering the terminal, he made his way to the car rental counter to pick up the vehicle he had reserved. He then walked to the parking lot where he retrieved the Ford Fusion he would use while in the city.

Hotel reservations had been made at the President Abraham Lincoln Springfield, a property chosen for its location at 701 East Adams Street, only three blocks from the Lincoln Home Historic Site. This would be Alex's initial stop the next morning and the beginning of a full day exploring the buildings where Lincoln lived, worked and was ultimately laid to rest.

Alex tossed his suitcase into the trunk of the car. In his excitement for this trip, he had already mapped out his route at home using MapQuest and now pulled out the written directions. Easing the car out of the airport parking lot, he made his way to the J. David Jones Parkway. As he drove, he took in the sights of this quaint Midwestern city. The street lamps revealed a definite lack of any buildings over five stories tall outside the downtown area, the ultimate destination. However, he did see one structure of which he made a mental note. Passing the Cozy Dog, he recalled seeing a segment about this establishment on the Food Network. It was deemed to be the restaurant where the corn dog was invented and he decided he'd have to stop there for a meal. He soon arrived at the hotel.

After parking his car, Alex entered the hotel and checked in. The front desk clerk, a pleasant gentleman in his early sixties, handed him his room key, along with a brochure with suggestions for sights to see while visiting Springfield. Alex smiled to himself, for his suitcase had pages of information about locales to be visited, courtesy of the Internet. It was after 10 p.m. when he opened the door to his room, and all he wanted to do was take a shower and get into bed. He set the automated hotel wake-up service for a 7 a.m. call, turned out the light, pulled the covers up to his chin and was soon asleep.

The hotel phone rang at precisely the pre-arranged time. Alex picked up the receiver and was greeted by a recording wishing him a good morning and advising that the weather forecast for the day was sunshine and 73 degrees. He stretched, got out of bed and proceeded to get ready for his first day of exploring.

Alex grabbed his satchel containing the maps and other information he would need for the day of sightseeing. Throwing the strap over his shoulder, he left his room. Upon entering the elevator, a couple was chatting. Pleasantries were exchanged and as they descended Alex listened silently while the couple continued their conversation, curious about the sites they were intent on seeing. When the doors opened onto the lobby, Alex exited behind the couple. He walked over to the hotel's convenience mart and bought a copy of the local newspaper, the *State Journal Register*. Then he headed for Lindsay's Restaurant.

A young lady in a white shirt and black slacks escorted him to a table. After reviewing the menu, Alex ordered coffee along with scrambled eggs, bacon, an English muffin and fruit. When he was through he charged the breakfast to his room and headed out to begin his day.

It was a beautiful morning and his clothing choice of jeans and a short-sleeved polo shirt was perfect. Removing his sunglasses from his satchel, Alex proceeded down 9th Street.

In a scant few minutes, Alex reached the Visitors' Center adjacent to the several square blocks comprising the Lincoln Home Historic Site and what is known as "Mr. Lincoln's Neighborhood." In the Visitors' Center, he went up to a counter, anticipating having to purchase a ticket for a tour of the home. He was somewhat surprised to hear that, while there was no charge, a time-designated ticket was required, indicating the time that his tour, led by a park ranger, would begin. The young woman at the counter gave him a ticket with the time of 10:30 stamped on it. Alex looked at his watch and saw that it was only 9:45.

"What can I do until the tour begins?" he asked.

"Well," she began, "there's a film you can watch about the properties adjacent to the Lincoln home, or you can walk on down to Jackson Street using the gravel path to 8th, where the Lincoln home and the other buildings are located. You certainly have time to stroll along 8th and view what we call the historic neighborhood. But be sure to keep an eye on the time, as you must meet your guide by the bench directly across from the Lincoln home a few minutes before ten-thirty. And be sure to come back here and visit our gift shop before you leave."

"Thank you," Alex replied and, ticket in hand, he walked

out of the building and proceeded toward Jackson Street, making his way toward the house. The entire area encompassing Mr. Lincoln's Neighborhood was blocked off to automobile traffic and was the sole province of pedestrians viewing the original and restored buildings.

Suddenly, Alex stopped in his tracks. There it was, in front of him: the structure the Lincolns had called home between 1844 and their departure for Washington City in 1861. Alex was momentarily transfixed. He had read about the home and seen pictures of it, but it was another thing altogether to be standing only yards away. He was struck by the tan building, its windows framed by green shutters, and by the front porch, the location of the famous photograph of Mr. Lincoln surrounded by a throng of people congratulating him after his nomination for president by the Republican Party. He tried to imagine himself as one of those revelers standing there more than 150 years ago.

Alex strolled past the house and began to look at some of the other buildings that made up the neighborhood. Each one had a mounted placard out front with a brief description of its history and significance. After reaching the end of the block, he turned around and headed back toward the Lincolns' house. When he glanced at his watch he saw that the time was 10:18, so he proceeded back to the corner of 8th and Jackson and the bench where he would meet up with the National Park Service Ranger who would be conducting the tour.

There were already seven people gathered around the tour leader and Alex ambled up to join them. The ranger began, "Good morning to you all. This is the 10:30 tour. My name is Richard and I'll be your guide as we go through the Lincoln

Home Historic Site. Before we go on, let's find out how far each of you has traveled to be here today."

Each of them responded when pointed to, announcing they had come from New York, St. Louis, Chicago and Los Angeles. Richard continued, "Now before we enter the house, some simple rules. Be sure to remain on the carpet runners and please do not touch any of the items on display. Photographs are permitted, but no flash photography. And, above all, if you have any questions or historical information that you would like to share with the group, do speak up. Now, please follow me."

The group walked toward the house and stopped at the gate fronting the cement steps that led up to the front door. Richard began his presentation:

"This is the only home that Mary and Abraham Lincoln ever owned. They bought it in 1844 from the Reverend Charles Dresser, the man who had actually married the couple two years earlier. They paid the sum of $1,500 for the property. When originally purchased by the Lincolns, it was a one-and-one-half-story cottage. Over the years, work was done to enlarge the house as their family grew, with the greatest change coming in 1855 when the second story was added. Most of the construction on the house was overseen by Mary Lincoln and was done while Mr. Lincoln was away, riding the 8th Judicial Circuit and practicing law. Now, look carefully at the front door. You will notice there is no house number. In those days, each house was identified by its owner, not by an address. Hence the plate affixed to the door inscribed 'A. Lincoln.'"

As Alex was taking pictures of the front of the house, Richard began to walk toward the front steps. "Now if you will follow me inside. And please, watch your step."

Richard led the group through the house. He pointed out the parlor at the front of the ground floor, where Lincoln entertained political guests and where he was notified that the Republican National Convention meeting in Chicago had nominated him for president. On the opposite side was the family living area, where the boys played. It was not unusual for Lincoln to get down on the floor and romp around with them. Next the group climbed the stairs to see the bedrooms. Abraham and Mary Lincoln had separate bedrooms, which was the common practice of the upper middle class. Richard pointed out a shaving kit and mirror sitting upon a bureau in Lincoln's bedroom that had actually been used by him. They walked through Mary's room and past the bedroom that had been shared by Willie and Tad. There was no particular room for Robert Lincoln as, by this time, Robert was away at school. They then peered into a small servant's room. Next, it was back down the stairs to the kitchen, where it was pointed out that the iron stove in the corner was original to the house. When the tour was over, the group left the house through a door to the backyard, where the privy still stood.

All during the tour, Alex tried to visualize Lincoln and his family in the house as they went about their daily lives. As he snapped pictures of the various rooms, he conjured images of the eventful meeting in 1860 when a group of men who had travelled from Chicago knocked on the door and, upon being ushered in, conveyed to Lincoln that he was now a candidate for president of the United States. Alex grinned as he recalled the stories of the Lincolns' tumultuous marriage and an incident when Mary Lincoln actually chased the future president out of the house brandishing a carving knife. Alex experienced a very

special and unique feeling as he walked through the same structure where Abraham Lincoln had spent so many years.

• • •

After thanking Richard for the tour, Alex checked the map for
directions to his next destination: the Great Western Railroad
Depot, now known as the Lincoln Depot, located at the corner
of 10th and Monroe. After proceeding only two blocks, he
arrived at the depot.

The ground floor of the building remained configured just
as the station might have looked in 1861. There was a blackboard with a train schedule attached to the wall, a ticket booth
and a waiting room. Upstairs, there were now exhibits reflecting
Lincoln's life in Springfield and a continuously running twenty-
minute film depicting his inaugural journey from Springfield
to Washington City.

However, it is what was said there, on a cold, rainy morning
on February 11, 1861, that will keep this building forever alive
in the Lincoln lore. Alex read a description of what transpired
on this very spot so many years before. A group of about a thousand friends and colleagues jammed the courtyard just outside
the station to see the great man off. After participating in a
makeshift receiving line inside the depot and shaking hands
with many of the well-wishers, the train to transport the presi-
dent-elect to the nation's capital pulled into the station. Mr.
Lincoln climbed the metal steps and paused at the rear of the
train, taking one last, long look at the city and its residents that
had meant so much to him.

Alex walked out of the depot and stood alongside the

parallel-running track, upon which had once stood the locomotive and several cars destined for Washington. He could almost hear the gentle puffing of the steam engine as it idled, awaiting the boarding of the passengers it would be entrusted to safely transport. He envisioned Lincoln standing on the rear platform of the train, slowly and mournfully telling the crowd what was in his heart. Recollecting Lincoln's Farewell Address to the citizens of Springfield always brought a lump to Alex's throat and he could only imagine the effect it had upon those who actually heard the words firsthand. In Alex's mind, the throng became very quiet, as Lincoln addressed them one last time:

> My friends, no one, not in my situation, can appreciate my feeling of sadness at this parting. To this place and the kindness of these people, I owe everything. Here I have lived a quarter of a century and have passed from a young to an old man. Here my children have been born and one is buried. I now leave, not knowing when, or whether ever, I may return, with a task before me greater than that which rested upon Washington. Without the assistance of that Divine Being, whoever attended him, I cannot succeed. With that assistance I cannot fail. Trusting in Him, who can go with me and remain with you and be everywhere for good, let us confidently hope that all will yet be well. To His care commending you, as I hope in your prayers you will commend me, I bid you an affectionate farewell.

Alex photographed the building from several vantage points. Then he stood for a moment and, before turning away, thought somewhat mournfully, "I wish I could have been there."

• • •

After one last lingering scan of the building, Alex turned and headed north on 9th Street for half a block before turning left on Monroe. The day was getting warmer and he was glad that he had left his jacket in the hotel room. As he walked, several tourists with maps in their hands and cameras draped around their necks passed him on their way toward the railroad station.

I wonder what goes through their minds as they view these sights, Alex mused. *Do they just see this as another historical locale to explore and, once all has been seen, forget about it? Or will these spots register something lasting within them, to be drawn upon later when they are back at home?* He hoped that some type of lasting impression would be made, especially with the children and teenagers walking beside their parents.

Alex reflected for a moment about how, when thinking about the man, he always referred to him as "Mr. Lincoln." Not just Lincoln, or Abe, or Honest Abe, or any of the other popular sobriquets, but rather, always, as "Mr. Lincoln." He truthfully could not think of why this was the case, other than it always seemed to be the right thing to do.

Looking at his own visitors' map, he smiled to himself as he silently read off the names of the streets that made up Mr. Lincoln's Neighborhood. The streets were named for the likes of Washington, Adams, Jefferson, Madison, Monroe and Jackson. Strange, he thought, how there was clearly one name glaringly missing.

Alex came across a small restaurant with a chalkboard out front advertising various sandwiches. He entered and had a casual lunch before continuing on to the next site.

Upon reaching 6th Street, he stopped to take in the view of the Old State Capitol and to snap several photographs. He could imagine the hustle and bustle about the building in the 1850s as lawyers, legislators, clerks and residents made their way in and out of the building to conduct whatever business was of importance to them. Alex thought about how Lincoln was instrumental in the 1837 negotiations that had culminated in the Illinois state capital being moved from the town of Vandalia to Lincoln's home city of Springfield.

Alex passed through the opening in the cast-iron gate and up the walkway toward the steps. Looking up at the two-story building, he focused on the dome perched atop a windowed cupola. Upon entering he took a brochure and quickly read it over before beginning to explore the interior rooms. The brochure explained that this building was actually a re-creation of the original Capitol building, built so as to appear as it did during Lincoln's time. Although he knew the room he most wanted to see was upstairs, Alex permitted himself to first look at the ground floor offices.

Peeking into the Auditor's Office, the informational placard said that this was where local finances were handled. Alex next stopped in front of the entrance to the office of the secretary of state and peered at the furnishings arranged as if the secretary himself had just left for the evening. The following room was the Law Library, which Alex learned was used as an informal meeting room as well as a repository for books. He then encountered the room where the Supreme Court had sat, which was punctuated by an ornate wood carved railing separating the justices from the lawyers appearing before them. A placard described how Lincoln and his law partner, William Herndon, had a large appellate practice and that Lincoln therefore often appeared in this very room to plead his clients' cases before the justices.

Alex then moved to the base of the impressive stairway leading to the second floor, where the room that held the most fascination for him was situated. Slowly, he climbed the stairs, looking around to take in the aura of his surroundings. He then strode directly toward the Representatives' Hall. It was in this room that the legislators of the day met to argue political points of view, make deals and give speeches whose contents were beneficial to either the state as a whole, or, as on most occasions, to the town each man represented.

As he stood just behind the last row of desks at the point beyond which visitors were not allowed to pass, Alex scanned the room with care, looking for the particular artifact that all who enter seek out. His gaze came to a stop at a desk in the second row, just to the left of the center of the room. There, silently occupying the desk and positioned so that the wide brim faced the ceiling, sat a stovepipe hat. This is purported to be the location of the desk that Lincoln occupied when he presented his "House Divided" speech. The words echoed in Alex's mind: *A house divided against itself cannot stand. I believe this government cannot endure, permanently half slave and half free . . . It will become all one thing or all the other.*

Alex was awestruck standing where such a monumental event took place over 150 years ago. He paused for a few more moments, made an about-face turn and exited the room.

The last room he spent any time looking into was the one known then as the Governor's Reception Room. It was here, after Lincoln's 1860 nomination as the Republican candidate for president, that he greeted both well-wishers and office seekers. Since Lincoln's own law office was too small to accommodate all those who wanted to meet with him, the governor offered the use of this room to serve Lincoln's needs.

Alex left the Capitol Building, glanced at his watch and saw that it was almost 4:30. He had covered quite a bit of ground and decided to finish his explorations during the second and final day of his visit. Alex made his way back to the hotel's parking lot and, as previously intended, drove to the Cozy Dog for dinner. Once inside and while waiting in line to order, Alex reviewed the menu. When it was his turn, he stepped up to the counter and ordered two Cozy Dogs, a large order of fries and a medium diet soda. Getting the order "to go," Alex returned to his car and made his way back to the President Abraham Lincoln Hotel.

In his room, he turned on the Golf Channel and watched it while he enjoyed his hot dogs. When he had finished eating, he called Sarah to tell her about his day. She could hear in his voice that this trip and the sites he had seen truly had made an impression. After a ten-minute conversation, they said good night.

Alex watched some more television, read for a while and then turned out the light for the evening.

SPRINGFIELD, ILLINOIS
PRESENT-DAY

SECOND DAY

Alex's second morning in Springfield was not much different from the first. He showered, got dressed and went down for breakfast. After finishing his meal and gathering his belongings, he made his way out to the parking lot. There were three stops on today's agenda. Alex drove downtown and parked in a lot near the Old State Capitol. This time, however, he made his way to the structure directly across the street—the three-story Tinsley Building. Alex went in through the side door, where bold lettering read "LINCOLN–HERNDON LAW OFFICES."

The famous building actually housed three separate venues of historical interest. On the first floor was the post office, where people would come to send mail, as well as pick up letters and packages because there were no home or business deliveries. Alex learned that, before 1845, the cost of mailing a letter was dependent upon the number of pages it contained. To mail a single sheet, the sender would fold it in half and the postmaster would charge accordingly. This procedure was changed in 1845, when the amount of postage due was based on the weight of the mailing. Thus, a single posting was now deemed to be anything weighing less than a half an ounce. With this modification, envelopes could now be used and the correspondent's privacy was more secure.

Alex next made his way to the second floor of the building. In Lincoln's time, this was home to the United States Federal District Court for Illinois and, when it was in town, the 7th United States Circuit Court. It had been restored in such detail that Mr. Lincoln would certainly have recognized the room upon entering.

Then it was up one more flight of stairs to the small office where Abraham Lincoln and William Herndon practiced as law partners from 1844 to 1861. Prior to becoming a lawyer, Herndon worked in the store of Joshua Speed, Lincoln's best friend in Springfield, while he was studying and reading the law. In 1844, Herndon was admitted to the bar and soon after, when the partnership between Steven Logan and Abraham Lincoln dissolved, Lincoln asked his young associate to become his junior partner.

Lincoln always addressed Herndon as "Billy," but Herndon in return addressed his senior partner only as "Mr. Lincoln." The two men became very close, both professionally and as friends. However, Mary Lincoln did not like Herndon and never invited him to the Lincolns' home in all the years the two men worked together. Lincoln and Herndon developed one of the most successful legal practices in Springfield and remained active partners until Lincoln was elected president.

The story goes that, upon Lincoln's election to the presidency, Herndon inquired as to whether this meant that their partnership was over. Lincoln made it clear to Herndon that this change in his own circumstance would not affect the two of them. He advised Herndon to keep their firm's sign-board hanging out and made a promise that, if he returned to Springfield alive, "We'll go right on practicing law as if nothing had ever happened." Despite Lincoln's absence from Springfield and the turns that history took, Herndon considered "Mr. Lincoln" to be his law partner until April 15, 1865.

Entering the third-floor offices, Alex saw a long table, covered with green felt, running from about midway in the room toward the window. Just in front of the window, it made a "T" with another table positioned parallel to the window wall. Situated on the table were books, legal documents, inkwells and candles, so that it appeared just as it was when the two men were present and working. Seeing a sofa off to the side, Alex recalled reading about how Lincoln would often stretch out on it to think, or to talk with Herndon about the legal cases at hand. The scene also brought to mind stories about Lincoln's young boys, Willie and Tad, who would run amok in the room when they visited, much to Herndon's consternation. The boys tossed papers and even knocked over inkwells, without ever raising the ire of their father.

The clock on the wall is a replica of the one that hung in that very spot in Lincoln's day, which was ordered from a factory in New Haven, Connecticut, in about 1850. The original still exists, now housed in the Abraham Lincoln Presidential Library and Museum and, to this day, still keeps accurate time. The clock mechanism needed daily winding and there is a worn spot where the winder's knuckles rubbed against the housing while performing this task.

Alex stood transfixed at the foot of the table and tried to transport himself back in time, to when the partners were there together. He tried to imagine Lincoln slapping his knee as he was telling one of his famous stories, while Herndon would do his best to complete whatever legal document he was tasked with drafting. Alex knew that Lincoln often went through mood swings, from happy and upbeat to sad and sullen. No matter what his state of mind, when he was there in the office, Lincoln never tried to mask his true feelings from his friend Billy.

• • •

Alex's next stop was the Abraham Lincoln Presidential Library and Museum. He was looking forward to seeing Mr. Lincoln's personal items that were on display, along with documents written in his own hand. Alex walked the short distance to the museum. Just past the entrance lobby is a façade of the front of the White House, which is positioned behind mannequins representing Mr. and Mrs. Lincoln and their three boys, Robert, Willie and Tad. Like everyone else, Alex had to have his picture taken with the "First Family." He asked a man who was standing nearby if he would be so kind as to take his picture and the man gladly consented. Alex handed him his cellphone and several snapshots were taken.

Alex then toured the museum. There were areas depicting various times in Lincoln's life, from boyhood to the presidency, as well as exhibits devoted to the Civil War. On view were personal effects that Lincoln had used over the years and glass cases displaying letters and documents Lincoln had penned. Alex spent a couple very enjoyable hours roaming about and viewing the many exhibits.

Midway through, Alex remembered the words Sarah had uttered when he first told her of his vacation plans and he could not conceal a smile. Sarah was right: here he'd been looking at these exhibits for well over an hour. She would no doubt have been sitting on a bench nearby, patiently waiting for him to finish.

The visit culminated in the museum shop, where he purchased a stoneware mug with the likeness of the president on it and a replica of a teacup and saucer from the Abraham Lincoln White House China Plate collection. It was emblazoned with an eagle and bordered in purple, Mary's favorite color. Both would fit perfectly into his whimsical keepsake collection back at the office.

As Alex left the museum and made his way back to the parking lot, he now had only one more location to visit to complete his tour. This was, of course, the spot where Mr. Lincoln lies in repose to this very day, his final resting place in the tomb in Oak Ridge Cemetery.

But first Alex wanted to grab a bite to eat. He dropped his purchases off at the hotel and freshened up a bit, then took the bag containing the brochures he had collected and went downstairs through the lobby to the Globe Tavern. He selected this restaurant not just because it was conveniently located inside the hotel, but because it was named for the original Globe Tavern, on Adams Street between 3rd and 4th Streets, where the newly married Abraham and Mary Lincoln took up lodgings on its second floor in 1842.

The tavern was not very crowded and Alex was shown to a table right away. "Can I get you something to drink?" asked the young lady who had escorted him to the table.

"Yes, iced tea, please," he replied.

"Very good, sir. Your server will be right with you."

Alex ordered a tuna melt which, at the suggestion of the

server, was accompanied by homemade potato chips.

As she went off to place his order, Alex took a long sip of his tea and began going through the brochures he had collected.

As he ate his lunch, his thoughts again reverted to the city of Springfield as it must have appeared 150 years ago, trying to see the descriptions in the brochures as windows into the past. He absent-mindedly ate the sandwich and chips, not really tasting either, as his mind was too preoccupied with his mental time travels. The server interrupted his almost trance-like state when she dropped off his check.

Alex finished his meal, collected his belongings and made his way to the cashier. After paying the bill, he left the hotel and walked to the parking lot to retrieve his car. He headed up 6th Street and made a left turn onto Grand Avenue. Within a half mile, he made a right turn onto Monument Avenue and proceeded to the entrance of Oak Ridge Cemetery, where he followed the signs to the Lincoln Tomb.

Suddenly, there it was in front of him: the tomb where Mr. Lincoln was buried. It was an impressive structure. Constructed of granite, it had a rectangular base and in the center was a statue of Lincoln. Rising directly behind him was an imposing 117-foot-tall obelisk, which was adorned and encircled by a number of statues depicting various events of the Civil War.

Alex parked and walked the short distance to the tomb. Halfway there, he stopped and quickly snapped a few pictures. Approaching the steps to the entrance, he encountered a large bust of the 16th president. While most of the sculpture was dark in color, Lincoln's nose was a bright gold. Alex could not resist pausing to rub it before continuing inside. He later learned that the reason the nose was so shiny was due to the multitude of visitors doing exactly what Alex had done as they passed by.

Alex entered the tomb and followed the circular hallway, stopping along the way to examine the artifacts displayed. Many of these displays were small statues dedicated to the life of the president. On the walls were plaques with excerpts from some of Lincoln's greatest speeches. As he continued he found himself facing an imposing rose-colored granite monument that marked the final resting place of Abraham Lincoln. Etched into the stone, in two lines, was the simple reminder of the giant who rested beneath: "Abraham Lincoln. 1809—1865." No other words, epithets or descriptions appeared on this beautiful stone. Behind the edifice in a semi-circle were the American flag, a flag depicting the seal of the president of the United States and various other flags representative of Lincoln's background. Engraved in the wall directly behind the granite monument, gold lettering read: "Now he belongs to the ages."

Alex learned that the last mortal remains of Abraham Lincoln are encased in a thick, concrete vault and buried 10 feet below the marble floor. Alex stood motionless, consumed by a feeling of supreme awe. For years he had read about Lincoln and collected books and pictures of him. Today he had visited places where the great man had once actually lived and breathed. But now Alex reflected in silent reverence his proximity to Abraham Lincoln. The only thing separating them was a marble floor and 10 feet of cement. Alex glanced down at the floor and imagined Lincoln's kind, tired face, preserved in the last photograph ever taken of him, now resting for eternity just below where he was standing.

"Oh, Mr. Lincoln," Alex said in a barely audible whisper, "If only I could have been there that evening to somehow prevent that awful act from ever having occurred. If only there was some way to change history, to go back in time and undo that terrible deed."

After a few more moments of reflection and introspection, Alex turned around and now faced crypts embedded in the wall containing the remains of Mary Lincoln, who passed away in 1882, and their children. Edward had died at the age of five; Willie, the president's favorite, at 12; and Tad at 18. The only son not resting in perpetuity with the rest of the family is Robert Lincoln, who was buried in Arlington National Cemetery following his death in 1926.

Alex had now visited all the historical locations directly associated with Lincoln's time in Springfield. A quick phone call home to tell Sarah about his day's activities, followed by an uneventful flight back to Los Angeles capped off the day.

Now Alex was all set to finalize his plans to visit Washington, D.C., and view the sites where Lincoln had spent the final years of his life.

APRIL 13, 1865
THE SOLDIERS' HOME

ABRAHAM LINCOLN

Beginning in June 1862, President Lincoln and his family began spending much of the summer at the Soldiers' Home. They resided in a cottage that had originally been constructed in 1842 by a wealthy banker. Then, in 1851, the cottage, with the land surrounding it, was purchased by the federal government as a place to house retired and disabled Army veterans. It became officially known as the Soldiers' Home.

The president enjoyed the time he spent there, which allowed him to escape the heat, humidity and odors of the Washington summer. It also gave him a respite from the political pressures of the White House, including not only the interminable tasks requiring his attention in the operations associated with the war, but also the constant barrage of office seekers who lined up daily hoping to plead their causes to the president.

At first, Lincoln rode the three miles from the White House to the hills of the Soldiers' Home alone. Although he was continually warned that it was too dangerous to make the ride by himself, Lincoln enjoyed the solitude. It gave him a chance to think about the war effort, or to allow his mind to wander to times when he did not have the burdens of the world upon his shoulders. However, this practice came to an abrupt end in

August 1864. One late evening he was on his way to the Soldiers' Home, astride his favorite horse, when, as he approached the entrance gate to the property, he heard what sounded like the report of a rifle. He was taken completely aback, especially when the consequence of the shot resulted in his stovepipe hat becoming separated from his head. Lincoln's horse broke into a gallop and delivered his charge safely to the cottage.

Upon hearing what had happened, a member of the president's detail rode toward the gate entrance and retraced Lincoln's path. Sure enough, there on the ground, not fifty feet from the property entrance, was the president's famous silk hat with a bullet hole halfway between the brim and the top. The soldier poked his finger through the hole, imagining what could have been.

The hat was given to one of the president's secretaries, who returned it to Mr. Lincoln. After keenly inspecting it, the president appeared quite unconcerned and attributed the event to some careless hunter. He asked that it be kept quiet and was especially adamant that Mrs. Lincoln not be told. All agreed to respect the president's request, but he no longer had the luxury of a solitary, quiet, leisurely ride from the White House to the cottage.

The president and Mrs. Lincoln relished their time at the cottage. Although Lincoln often journeyed there without his wife—who might be in New York or Philadelphia shopping for clothes or furnishings for the White House—she liked it as much as he did. In 1865, Mary Lincoln wrote, in a letter to a friend, "How dearly I love the Soldiers' Home. We are truly delighted with this retreat. The walks around the grounds are delightful."

On the morning of April 13, 1865, Lincoln awoke in his bed in the White House. Mary, who had accompanied her husband to the cottage several days earlier, had decided to remain there while her husband divided his time between the cottage and the White House. When he left the day before to return to Washington, Lincoln promised his wife that, after attending to business the following day, he would ride out to join her. His morning was spent not unlike many of his days. After an early morning breakfast of one egg and a cup of black coffee, the president made his way to the telegraph office at the War Department to get the latest news about the war. Lincoln always looked forward to spending time with the young telegraphers, having a chance to talk with them and relay some of the stories that he had gathered over a lifetime of experiences. Unfortunately, the mood was always eventually broken by the clacking of the telegraph key, bringing him back to the problems and issues of the day.

Midmorning found the president in the office of his Secretary of War, Edwin Stanton. A host of men were also present and discussions were conducted regarding a variety of military problems. While he could have spent all day there in conference, Lincoln could not forget or ignore his promise to Mary to join her at the cottage. Glancing at his pocket watch, Lincoln slowly pushed himself up from his chair so that he was fully at his six-foot-four-inch height. "Gentlemen," he said in his slow, familiar drawl, "while I consider this meeting and its subject matter to be of paramount importance, I am committed to another meeting some three miles from here. And, whereas I know that you will be generous in excusing my failure to avoid making my exit, I also know that my next engagement will not be so generous in excusing my failure to ensure my making my entrance." The room erupted in laughter and Mr. Lincoln took his leave.

He walked back to the White House and asked for his horse and carriage. Then he went upstairs to get his overcoat and gloves and, as there was a bit of a chill in the air, he also took his shawl. Slowly and deliberately plodding down the stairs, Lincoln proceeded to the back door exit adjacent to the stable area, where the horse and carriage awaited him, flanked by two armed soldiers. "Well, boys," the president announced, "I have kept Mother waiting long enough." With that he climbed into the carriage, took the reins and followed the soldiers, who had mounted their horses and begun to move out. They proceeded down the gravel path from the White House toward the main road, to begin the one-hour ride that would take them to the Soldiers' Home. The sky was blue, with a few puffy clouds in the distance and on this cool spring day the stench that bedeviled the city during the summer months was not present.

The entourage headed northeast on Vermont Avenue, where a bend to the right put them on Rhode Island Avenue. The dirt roadway was dry and the horses riding ahead of the president's rig kicked up a bit of dust that wafted into the carriage. They continued to 7th Street, where Lincoln eased the horse to the left. Along this stretch of roadway, the wheels fell into the rut left by those carriages and larger coaches that had previously followed this route. The president's carriage virtually steered itself along the roadway, the driver needing to do very little to keep the horse in a straight path. As he drove, Lincoln reflected on the fact that the Civil War was finally over and that now the earnest task of Reconstruction was to begin. He recognized the toll so many families had suffered by the loss of loved ones to the gun and artillery ball salvos from the Southern troops. And, as he always did, he thought deeply and lovingly about his dear son, Willie, gone now for just over a year.

After a stretch along 7th Street, the group came upon Rock Creek Church Road and the last one-and-a-half miles to their destination. The air was sweet with the smell of the trees and brush that framed the narrow roadway. Birds flew overhead and small animals rustled in the bushes. Suddenly, the cottage came into view and the journey was complete.

• • •

"Why Mr. Lincoln," exclaimed Mary, who was waiting on the porch as the men rode up the path toward her. "I was beginning to wonder if I was going to see you at all today."

"Now, Molly," the president replied, using one of his affectionate names for his wife. "It is only two o'clock. We have plenty of time to spend together."

Mr. Lincoln disembarked from the carriage and they walked arm-in-arm into the house. "You look tired today, Father." She patted his hand tenderly. "Arthur has supper planned for four o'clock, so why don't you relax for a couple of hours?"

"You know, Mary, that is actually a good idea. I am quite partial to that sycamore tree in the middle of the yard. I think I may spend some quiet time over there with Mr. Shakespeare."

Ever since he was a young man, Lincoln had revered Shakespeare's writings and had committed numerous passages from the plays to memory. His favorite was *Hamlet* and he must have read, and reread, the tale of the Dane hundreds of times. In the library, Lincoln selected a copy of the play from a row of books on a shelf above the fireplace. With a smile, he walked out the front door, down the steps and onto the grass. In that familiar gait, where his entire foot came in contact with the ground at once, as opposed to a heel-toe cadence, he made his way to the large sycamore tree.

He found a spot where the sun was behind him and sat on the ground with his back against the majestic tree. The sycamore was in full bloom and the rays of sunlight peeked and darted through the leaves. He thought for a moment of the many youthful hours he had spent this way, first as a boy and later as a young man in New Salem. Whether reading the classics, the Bible or Blackstone's *Commentaries*, he had always found that the support of a fine tree added to his enjoyment.

He looked at the cover of the book for a moment and then opened it to read once more the intricacies of the plot lines woven by the Bard. He must have fallen asleep, for he suddenly realized that Mary was calling him from the house.

"Mr. Lincoln! Mr. Lincoln! Are you just going to laze under that tree, or are you going to answer me?"

"Um, yes, I hear you," the president said, jolted from his reverie. "What is it that you want?"

"I've been calling you for well over a minute." She was obviously annoyed. "Arthur has supper prepared and it is being set out on the dining room table. Please come and join us."

"I am on my way," the president replied.

His book had fallen to the ground. He picked it up and brushed off some leaves that had attached to the cover. As he got to his feet he noticed that his right leg had fallen asleep. Lincoln turned to his right toward the cottage and after taking just two steps, the toe of his right boot encountered an exposed tree root. He lost his balance and pitched forward.

"Carn-sarn-it!" he exclaimed, landing on his hands and knees, more embarrassed than anything else.

Suddenly, he heard a voice. "Mr. President, are you all right?"

"Yes, Crook, I am fine. Just help me up from this uncomely position before someone sees me."

The man Lincoln addressed was William H. Crook, his White House guard and one of his most trusted confidants. Crook often traveled with the president, acting both as a guard and as an intermediary between Lincoln and those who might want to impose upon him. When not travelling with the president, Crook could often be found at the main entrance to the White House, screening prospective visitors. He had accompanied Lincoln in March 1864 when the president boarded the side-wheel steamer *River Queen* to sail down the Potomac for his famous meeting with General Grant at his army headquarters at Center Point.

Crook extended his right hand for the president to grasp and, with this assistance, Lincoln regained his footing. Brushing the leaves and dust from his trousers, he jokingly exclaimed, "I can only imagine what old Jeff Davis might say if he had chanced to observe the prominence of the tail of the government superseding its head!"

Both men laughed heartily as they made their way to the cottage to join the family at the supper table.

APRIL 13 – PRESENT-DAY
WASHINGTON, D.C.

MORNING

Alex had arrived in Washington the previous day. Since he was not in town with his wife and children, this trip, like the one to Springfield, was not going to be treated as a vacation. Rather, he had specific places he wanted to see and was going to do so over the course of several days.

He had thought quite a bit about the Lincoln sites that the visit should comprise. Discussing it with Sarah, Alex had narrowed down his choices to those where a significant event in the president's life had occurred. He therefore decided that he might not necessarily see the White House. Although the Lincolns did occupy the structure for four years, the building had been renovated several times since then. Theodore Roosevelt added the West Wing for his office and others had made changes over the years. Of course, the most dramatic change was made during the Truman administration, when the inside of the house was gutted and completely rebuilt. If Mr. Lincoln walked into the White House in the 1950s, he would never recognize it. Thus, for Alex's purposes, a tour of the White House would not transport him back in time to when the Lincolns were its occupants.

His visit began instead at the U.S. Capitol building. In doing research for the trip, Alex learned that, though Lincoln spent one term as a congressman, from December 1847 to March 1849, he did not walk the hallowed halls as they appear today. In his time, there were no separate wings on either end of the building housing the Senate Chamber and the House of Representatives. Rather, the House met in what is today the National Statuary Hall, where desks were strategically arranged for its members. Alex gleaned from the U.S. Capitol's website that there was a one-hour tour focused on those portions of the building that were of interest to him in his Lincoln quest and would fit his needs perfectly.

He arrived at the Capitol early for the first such tour of the day, which began just before 9 a.m. A sign told him that it started in the Visitors' Center and that he would need to stop there to obtain a ticket. A woman gave him a ticket for the 8:50 tour and directed him to a theater to view a short film on the history of the United States. There was time before the film was set to start, so Alex strolled through the Exhibition Hall, where one item in particular caught his eye.

Against the wall, encased in glass, opposite a scale model of the Capitol dome, was a platform covered in black velvet. The descriptive plaque posted before it explained that this was the catafalque upon which the coffin of Abraham Lincoln was placed while his body lay in repose in the Capitol Rotunda. For several days after the assassination, thousands of people had filed by to pay their last respects to the fallen leader. While the framework of the structure is from Lincoln's day, the velvet covering had been replaced over the years. Viewing this object, Alex was transfixed, recreating the scene that took place here back in April 1865, his gaze interrupted only by the flash of cameras as people took pictures of the bier.

Alex was suddenly brought back to the present when he heard an announcement that his tour was about to begin.

At the theater, the two dozen visitors were welcomed by a short, stout, bearded man in his 40s who introduced himself as Todd and stated he would be their tour guide. Alex smiled to himself at the irony: the guide's name and Mary Lincoln's maiden name were the same. He entered the theater and took his seat.

Alex found his mind drifting off as the short film played, anticipating viewing the parts of the Capitol where Lincoln had spent time as both legislator and president. At the end of the film, the lights came on and Todd invited the visitors to assemble just outside the theater.

Todd announced that this particular tour would focus on two specific places. The first stop was Statuary Hall, the space where the House of Representatives had met from 1807 to 1857. Todd told them that, once the House wing was completed, it was decided to turn this spot into a place to display statues of famous Americans. Each state is now permitted to have two statues depicting the men or women who contributed significantly to its history.

Next, Todd led them to the infamous spot where John Quincy Adams had his desk positioned while serving in the House of Representatives after his term as president. Asking the group to remain where they were, Todd moved to another location within the Hall. He then whispered, "So, how is everyone doing?" To everyone's amazement, they heard his words perfectly. Upon returning, Todd related with a smile that, since Adams was a former president, he was permitted to choose the location of his desk. Adams had picked that spot precisely because the acoustics permitted him to eavesdrop on the conversations of others.

After the guide delivered his talk and pointed out a few of the more interesting statues, he told the guests that they could spend fifteen minutes looking at the likenesses before they moved on to the Rotunda. Alex approached the guide and said, "Excuse me, Todd, can I ask you a few questions about Lincoln's time here in the Capitol?"

"Why, of course. And what might your name be and where are you from?"

"Oh, excuse me. My name is Alex and I'm visiting from Los Angeles."

"OK, Alex, fire away. I also happen to be a big fan our 16th president and I hope I can answer your questions."

"I was wondering how the seats were assigned and arranged in Lincoln's day."

"Well, the desks were arranged in a sort of a semi-circle. House members drew their seats by lots and in 1847 Lincoln drew seat number 191. We've placed bronze markers on the floor where the desks of those who went on to become president were situated. If you look over there," he said, pointing to his right, "you will find the marker where we believe Lincoln's desk sat during the one term he served in Congress."

"It's kind of hard to believe that's where his desk actually was," Alex marveled. "I'll have to go over there and take a look. I was also curious as to whether it's true that he lived near the Capitol during his time in Congress?"

"Yes," replied Todd, always welcoming the chance to share a historical tidbit on topics he enjoyed. "Lincoln lived in what was then a boarding house owned by a Mrs. Spriggs. At that time, it was located across the street and was one of several row houses on the property where they have since built the Library of Congress. While Mrs. Lincoln and their two younger sons stayed there with him for a short time, he was mostly residing alone for the couple of years he was in Congress. I will tell you something else very interesting. Lincoln was present in this chamber on February 21, 1848, the day that John Quincy Adams collapsed while seated at his desk. Mr. Adams died two days later and Lincoln attended his funeral. Now," Todd concluded, "you'll have to excuse me so we can continue on to the Rotunda."

Alex thanked him and crossed the room to see the bronze marker noting the location of Abraham Lincoln's desk when he served in the Thirtieth Congress. This was one of those special places that he really wanted to see while in Washington and Alex stood in reflective silence until his thoughts were interrupted by the kind voice of the tour guide.

"Come now, Alex from Los Angeles, we need to move on. There is another tour right behind us." Some of the other tour members giggled and Alex, smiling and waving, joined the group as they entered the Rotunda.

This was, of course, where Abraham Lincoln's body had lain in state after the assassination. Todd explained that Lincoln was actually the second man to lie in repose there; the first was Henry Clay, who happened to be Lincoln's idol. Todd then related a few facts about the Lincoln funeral. The president's body arrived on the afternoon of April 19, 1865 and remained for two days in an open coffin so that Cabinet members, government officials and members of the public could pay their last respects. One person who did not attend was Mary Lincoln.

Todd then talked about other historical events that took place in the Rotunda, including the lying-in-state of presidents James Garfield, William McKinley, William Taft, John F. Kennedy, Lyndon Johnson and Ronald Reagan.

"And," Todd explained, "the exact same catafalque upon which Lincoln's coffin rested also supported the coffins of each of these presidents. As for the Rotunda itself," he continued, "due to lack of funds and the War of 1812, work on it did not begin until 1818 and it took six years to complete. The beautiful dome that you see atop the Rotunda was built between 1856 and 1866. Also, during the Civil War, the spot where you are now standing was a military hospital that cared for Union soldiers injured in the fighting."

The tour was over and Todd said, "I want to thank you all for coming. I can give you a few minutes to look around and ask any questions you may have. Then please follow the exit sign and enjoy the rest of your day." The group gave Todd an appreciative round of applause and dispersed to explore the various sites within the Rotunda.

Alex stood in place for several minutes, looking at the spot where Lincoln's body had lain in state so many years ago. He retrieved his cellphone to take several pictures. Then, with a sigh, he made his way toward the exit and out of the building. There was one more vantage point he wanted to see before leaving Capitol Hill. After asking a Capitol police officer for directions, Alex made his way to the designated steps and found himself looking up at the East Portico where, in 1861 and 1865, Lincoln was sworn in as president and where he gave his inaugural addresses. It is, of course, his Second Inaugural Address that is probably the most famous such speech ever delivered.

Alex recalled the last words of the speech, imagining Lincoln, in his black suit, standing on the platform specially erected for the inauguration and speaking in his rather high-pitched voice, reading from the text he had painstakingly prepared:

> With malice toward none, with charity for all, with firmness in the right as God gives us to see the right, let us strive on to finish the work we are in, to bind up the nation's wounds, to care for him who shall have borne the battle and for his widow and his orphan, to do all which may achieve and cherish a just and lasting peace among ourselves and with all nations.

After spending several minutes there, Alex walked down the Capitol steps. He then reached into his pocket for the tourist map that would help him find his next destination.

• • •

The next location that Alex wanted to visit was Ford's Theatre, about a thirty-minute walk along Pennsylvania Avenue to 10th Street. It was such a beautiful spring day, he chose to walk rather than catch the trolley or hail a cab.

Pennsylvania Avenue was alive with pedestrians. It was easy to tell the tourists from the people in the middle of their workday. Sightseers were dressed very casually with the clear giveaway being either the ubiquitous map in hand or camera around the neck. These people strolled along the avenue, chatting amiably and pointing to the Federal buildings that lined the street.

Conversely, those walking along the avenue during their

workday were equally easy to identify. The men wore suits and the women were attired in colorful dresses or very conservative pantsuits. Many were walking in tandem, but most were striding alone, at the familiar quick business-like pace. One could clearly sense a purpose to their gait.

Fortunately, thought Alex, today I am in the tourist category. Alex was enjoying the unusually warm spring weather and the sights he saw along Pennsylvania Avenue. From the map, he noticed that he would reach 10th Street before he got to the White House and he made a mental note to take a small detour and pass by the White House on the way back to his hotel.

At the intersection of Pennsylvania and 10th, Alex crossed the street, heading north and walked about a block and a half to his destination. The theater was between E and F Streets, on the east side. After arriving, Alex stopped to view the architecture of the building. It was just as he had seen it in books. The lower portion of the building was composed of what appeared to be five arched entryways, all painted a gleaming white. Old-style gas lamps stood sentry at the curb. Above the archways rose a two-story brick facade with five windows separated by brick pilasters. After taking a few photos, Alex walked under the center arch and into the building, the last building Abraham Lincoln ever entered alive.

Entering the lobby, he proceeded to the ticket booth and handed the woman a ten-dollar bill. He received a five-dollar note in change which he returned to his wallet. After being handed a ticket for the self-guided tour, he took a brochure and began his exploration of the theater.

Alex was surprised by the number of items housed in the museum, including a replica of the disguise (a cloak and tam o' shanter hat) that Lincoln wore when he was spirited into Washington for his inauguration in 1861 after Allan Pinkerton and Kate Ware had discovered an assassination plot brewing in Baltimore. Alex walked past glass cases displaying items that Mary Lincoln had purchased for the family's use while they lived in the White House.

As he continued through the museum, Alex came upon the artifacts relating to the events surrounding the assassination, including background stories of the conspirators and a playbill from the production of *Our American Cousin*. Then the real treasures of the collection and the items that truly made him pause and ponder came into view. There was John Wilkes Booth's diary, which included entries he had made to justify his killing of the president. Also present was the compass that Booth used during the several weeks in which he was attempting to escape to what he thought would be sanctuary in the South. Alex viewed with interest the large Bowie knife that Booth used to attack Major Rathbone during their brief scuffle when the major tried to detain Booth following the assassination.

Then Alex stood awestruck by the somewhat innocent-looking but deadly weapon inside the display case. Here was the .44 caliber Derringer, small enough for Booth to carry in his vest pocket, which delivered the tiny metal ball that ended the president's life. Alex had to convince himself as he played out the scene in his mind that this was indeed the actual weapon that Booth had in his hand as he entered the box, held in an outstretched arm and fired at the back of Lincoln's head from point-blank range.

Alex concluded his tour of the museum by examining the very suit the president was wearing on that fateful evening: a black frock coat, waistcoat, trousers and boots. Again, Alex struggled a bit to make his mind appreciate the fact that these were not costumes worn by an actor in a theatrical production, but instead the very clothes Lincoln had slowly and deliberately put on in his bedroom at the White House. Did he and Mary talk about what he was to wear that night? Or were these the usual clothes the president wore when he went out in the evening? Also displayed were the white kid gloves that, history tells us, Lincoln was not fond of wearing. Next to the standing mannequin wearing the famous clothing was a blood-covered pillow. This was the pillow that supported Lincoln's head during his final hours as he lay dying in a much-too-small bed in the back room of the Petersen House. Finally, there was the actual door that Lincoln and Booth had used to enter the presidential box. Also visible was the hole Booth drilled in the door as part of the preparation for the assassination.

After spending a significant time inside the museum, Alex went back upstairs so that he could stand and look at the presidential box itself where the fatal events took place. From the first floor he looked up to see the bunting and photograph of George Washington, just as they had been set out on the night when the Lincolns and their guests arrived for what was intended to be a pleasant, diversionary night at the theater. Alex took pictures from several vantage points and then followed a small group of people up the stairs leading to the second floor. Behind the last row of seats they encountered a short staircase, the top of which put them just a few strides from the door to the presidential box itself, which was fashioned as it had been on the evening of April 14, 1865. The visitors were permitted to stand just a few feet away from the exact rocking chair

Lincoln had occupied. Being so close to where the assassination occurred made Alex pause, close his eyes and reflect on the chaotic scene that had played out in this very spot all those years ago.

"If only . . ." Alex mused, not really sure how to complete this thought. "If only . . ."

Shaking his head and having satisfied himself that he had done justice to the artifacts available to view, Alex left the theater and went across the street to the Petersen House so he could view the room where Lincoln succumbed to the head wound at 7:22 a.m. on April 15, 1865.

The Petersen House, built in 1849 by William Petersen, a German tailor, is a three-story row house, with a curving cement staircase bordered by a cast-iron railing that leads to the front entrance. Inside, Alex saw the parlor where Mary Lincoln spent much of the night and early morning after she became too hysterical to remain in the same room as her dying husband.

He then went to see the small bedroom at the rear of the house, where Lincoln's six-foot-four-inch frame had been laid diagonally across a small bed. Although he never regained consciousness, every effort was made to make the president as comfortable as possible. Charles Leale, a young Army surgeon who happened to be in Ford's Theatre at the time of the shooting, had directed the president be taken to a location away from the throng of people. The men carrying the unconscious president were waved across the street and into the Petersen House, where Dr. Leale remained to render what little medical care he could.

Alex viewed the reproduction of the room as it would have appeared that night. The actual bed that Lincoln lay upon is now on display at the Chicago Historical Society. Alex smiled to himself, wondering how Sarah and Mark would react when he told them that he would now have to travel to Chicago.

The placard in the room briefly described the events of the nine hours that Lincoln lay there fighting for his life and about those who were present in the room at the end. They included Robert Lincoln, Edwin Stanton, Lincoln's close friend Senator Charles Sumner and several military persons. Mary Lincoln was not in the room when her husband died. There was a picture of the room as it appeared shortly after the president's body was removed, as well as a placard of the famous quote by Secretary of State Stanton: "Now he belongs to the ages."

While this was indeed a moving place to visit, it did not take Alex very long to see the room and parlor. He exited the building and suddenly realized that he was hungry.

APRIL 13 – PRESENT-DAY WASHINGTON, D.C.

AFTERNOON

Alex had not eaten since breakfast. It was now 12:30 and he wanted to find a place to grab a quick lunch. A person working at the Petersen House suggested Burger World and offered directions. Alex made the short walk and within less than five minutes arrived at the restaurant, which appeared to be a very popular destination as almost all of the tables were taken.

Upon entering, Alex approached the counter and ordered a cheeseburger, fries and soda. He found an available seat nearby and waited for his food to be brought out.

He pulled out the street map of Washington. It was still early enough to visit one more location today and he pondered which one it should be.

Alex decided that he wanted to see the Lincoln Cottage at the Soldiers' Home. He really did not have any idea of where it was in relation to his current location, so he pulled out his smartphone and went to the Google Maps app. He simply entered "Lincoln Cottage" and the suggestion of President Lincoln's Cottage on Rock Creek Church Road came up first. The map opened up, showing the Cottage. Between bites of his hamburger and fries, Alex clicked on the link, where one bit of information caught his eye: the cottage was only four miles from the White House.

It was then that he had a very interesting idea.

His thoughts were interrupted by a restaurant employee's inquiry as to how he was enjoying his meal.

"Fine, thanks. But let me ask you something. Is there a place near here that rents bicycles?"

"Why, yes, there is. Washington Pedalers is only a few blocks from here. Let me get the address for you."

Alex decided that it would be most interesting to ride a bike to the Soldiers' Home and perhaps try to trace a path similar to the one Lincoln might have taken on his carriage rides between the White House and the Cottage. Alex noticed that the woman seated at the table next to him was writing on a yellow pad.

"Excuse me," he said to her. "May I have a piece of paper?"

"Sure." She tore off a sheet and handed it to him.

Alex thanked her and, returning his attention to his phone, clicked on the directions link and set the starting point as "the White House." It was a fairly straightforward route and he was confident he could make it by bicycle. He then clicked on the "bicycle" icon to get turn-by-turn directions for his ride. Instantly, the screen displayed the suggested route and indicated that it would take just 30 minutes. Even though Alex had a GPS feature on his phone, he was old-school and still liked the idea of writing directions down. Pulling out his pen, Alex wrote out the directions.

The employee returned and handed Alex the address for the bike shop. Alex thanked him and then set out for Washington Pedalers.

After a short walk, he saw a group of bicycles on display on the sidewalk in front of a large plate glass window stenciled with the words "The Washington Pedalers." Underneath in a smaller font it read, "Bikes for Sale and Hire."

Alex was greeted by a bearded young man with red hair pulled back and tied in a ponytail. "Welcome to Washington Pedalers. So, what can I do for you?"

Alex said, "I am interested in renting a touring bike for the rest of the afternoon. What can you recommend?"

"If it's comfort and not speed that you're looking for, I would suggest this one."

The young man walked over to a line of bicycles and rolled one back to where Alex was standing. "This is a Dawes Galaxy AL. It's a British bike and I think that you will find it very comfortable for touring around the city. It rents for thirty-five dollars for the day. What do you think?"

"Sounds good to me," replied Alex. "How late are you open for me to return it?"

"We're open until nine p.m. Would you also like to rent a helmet? Not a bad idea if you plan to ride in D.C. traffic."

"How much is that?"

"Seven dollars."

"OK. Let's do it."

"There's also an attachment that provides a holder for your cellphone so you can use your GPS while you ride. No extra charge. Would you like me to put that on?"

"Yes, that would be great."

"I just need you to fill out the rental form and provide me with your driver's license so I can make a copy for our files. You also need to pay everything up front."

"No problem."

Within a short time Alex was riding toward the White

House, using the GPS on his phone to direct him. As he rode, he thought about another landmark he could visit first. He accessed the GPS on his phone and keyed in "Lincoln Memorial." Within seconds the directions were displayed, showing it was only a few minutes away. He pedaled in the direction of Lincoln Memorial Circle and soon was riding up to the edifice dedicated to the 16th president.

At a bike rack at the far end of the parking lot, Alex locked his bike and walked toward the white marble monument. He paused at the base before climbing the stairs, gazing at the imposing columns that buttressed the entire structure. After taking several pictures from this vantage point, Alex began to ascend the 58 steps up to the entrance and the statue of Lincoln. While he chose to mount the steps slowly and take in the beauty of the architecture, he nevertheless found the need to constantly avoid bumping into people who were poised on the steps pointing their cameras at the memorial.

Upon reaching the chamber level, Alex was awed by the magnificent marble sculpture of the president. The detail in Lincoln's facial features and the positioning of his hands were truly wonders to behold. He marveled at the president's likeness from various vantage points and then silently read the inscription carved into the stone directly behind the figure.

"In this temple, as in the hearts of the people for whom he saved the Union, the memory of Abraham Lincoln is enshrined forever."

Alex retrieved his phone and again took pictures from several angles.

Next, he walked about the base of the statue and read the words preserved on the other two walls: the Gettysburg Address and Lincoln's Second Inaugural Address. As Alex moved between each of the walls, he stood still for several minutes before each of the panels of engraved words, reading them slowly as if for the first time. Finally, he walked away from the statue to the steps leading back down to the plaza. Of course, before leaving the chamber, he had to turn and take one last look at the immortalized Abraham Lincoln.

Back in the plaza, Alex made his way to the bicycle rack. He unlocked the bike and wrapped the chain around the base of the seat, ready to proceed to his next destination.

Alex pulled out the directions to the Soldiers' Home and, climbing aboard the bike, retraced his route until he was making his way along 15th Street. At New York Avenue, he turned left, then left again on 11th Street, right on Rhode Island Avenue and left on 7th Street. Although he really tried to envision the scenery as Mr. Lincoln would have viewed it from his carriage while following the same basic route, the modern structures, vehicles and sounds of the city just did not translate to its more humble and agrarian 19th-century counterpart. Alex sighed and decided to instead enjoy the sights that the present-day city did have to offer. The wonderful weather was most cooperative for his half-hour ride to the Cottage.

Alex continued along 7th Street until he reached the intersection with Rock Creek Church Road, where he made a right. Just ahead was a sign with the information that the Soldiers' Home and the Lincoln Cottage were three-quarters of a mile ahead and advising visitors to use the Eagle Gate. Within a few short minutes, Alex arrived at the intersection of Rock Creek Church Road NW and Upshur Street NW and passed through the Eagle Gate entrance.

Once inside, he followed the signs to the parking lot. At the edge of the lot, by a path leading to the cottage, there stood several flagpoles. Alex locked the bicycle and helmet to one of them and walked to the Cottage.

At the steps leading into the building, he saw a sign advising that the next, and final, tour would start a 3 p.m., just a half hour away. After purchasing his tour ticket, he still had time to kill and he decided to stroll around the grounds.

He began walking on a well-manicured lawn. There were half a dozen benches scattered on it, but Alex's eye was caught by the sight of a large, beautiful sycamore tree situated almost in the center of the lawn. The stately tree had a thick trunk, gnarled branches and several exposed roots, indicating it had been there for many decades. The tree was in full bloom and he sat down under its welcoming branches, reclining with his back pressed against the trunk, facing away from the Cottage, so the sunlight would not be hitting him in the face. He stretched his arms above his head and then gently dropped them to his side, as he closed his eyes and enjoyed the quiet and the feel of the grass.

His reverie was interrupted a short time later by a woman's voice calling from the porch of the Cottage. "All of those who have a ticket for the three o'clock tour, please come forward and assemble at the foot of the stairs."

Alex was almost disappointed that the serenity of the moment was interrupted by the announcement that the tour was beginning. He drew his legs toward him and, placing his hands on the ground, pushed himself up. He slowly rose and turned to his right to walk back to the Cottage. After taking just two steps, the toe of his right tennis shoe encountered an exposed tree root and caused him to pitch forward.

"Carn-sarn-it!" He fell to the ground landing on his hands and knees, more embarrassed over the episode than anything else. Suddenly, Alex felt a chill go through him and for a few seconds experienced significant dizziness. As his head began to clear, he heard approaching footsteps accompanied by a man's gravelly voice.

April 13, 1865
The Soldiers' Home

Alex Linwood

Alex, whose eyes were focused on the ground ahead of him, saw two boots come to a stop inches from where he had come to rest. They were unlike any boots he had ever seen before. There was no stitching anywhere and the toe was not at all contrasting to the rest of the shoe. Rather, each boot seemed to be cut and molded from a single piece of leather. They were clearly well-worn.

A voice asked, "Young man, are you all right?"

"Yes, I am fine," said Alex, looking up at the speaker. The man appeared to be in his seventies, broad shouldered and slightly hunched over at the waist. His bald pate was framed by thick hair on either side of his head, and he wore thin eyeglasses and sported a full beard accented by a heavy moustache that curled up at the ends. His clothing was of a variety and style that Alex had never seen outside of a museum or a period movie.

The man extended his right hand encased in a worn, tan-colored glove. "Here, let me help you up."

"Um, thank you," Alex said hesitantly. While still grasping the man's hand, Alex looked at his surroundings. What had been a beautiful lawn was now a plot of grass patched with bare spots of dirt and some weeds. Benches no longer dotted the perimeter, and just beyond, where once there had been a parking lot, there was now a circular drive to a building clearly in need of a fresh coat of paint and new shutters.

With the man's assistance, Alex rose to his feet. "Where am I? What is this? What's happening?" He could not get the words out fast enough. "And—," he hesitated a moment as he brushed the debris from his clothing, "who are you?"

The man's face exhibited a sad smile. "Now, please relax, young man," he said soothingly. He looked at Alex to see if he was prepared for what he had to say. "You are still on the grounds of the Soldiers' Home. But," he continued in a slow, drawn-out manner, purposefully pausing for emphasis, "the real question you should be asking is not '*Where* is this?' but rather, '*When* is this?' You see, today is April 13, 1865."

It took Alex what seemed like several minutes to process the information he had just heard. Closing his eyes, he thought to himself, *I must be dreaming, or I must have hit my head on something. Now, just take a deep breath and open your eyes. Everything will be fine.*

As if commanding himself to do so, Alex slowly opened his eyes. But the old man was still there. "Wait a minute. What did you say? That I am standing here in the year 1865?"

"Yes. You are in Washington City and today is April 13, 1865. I should introduce myself. My name is William Crook and I am President Lincoln's bodyguard. And who might you be?"

Alex began stammering, almost under his breath, and repeated several times to himself, "William Crook? How do I know that name?" Then, almost absentmindedly, Alex stated meekly, "I'm Alex Linwood."

And then it dawned on him and he turned toward the older man, alarmed at what he had just been told, and tripping over his words said, "Wait a minute! Are you telling me that you are *the* William Crook; the man who was President Lincoln's bodyguard at the White House?"

"Oh, so you do recognize my name."

"But I don't understand," said Alex in a perplexed voice. "Are you telling me that after I tripped over that tree root I landed in 1865?"

"Actually, yes," replied Crook. "You see that sycamore tree that you were resting under? I was sitting here watching you, but, of course, you could not see me. When you got up, you tripped over a root, shouted out a most unique epithet and fell to the ground. The exact same thing happened at this precise spot to the president and also on April 13, 1865. He tripped attempting to get up after relaxing for a short time under this very tree."

"When you say 'the president' . . . you mean President Lincoln?"

"Why, yes. And when you tripped you uttered a most unusual phrase."

"I remember," Alex replied. "I said 'carn-sarn-it.' I cannot for the life of me think of why I said that. I don't recall ever saying it before."

"Maybe," said Crook in a hushed, barely audible voice, "it wasn't for the life of *you* that those words were uttered."

"What does that mean?" asked Alex, sensing uneasiness within him.

"Let me try to explain." Crook did his best to use a sympathetic voice. "If you know who I am, you know my story. But let me give you some background so that there is no misunderstanding.

"As I said, I was Mr. Lincoln's bodyguard and, even though I had been with him for only a short time, I considered myself to be his friend. Now, Mr. Lincoln had many so-called friends, but none that spent as much time with him on a daily basis, or had as much personal contact with him, as I did. As I look back, I now understand that I ignored the clues that Providence was trying to send my way. I should have been more insistent and tried to persuade him not to go to Ford's Theatre that night."

"That night," said Alex, repeating Crook's words. "You mean the night of the assassination?" Alex's demeanor suddenly changed from one of incredulity, to one of intrigue. "What clues are you talking about?"

"The first," said Crook with a touch of anger in his voice, "was the tardiness of that scoundrel John Parker. He was supposed to relieve me at four o'clock and take up the duties of guarding the president for the remainder of the evening. The fact that he failed to show up on time should have set off an alarm in my brain. You see, Parker had a rather, shall we say, sketchy history. He was a member of the Metropolitan Police Department of the District of Columbia. However, he had had some problems during the course of his service. He was charged with both dereliction of duty and conduct unbecoming an officer for several offenses, including once when he was found drunk on duty and, on another occasion, for sleeping on streetcars while at work. In fact, so the story goes, there was the time he went missing and was finally located at one of the city's brothels. When asked what he was doing there, Parker claimed the madam of the establishment had sent for him. Although

Parker was reprimanded for these unbecoming acts, he was never fired."

Crook paused, closed his eyes and spoke very softly. "And this is the man that I was compelled to step aside for and to trust with the life of President Lincoln. The fact that he couldn't show up on time should have alerted me to remain on my post."

"You said 'clues.' What other ones were there?" Alex inquired.

"When Parker finally arrived and I was gathering my hat and coat to leave, Mr. Lincoln took hold of my hand, looked me square in the eye and said, 'Good-bye, Crook.'" Crook's voice trailed off as the last few words escaped from his lips.

"So?" asked Alex. "Why was that significant?"

"Let me back up. In late 1864, after being hounded about fears and concerns for his safety by members of his cabinet, certain friends in Congress and even Mrs. Lincoln, the president finally relented and agreed to allow a detail of personnel to be assigned to watch out for his welfare. There were four of us assigned and we were scheduled such that our work detail would consist of an eight-hour shift in order to provide twenty-four hour protection. After a short time, one of the men was reassigned to other duties and I was selected to fill his spot. I was truly honored with my new assignment. My first day on the job was the fourth of January, 1865, and I was given the day shift, from eight in the morning until four in the afternoon. Then Parker was to come on at four o'clock."

Crook paused with a faraway look in his eyes before continuing with his story. "Every day, without exception, when my duties with the president were through, he would smile at me and say, 'Good night, Crook.' And I would reply, 'Good night,

Mr. President.' But, on the day of the assassination, upon taking my leave, his demeanor was somewhat odd and he looked at me with his sad and forlorn gray eyes and said, 'Good-bye, Crook.' I should have known that he was trying to tell me he had a premonition.

"If I had prevented the president from attending the theater that evening without my accompanying him, he may have lived through the night. My failure to insist that I do so has resulted in my spending eternity by this tree in hopes that someone would come along and do for Mr. Lincoln what I could not. There have been others before you, appearing at this very spot, showing up suddenly as if being birthed through a wavy, shadowy hole in the air. You see, although they have tried, none have succeeded."

"Tried . . . succeeded . . . at what?

"At saving the life of Abraham Lincoln."

Alex's legs went limp and he would have crumpled to the ground had Crook not reached out and grabbed his arm.

"Wait, I am confused," said Alex. "If the assassination has not yet taken place, how do you know it is going to happen?"

"I know this is a lot to take in," Crook said, "but hear me out. I am the ethereal spirit of William Crook. Ever since my death in 1915, it has been my self-imposed penance to patrol these grounds, awaiting the arrival of a person to do that which I could not.

"I don't know how this is possible," Crook continued, "but you, like the few before, passed through some type of time shift that transported you from whatever year you came from to what is the here and now. Somehow you were specially selected and sent here for a specific purpose. Now, the fact that you know who I am tells me that your presence here is no accident. You were sent here. Your mission, and the reason for being here in this very spot and place in time, is to do whatever is in your power to prevent the assassination of our beloved president, Abraham Lincoln."

"But . . . but . . ."

Crook held up his hand and continued without allowing Alex to interject. "If you are willing to accept this challenge, without reservation, there are some very specific ground rules that you must adhere to while on your quest. If you violate any of these rules, your presence here will be instantaneously terminated and you will be sent back to your own time. Now, any questions so far?"

"Only a million!" Alex exclaimed. Then, recovering his composure and looking Crook in the eye, he said somewhat sheepishly, "I—I'm sorry. But please understand. I am trying to process what you're telling me."

"Believe me, I certainly do understand," said Crook with compassion. "It is now ten-thirty on the morning of Thursday, April 13, 1865. You have just thirty-six hours to put into practice whatever plan you may devise to prevent the dastardly act of the traitor, John Wilkes Booth. However, remember, you cannot tell anyone that you are not of this time, or why you are here. And most importantly, you cannot say anything about knowing what the future holds in store for the president. Also, you cannot have any direct interaction at all with President Lincoln, though you may speak to everyone else. But be forewarned, and I cannot stress this strongly enough, if you violate even one of these rules, your opportunity to save the president's life will immediately end."

"Let me understand this," Alex said pensively, trying to convince himself. "I am really now in Washington in the year 1865. And, at this very moment, Abraham Lincoln is a living, breathing man? And I, and only I, know what will happen to him at Ford's Theatre tomorrow night; and I, and only I, am the one person who has the potential to prevent it?"

"Exactly right," Crook replied.

"Crook," said Alex, in a more suspicious tone of voice than he had intended. "Why should I believe that this is really happening and that I didn't crack my skull open when I tripped on that tree root and am just dreaming this?"

"That question is always asked of me and my answer is always the same." Crook looked at Alex with understanding and calming eyes. "Only you can find this out for yourself. Go and do what you were sent here to accomplish and you will quickly realize what I am telling you is the truth and that you are not experiencing a hallucination."

"Suppose I do as you ask," said Alex, finally accepting what Crook had been telling him. "I still have one question. Am I allowed to see President Lincoln? If this is really happening and I am now present during the time that Mr. Lincoln still lives, can I at least see him? I can't imagine being in this place and time and not having the opportunity to see him in person."

"I certainly understand," replied Crook. "And yes, you may see the president, but only from a distance, so that there is never an actual encounter between the two of you. And," he added with emphasis, "so long as he never suspects who you are or why you are here. Is that understood?"

"Oh yes, absolutely," Alex said with delight. He then silently

promised himself that no matter what else happened, he was
going to actually see Abraham Lincoln.

"Now," said Crook," we need to prepare you to exist and
function in the year 1865. First, we need to get you some contemporary clothes. Come over here."

Alex followed Crook to several baskets on the ground on the
other side of the tree. Sizing Alex up, Crook reached into the
first basket and pulled out a tan shirt made of rather heavy cloth.

"Try this on."

Alex removed his polo shirt and replaced it with the gar-
ment that Crook had handed him. To his surprise, the shirt
actually fit.

"How could you tell what size I am?" he asked incredu-
lously.

Crook smiled. "Remember, this is not the first time I've
done this. After a while, I can pretty well determine what will
fit." Then, laughing aloud, Crook said, "If ever I am relieved of
this arduous duty that I have become destined to perform,
maybe I'll come back as a tailor!"

Crook moved to the next basket. "This is a little trickier,"
he said, as he looked into another basket, this one full of pants.
"You see, the one thing that I do not have available to give you
is a pair of boots. Boots are just too difficult to make in differing
sizes. So, what we need to do is give you a pair of pants that are
long enough to hide, as best as we can, the, um, whatever you
call those things that you have on your feet."

"They're called tennis shoes. They are made out of canvas
and leather."

"All right. But as I said, we must find a pair of pants that
cover them without causing you to trip when you walk."

Crook carefully surveyed Alex's lower body and legs, and, reaching into the basket of pants, pulled out a pair. They were black and also made out of a heavy material, with two buttons at the waist and a rope-type belt. "Here, please try these on."

Alex looked around, hesitating to remove his pants in public. Crook let loose with a laugh, the first time Alex had heard him demonstrate such an outburst.

"Look around," said Crook. "There is no one here. If you want me to turn my back, let me know."

"No, that's okay." Alex stepped out of his tennis shoes, stripped off his jeans and pulled on the pair of pants Crook gave him. When he put his shoes back on, he saw that the bottom of the pants covered all but the toe of his tennis shoes.

"That should work just fine," said Crook. "Now, you will need these," he said, handing Alex a contemporary hat and coat. "And, of course, you must have some money."

"Oh, that's not necessary," said Alex. "I have money." He picked up his jeans that were now lying on the ground, reached into the back pocket, withdrew his wallet and pulled out several bills. As he handed Crook a five-dollar bill, he realized his error. "I suppose that this is no good here."

Crook closely examined the note embossed with the face of the slain president and shook his head. "No, I would think not. Better use these instead." He handed Alex several denominations of bills in what had become known as "greenbacks."

Alex took the bills and placed them atop the Lincoln five-dollar bill, folded the wad and stashed it in his right front pants pocket.

Crook pointed to another basket, "You can put your original clothes in here."

When Alex had picked up his jeans, his cellphone fell out of the pocket. Crook did not appear to notice this. Since Alex was keenly aware that the cellphone would be useless to him now, he put it back into the left front pants pocket of his jeans which he then dropped into the basket. Then he retrieved his wallet, which was now lying on the ground next to the basket and tucked it into his inside coat pocket.

"And, Alex Linwood, one last thing," Crook said, pointing, "Over there is a horse for you to use to ride into Washington City. Now you are ready for your journey to begin. I truly hope you are successful in saving Mr. Lincoln and altering the course of history. Remember, you have"—Crook paused as he pulled out his pocket watch—"a little more than thirty-five hours to complete your task and not one second more." The last words were uttered with great emphasis.

Crook took Alex's hand affectionately in his, clasping it a bit longer than would be done in an ordinary handshake. Looking Alex in the eye, he remarked, "Good luck, son, and God-speed."

With that, Crook turned and walked away, leaving Alex alone to ponder for a few minutes what had just happened and what lay ahead. With a shake of his head, he emerged from his introspection and headed toward the horse that was tied to a hitching post at the side of the house. He then quickly turned around and called out, "Wait a minute. How will I get back to *my* time?" But Crook was gone.

Alex had not ridden a horse for quite a long time. In fact, the last time he did so was when he worked as a summer camp counselor, years before. He climbed gingerly into the saddle and tried to make himself comfortable. The horse turned its head back and looked at Alex, seemingly saying, "Don't worry. It will be fine."

Alex turned the animal toward the path leading away from the Soldiers' Home and in the direction of the main road to the city.

APRIL 13, 1865
WASHINGTON CITY

AFTERNOON

Alex quickly found out that riding a horse was not like riding a bicycle. Although the animal was gentle in demeanor, the ride on the uneven dirt road was bumpy and most uncomfortable, especially where the person meets the saddle. He saw some rudimentary signposts that directed him toward the city and he finally reached an intersection where he turned onto 7th Street. This was clearly not the same 7th Street that, only an hour or so earlier, provided him with a smooth, even ride as he pedaled his rented bicycle. The modern structures he had passed on the way to the Soldiers' Home had vanished, replaced by trees, brush and small out-buildings. A narrow wooden bridge appeared ahead, straddling a creek that simply had not existed when, just a scant time before, he was astride his two-wheeler. As the horse stepped onto the wooden planks and continued across the bridge, Alex was truly delighted by the clip-clop of the hooves upon the hard surface.

Shortly, he came upon two other riders, who were clearly much more comfortable aboard their respective mounts. The two eyed Alex and could readily see that he was struggling a bit while perched in the saddle.

"Hey, there," one of the men called out. "First time in the city?"

"You could say that," Alex replied.

"I did say that," came the retort, as the man exhibited a somewhat puzzled look.

"Sorry," said Alex. "About how long a ride is it to the Federal buildings?"

"Oh, about an hour. You gonna be OK up there for that long?"

"I'll be fine," said Alex, less confident than his voice indicated.

"Well, we will leave you to your own pace. Good luck," he said, and the two men disappeared as they rode off around a bend in the road.

Alex continued on toward the city, giving himself time to reflect upon what had recently happened to him and what lay ahead. Often, when people are asked about their reaction to a significant event, the response is, "I don't really know. It has not hit me yet." Mounted on a totally unfamiliar mode of transportation, beginning to accept the fact that he was now existing in the year 1865, and fully aware of the task vested in him by William Crook, it finally hit him.

As Alex rode on, he tried to formulate in his own mind exactly what course of action to take when he got into the city. He had asked Crook for any helpful advice he might have, but Crook just shook his head and told Alex this was something he had to figure out for himself. Alex knew that at some point he would have to confront John Wilkes Booth, but the where and how needed to be carefully planned. Also, Crook told him that he was here only to save the president, which meant that the awful attack that befell William Seward and caused him such extensive injuries would still take place. Fortunately, Seward survived and even continued on in his position as secretary of state in the Andrew Johnson administration, where his crowning achievement was negotiating the purchase of Alaska from the Russian government.

Alex finally comprehended his purpose for being in 1865. When this realization of the where, when and why he was where he was sank in, a feeling of apprehension and anxiousness flooded him like an adrenaline rush. For the first time, Alex fully appreciated the fact that he had been transported to a bygone place and time where he knew absolutely no one and no one knew he even existed. And, what was more, he was burdened with the onerous and almost unbearable responsibility of being the only person with the potential to save the life of Abraham Lincoln.

Finally coming to grips with his new reality, Alex knew that he had to formulate some type of scheme to complete the task impressed upon him by Crook. But just how was he to prevent John Wilkes Booth from murdering the president? The first thought that popped into his head was to simply kill Booth. A curious smile then crossed his lips and he shook his head. "Simply kill Booth," he almost muttered aloud. How could taking the life of another person be characterized as simple?

Nevertheless, his mind pursued the idea. Shoot Booth? Was this the way to thwart the assassination of Lincoln? The problem was that Alex had never owned a gun. Further, he was not convinced he could actually point a gun and shoot at another person, not even John Wilkes Booth. He knew almost instantly that this approach was not realistic and he dismissed shooting Booth as the answer.

So what were the other alternatives? He could hint to Booth

that he knew about the plot to kill Lincoln, with the hope that this revelation would alter the would-be assassin's course of conduct. But then he had the fatalistic feeling that, rather than be deterred, Booth would simply add Alex's name to the list of people, including Lincoln, Secretary of State Seward and Vice President Johnson, who were designated for elimination. He quickly abandoned this idea as well.

Another notion then surfaced. Suppose Alex told the living and breathing Crook what the ethereal Crook already knew and thereby passed the responsibility of saving Lincoln to someone to whom such a duty rightfully belonged? No, thought Alex, that was too dangerous. First, he might disappear, as Crook had warned, even before the message could be fully relayed. Or, even worse, Officer Crook would want to know how Alex came upon such information and might even detain him while conducting his own investigation. Even if Crook could eventually be convinced that what Alex was telling him was true, by the time the investigation was over, so would be the president's life.

Alex knew that Booth and his cohorts had originally intended to kidnap President Lincoln and offer him in exchange for captured Confederate soldiers. Perhaps he could try to convince Booth to continue to pursue this strategy. But what if Booth could not be deterred from his intention to kill Lincoln, or, worse yet, what if Alex never had the opportunity to even broach this subject with the actor? Alex knew he had to have a backup strategy.

Then, unexpectedly, the answer came to him. Delay! That was it! Alex had to somehow figure out how he could delay Booth from being present at the presidential box on the evening of April 14th and thus be prevented from carrying out his heinous act. Alex was now firmly convinced that this was his best course of action and he sat up in the saddle with renewed confidence and purpose.

But the first order of business was to find Booth. As if emerging from a trance, Alex again became aware of his surroundings, including the clip-clop of the horse's hooves on the dry, hard dirt path. With the dust that was being kicked up by his horse dissipating behind him, Alex actually felt a sense of relief. He now had a realistic and viable plan.

Soon, the city of Washington came into view. Alex brought his horse to a quick stop and observed what lay before him. Rather than a metropolis made of glass and steel, or monuments made of marble glistening in the sun, the buildings were mostly constructed of wood, the majority of them no more than three or four stories tall. Row houses lined 7th Street as he entered the city proper. There were taverns on almost every corner, with men continuously entering or leaving. In the dirt roadway, animals roamed freely: pigs, a couple of goats and even a cow in addition to the usual dogs and cats. And then there was the smell, an overpowering acrid stench that seemed to hang in the air.

How do they become accustomed to that smell? Alex thought to himself. It reminded him of the dairy farm odor that would waft onto the freeways as one drove through Central California. While that only bothered the olfactory organs for a short time, there could be no escaping what he was exposed to now. He had, of course, read about this in many books describing the living conditions in 1860s Washington. But to experience it firsthand was truly something different.

As he rode on, it suddenly occurred to him that his first stop should be Mary Surratt's boardinghouse. Although Booth did not live there, he had spent considerable time at that location, meeting with the co-conspirators in the days leading up to the assassination. Despite the fact that the war was technically over and there were no longer any imprisoned rebels, perhaps if Alex could actually speak to Booth, he could convince him to continue on with the original kidnapping plot rather than alter his plan to one of murder.

There were clearly obvious problems that would have to be overcome. The most pressing was how could Alex even engage in such a conversation with Booth? How could a complete stranger have enough in-depth and inside information about the conspiracy to even broach the subject? Would Booth be so startled that he would suspect there was a breach somewhere among his cohorts, thereby actually putting Alex's life in danger? Alex had to figure out a very delicate way to broach the subject.

Then, assuming there was such a discourse, what reason would Alex come up with for the purpose of kidnapping the president if the war was over? Perhaps he could convince Booth that, if the scheme of kidnapping the president remained, the demand for Lincoln's safe release might constitute a significant concession by the Union leaders when the terms for Reconstruction were negotiated. Additionally, those former members of Congress from previously rebellious states, who held legislative seats when the South seceded, could return to their posts in the House and Senate. Or perhaps some type of assistance could be given to Southerners whose farms and businesses had been destroyed during the course of the fighting. Alex knew he had to come up with some type of "carrot" to encourage Booth to forget his current assassination plan and reinstate the former kidnapping scheme.

But first he had to find Booth. Alex reined in the horse and dismounted in front of a general store. He decided to ask passers-by if anyone knew where the Surratt Boarding House was located. He knew that it was a long shot, but he had to begin somewhere. After more than thirty minutes and several dozen people, he was no closer to learning of its whereabouts than when he started. Obviously, the boarding house was not in the vicinity. He removed the wristwatch that he had tucked away in his pants pocket and checked the time. It was 4:30 and he wanted to find the Surratt home before it became dark.

Alex decided to continue riding along 7th Street, scanning the buildings, hoping to see something that would assist him in his search. Then, suddenly, at the corner of 7th and F Streets was a Post Office Department. Alex jumped down, tied the horse to a hitching post and ran inside. He observed a long counter, with multiple arched windows. Behind each window stood a postal clerk, attending to the requests of the customer standing before him. Racks along one wall held newspapers and other circulars, and a large pot-bellied stove was situated in the middle of the room. The noise created by all of the people seeking information or wanting to post letters and packages was nothing short of a cacophony.

Alex got into the shortest line behind a rather rotund woman. There were five people ahead of him. Alex, whose middle name was not patience, kept glancing at the clock on the wall and watching the other lines, just in case his choice had been a poor one and required him to move. After what seemed a long time, but was really only about 10 minutes, the woman walked away from the counter and it was Alex's turn.

"Next," called out the clerk, a man in his late forties, whose coat and cravat were visible above the counter. Alex approached the postal clerk who peered at him somewhat quizzically since Alex had neither a letter nor a parcel for mailing. "How can I help you?" he asked.

"I am trying to find an address and I was hoping that if I gave you the name of the owner of the building, you could tell me its location."

"Sure thing," replied the man. "Whose address are you looking for?"

"I am trying to find the location of the boarding house owned by Mary Surratt."

"Let me see if it is listed in the city directory." The clerk reached under the counter and pulled out a well-worn bound tome. "What was that name again?"

"Surratt. S-U-R-R-A-T-T. The first name is Mary."

The man donned a pair of spectacles and turned the pages of the book, presumably to the listings beginning with the letter "S," and upon locating the correct page, ran his forefinger down the listings. Finding nothing initially, he turned the page and repeated the process. This went on for several pages and Alex's hopes began to quickly diminish.

"Ah, here it is," the postal worker exclaimed mildly. "I'll write it down for you."

Removing the pencil that had been tucked behind his ear, he touched the lead tip to his tongue, scrawled down the information and then slid the slip of paper under the caged divider. Alex thanked him and turned away. As he was walking toward the door, he looked at the note: "Mary Surratt—604 H Street, NW."

Alex's heart began to pound in his chest as he strode toward where he had tethered the horse. Was he actually on his way to coming face-to-face with John Wilkes Booth? Could this really be happening? Could he actually be taking steps to prevent the killing of the president? In any event, he was now about to head toward the site where the conspirators had met and devised their diabolical plan. Just as he put one foot in the stirrup to climb into the saddle, he suddenly realized something: he did not know where 604 H Street was. He shook his head and got back down, hoping that a passerby could point him in the correct direction.

The first two people were unable to help. The third person he asked was a very young soldier, sporting a moustache and mutton chop sideburns and carrying a medical bag at his side. "Pardon me," Alex said casually while impeding the young man's path of travel. "By any chance would you know how to get to 604 H Street, Northwest, from here?"

"Why certainly, sir." The soldier pointed to the part of 7th Street that Alex had not yet travelled. "If you continue about two blocks, you will come to the intersection with H Street. Turn to your right and the next street will be 6th Street. The address you seek should be near the corner of 6th and H."

Alex thanked him and, as he reached out to shake his hand, glanced down at the black medical bag, the handle of which was in the young officer's left hand. A gold monogram embossed just below the bag's latch bore the lettering "C.A. Leale." Although there was something very familiar about the man's name, Alex could not put his finger on it. Bidding him good-day, Alex returned to the edge of the wooden sidewalk where his horse was waiting, pulled himself up onto the saddle and directed the horse down 7th Street.

APRIL 13, 1865
TWO WOMEN

It was a very short ride from the Post Office building to 6th and H Streets. Alex turned the corner and studied the buildings on H Street carefully, looking for 604. After passing a barber shop and a gunsmith, he saw the number etched on a wooden board that swayed from a metal signpost.

It was now approaching 6 o'clock. Alex alit from the horse and stood transfixed, staring at the building. It was an unassuming, wooden three-story structure, with shutters and two dormers. Although there was a door on the ground floor, a set of wooden steps ran up and parallel to the front of the house, leading to a second-floor landing and an ornately framed door that was clearly to be used to gain entry. Alex steeled himself and, in an almost surreal state, began to ascend the stairs.

He reached the top landing and turned to his left to face the door. Suddenly he realized that he had never been to a boardinghouse before. What was the proper protocol? Did one just walk in as if it were a hotel, or knock and wait for someone to open the door? Deferring to the course that seemed least intrusive, Alex knocked.

A woman's voice called, "It's open. Come on in."

Gradually opening the door, Alex saw a middle-aged woman walking toward him. He froze with his left hand still on the doorknob and stared. It was actually her. In the books he had read, especially those dealing particularly with the assassination, there were photographs of all the conspirators. He had read these enough times to be able to recall the faces of the primary people involved in the plot. The approaching woman looked just like the photographs Alex had seen. She was unmistakably Mary Surratt. A chill went up and down Alex's spine as he thought, *This just got real.*

Mary Surratt was of medium height and somewhat stout. Her thick, straight brown hair was parted in the middle and pulled back so that it barely covered her ears. She had penetrating dark eyes and a stern expression punctuated by somewhat heavy eyebrows. As with many people of this era, she appeared older than her 35 years of age.

Alex continued to stare at the woman until her voice brought him back to consciousness. "Can I help you?" Her tone clearly suggested it was not the first time she had asked him this question. Just as he was about to speak, he heard footsteps coming up the stairs behind him, and a man brushed past him and entered the building.

"Hello, Mrs. Surratt," said the man. And then turning his head back toward Alex he asked, "Who is this?"

"Oh, hello Davey," replied Mary Surratt.

Alex could not believe his ears or his eyes. David Herold had just pushed past him and into the house. This was the same David Herold who, in less than thirty hours, would be accompanying Booth into the Maryland countryside after the assassination. The same David Herold who, with Booth, spent the night at the home of Dr. Samuel Mudd after the doctor set Booth's broken leg. The same David Herold who was with Booth in the barn on the Garrett Farm when Booth was shot and killed by Union troops, and who himself surrendered rather than face the same fate. And the same David Herold destined to be tried, convicted and hanged as one of the co-conspirators.

"How was your day?" Mary asked him. "And, as for this fellow," she said a bit more gruffly, jerking a thumb in Alex's direction, "I am trying to find that out."

Herold continued toward the back of the building. Mary Surratt stood glaring at Alex. "Well?" Her voice clearly implied that she was not going to ask again.

Alex somehow regained his composure and began to speak. "Good evening, ma'am," Alex said. "Is John Wilkes Booth in?" incredulous that these words actually passed through his lips.

Mary looked at him suspiciously and took a half-step back. "What do you want with Wilkes?"

"Well," Alex began, stumbling slightly over his words as he had not rehearsed this part in his head. "I am a big admirer of his and I have seen him perform many times. I heard that he frequents this home and I was hoping to say hello and get one of his calling cards and an autograph."

Mary's jaw seemed to relax a bit and her demeanor softened slightly. "He is not in just now. I'm afraid that I do not know where he may be, or when he may be returning. I am sorry I cannot be of any further help to you."

She then stood stock-still and stared into Alex's eyes, saying nothing, but it was clear from her body language that it was now time for Alex to take his leave.

"Thank you," he said. "Sorry for the intrusion."

Alex exited through the door onto the exterior landing. Mary Surratt did not say another word and the door closed behind him.

• • •

Alex suddenly realized he was famished. With all that had already happened today, he now finally had time to think about getting something to eat. He hoped that perhaps there was a restaurant in the area and he decided to walk a couple of blocks in each direction to see what he could find. It was also getting a bit chilly and he was thankful for the coat that Crook had given to him.

Alex walked two blocks along H Street and saw, up ahead and across the street from where he was, a green awning, across the face of which was a sign reading, "Chambers' House and Grille." This sounded like a promising establishment. Alex crossed the street carefully, mindful of horse and carriage traffic, as well as that which the animals had deposited on the street, and went up to the restaurant. The aroma wafting from within was actually quite inviting.

Inside was an enormous bar, staffed by three bartenders moving busily from one end to the other, miraculously without knocking into one another or spilling anything. A crowd of men stood before them, enjoying libations and cigars while engaged in animated conversation. At the far end of the bar was a podium, where stood an attractive woman who appeared to be in her late thirties, wearing a dark green dress, who Alex assumed to be the restaurant hostess. Alex noted that the dress, which came down almost to the floor, had a high neckline along with long sleeves bordered in white at the wrist. A portion of her high buckled shoes peeked out from below the hemline. She wore her dark hair pinned up, flattering her soft facial features. As Alex approached the podium, the woman smiled, which made her face light up. Alex also noticed she had green eyes.

"Welcome to Chambers," she said in a somewhat husky voice. "My name is Lucy. How can I help you?"

Alex was somewhat disarmed by this attractive and obviously very self-assured woman. "Good evening, I would like to have dinner here tonight."

"Very nice," she replied. "Are you dining alone, or are you expecting a guest?"

"No, it's just me."

"Very well, please follow me." Lucy removed a menu from a stack sitting atop a counter and walked into the dining room. Alex followed her to a table against the wall about halfway into the large dining area. The table was set for two people with utensils, plates and coffee cups. She placed the menu upon a napkin sitting between the eating implements. At the far corner of the table rested a complimentary copy of the *Washington Evening Star*.

"Bon appétit," said Lucy, as Alex sat down. "I will check back to see how you are doing. Your waiter will be with you in a minute."

Alex watched as she made her way back to her station near the end of the bar, unable to take his eyes off of her. His focus was interrupted by a male voice.

"Good evening, sir. I am Thomas. Are you ready to order?" asked the waiter, who had suddenly appeared tableside. Thomas was a tall, young black man, impeccably dressed in a black suit. He was wearing white gloves and holding a pad and pencil.

"Um, I think I need a couple of minutes to look at the menu. But in the meantime, could you bring me a beer?"

"But of course. Do you have a preference? The back of our

menu has a complete list of the beers that we offer."

Alex picked up the menu, turned it over and looked at the available choices. Nothing was familiar to him, but he did not want to give the impression that he really had no idea what his options were. "I will have the Scotch Ale, please."

"Good choice, sir. I will get that for you and be back to take your order."

Alex flipped open the menu and was somewhat taken aback by the selections. Many of the choices were unlike anything he had ever seen. There was a soup course, with the options including tomato, pea or puree of fowl; a selection of boiled foods like leg of mutton, beef tongue and ham; entrees consisting of wild red-head duck and stewed veal; and vegetable selections of parsnips, beets, onions and turnips. Fortunately, there were also a few tried-and-true items that allowed Alex to feel that he was ordering a meal that would not require him to be too adventurous.

The waiter returned and set down a tall glass of amber beer. "Have you decided on dinner, sir?"

"Yes," replied Alex. "I would like to start with the tomato soup and then I would like the roast turkey and mashed potatoes. Oh, and some bread and butter, too, please."

The man meticulously wrote down the order on his pad. "Thank you, sir," he said and made his way back to the kitchen.

Alex reached for the newspaper. He had always enjoyed reading newspapers and made a point of picking up the local edition whenever he traveled. However, a paper printed over 150 years ago was even more fascinating. As he waited for the meal to be served, Alex could not help but continually glance from the inked pages over to the hostess podium where Lucy was standing. Once, she caught him staring and smiled at him. Alex quickly averted his eyes back to the newspaper, embarrassed that his ogling had been detected.

The waiter returned with a steaming bowl of soup and a basket containing a small loaf of fresh, hot bread that smelled wonderful. Alex tore off a piece, applied some butter and took a bite. If it was possible, the bread tasted even better than it smelled. The soup was also quite good. Alex wondered why he had assumed that the food would not be as delicious as it was. He quickly devoured the soup, not realizing how hungry he had been. The waiter returned shortly and replaced the soup bowl with the roast turkey and mashed potatoes, both awash in a thick gravy.

The plate on which the food was served was itself quite interesting. It was a white porcelain plate, glazed with a cobalt-blue design of a pastoral landscape. Alex was unaware that the plate was actually Blue Canton dinnerware that dated back to Colonial times. As he took his first forkful of potatoes, he heard a woman's voice.

"Hello again. I am Lucy Chambers."

"Oh, do you own this restaurant?" asked Alex.

"Actually, my father is the owner. That's our picture there hanging over the bar. But seeing as he is getting up in years, I have taken to running it. Are you enjoying your meal?"

"Yes, very much, thank you. Oh, and I am Alex Linwood. It is a pleasure to meet you."

"I have a minute free. May I join you?"

"Of course," said Alex, rising from his chair as Lucy lowered herself into the chair across from him.

"Pardon me for saying so, but you appear a bit lost. Have

you recently arrived in Washington?"

"Yes, actually I have only been in the city a short while."

"Are you here on business?" she asked. "Perhaps a speculator of some sorts looking to take advantage of the postwar possibilities?"

"Oh no, it's nothing like that. But I do have some business that I must attend to . . ." His voice trailed off before he said something he shouldn't.

Lucy sat with him for a couple of minutes and they had a brief, but very comfortable, conversation until Lucy looked over to the bar and saw some customers waiting for a table.

"I must be off," she said, as she slid her chair back. "Enjoy your time in the city."

"Thank you." Alex once again rose from his chair and remained standing, watching her as she walked off.

Then he sat back down and finished off the turkey and potatoes. He soaked up the last bit of gravy with a piece of bread, washing it down with the final swallow of beer. The waiter returned and told him that dessert was part of the meal and offered either lemon pie or ice cream. Alex chose the pie, with a cup of coffee. The pie was fine, but the coffee was much bitterer than he was used to drinking. There was no sugar on the table, so he just sipped it slowly. When he was through, the waiter removed the plates and placed the bill on the table. Alex read over the check and had to suppress a smile: the ale was 50 cents, turkey 60 cents, mashed potatoes 15 cents and the bread 10 cents.

As Alex was fishing in his pocket for money, Lucy passed by his table again as she was returning from having seated a couple of customers. "Thank you for dining with us, Mr.

Linwood," she said with a warm smile. "I hope you enjoyed your meal."

"Oh, I did very much," he replied. "And I also enjoyed talking with you."

Lucy touched his arm gently and walked off. Alex carefully removed a couple of period one-dollar bills from his pocket and laid them on the table. Wiping his mouth one last time with his napkin, he got up. As he left the restaurant, he glanced up at the picture of Lucy and her father displayed over the bar.

EVENING

It was almost 8 o'clock in the evening, and too late, or perhaps too early, to seek out Booth to try to interrupt the intended plan. Alex went back to where he had left his horse tied and saw a young black boy who happened to be standing nearby.

"Hello, young fellow," said Alex. "Do you by chance know of a place where I can get my horse fed, watered and boarded for the night?" This jargon was right out of the old Western novels he had read as a kid. He was unsure if he had even made the request correctly.

"Oh, yes, sir," the boy replied. "My uncle Horace owns the livery stable just down the street. I could take your horse there for you if you like."

"Ah, I remember passing it earlier today. That would be fine and much appreciated," said Alex. "Tell your uncle my name is Alex and I will pick up the horse tomorrow morning." Alex reached into his pocket and withdrew a coin that he pressed into the boy's palm.

"Thank you, sir," said the boy. "I certainly will."

"Oh, and one more thing. Do you know of a hotel where I can get a room for the night?" asked Alex.

"Well sir, the Capitol House is just a few blocks that way," the boy said, pointing in the direction from which Alex had just come.

"Thanks very much."

The lad untied the horse and guided it toward the stable. Alex began walking along H Street. Although it was still relatively early, it had been a long and very stressful day and Alex was suddenly exhausted. He looked forward to getting a good night's rest and resuming his quest the next morning.

As he moved along the sidewalk, he took particular notice of the ambient gas streetlights illuminating the way. They gave off a very different glow than electric light posts, as they were softer and, of course, not nearly as effective as the lights to which he was accustomed. There was a pretty good amount of foot traffic along the avenue and he observed all types of people. There were men in suits likely returning home from an office job, as well as men in rougher clothes who possibly performed some type of manual labor to earn a living. He also saw well-dressed women adorned in fancy hats, walking either in pairs or at the side of a gentleman. Likewise, there were women whose clothing and demeanor clearly suggested a harsher way of life to make ends meet.

Finally, Alex spotted the Capitol House. It was a four-story brick building with a restaurant on the ground floor and a separate entrance for the stairs leading to the hotel lobby. Alex entered through the double glass doors and, climbing the single flight of stairs, found himself standing in a very modest but clean lobby. The clerk stood behind a small desk, on the wall behind which was a shelving unit of multiple pigeonholes. Beneath each unit was a room number. Some of the compartments were filled with mail, while in others there was just a room key.

Alex approached the desk and was glad to see keys in several of the boxes and assumed he would not have to look elsewhere for lodging. The man behind the desk was older, with thinning gray hair, an almost-white moustache and horn-rimmed glasses. He looked up from his ledger book as Alex advanced.

"Good evening, sir. How may I help you?" he asked in a comfortable and welcoming voice.

"I would very much like a room for the night."

"We can certainly accommodate you there," the clerk replied. Then he looked at Alex more carefully and at the floor where Alex was standing. "Do you have any bags?"

"Um, no, I don't," said Alex. "I am only going to be staying one night."

"Very well," responded the clerk, this time in a bit more of a suspicious tone. "The room lets for four dollars a night, which includes clean sheets and it is two dollars extra for breakfast in the morning at the restaurant downstairs."

"Fine," said Alex, as he stood waiting for his key. He could feel fatigue setting in.

"That will be six dollars, in advance," said the clerk, putting sufficient emphasis on the last two words uttered. "I will also need for you to sign the register." He picked up a pen, dipped it into the inkwell next to the book and extended it to Alex. The clerk then rotated the registration book so that Alex could sign in. Alex printed his name in the register, along with the date he was checking in and tomorrow's date, when he would be leaving. Turning the book back, the clerk eyed what he had written and then took a key from one of the slots. "You'll be in room 20. That'll be six dollars, please."

Alex reached into his pocket and looked with bleary eyes at

the several bills he pulled out. He peeled off a one-dollar bill and the mostly masked five-dollar note behind it and handed them to the clerk.

The clerk gave him the key. "Your room is two fights up, middle of the hall. Washroom is down the hall from your room. The stairs are over there." He pointed to the far end of the lobby. "Breakfast is served from six to ten a.m."

Alex thanked him, stifling a yawn as he headed to the stairs. He climbed the two flights of steps and walked down a dimly lit hallway until he found his room. He inserted the key, turned the latch and entered. The room was softly aglow from the sconce on the hallway wall. Inside, he saw a lamp and a box of matches on a table. He struck the match, lifted the glass globe and touched the match to the wick. Once it began to burn, he returned the globe to its original position. Then he turned and closed the door.

Alex saw that his quarters consisted of a large room with a bed, two chairs and a long dresser. Atop the dresser was a pitcher of water, an empty bowl and a towel. On the floor beside the bed there was a chamber pot. Alex pulled back the covers and, fully clothed, fell into bed. He pulled the bed sheets up to his neck and heaved a sigh. After about fifteen minutes, he was very close to falling asleep. Suddenly there was an insistent knock at the door.

"Who could that possibly be?" Alex wondered, suddenly jarred awake.

He got out of bed, crossed the room and looked for the familiar peephole in the door. Of course, there was none, so he cautiously opened it. Two men stood before him, one in a black suit and the other in the uniform of a Washington police officer.

The man in the suit spoke first, dispensing with any salutation.

"Are you Alex Linwood and did you just check in a few minutes ago?"

"Why, yes, I did," Alex replied. "Is there some sort of problem?"

"And did you pay for your room in advance?"

Again Alex replied in the affirmative.

"And did your payment include this five-dollar bill?"

The man in the suit held out the bill pinched between the thumb and forefingers of his hands. To his shock, Alex saw that it was a Lincoln five-dollar bill.

The police officer asked, "May we come in and ask you a few questions, sir?" It was more an order than a request.

Alex's heart dropped into his stomach. He tried to think of something to say that would make them simply turn and leave, but nothing came to mind.

"Sir?" repeated the officer.

"Yes, gentlemen, please come in." Alex hoped responding in a demure fashion might help his situation.

"Sit down," instructed the man in the suit, "and keep your hands where I can see them." Alex walked over to one of the chairs and sat with his hands positioned on the arms. One of the men stood directly in front of him, while the other situated himself behind. Both men presented rather imposing figures and Alex felt helpless.

"May I ask what this is all about?" Alex inquired to the man standing in front of him, while also glancing over his shoulder at the second person. He thought that if he feigned ignorance things might turn in his favor. But such was not to be the case.

"Don't you know that passing counterfeit money is against

the law?" intoned the man in the suit, glaring down at Alex and holding up the five-dollar bill.

How could Alex explain that the bill he'd given to the desk clerk would someday actually be accepted as legal tender? He was about to try to piece the words together, but his thought process was jarringly interrupted.

The man standing in front of Alex moved a bit closer and said, "My name is Henderson, Secret Service, and this is Officer Baker. We are placing you under arrest."

The words hit Alex like a sharp slap. His mind continued to race as he tried to come up with a plausible explanation.

"Wait, wait," Alex stammered. He could scarcely believe this was really happening. "I can explain." But how could he really explain?

Henderson was not in the mood for any story. "You can tell it to the judge on Monday morning," he said. "In the meantime, you are going to be the guest of the city for the weekend. Now get up and come with us."

"But—but—" Alex pleaded as he rose from the chair. He simply could not think of anything to say. How could he have been so careless as to use modern money to pay the hotel bill?

The police officer, a burly man with a barrel chest, reached out from behind and grabbed him by the forearm. "Hard way or easy way?"

"Easy way," Alex muttered in a resigned voice, head bent.

"Good," said the policeman. "Then no need to use the cuffs. Let's go."

The three men exited the room and walked down the hall. The Secret Service agent led the way, with Alex in the middle, his arm still being held by the police officer following just slightly behind.

How ironic, Alex thought as he was being led away. The Secret Service, which in modern days is charged with protecting the life of the president, has now taken into custody the man whose purpose for being here is to save the life of the president.

They walked down the two flights of stairs to the lobby. As they crossed to the exit door, the desk clerk glared at Alex. "Thought you could cheat me, eh? Thought I wouldn't notice? Imagine the likeness of Abraham Lincoln on a five-dollar bill! I don't know what your game is . . ." His voice trailed off as the three men disappeared through the exit door.

Upon reaching the ground floor, Alex was astonished by what he saw. There at the curb was a black paddy wagon with the word POLICE emblazoned across the side. Hitched to it was a brown horse, wearing blinders. It was just like something he had seen a hundred times in the movies—but this was real. The Secret Service man stood close to Alex, while the policeman opened the rear door. "In you go," he barked.

Alex had no choice. He walked to the far end of the wagon, grasped hold of the handle, placed his foot on the step and pulled himself in. The interior of the vehicle was small, with only two benches, each attached to a side of the wagon. The air inside was thick and acrid, full of unpleasant odors, making it difficult to breathe. Alex sat down on the right-hand bench. He was alone. The double doors closed and he heard the clank of the latch.

"Thanks for your help, Joe," said the Secret Service agent.

"No problem," the officer replied. "I will take him to the 9th Street Precinct for booking. Have a nice evening, Fred."

With that, the officer climbed into the driver's seat and the wagon began to move. Alex jolted from side to side as the horse moved along the uneven street. He felt a combination of fear and dread, but he was more stunned than anything else. He knew, from the time he spoke to Crook, that anything was likely to happen to him in this unfamiliar time and place, but this series of events was something that had never even crossed his mind. What could possibly go wrong next? Crook said he had only 36 hours to try to stop Booth and now it looked as if he would spend the remaining time sitting in a Washington jail cell. His mouth was dry and he had a slight ringing in his ears. The words "You can't change history" played over and over in his head.

After a short while, the vehicle arrived at the police station. There was a creak as Baker got down from the driver's seat. Then, instead of hearing the rear door opening as he had expected, Alex heard two men speaking to one another just outside.

"Baker, what have you got there?"

"Agent Henderson and I picked up this counterfeiter at the Capitol House. I am going to book him and put him in a cell until Judge Bowman can deal with him on Monday." Alex still could not believe this was happening.

"Haven't you heard?" the other officer asked. "You need to take this guy to the 12th Street Precinct. Judge Bowman now has a courtroom there to handle cases like this."

"No one told me," replied Baker, clearly annoyed. "OK, I'll see you later." With that he walked around the wagon and once again took his position in the driver's seat.

Inside, Alex felt as if the walls were closing in on him. He had to fight the urge to stand up and scream. He now had more time to imagine what lay ahead and he banged his fists on the bench, feeling utterly frustrated and helpless. All he could think about was what a 19th-century jail cell might be like.

Once again, the paddy wagon moved slowly along the street. When the wagon passed under a streetlamp, shards of light briefly entered the interior through the space between the rear doors. Alex despaired, resigned to the fact that there was nothing he could do to alter his predicament.

His current nightmare was suddenly interrupted by a tremendous jerking motion that nearly threw him off the bench and onto the floor. The wagon was unexpectedly going faster. Alex clutched the portion of wooden bench between his legs to keep from falling.

Just ahead, a commotion was brewing. "Help, help!" A slender young woman was screaming. "They are robbing us! Please help! They are beating up my husband!"

Officer Baker heard the wild cries and instantly hollered to the horse to move, while furiously shaking the reins. The horse responded almost immediately and its gait changed from a walk to nearly a gallop. Alex, inside the darkened police wagon, could not imagine what was happening. There were no straps or handles to hang onto and the bench provided little assistance. The wagon suddenly made a violent turn to the right, throwing Alex off the bench. He struck the right side of his head on the wall and fell to the floor. As the patrol wagon resumed a straight course, Alex picked himself up and sat down again. Then he felt the momentum of the wagon begin to slow.

Just as the paddy wagon was about to arrive at the site of the turmoil, another officer came running toward it from the opposite direction. Officer Baker reined in the horse to a stop and leapt from the seat. He ran around to the back of the wagon and arrived to see three men, dressed in old and dirty clothes, accosting a young, well-dressed man. At almost the same instant, his fellow officer came upon the scene.

"Officers! Oh, thank God! Please help us!" the woman cried.

Without a word, the two Washington peace officers jumped into the fray. The three assailants were screaming incomprehensibly and flailing away at the young man.

"Quick!" Baker yelled to his comrade. "Open the door to the wagon so we can throw these guys in."

The second officer rushed to the rear of the paddy wagon, undid the latch and flung open the doors, totally ignoring Alex. He then returned to assist in subduing the three hoodlums. It was clear at this point that Officer Baker was paying no attention to the man he had previously locked in the wagon. He was about ten yards away from the now-opened rear doors and his hands were full attempting to assist the young man who was the object of the assault. The young woman continued to scream and by now a small crowd was gathering to watch the commotion.

Alex saw his chance. Without a second thought, he leaped out of the paddy wagon, pushed his way through the throng and ran down the street as fast as he could. All eyes were on the ruckus involving the combatants and his escape went unnoticed.

Alex had no idea where he was going, but he knew that he could not stop. After running for several blocks, he suddenly saw, just ahead of him, a large stable. A crude sign perched slightly askew over the double barn-style door read: "Horses for Hire and Boarding. Horace Adams, Proprietor." Alex made a beeline across the street, dodging a horse-drawn streetcar, and entered the stable. There were several lamps lit, giving off an eerie glow. Alex stopped, bent over at the waist and put his hands on his knees, trying to catch his breath. He now could feel the throbbing in his head.

All at once, a young boy appeared at his side. "Mista, are you all right?"

Alex raised his head to respond, but before he could utter a sound the boy exclaimed: "Hey, I know you. Ain't you Mista Alex, the man who had me bring his horse here?"

"Yes, son," Alex replied. "It's me. It seems I got myself into a bit of trouble. Mind if I spend the night here in the stable?"

Before the boy could answer, a horse-drawn buggy emerged from the shadows. "Why don't you come with me, instead?"

Alex recognized the voice and in a second saw the driver of the buggy. It was Lucy.

"I would very much appreciate that," Alex said, still fighting to catch his breath.

"Then get in," Lucy said in a warm and inviting tone.

Alex pulled himself into the buggy and collapsed next to her on the left side of the bench seat. Lucy waved to the boy and made a clicking sound, to which the horse responded by beginning to walk. Lucy guided the buggy out of the stable and into the night.

• • •

The three ruffians had been brought under control with the help of two other officers who had arrived on the scene. "Bring them over here," Officer Baker called. "Put them in the back of the wagon. I'm sure the prisoner inside won't mind a little company."

One of the officers led the first man to the rear of the paddy wagon and peered inside as he ushered the man up the step. "What prisoner?" he called out.

Officer Baker rushed to the back of the wagon and, looking inside, saw that Alex was gone. He simply put his hands on his hips and shook his head.

LUCY

Lucy Chambers was born in West Chester, Pennsylvania, in 1828. This small town, about 40 miles from Philadelphia, was often a resting point for people traveling there from Lancaster County. Her father was the co-owner of an inn and tavern that was a frequent destination of persons making that journey.

As a teenager, Lucy began working at her father's business. He taught her all facets of the trade, from food preparation and service to how to deal with customers both gracious and rowdy. When she was behind the bar, the tapper—the name given the person who taps kegs or casks—would instruct her in the proper way to pour beer and spirits. He had jokingly reminded her to "mind her P's and Q's," an archaic reference when serving beer to a customer in either a pint or a quart stein. Lucy's father always said that she was a natural in every aspect of this endeavor and someday hoped that she would take over the business.

In 1857, Lucy became engaged to a young man from Philadelphia. He was completing his studies at the Jefferson Medical College and told her that, once he graduated, they could marry. Unfortunately, her betrothed contracted influenza during the pandemic that lasted from 1857 to 1859; he succumbed to the disease in 1858. With his death, Lucy turned her full attention to assisting her father and his partner in the operation of the tavern.

Then, in 1860, the two co-owners had a falling out. Lucy's

mother had died 10 years earlier, so there was nothing to keep them in Pennsylvania. Her father, who had a keen interest in national politics, had always wanted to go to Washington. So, after selling his interest in the business, Lucy and her father relocated to Washington City. Almost immediately, her father bought a small restaurant and renamed it Chambers' House and Grille. Lucy went to work with him, taking the de facto title of partner. Over the years, the restaurant expanded and was soon a very popular spot for both Washington's businessmen and members of Congress.

Lucy's father was very proud of his new establishment and the fact that he was now sharing the enterprise with his only child. To memorialize the event, he engaged the services of a local photographer, who met them early one autumn morning at the restaurant. Lucy and her father struck a pose by the large window embossed with the restaurant name and their likenesses were preserved for posterity. The framed photograph was proudly displayed over the bar with the inscription, "Est. 1860."

In 1864, her father suffered a serious injury in a horseback riding accident and was no longer able to work. Lucy took over the daily operations of the restaurant and it continued to thrive under her stewardship. She worked long hours and enjoyed interacting with the interesting people who frequented the eatery. However, there was never again a beau in Lucy's life.

• • •

Once they were on the street, Lucy encouraged the horse to pick up the pace and the carriage moved along at a steady clip.

"Are you all right?" Lucy asked, with genuine concern in her voice.

"I think so," Alex replied, although he still felt pain to the side of his head.

As the carriage passed under a streetlamp Lucy glanced at the man seated to her left. "You're bleeding!" she exclaimed in surprise, squinting to see in the minimum available light. She noticed the red trickle of blood running down his neck and onto his shirt collar. She removed a scarf that had been wrapped around her neck. "Here, take this. Press it to the side of your head."

Alex took the scarf and applied it to the laceration, which was just above his ear. He felt a little pain as he applied pressure. "Thank you," he said, taking a deep breath. He could smell her perfume on the scarf. It had a lovely lavender scent. "That should stop the blood."

"We'll be at my house in just a few minutes," Lucy said in a calmer tone. "I'll clean you up when we get there."

They rode in silence for a few minutes, until Lucy guided the horse and carriage off the main road and through an open gate attached to two stone pillars. The rig then entered a small courtyard where a tall, thin black man greeted them.

"Hello, Jonah," said Lucy. "Can you help us into the house and then come back out to unhitch and feed Bess?"

"Yes, ma'am," Jonah replied in a deep baritone voice. "Here, sir, take my hand." He reached out toward Alex, who clasped the offered hand and gingerly climbed down from the carriage. Though the bleeding had subsided somewhat, Alex was beginning to feel a bit lightheaded. Jonah wrapped his large arm around Alex's shoulder and guided him toward the rear entrance of the house, with Lucy leading the way. They climbed the stairs and Lucy opened the door onto a small service porch. Just inside was a wash basin perched atop a small table.

"Please take him into the parlor and help him to a seat on the sofa."

They entered the next room and Jonah eased Alex onto a red velvet sofa. Several lamps provided a warm glow and a fire in the fireplace made the room very comfortable.

"Thank you very much," Lucy said to Jonah. "If I need any other assistance I will let you know."

"Y'all welcome, Miss Lucy. I will go out and tend to Bess." With that, Jonah left the parlor. The sound of the back door closing could be heard as he exited the house.

"Now, let me look at that that head of yours," said Lucy. She sat down next to Alex and removed the scarf that he was still pressing against his wound. "Can you move so that you are a little closer to the lamp?"

Alex slid to his left, to the end of the couch and tilted his head forward so that it was nearly touching the large glass globe. Lucy crouched down beside him and gently applied her hands to the area of the wound, carefully parting Alex's hair to get a better view of the laceration. Alex found her cool, tender touch was very pleasant and caring.

"It looks like the bleeding has stopped," she said. "Let me get something to clean you up."

Lucy left the parlor through an open doorway and Alex looked around. The room was rectangular, adorned with red wallpaper with a raised pattern. A large rug lay on the dark, wooden floor in front of the sofa. Several landscape paintings hung on the walls and the ceiling was white plaster. Alex was surprised at how at ease he felt sitting in the home of a woman he had just met. He was touching his forefinger to his wound when Lucy walked back in.

"Leave that alone!" she said, almost scolding him. "You don't want to open it up again." She was carrying a small basin in her left hand and a bottle of iodine along with a gauze bandage in her right. Draped over her right arm was a white cloth. Lucy set the items down on the low wooden table in front of the sofa, then turned and walked to the opposite end of the room, where, on a waist-high mahogany server with a marble top, sat several cut-glass carafes and four cocktail glasses. Lucy removed the glass stopper from one of the bottles and poured some of its contents into one of the glasses and, replacing the stopper, returned to where Alex was seated.

"Here, drink this."

Alex noted the unmistakable aroma of brandy. He took a sip. It was smooth and warm as he swallowed. He licked his lips and took another sip. "Won't you join me?" he asked Lucy.

"Just let me do this first and then I will."

Lucy dipped the tip of the cloth in the basin of water and gently began sponging away the clotted blood from Alex's scalp. She dabbed carefully at the wound and looked at the cloth when she removed it. There was nothing on the cloth to indicate he was still bleeding. Lucy moved back to the table, took the cork out of the iodine bottle and poured a little onto a clean section of the cloth.

"This may sting a little." She then applied the tincture of iodine. Alex winced when the medicine came in contact with his scalp.

"Sting a little? It burns!" he said in mock pain.

"Oh, stop being a baby," Lucy replied and they both laughed. "One more and I'm done." Lucy once again touched the medicine-soaked cloth to the wound. Alex did not react to the application of the medicine, but instead stared into Lucy's eyes.

"There," she said. "Let me wrap it with the bandage and you should be fine." She went back to the table for a clean piece of gauze, wrapped it twice around Alex's head and tied the ends together.

"Now, can you tell me what happened?"

Alex knew he was in a dilemma. He wanted to be as honest as he could with Lucy, but he obviously had to weigh his words and his story very carefully. He got up, took his empty glass and deliberately walked across the room to the server. He poured himself a second glass of brandy. "Will you join me now?" he asked, looking at Lucy over his shoulder.

"Of course," she replied. Alex filled a second glass with the amber fluid and returned to the couch where Lucy was seated. He set the glass of brandy on the table in front of her, sat down and turned to face her. He noticed that she had undone three of the top buttons on her dress to reveal an ample bosom and had raised her skirt enough to show a finely shaped calf in dark stockings.

"Now, tell me what is going on with you," she said impatiently.

Alex was clearly surprised by Lucy's actions and his roving eyes did not hide this fact. Her slightly tilted head and half-smile made it silently understood that she did not mind his ogling her.

Alex cleared his throat. "Well," he began. "I arrived here in

Washington just this morning. I am looking for someone, but have not yet been able to find him. I decided to take a room for the night and get a fresh start in the morning, but I ran into a bit of trouble."

"Who are you looking for? In my business, I know most of what you would call the prominent men in town—I assume it is a well-known individual. Maybe I can help you find him."

Alex knew he had no real leads on Booth's whereabouts. He also, unwittingly, had begun to let his guard down as he sat beside Lucy.

"Please." Lucy put her hand on Alex's leg just above his knee. "Let me help you. You can trust me."

"OK," said Alex. "You see, I am looking for an actor . . ."

Suddenly, he felt a bit dizzy and a wavy portal appeared in front of him, just like the one he had seen at the Soldiers' Home before being transported to the year 1865. Simultaneously, he could hear the graveled voice of William Crook admonishing him: "You cannot tell anyone that you are not of this time, or why you are here. If you violate any of these rules, your presence here will be instantaneously terminated and you will be sent back to your own time."

Alex had thought that maybe he could coyly seek Lucy's help. Now he knew that, in order to be permitted to remain in the current time and place, he had to do this strictly on his own.

"Alex? Alex?" he could hear Lucy saying as he emerged from the fog he had been in. "Are you all right?"

"Yes, I am fine. I just think that the long day has finally caught up to me."

"I understand," said Lucy. She rose from the sofa and, bending slightly at the waist, extended her hand. "Let's go to bed."

Alex felt his ears become noticeably warm and his throat go dry. Then a strange thought came to him. Would it really be cheating if he had sex with another woman more than a hundred years before Sarah was even born?

He looked at the outstretched hand and the beautiful woman beckoning to him. "I am really flattered and believe me, very tempted," he said, feeling his heart beating in his chest. "But," raising his left hand to show Lucy his wedding ring, he said, "I'm afraid I can't."

Lucy's hand remained extended and she said with an understanding and disappointed smile, "Come with me and I will show you to the guest bedroom."

Alex took her hand and they walked out of the parlor and up the staircase. At the top, they walked halfway down a short hallway.

"This is your room," said Lucy. She leaned in and gave him a peck on the cheek. "Sleep tight." She continued walking down the hall.

"Thanks," replied Alex. "You too."

Alex entered the room and closed the door. He took off his shoes, turned back the covers on the bed and collapsed onto the mattress. He pulled the covers tight against his chin and within a minute was fast asleep.

APRIL 14, 1865
MORNING

ABRAHAM LINCOLN

President Lincoln awoke around 7 a.m. on Good Friday and was greeted by a lovely spring morning in the nation's capital. He began his workday, before breakfast, at the mahogany desk in his private office where he dealt with a pile of documents that needed his immediate attention, but that he wished he did not have to address. These were all pleas for pardons; some made on behalf of the offending soldier himself and others from a worried mother or father. The offenses for which clemency was sought ran the gamut from minor infractions, such as falling asleep at one's post, to the most severe, that of desertion. Yet even the harshest violator seemed to advance his cause by presenting a good reason for the soldier's purported unacceptable conduct. Even though the war was, for all intents and purposes, over, these charges still remained pending and had to be reconciled.

Lincoln picked up a request from a 25-year-old man whose reported sin was being out of uniform at the morning inspection. In the petition to the president, the soldier explained that he had experienced a terrible bout of dysentery the night before, and, in his words, "Truth be told, it is nothing short of a miracle that this much of me was able to make it here on time at all." The president had to laugh as he imagined the poor creature doing his best to obey the call for the morning's inspection. Across the bottom of the petition, he scrawled, "Pardoned. A. Lincoln."

After reviewing several equally inconsequential infractions, he came across a furtive plea that caught his full attention and caused significant concern. It was a request for the president to reverse a sentence of death imposed upon a 19-year-old boy for the crime of desertion. This was the kind of application that caused Lincoln the most distress. While he knew it had been vital to maintain order among the ranks, he also understood, with the compassion of a father whose own son had served his country during the war, that such a lethal sentence had to be tempered in consideration of the surrounding circumstances. He had received the document from the soldier's mother, who begged the president to spare the only son she had left, as her other two sons had died in the war. Lincoln was keenly aware that his secretary of war, Edwin Stanton, believed desertion should be punished with the utmost severity. He told Lincoln many times that, if deserters were not made to pay the ultimate price for their actions, it could result in innumerable followers.

But, after some agonizing soul searching, Lincoln's compassionate side won out over his role as commander in chief. Knowing that Stanton himself often looked over the pardons issued to deserters, Lincoln left a personal message in hopes of explaining his decision: "If Almighty God gives a man a cowardly pair of legs, how can he help their running away with him? Pardoned. A. Lincoln."

The president stretched his arms above his head and looked up at the clock on the wall. It was just before 8 a.m. and he had promised to take breakfast with his family. Removing his spectacles and placing them in his topcoat pocket, he made his way to the family dining room.

Mrs. Lincoln was already seated at the foot of the table, with Robert and Tad positioned opposite one another at its sides. Mr. Lincoln occupied the chair at the head of the table, where his breakfast of one soft-boiled egg, toast and a cup of steaming hot coffee awaited him. His sons were consuming hot cakes, scrambled eggs and sausage, while Mary nibbled on a small helping of eggs and toast with apple butter.

"Good morning, Mrs. Lincoln," said the president. Then, turning to each of his sons, he remarked on how good it was that each of them was there and that the four of them were actually taking breakfast as a family.

"Robert," he said to his older son. "Tell me about the time you spent under the command of General Grant." Robert, a captain in the Union Army, had cajoled his father into letting him enlist, much to the distress of his mother. However, as a compromise, the president made sure that his son would be in the detachment of General Grant and not in immediate harm's way.

"Oh yes!" exclaimed Tad. "Please do and be sure not to leave anything out." It was well known that Tad was enamored of the soldiers serving in the war and often times had dressed in his own Union blues and mingled with the troops assigned to the White House detail.

Robert had been present five days earlier at Appomattox Courthouse when General Robert E. Lee formally surrendered to General Ulysses S. Grant, and he told his family how impressed he had been when Grant demanded that his men exhibit the utmost respect to the vanquished Southern leader.

Tad sat in rapt attention as his older brother relived the historic scene.

When the boys had finished their meal, they were excused from the table by their mother. Then Mary addressed her husband from across the table. "We do have tickets to see tonight's play at Grover's Theatre, Father. But I would much rather see the closing performance of *Our American Cousin* at Ford's Theatre. I'd like to extend an invitation to General and Mrs. Grant to join us." Her tone was more like a directive rather than a request for acquiescence.

"That will be fine, Mother," her husband replied. "What time are we to be there?"

"We should get to the theater as close to eight as we can. I'll send word to the Grants. Will you take care of securing the tickets?"

Lincoln promised he would make the arrangements and sighed as he rose from the table. It was time to get back to work. He kissed Mary on the cheek and, lumbering out, went back to his office. There he summoned a messenger and told him to go to Ford's Theatre and reserve the State Box that evening for himself, Mrs. Lincoln and their two guests. Then, as he always did, he settled down with the morning newspapers until Speaker of the House Schuyler Colfax appeared for his appointment with the president to discuss plans for Reconstruction. Throughout their conversation, Lincoln maintained his position that he did not want the reunification of the South to include punishment.

By the time Colfax left, it was 10 a.m. While this conference had been taking place, unbeknownst to Lincoln, General Grant had been engrossed in a discussion with Secretary Stanton.

During the course of their meeting, he had informed Stanton that he and his wife were going to decline the Lincolns' invitation, which he had just received, to accompany them to the theater that evening.

As the morning progressed, the president participated in a variety of meetings. These included consultations with members of Congress, including New Hampshire Senator John P. Hale, whom Lincoln had just appointed Ambassador to Spain and whose daughter, ironically, was the fiancée of John Wilkes Booth.

Meanwhile, the previously dispatched young messenger rushed as fast as he could from the White House to the theater. Upon arriving, he asked to speak with John Ford, the theater owner. Being told the elder Ford was out of town, and that his younger brother, Henry Clay Ford, was in charge, the lad was directed to his office.

"Mr. Ford," the messenger exclaimed as he burst unceremoniously into the inner office. "I was sent here by the president to tell you that he and Mrs. Lincoln along with their two guests will be coming tonight to see the play. The president asked if they could use the State Box."

Ford was surprised and elated. "Wonderful! I will make sure the State Box at stage left is reserved for him. And I won't even insist upon payment of the ten-dollar ticket price. Say," he added, clapping his hands together. "I have a terrific idea. We must appropriately decorate the box for our distinguished visitors."

"How will you decorate it?" asked the boy.

"Well, let me think. You know, this will be the very first time that we have ever done anything like this. That area has never been dressed up before and especially not for anyone of the stature and importance of Mr. Lincoln. He pursed his lips and looked upward. Thinking out loud he said, "I suspect I will have the American flag displayed within the box and drape bunting of red, white and blue over the railing. I also have a painting of George Washington here in the office that should add a nice presidential touch." He vigorously pumped the boy's hand. "Thank you very much for such exciting news. Now I know how to ensure that we will have a full house tonight!"

JOHN WILKES BOOTH

At 9 o'clock, John Wilkes Booth awoke in his room at the National Hotel at 6th Street and Pennsylvania Avenue, in Washington City. He dressed quickly and went downstairs for a light breakfast of coffee and toast.

After finishing his meal, Booth left the hotel and moved about downtown Washington, getting his hair cut and making several other stops. He then walked toward Ford's Theatre. Booth knew the owner, John Ford, well, as he had performed at the theater as an actor in numerous stage productions. He had made arrangements with Ford to allow his mail to be delivered to the theater and held there for him. Booth would appear almost daily to pick up letters, circulars and whatever else might have arrived for him.

He arrived at Ford's Theatre just after 11 a.m. As he entered, he was met by 21-year-old Henry Clay Ford, who was acting as manager during his older brother's absence from the city. "Good morning, Mr. Booth!" He spoke warmly, somewhat awestruck by the fame of the handsome, dapper actor. "How are you, sir?" "Just fine, Henry," Booth replied. "I have just come to collect my mail. Is there anything for me?"

"Let me check for you, sir." Ford disappeared into the office, checked the mailboxes and emerged to say, "I do not see anything there for you today, Mr. Booth."

Booth thanked him, and, as he was about to leave, Ford called out to him. "Oh, by the way, have you heard the exciting news, Mr. Booth?" Henry was unable to hide the excitement in his voice. "President and Mrs. Lincoln have sent word that they will be here this evening to attend the final performance of *Our American Cousin*. I hear that the president is an admirer of Laura Keene and he doesn't want to miss seeing her."

Booth was taken aback by this pronouncement. Several evenings earlier, after Lee's surrender to Grant ended the Civil War, Booth, Herald and Powell had been among the throng who heard the president deliver an impromptu speech from an upper-story window in the White House. During the course of his brief address, the president had said that one of his priorities was conferring voting rights upon certain former slaves. These words had made Booth's blood boil. He turned to the other two men and, in a hushed, sinister, voice, exclaimed, "Now, by God, I'll put him through. That is the last speech he will ever make."

When he made this off-the-cuff remark, Booth had no specific plan to carry out his veiled threat. For months he had been meeting with his co-conspirators, David Herald, Lewis Powell (also known as Lewis Payne), George Atzerodt and John Surratt, discussing plans to kidnap President Lincoln. Several of these meetings had taken place at the boardinghouse operated by

Mary Surratt, John's mother. They had formulated two plots, but each of them had been thwarted when Lincoln failed to appear at the location where they lay in wait. Up to this time, there had been no talk of assassination, or of seeking out and attacking any other high office holder.

Lincoln's remarks had now been seared into his mind and he was determined to find a confluence of time and place that would foster this act. With the information imparted to him by the young Ford, a new plot began to formulate in his mind—not to kidnap Lincoln, but to murder him.

After politely excusing himself and shaking Henry's hand, Booth spent some time wandering about the interior of the theater. He was greeted by several stagehands, none of them surprised by his presence. Booth was thinking hard. He was very familiar with the play to be performed that evening and had committed almost every line to memory. He ran the dialogue through his mind, trying to determine which words would generate the loudest laughter and cover up the sound of a pistol shot. He ultimately decided upon a series of lines to be delivered by Harry Hawk at a moment when he was alone on stage. Booth recited the words in a whisper: "Don't know the manners of good society, eh? Well, I guess I know enough to turn you inside out, old gal—you sockdologizing old man-trap." Booth calculated that, if the curtain went up at 8 p.m., these now infamous remarks would be spoken with the anticipated effect around 10:15.

Booth was now fully committed to ending the life of Abraham Lincoln amid the laughter of the audience. With a plan now firmly in mind, he left the theater and walked to Washington's Best General Store, located a few blocks away.

He needed to purchase two things that would give him the time required to accomplish the deed and make his escape. He knew that the Lincolns would be seated in the upper box, stage left, which was entered by walking up the staircase to the balcony level and then behind the last row of seats. There a short staircase led to a white door that opened into a small foyer leading to the presidential box.

The first item that Booth needed was a gimlet, a small boring tool having a spiraled shank, a screw tip and a cross handle. This would be used to make one hole at the inside base of the door and another at the same height in the side wall. The other necessity was a wooden dowel. Once the holes had been drilled, Booth would insert the ends of the dowel into these two cavities, preventing the white door from being opened from the audience side into the foyer. He intended to use this to barricade the door, shoot the president in the back of the head at close range with a six-inch-long .44 caliber Derringer and then leap to the stage below. He anticipated that the startled patrons in the theater would be slow to react to what had just occurred and in the confusion he would escape through a service door at the back of the theater and ride off on a horse that would be waiting for him.

Booth arrived at the store and within a mere fifteen minutes had purchased the gimlet and a wooden dowel that could be trimmed to the required length. Now he had everything he needed to guarantee the means to both commit the murder and then make his escape.

ALEX LINWOOD

The eventful last day Alex spent in the year 1865 began when he awoke in Lucy's guestroom feeling fully refreshed. He had slept straight through the night, something he rarely did in his own bed at home. He found a pitcher of water and a towel on the dresser and, after washing up and putting on his shoes, he opened the door and was met by the wonderful aroma of brewing coffee. Making his way downstairs, he followed the enticing smell to the kitchen at the rear of the house. There stood Lucy in a simple cotton dress with long sleeves and a high neckline.

"Well, good morning. It's about time you woke up. How are you feeling?"

Alex looked at the clock perched on the shelf above the stove indicating it was 9:15 a.m. "I'm actually feeling great, thanks. How about you?"

"Very well, sir, thank you," Lucy replied with mock formality. They both laughed

"How is your head this morning, Alex? Let me take a look at it."

"Well, I don't have a headache so that's a good thing," he said. Lucy moved in closer and carefully unwrapped the bandage. The bleeding had stopped, but there was some dried blood in Alex's hair. "Here, let me clean that for you," Lucy remarked as she took a clean cloth from a drawer, dipped it into a pot of water that had been sitting on the back of the stove and gently dabbed at the wound. Her touch was very soothing. "There, how does that feel?"

Alex touched his head with his index finger. "It feels pretty good. Thanks."

"Looks like it wasn't too bad after all. It should be all healed in a few days. How about some coffee?" Lucy asked as she turned to the stove.

"Sure."

Alex sat down at the kitchen table and Lucy poured the black, steaming liquid into a white china cup. "Sugar and cream?"

"No, black is fine, thank you."

Lucy poured a cup of coffee for herself and sat opposite him. "Help yourself to a fresh buttermilk biscuit or two. There's the honey."

The biscuits were delicious and for a few minutes all that could be heard was the sound of coffee being sipped and a knife scraping against a plate to scoop up honey. Alex ate two, while Lucy watched him with satisfaction. Finally, she said, "So, can you tell me anything more than you told me last night about why you're here in the city? You said something about looking for an actor."

Alex took another sip of the strong, black coffee and set down his cup. He looked directly at Lucy. She appeared genuinely concerned about him and that made it all the more difficult to lie to her. Again recalling Crook's admonition, Alex had to phrase his response carefully.

"I am here on behalf of a theatrical company based in New York City." He hoped that she had never been to New York and would not ask him any specific questions about the city that he could not answer, especially since he knew nothing about New York in 1865.

"I've always wanted to go to New York City. It must be very exciting there with all the shopping and the theaters. But I didn't mean to interrupt. Please go on."

"My employer is looking for new talent for a play he will be producing and asked me to see if there might be someone here to fit the bill."

"There are quite a few playhouses here," Lucy said. "I am sure that you will find someone." She reached across the table and took his hand. "How long will you be here in Washington?"

"I'm afraid I must leave tonight," replied Alex.

"That doesn't give you much time, does it? How does your employer expect you to find someone that fast?"

Alex knew he had to cut this topic of conversation short before she realized it was not the truth. "He gave me a couple of names to check out with the local theater owners."

All Lucy said was, "Hmm." She either bought his story or was smart enough not to pursue it any further.

They finished their breakfast mostly in silence. After consuming a second cup of coffee and a third biscuit, Alex pushed his chair back from the table and stood up.

"I am never going to see you again, am I?" Lucy's eyes were downcast.

"I don't think so," Alex replied softly. This time he took her hands in his. "I want to thank you for all that you did for me. I don't know what I would have done last night without your help and kindness."

He put his arms around her in an affectionate embrace, but not an amorous one, and kissed her quickly on the lips. Then they pulled apart.

"I won't forget you," he said.

Lucy walked with him down the corridor to the front door and they parted without another word. She watched as he turned down the path to the street and then she went inside and closed the door.

• • •

Alex was not really sure what do to next. He couldn't return to the Surratt boarding house, as a second appearance might arouse suspicion. He peeked at the watch in his pocket. It was now 10:15. He had just twelve hours left to figure out how to prevent Booth from shooting the president.

After a very long walk back into town, Alex suddenly saw ahead of him the White House, or as it was then known, the President's House. How different it looked from the White House of his era. Gone was the protective wrought iron fence that provided security for the president and his family. There was no guard shack to pass through before entering the grounds. A U-shaped gravel path off the street allowed people to move toward the front door of the building from two sides. And, strangest and most unusual of all, a steady stream of visitors was simply walking in and out of the front door of the mansion.

Even though the clock was ticking, he could not pass up the opportunity of a chance encounter with the president. After all, Crook said that Alex would be permitted to see President Lincoln, so long as there was no actual interaction between them. Alex crossed Pennsylvania Avenue and walked up the path leading to the front door, the gravel crunching under his shoes. Going in and out were delivery men carrying various wares, as well as soldiers, men in suits with calling cards and more simply dressed men and women—all hoping for a brief audience with the president. For all he knew, some of them could be members of Congress or even someone in the Cabinet.

He soon arrived at the steps leading to the covered portico and the double entry doors. A gravel-voiced doorman in uniform asked, "May I help you with something, sir?"

Alex looked at him and gasped. The man did not notice his surprise, but clearly was waiting for an answer. "Please state your business," he said in a firm, authoritative voice.

The doorman was a young William Crook! And, while Crook clearly did not know who Alex was, it was eerie to be confronted by the living man whose spirit had, only yesterday, given Alex his assignment. Alex stumbled with his words as he replied.

"I would very much like to see the president," Alex said finally. And then, recalling one of the reasons why men called upon the president, he added, "I am interested in a position with the federal government."

"The president is unavailable." Crook stood erect and stared sternly at Alex and his dismissive tone obviously meant this meeting was at an end. But Alex had come this far and he held his ground. He would tempt the fates with a simple request.

"Is there something else?" asked the doorman, not used to having his authority challenged.

"Yes," Alex replied somewhat pensively. "May I go upstairs and take a look at the Shop?"

Alex knew that the "Shop" was the slang reference to the upstairs room that President Lincoln used as both an office and the Cabinet Room. In the present day, that very room is referred to as the Lincoln Bedroom.

"I am not supposed to allow anyone up there if the president is not there," said Crook, peering closely at Alex, his brow furrowing, as if he were trying to retrieve something from the recesses of his memory.

"Do I know you?" he asked, in a much softer tone. "There is something very familiar about you, but I can't quite put my finger on it."

"No, I don't think so," replied Alex, feeling a bead of perspiration run down the back of his neck.

"Hmpf." Crook was clearly annoyed with himself for not being able to remember where he had seen this face before. "Well, go ahead, but best be quick about it. Up the stairs and turn to the left. It will be the first door you come to."

"Thank you very much, sir."

Alex darted up the stairs before the doorman could change his mind. When he reached the top he stopped. Alex realized that he was about to enter a room where so much history occurred. Discussions about the war, Cabinet meetings on a variety of issues facing the nation and the first reading of the Emancipation Proclamation had all taken place in this office.

He entered. The room was just as he had seen it in photographs and drawings. Along the wall to his right was the large table, surrounded by chairs, that was used for Cabinet meetings as well as by the president for entertaining office seekers, congressmen and other guests. The chair at the far end of the table was the one that Mr. Lincoln occupied when he was present. The table was strewn with books and papers, and a lamp sat in the middle. Behind this table was a desk in front of a doorway. It was said that this doorway was used by the president as his private access to the family quarters.

Alex wistfully wished he had kept his cellphone with him so he could capture the office as it appeared at this momentous period. But to whom could he show the pictures?

On the far wall were two large windows. Alex could almost visualize the president standing there looking out at the city while pondering myriad issues and concerns. On the wall to his left, Alex saw many maps depicting which troop movements had been followed and battle strategy charted. He was amazed at the vibrant colors of the wallpaper and carpet; the photographs he had seen of the room were, of course, only in black and white.

He was about to go further into the room and touch the large table, when a man gently brushed past him.

"Can I help you with something?" he asked cordially. "The president is not in."

Unbeknownst to Alex, the speaker was John Hay, one of the two personal secretaries to President Lincoln. He and John Nicolay were truly the president's right-hand men, upon whom he relied for responding to correspondence, keeping track of his appointments and providing companionship and advice— whether solicited or not.

John Hay had a long career in politics after the tragic end of the Lincoln administration. He was a secretary to President James Garfield, as well as secretary of state under William McKinley and Theodore Roosevelt. Thus, John Hay was, in actuality, a historical witness to the first three presidential assassinations.

Alex was hesitant to interact with the man, fearing that it might somehow end his time in 1865. He simply told the gentleman that he was on his way out, left the office and made his way back down the stairs. Fortunately, he had not been gone long enough to raise the ire of the doorman.

"Thank you, Mister . . ." His voice trailed off before he made the blunder of calling Crook by name. "Uh, thank you, sir."

Crook nodded and Alex made an adroit about-face, descended the exterior stairs post-haste and walked off the White House grounds. But the feeling of knowing that he had been in the very office where Mr. Lincoln had spent so much time and where so much was accomplished was simply indescribable.

APRIL 14, 1865
AFTERNOON

ABRAHAM LINCOLN

A lengthy meeting between Lincoln and his Cabinet took up most of the early afternoon. They discussed how to return the country to normalcy now that the war was over and the fact that providing economic assistance to the South would, in turn, be beneficial to the North. At around 1 o'clock, while the meeting was in progress, General Grant entered the Cabinet room and took a seat near the window. He had specifically been asked by the president to attend the session. Once the pending business had been concluded, the president arose from his chair and turned toward Grant.

"General Grant, we all wish to welcome you here today. I know that I am most eager to have you describe for us that which took place at the McLean House when you and General Lee met to discuss the terms of surrender. And I am certain that these assembled gentlemen share in this as well."

"Thank you for inviting me here today, Mr. President," Grant began and then proceeded to relate what had transpired between him and General Lee only five days earlier. The president and the Cabinet members were enthralled by the tale Grant shared with them.

After about an hour, Grant made his concluding remarks and was congratulated and thanked by each Cabinet member with warm handshakes and personal remarks. After the Cabinet members had taken their leave, Grant and Lincoln had a brief conversation, which ended with the subject of Mrs. Lincoln's invitation to the theater.

"Mr. President," Grant began, "I regret to inform you that Mrs. Grant and I will be unable to accept the theater invitation. You see, we will be leaving Washington on the evening train to visit our children. Please relay my sincere regrets to Mrs. Lincoln."

"I know that Mrs. Lincoln will be very disappointed," replied the president. "But most assuredly she will understand, especially when children are concerned. I wish you and Mrs. Grant a safe journey."

The two men shook hands and Lincoln escorted Grant to the office door. "Thank you again, General, for all you have done for your country. I look forward to our next meeting." The old soldier, after replacing his hat upon his head, tipped it toward the president and made his exit.

Lincoln then returned to his desk and after about twenty minutes made his way to the residence portion of the White House for lunch with Mary. The meal consisted of biscuits, cheese, a pitcher of cold milk and apples, the president's favorite fruit.

As they ate, Lincoln said, "Mother, I'm afraid General Grant told me they won't be able to accompany us to the theater tonight."

"But why not?" Mary asked, with a clear sense of hurt in her voice.

"They are leaving the city tonight to visit their children. Surely you can appreciate how that would take precedence over their spending an evening with us," said the president with a wry grin.

"Oh, I bet they refused because that Julia Grant and I don't see eye to eye."

"No, no, I would not read anything into this. Please do not upset yourself," he said reassuringly.

They continued to eat their lunch, mostly in silence. Once the meal was concluded, the president patted his wife tenderly on the shoulder and returned to his office.

Mary Lincoln still wanted to find another couple to accompany them to see *Our American Cousin*. She thought that Secretary and Mrs. Stanton might enjoy being their guests and had a message relayed to them through the office of the secretary of war. But Secretary Stanton sent a response saying that he and his wife must "most regrettably and respectfully" decline this invitation.

Lincoln continued to work in his office throughout the afternoon. He met with Vice President Johnson, as well as with several persons who had waited patiently downstairs for a few moments of his time. At 3 p.m., he ended his day's work and walked slowly down the hall to the family quarters. He was met by Mary, who told him that she wished to go for a carriage ride before dinner. The president happily agreed.

Following a short trip around the city, the couple made a stop at the Navy Yard just before 4 o'clock. While there, the president and Mrs. Lincoln viewed several ships, including a tour of the ironclad vessel *Montauk* that had seen active duty during the war. When they returned to the front porch of the White House, they were greeted there by two good friends from Illinois, Dick Oglesby and General Isham Haynie. Bidding adieu to Mrs. Lincoln, the president and his guests went upstairs to the president's office, where they sat and reminisced about old times. At 6 o'clock, when word arrived that dinner was about to be served, the visitors departed and Mr. Lincoln made his way back to the residence to dine with his family.

Lincoln was a very picky eater and generally indifferent to food. In fact, he often had to be reminded to eat, so consumed was he with the issues surrounding the war. On this evening, however, the staff served one of his favorite meals, chicken fricassee, prepared just as he liked it, with the chicken cut up in small pieces, fried and seasoned with nutmeg and accompanied by gravy made of chicken drippings. The meal was topped off by his favorite dessert, apple pie.

As his plate was being filled, Lincoln smiled appreciatively at Mary, keenly aware that it was she who had requested the White House cook to prepare this repast.

Mary smiled back and said, "Mr. Lincoln, I have found a couple to join us at Ford's Theatre tonight. Clara Harris and her fiancé, Major Henry Rathbone, enthusiastically accepted my invitation."

Miss Harris and Major Rathbone had been friends of the Lincolns ever since their arrival in Washington from Springfield. "It will be very nice to see them," Lincoln said and they then shared a pleasant family meal.

JOHN WILKES BOOTH

Now that Booth had firmly decided on the permanent elimination of Lincoln, he also wanted to throw the government into complete disarray. This would be accomplished by the next two most powerful men in the Union suffering the same ultimate fate. It was therefore imperative that he meet with Atzerodt and Powell to instruct them in their new roles in the scheme. Atzerodt's role would be to kill Vice President Johnson, while Powell would take care of Secretary of State Seward.

Booth proceeded to the Herndon House where Lewis Powell was renting a room. Once inside the small quarters and without any inconsequential conversation, Booth told him about the plan. "The end result has changed," he stated authoritatively. "I am going to assassinate that Negro-loving Lincoln tonight while he sits idly watching a play. But that is just one part of the plan. We need to throw the Federal government into total chaos. Therefore, I want you to go to the home of Secretary Seward—" Booth paused for dramatic effect, "and kill him."

Powell's eyes widened. Although a man of incredible physical strength, Powell was not one for independent thinking and so he agreed without hesitation. Booth instructed him to strike at 10:15 that evening, so that the lives of Lincoln and Seward would end simultaneously. He left the particulars of how this was to be accomplished to Powell.

Satisfied that two prongs of the plan had now been arranged, Booth had one more stop to make. He headed to Kirkwood House, where George Atzerodt had lodgings, to notify him of his new assignment: the assassination of Vice President Johnson. Ironically, the vice president was also a boarder at Kirkwood House. However, upon his arrival, Booth learned that Atzerodt was not at home, so he made his way along 14th Street near Willard's Hotel. As he turned down a side street, he saw George Atzerodt approaching. There in the shadows, Booth told him about the new plan, which now included Atzerodt murdering the vice president.

Atzerodt voiced his reluctance. He told Booth that he was not opposed to the Lincoln kidnapping scheme, but murder was something else. Booth would not take no for an answer and he pressed Atzerodt insistently until he finally gave in. Booth said the deed had to be done at 10:15 that evening. Once Atzerodt assured him that he would follow through with his assignment, Booth calmly walked off.

ALEX LINWOOD

Alex returned to the stable where he had boarded his horse. Inside he was met with the pungent smell of horse manure and, hearing the sounds of someone mucking out a stall, he called out, "Hello? Anyone here?"

There appeared the boy who had taken Alex's horse from the restaurant to the stable. "Oh, hello, Mista Alex. Come for your horse? Let me git 'im for ya. He been fed, watered and brushed down. A fine animal he is."

"Thank you," Alex replied. "How much do I owe you?"

"Well, sir, it'll be two dollars."

Alex reached into his pocket and this time very was careful to remove two of the appropriate dollar notes. He handed them to the boy.

"Thank you, sir. Would you like me to saddle 'im up for ya?"

"Yes, if you would. Thanks."

The young boy disappeared toward the rear of the stable. Alex could hear the sounds of the horse being walked and the grunts of the boy as he threw on the saddle. In a few minutes, he returned, with the horse in tow.

"Here you go," the boy said cheerfully.

"Thank you again," Alex said as he mounted the horse, "and good-bye."

"Bye." The boy continued to wave as Alex rode out of the stable.

He decided to stop by Ford's Theatre to see if by chance Booth might be there as he knew that he frequented the theater just to retrieve his mail. He could think of no other place to look for the would-be assassin. He remembered that it was at the corner of 10th and F Streets and could be easily found by following the street signs.

As he rode along, he tried to think of some clever reason why he was asking for Booth. Nothing really plausible came immediately to mind and he hoped that when the time came, a reason would spring into his head.

The traffic along 10th Street was rather heavy with a steady flow of drays carrying all sorts of merchandise, jockeying for roadway space with horse-drawn streetcars and private carriages. There were others, like him, riding horseback, as well as a host of pedestrians. At some points along the way, the sidewalks were impassible, sometimes because deliveries to stores were stacked up in front of the establishments, sometimes simply due to trash that had been tossed onto the sidewalk. People constantly had to walk in the street and do battle with the horses and vehicles to avoid stepping into something best left undisturbed.

Soon Alex saw the street sign indicating that he was at the intersection of 10th and F Streets, and there in the middle of the block was Ford's Theatre. He was surprised that the appearance of the facade wasn't much different than it had been when he visited the theater as a tourist in his own time. Dismounting and tying the horse to a hitching post, he entered the lobby.

There were several people busily moving about, all appearing quite focused on the task at hand. A man, who he later learned was Henry Clay Ford, was pointing and yelling out instructions. Alex heard him say, "We want that box to be as decorated as we can, befitting the attendance of the president. Get that rocking chair up there. We want Mr. Lincoln to be as comfortable as possible while he watches the play. And be sure to put up the bunting. I want everyone in attendance to know that someone important is seated there."

Alex attempted to speak to Ford about the whereabouts of Booth, but the theater manager dismissively waved him off, saying he was too busy to talk. The other men scurrying about also looked too involved in their work to be bothered. But, over in a corner, sat a young man who seemed to belong there but who was not engaged in the whirlwind of preparing the theater for the president's visit.

Alex walked up to him and said, "Hello, young man. Do you work here?"

"Not really, but I spend enough time here that you'd think I did. You need something?"

Alex tried to quickly conjure a reason for inquiring about Booth, but instead decided to take the direct approach. "Do you know if John Wilkes Booth is here in the theater?" he asked as nonchalantly as he could.

The man replied matter-of-factly, "You just missed him. He came to get his mail this morning and then he left."

"Any idea where I might find him?"

The young man answered readily. "Well, he could be at any one of the theaters around here. I am not sure if he is currently appearin' anywhere. I do know that he takes a lot of pride in his appearance and often goes to Booker and Stewart's barbershop."

"Can you tell me where that is?"

"Sure. It's on E Street near Grover's. Just a couple blocks north of here."

"Grover's?" Alex asked.

"You know. Grover's Theatre. If he ain't there, maybe he's at the National Hotel where he has a room."

How ironic, Alex thought. Grover's Theatre was where Tad Lincoln would be that evening, attending a production of the play *Aladdin! Or His Wonderful Lamp*, when he learned that his father had been shot.

Suddenly the young man leaped to his feet in response to Ford calling out his name. "Gotta go, mister!" and he ran off in the direction of the voice.

Alex left the theater and got back onto his horse. He was certainly stopping at the places which Booth frequented, but his timing was lousy.

Turned his horse in the direction of the barbershop, Alex continued on with his quest. The barbershop was not far away. In front was the familiar red-and-white-striped barber's pole. He walked in and was mesmerized by being inside an actual 19th-century barbershop! There were four barber's chairs, three of which were occupied, and a large cabinet holding an array of elixirs, potions, creams, scents, powders and pills guaranteed to cure whatever might ail you.

Alex approached the one man who was not currently tending to a customer.

"Shave and a haircut, sir? Hop right into the chair."

Alex thought that it might be best to engage the barber in conversation about Booth by doing so casually and while being groomed.

Alex stroked his cheeks and chin. "Yes, I could use a shave."

"Sure thing." The barber picked up a cloth apron, flicked it across the chair a couple of times and invited Alex to have a seat. Once he was settled, the barber mixed up some powdered shaving cream and water in a cup and pulled the leather strop taut to sharpen the razor. Then he applied the shaving cream with a small brush and began deftly maneuvering the straight razor along Alex's face.

Alex started the conversation by asking the barber his name (it was Pete) and then talking about the weather and other innocuous topics. Finally, when Pete was nearly done, Alex posed some more pertinent questions.

"Ever have anyone famous come in here?"

"What do you mean by famous?" replied Pete.

"Oh, I don't know. With all of the theaters near here, I suspect that some famous actors might come in from time to time."

"Now that you mention it, we do have a regular that I suppose you would say is kinda famous. That actor fella, Wilkes Booth, comes in for a haircut. 'Course he always waits for Charles. He's the guy at chair number one up front."

A short, stocky man with a large head and broad shoulders, Charles Wood was engaged in cutting the hair of a man in a business suit.

"Do you think this Booth fellow will come in today?" asked Alex, as if it were just an afterthought.

"Don't know. Let me ask." Raising his voice, Pete called out,

"Charles, you think Wilkes will be in today?"

"He was already here—about ten o'clock this morning. I gave him a quick shave and a trim. He left just before you got in. Unlike you, some of us have to get up and out when there's a living to be earned!"

"Ah, suck a lemon!" Pete called back, grinning. Then turning back to Alex he said, "Well, there's your answer."

Alex could not believe it. Booth always seemed to be one step ahead of him, almost as if something was preventing the two of them from being in the same place at the same time. Pete finished shaving Alex and applied a hot towel to his face. The wet heat against his newly-shaven face felt incredibly soothing. After a minute or so, Pete removed the towel, splashed Alex's face with some witch hazel and removed the apron.

"How's that?"

"Feels great," replied Alex. "How much do I owe you?"

"It'll be two bits," replied Pete.

Alex reached into his pocket as the two men walked up front to where the cash box was located. Alex was not sure if a tip was expected, but he felt it was better to leave one than not. He handed Pete a circa 1865 one-dollar bill. Pete gave him change and waited, staring at Alex. It seems that Pete was expecting a tip after all. Alex handed him a dime.

"Thank you, sir," said Pete. "Hope to see you again soon."

It was now just after 3 p.m. and Alex was nowhere close to finding Booth. Despite his large breakfast with Lucy, he had worked up an appetite from all the riding and walking during the morning. He stopped into a small restaurant where he enjoyed a simple meal of bread, cheese and ale. He then wandered about the city for several hours, stopping in at theaters as well as the taverns and restaurants in the vicinity, each time being told that the man he was looking for had either not been there at all or had come and gone.

Alex was now beginning to wonder if the task assigned to him was even possible to complete. Washington was a good-sized city and time was running out. The chances of finding Booth were diminishing quickly. Alex could only think of one more place to try and find his elusive subject. His next stop would be the National Hotel.

APRIL 14, 1865
EARLY EVENING

ABRAHAM LINCOLN

William Crook came on duty at 8 o'clock that morning. He had been acting as bodyguard and protector of the president for only about four months. He was previously a Union Army soldier and, at the time of his new assignment, a member of the Washington police. Lincoln, as was his nature, quickly became quite fond of Crook. Prior to this, there had been no detail specifically assigned to protect any president against an actual or perceived threat. The duties of the Secret Service in 1865 did not include being guardians of the president, as the organization's primary function was to combat the widespread counterfeiting of U.S. currency.

During most of Lincoln's time in office, the doors to the White House were unguarded, open all day and often into the night. Office seekers, friends and those with any type of business simply walked into the foyer of the mansion and waited to be beckoned to meet with the president. With the concluding battles of the Civil War, coupled with the fact that Washington was a Southern city, home to many Southern sympathizers, it was often suggested to Lincoln that a guard be stationed at the entrance to the White House for his own protection. After months of protestations, the president finally acquiesced. Thus, in November 1864, four around-the-clock bodyguards were assigned to monitor the White House environs. One so entrusted was William Crook.

Crook was due to be relieved for the day at 4 p.m. by John Parker. However, Parker was late in arriving and Crook, true to form, refused to depart his location until he was formally relieved. Three hours later, at 7 p.m., Parker finally arrived at the White House to take up his position. Crook knew that the Lincolns were attending a performance at Ford's Theatre that night and, to ensure the safety of the president, instructed Parker to be at the theater no later than 8 o'clock. After satisfying himself that the president's needs would be met, he prepared to withdraw and go home.

As he was leaving, Crook saw Lincoln standing by the doorway. "Good night, Mr. President," he said, as he always did at the conclusion of his shift.

"Good-bye, Crook," the president replied solemnly.

Crook would always maintain that this was the very first time the president had ever responded to him in such a manner. Rather, Lincoln had always similarly returned the salutation with his own, "Good night, Crook."

Lincoln returned to his office, where he met with former congressman George Ashmun, concluding the meeting at 8 o'clock, knowing it was time to leave for the theater. He collected his hat, coat and kid gloves and proceeded downstairs to the foyer where he was to meet his wife. Mary was resplendent in a black-and-white-striped silk dress with a matching bonnet of black lace nestled on her dark brown hair. Mary loved fine clothes and liked making herself attractive for her husband, and Lincoln was genuinely proud of her good looks.

Mrs. Lincoln took his arm and they descended the White

House steps and climbed into the waiting carriage. On the way to the theater, the coach stopped at H Street near 14th, the residence of Clara Harris, where she and Major Rathbone were waiting. The presidential party arrived at Ford's Theatre at approximately 8:30 p.m.

When they entered the theater, the performance was already underway. John Buckingham, the main doorkeeper and ticket collector, formally acknowledged the esteemed guests. John Parker, the assigned bodyguard, had already arrived. The Lincolns, together with Miss Harris and Major Rathbone, followed Buckingham up the stairs to the balcony level and along the passageway leading to the access door to the State Box. A cast member spotted the president and, breaking out of character, began to applaud. The orchestra leader, looking back and seeing the president, had the ensemble play "Hail to the Chief." This was accompanied by an ovation from the now standing audience in acknowledgment of the president's arrival. The president tipped his tall stovepipe hat in appreciation of the warm reception. He and Mrs. Lincoln, then Miss Harris and Major Rathbone, walked past Parker, who had now assumed his security position outside the door leading into the State Box. Upon entering, they all sat down, Lincoln lowering himself into the rocking chair that Henry Ford had brought in especially for him. With the four late arrivals now settled in, the play continued.

A short time later, Parker, who could not see the play from his vantage point, decided to relocate to a seat in the lower gallery. As he left, Parker closed the door to the box with more force than he had intended. As a result, a dowel that had been positioned there tumbled to the floor and rolled under the door, coming to rest less than a foot from the top of the short staircase and just a few steps from the door. Not noticing the dowel, Parker proceeded down the main staircase.

At the close of Act II, John Parker left the theater for drinks in the adjacent Star Saloon.

JOHN WILKES BOOTH

At approximately 6 p.m., Booth arrived back at Ford's Theatre. After buying drinks for several theater employees at the adjacent Taltavull's Star Saloon, he returned alone to the theater. He carefully walked the same path the president would take later that evening. The theater was silent except for the sound of his footsteps on the carpeted floor. Inconspicuously, Booth entered the presidential box through the now-open door. Inside, he saw a rocking chair with a tall red-velvet back, along with several more modest chairs. Booth peered over the railing to the stage below, estimating the drop to be about 10 feet. He was confident that he could make the leap to the floorboards below and then quickly retreat, unmolested, out the rear door of the theater.

Booth reached into his pocket and withdrew the gimlet and dowel. Closing the door, he knelt down and, using the gimlet, proceeded to drill an angled, inch-deep hole in the lower part of the wall close to the door hinge. He tried to insert one tip of the dowel, but the hole wasn't quite big enough. So, removing his knife from its sheath, he inserted the blade into the hole and, with a couple of twists, managed to enlarge it. He then re-inserted the dowel. Although it took a little muscle and rotating of the wooden pole, the tip of the dowel finally entered the hole.

Booth next swung the dowel toward the door to determine the length required to secure the door in the closed position. He broke off the necessary piece and used a pencil to make an alignment mark. Then he once again made use of the gimlet, twisting it clockwise and counter-clockwise to bore the corresponding hole. Fortunately the door was made of a softer wood and so the job was easier. Booth inserted the other end of the dowel securely in place, rose from his knees and, rotating the door knob, gave it a pull. The door did not budge.

Satisfied with his handiwork, he once again knelt down, removed both ends of the dowel from the holes and partially opened the door. Booth then carefully and deliberately positioned the dowel behind the door, leaning it on end next to the door's lower hinge. Now that the rod was hidden, he again positioned the door so that it was completely open. Confident that his security within the box was now fully ensured, he returned the knife to its holder and the gimlet to his pocket. Then he went down the stairs and strode out of the theater.

Booth stopped for supper at a nearby restaurant in anticipation of the most important performance of his life. Accompanied by an attractive female companion, who also happened to be a guest at the National Hotel, he dined on puree of fowl, cold ham, roasted wild duck, mashed potatoes and red wine.

Booth barely looked at the beautiful woman seated across from him and the conversation was stilted. He was immersed in thought, pondering the undertaking that he faced later that night, as well as the tasks now entrusted to Powell and Atzerodt. Empty dishes were cleared, replaced with subsequent courses and his wine glass refilled. After about an hour, he finished his meal and paid the bill. Rising from his chair, he apologized to his dinner companion, telling her that important business required his immediate attention and instructed the waiter to serve her anything else she wanted and to put it on his tab. Then, turning toward the visibly surprised lady, Booth bowed his head, tipped his hat and walked out of the restaurant. Stopping underneath a streetlamp, he looked at his pocket watch. It was still too early to return to Ford's Theatre, so he decided to walk for a while.

At just before 9 o'clock, Booth arrived at the rear of Ford's Theatre. He entered the back door and immediately proceeded underneath the stage and exited through a side-door access to the alleyway to Taltavull's Star Saloon. He regally walked to the bar with head held high, befitting what he perceived as his standing as not only the accomplished actor that everyone knew him to be, but also the yet unrecognized historical figure he would soon become. Booth ordered a shot of whiskey and a glass of water. A stocky man standing next to him looked Booth up and down several times and finally remarked, "You'll never be the actor your father was."

Without missing a beat, Booth smiled slyly and replied, "When I leave the stage, I will be the most famous man in America." Waving him off dismissively, the man moved to the other end of the bar.

Suddenly, another man came through the double doors. He wore a high-collared white shirt without a cravat, high-waisted trousers that seemed a little too long, a gray frock coat that was clearly too large in the shoulders and shoes that were quite different from those worn by anyone else in the establishment. He stopped and scanned the patrons, his gaze coming to rest on the individual sipping whiskey at the bar. The newcomer stood transfixed. Only fifteen feet separated the two gentlemen. Booth, leaning against the bar, noticed the attention he was drawing and, assuming this was just another admirer, paid little heed. Taking a deep breath, the newly arrived man regained some of his composure and consciously forced himself to move toward the bar.

ALEX LINWOOD

Alex was now traveling on horseback toward the National Hotel located at 6th Street and Pennsylvania Avenue. This was where Booth had lodgings up to the time of the assassination. It took Alex a little longer to get there than he had expected. His journey was interrupted by a disturbance caused by a wagon heavily laden with produce and sundries, which had tipped over at the intersection of 9th and Pennsylvania. A group of men was helping the distraught merchant retrieve the apples, corncobs, beans, carrots and a few eggs that had survived the mishap. Sacks of coffee, salt and flour were strewn about. Others were trying to turn the wagon upright. The grocer himself was busy chasing off several boys who were trying to make off with the goods that had fallen into the road. Streetcars, passenger carriages, horses and pedestrians all had to take turns maneuvering around the pandemonium. Although he was sorry for the unfortunate grocer, Alex chuckled to himself. The scene before him was not totally unlike something that could happen in a 21st-century accident.

Alex was finally able to continue on his way. After riding several more blocks, he arrived at the National. Since its construction in 1827, it was one of the most famous and luxurious hotels in Washington. Every president from Andrew Jackson to Abraham Lincoln had been a guest; usually while awaiting inauguration and relocating to the President's House. It also housed one of the finest restaurants in the city. Henry Clay and Daniel Webster were among the luminaries who had dined and spoken there. The hotel had even hosted a banquet for President Lincoln the day after his first inauguration, sponsored by the members of Congress from the state of New York. The building stood four stories tall and encompassed almost an entire city block. By 1865, it had been expanded so that it was able to accommodate over a thousand guests.

Alex had his horse tended to and entered the lobby. Its grandeur astonished him. There was a long reception counter intricately carved with flowers and leaves and a grouping of tufted circular settees of red velvet in the middle section of the lobby. These were accompanied by tables adorned with fresh flowers, hotel stationery and decorative quill pens and embossed pencils. Ornate chandeliers of gold and cut glass hung throughout and made for a well-lit environment. The lobby was abuzz with people, primarily men talking business or politics. Alex recalled that the term "lobbyist" was derived from just this type of interaction. As he passed a table, Alex took a few sheets of paper and a pencil and stuffed them into his pocket, as was his habit, in case the need for such implements should arise.

Alex then approached a desk clerk. "Yes, sir, how may I assist you?"

"I have some business with Mr. Booth," replied Alex, trying to envision just how a proper gentleman of the time would make the inquiry. "Is he in?"

The clerk turned and looked behind him, placing his hand inside the box marked 228. "His key is here, so I suspect he is out."

Although he now knew the room number, Alex did not want to simply leave as he thought it might draw undesired suspicion on himself. He again tried to recall a proper response and said to the clerk in a matter-of-fact manner, "Can you kindly tell me what room he occupies? I should like to leave my carte de visite." Alex, of course, had no such card, which in those days was a business-type card printed with the likeness of the bearer, but he hoped the clerk would give him the room number so that he could proceed there with the clerk's knowledge and consent.

"I would be happy to receive your card and ensure that it gets to Mr. Booth," replied the clerk. He stood with his palm outstretched awaiting the card.

Alex thought he would give it one last try. "I appreciate your assistance, but it is rather important that Mr. Booth is made aware that I came to see him. I would much prefer to slip it under his door myself."

"As you wish, sir," the clerk responded. "Mr. Booth occupies room number 228. I will be happy to place it in his box so that it gets to him upon his return."

"I appreciate your offer, but I prefer to deliver it personally."

"Suit yourself," responded the clerk and he turned to attend to the next guest.

Alex left the hotel and took a walk in order to gather his thoughts. If he did go up to Booth's room, what would he gain if its occupant was absent? Finally, he went back into the building via the revolving door fronting Pennsylvania Avenue and walked toward the staircase leading to the second floor. He climbed the stairs, went down the hallway and stopped in front of the door marked 228.

Now what? Knock? Peek through the keyhole?

His dilemma was interrupted by an attractive woman approaching from down the hall. "If you are looking for Mr. Booth, you missed him. He and I just finished dining, although I must say, he was rather distracted and did not make much of a dinner companion. He left all of a sudden and said he had some business to attend to. Rather mysterious, if you ask me." This last comment was made almost as if she was talking to herself. Then, refocusing her attention on Alex, she brightened up and asked, "May I tell him who came asking for him?"

"Thank you, but that won't be necessary. I will try again another time." Alex bowed, went back down the stairs and out of the hotel.

No matter what he did, Booth was always one step ahead of him. If he was going to accomplish his mission entrusted to him by Crook, it would have to be done at one of the two remaining places: at the tavern Booth had visited right before the assassination, or directly at Ford's Theatre.

Alex mounted his horse again for the long ride across town to Taltavull's Star Saloon.

APRIL 14, 1865
FORD'S THEATRE

BEFORE 10:30 P.M.

A lex Linwood could not believe his eyes. He was actually approaching the one and only John Wilkes Booth. Alex could feel his heart pound and his pulse quicken. Booth was a more striking figure than his pictures portrayed. His entire countenance exuded what Alex could only interpret as arrogant aristocracy. His dark, piercing eyes stared directly at Alex. Booth was impeccably dressed. He had taken off his hat, revealing his thick, black, wavy hair. A well-waxed moustache curled over his lips.

Alex swallowed hard as he strode toward the bar and approached one of the most infamous men in American history. When he was within arm's length of the would-be assassin, he stopped. Without a word, the two men weighed one another, each waiting for the other to break the silence. Several people at a nearby table stopped talking and fixed their attention upon them. Alex knew that he had to say something, as he did not want to cause a scene, nor did he want Booth to walk away dismissively.

"Mr. Booth," said Alex, in a slightly high-pitched voice that surprised his own ears.

"Yes. And who might you be?" the actor inquired.

His mind in a whirl, Alex tried to summon a plausible identity and a reason for being there. Then it came to him. Booth, like any other celebrity of his stature, liked nothing more than to talk about himself and to have a captive audience for his braggadocio. So, playing upon Booth's vanity, Alex pressed forward.

"Sir, my name is Francis Larson, but you can call me Frank," he said, recalling the name of a college history professor. "I'm a reporter with the *Philadelphia Intelligencer*. I heard that President Lincoln was going to be attending the theater tonight and I wanted to be here in case he made some sort of a speech or addressed those in attendance. Imagine my delight when I passed by this establishment and saw a man of your prominence in the theater standing at the bar! May I ask you a few questions for our readers?"

"You are quite a ways from home, Mr. Larson," responded Booth somewhat warily.

"Oh, you see, sir, Washington City is my beat. I usually cover politics and human interest stories at the Capitol." Alex tried to be as calm and matter-of-fact as possible, but his hands were shaking and his knees trembling.

Booth appeared tense and seemed to be taking stock of the man standing in front of him. Then his jaw seemed to relax, although his general demeanor did anything but. As he spoke to Alex, it was clear from the tone of his voice that Booth was addressing Alex in a formal and businesslike manner and not as acquaintances or equals.

"What would you like to know?"

"Well, first of all, what is your favorite role to play?"

"As you probably know, I pride myself on being an accomplished Shakespearean actor. As for the role, it is the one that I am portraying at any given time. It is the play in production that is the most important and I guess you could say my favorite." Booth hesitated a moment, his brow furrowed. "Aren't you going to write any of this down? I thought this was an interview for a newspaper."

"Ah." Alex could feel himself blanch and he suddenly thrust his hand into his pocket and pulled out the pencil and paper he had picked up at the hotel. He was careful not to let Booth see the embossed heading for the National Hotel. "Pardon me, Mr. Booth, but I was so enamored of you that I completely forgot about the tools of my trade."

Alex pretended to be writing as the actor held court, regaling the faux reporter standing before him with detailed accounts of his preparation for a theatrical role, his recent accomplishments and famous women with whom he had appeared. After speaking for a while, Booth saw that his glass was empty.

"I think it would be appropriate for the *Philadelphia Intelligencer* to buy me a drink, don't you?"

"Of course." Alex motioned to the bartender.

Booth's glass was refilled and the questions and answers continued for a bit longer. Suddenly, the actor waved his arm and cut Alex off in mid-sentence. "That is all that I have time for this evening." He finished the last of his whiskey and reached for his hat.

"But, Mr. Booth, we have only scratched the surface," replied Alex somewhat excitedly. "There is so much more that my readers want to know."

"Not tonight. I have a very important business engagement—an appointment with destiny, you might say," replied Booth with his chin uplifted, ever the performer.

As Booth strode from the bar, Alex could think of no way

to stop him from leaving. He had hoped that, if he engaged Booth in talking about himself, the actor would lose track of time and the schedule he had to keep. Now what was he to do? It was not in him to tackle the man. Besides, Alex knew that Booth was concealing a large Bowie knife and would not hesitate to use it.

The saloon had a set of double doors exiting onto the sidewalk and was only about a dozen steps from the theater's entrance. Booth paused just short of the doors to straighten his clothing, adjust his tie and set his hat at just the right angle. Mesmerized, Alex observed his performance: it was like watching a peacock preen itself. When he was satisfied with his appearance, Booth exited the bar, turned to his right and walked the short distance to the theater.

After a brief delay, Alex followed him, but not too closely, careful not to be seen. Booth peered inside the doors at the back of the theater. Alex assumed it was to determine exactly how far along the play was, so that Booth could determine when the famous laugh-producing line would be delivered. Booth quickly processed the information, spun back and moved toward the carpeted staircase that led to the second level and the presidential box.

As Booth was a couple of strides from the staircase, he spotted out of the corner of his eye, the reporter from Philadelphia. He paid no heed, as undoubtedly the reporter was lingering in the lobby in case the president addressed the audience at the conclusion of the play. Booth chuckled to himself at the thought that the reporter was, unwittingly, going to get the story of the century.

Watching Booth approach the stairs, Alex's mind raced, trying to improvise a plan. Abruptly, and inexplicably, he thought of

Mary Lincoln, and how, if he could prevent the assassination of her husband, he would also save her life in the process. He knew that the death of the president had resulted in her living grief-stricken for the remainder of her days, and that the debts incurred as First Lady could never be repaid to her creditors. He also knew that her own son, Robert, ultimately had her committed to Belle-vue Place insane asylum for nearly four months and that she finally died a recluse. This downward spiral would be changed forever should the president survive the night.

Alex struck upon what he felt was his one last, best hope to avert the impending disaster. As Booth made his way up the stair-case, Alex began moving swiftly toward the door to the back of the house. As Alex moved quickly, Booth moved stealthily, almost as if the two men were engaged in a macabre dance. Step by step, they moved through the theater, with their presence known only to themselves. Booth, ascending the stairs toward his intended victim, and Alex entering behind the last row of seats to foil a horrendous plan. Alex was vividly conscious of Booth, directly above him, moving ever closer to the president.

Then, in a flash, Alex knew how he could thwart the assas-sination. He rushed from the back of the house toward the stage. An usher, in an effort to intercept him, remarked in a stage whisper that certainly did not befit the situation, "Hey, where are you going?" Alex said nothing and nearly knocked the poor fellow to the floor as he brushed past.

Midway down the aisle, he glanced back over his shoulder. He could see that Booth had made his way completely across the back rows of seats in the balcony and would soon be at the presidential box.

Alex had no time to lose. When he was almost to the stage,

he turned toward the audience and shouted at the top of his lungs, "Ladies and gentlemen! Ladies and gentlemen! Your attention, please."

Booth heard the shouts and directed his gaze toward the stage. To his shock and surprise, he saw the reporter screaming like a madman. What was happening? Why would this Philadelphia reporter act in such a manner?

Booth's movement toward the box was halted and he backed up a bit to get a better look at what was happening down below, ending up directly behind the last row of seats.

Alex kept yelling as he brushed past an astonished conductor in the orchestra pit, nearly toppling him into the brass section. Alex dodged among the musicians, some staring in surprise, others in disgust. He ran up the three wooden steps, leapt upon the stage and, turning to face the audience, found himself next to the famous actress Laura Keene.

There was an audible gasp from the audience. Was this part of the performance? In his box, President Lincoln leaned forward in his rocking chair and gazed below. Mary grasped his arm, visibly frightened by this sudden outburst.

It was as if time stood still for a moment. Here was Alex, standing on the stage like an intruder, while the man he was trying to save stared down at him, trying to understand exactly what was happening. Alex was just about to catch the full wrath of the show's star, but before she could speak, he yelled at the top of his lungs, trying to muster all the theatrical flair that he could.

"Ladies and gentlemen," he said loudly, waving his arms. "Tonight, you all have a unique opportunity rarely given to the theater-going public. Here and now, I ask you to show your appreciation for one of the greatest actors in the American theater today. Up there," he continued, pointing to the balcony where Booth stood. "Up there, in the flesh, is John Wilkes Booth!"

The audience rose and turned toward the direction in which Alex had been pointing. "There he is, I see him," shouted more than one voice.

A high-pitched female voice called out, "Oh, Mr. Booth!"

"Three cheers for Mr. Booth!" yelled another patron.

With that, the crowd burst into applause. And Booth stood stock-still. Shock and surprise engulfed him. How could this be happening?

Although no one knew it, Booth was caught so completely off guard that he failed to give the crowd what it really wanted—one of his famous bows.

In this moment frozen in time, Alex's eyes turned toward the presidential box. Despite the din in the theater, he was aware of nothing but silence. There, at the other end of his gaze, standing tall and regal and full of life was Abraham Lincoln. Alex was completely awestruck and could not believe his own eyes. Just above and no more than a dozen feet away, stood the object of the countless books and articles he had devoured over the many years since his Aunt Rosamond gave him the first book. But he wasn't looking at some detached, unearthly photograph from the past. Here stood the actual man himself, alive and animated.

Alex felt his legs wobble at the realization that Mr. Lincoln was dividing his attention between Alex himself and the man who, if it wasn't for Alex, would have ended the president's life. The president stood and, like the rest of the audience, paid homage to the actor standing just a short distance from the door leading to the box he occupied. Lincoln's kindly face displayed a smile Alex had never seen before, since there is no photograph of the president smiling. It was indeed the angelic smile that had been described by so many of his contemporaries who had had the good fortune to see it. The president continued applauding and turned and spoke to Mary.

Alex continued to be mesmerized by the sight of the president. How many times had he said to himself, "If only I had been there?" And now, here he was, about to accomplish the impossible—saving the life of Abraham Lincoln.

Just as he was about to direct his attention to Mary Lincoln, Alex's trance-like state was broken. He sensed someone rushing toward him. It was Booth, who had entered the rear of the orchestra level seating area and was racing down the aisle brandishing the Bowie knife.

Instinct took over. Alex turned and fled through a door that was part of the scenery. He headed for the theater's rear exit about 50 feet away, nearly tripping over a cart filled with costumes and props. An angry stagehand yelled an obscenity. As he ran out of the theater, Alex passed a man holding a horse and looking around, as if waiting for someone. Alex burst into the cool night air, turned and began racing down the alley toward 10th Street.

A moment later, Booth emerged through the same exit and dashed into the alley, so enraged and intent upon catching up to Alex that he was oblivious of Ned Spangler standing there holding the horse that Booth had planned to use for his escape after shooting the President.

Alex was keenly aware of Booth behind him in the alley and beginning to bear down. The cold air made his lungs burn as he tore down the alleyway. His tennis shoes allowed him to keep ahead of the younger, stronger, but heavy-booted man chasing him. Though unable to escape the feeling that at any moment he was going to feel Booth's grip wrestling him to the ground, Alex dared not turn to look over his shoulder.

Then a voice screamed out wildly: "I don't know who you are, or how you found out, but you've ruined all of my plans. If I can't kill him, I can surely kill you!"

At the end of the alley, Alex impulsively turned left on 10th Street. He had hoped to disappear into a crowd of people, but the street was not very busy. Booth was now close on his heels.

Suddenly, as if out of thin air, a carriage appeared and a woman's voice called out: "Get in!"

It was Lucy! This was the second time she had miraculously come to his rescue. As she slowed the carriage, Alex leapt into the seat beside her. "Get-up!" she screamed. She violently shook the reins and the horse instantly began to gallop.

"What are you doing here?" Alex was beyond being incredulous, but not beyond being thankful.

"You told me last night that you were here to see an actor and then it occurred to me that this is the part of the city where most of the actors can be found. I don't exactly know why, but something told me that I had to be here for you tonight."

Alex could not believe how his life had been saved by a woman's intuition. He grasped hold of the metal seat frame as the coach sped away. In that moment, it all sank in. He had done it. He had actually carried out the arduous responsibility Crook had thrust upon him. Alex Linwood had saved the life of Abraham Lincoln. Now his emotions were catching up to him and a lump rose in his throat. He looked over at Lucy. If not for her, he might not have survived Booth's pursuit.

The carriage rocked back and forth as the wheels rolled over the uneven dirt street, with Alex hanging on for fear of being thrown out. Out of pure gratitude, Alex felt the uncontrollable urge to wrap his arms around Lucy. As he leaned closer to her, a wheel struck something in the roadway. The carriage swerved violently and Alex's body pitched in the opposite direction. Simultaneously, he felt an unseen force pulling him out of the carriage. With the sound of Lucy's screams in the background and the peal of a distant clock chiming half-past ten, a wavy portal appeared, opened and swallowed Alex in midair.

• • •

Booth saw the carriage appear and the so-called reporter leap into it. The coach then took off and rounded the next corner, leaving Booth behind in its wake. He slowed to a stop and stood staring for a few seconds. He knew that he would not be able to catch the man whose interference had kept him from killing Lincoln. He pulled out his pocket watch and looked at the time. He might still have his opportunity if he hurried back to the theater.

Booth turned and ran back toward Ford's Theatre. Entering the front door, he knew he no longer had the luxury of being discreet. With his hand on the butt end of the Derringer, he bounded up the stairs with reckless abandon. After traversing the back row of the balcony seats, he stopped. Standing there at the foot of the staircase to the president's box was John Parker, the president's bodyguard, chatting amiably with another man. During the interim fiasco created by Alex, Parker had returned from the saloon and now stood poised between Booth and an open pathway to Abraham Lincoln.

Booth was filled with rage and despair. All his detailed plans had gone for naught. He would not be able to carry out the scheme he had painstakingly devised. Slowly, he turned, retraced his steps and slunk out of the theater.

• • •

When Alex was thrown out of the carriage, Lucy reached out her hand to grab him, hoping he would in turn be reaching for her. But there was no touch of his hand upon hers.

Lucy then brought the carriage to a stop as quickly as possible and jumped to the dirt street below. She ran as fast as she could back to the exact spot where Alex had been thrown from the coach, frantically calling his name over and over.

There was no response, and as she got closer, she was filled with dread, expecting to come upon Alex's body lying motionless upon the ground. But a strange thing happened: she did not see him. She stopped in the middle of the street and turned in a slow circle, looking in all directions for several minutes. Alex was nowhere in sight. He seemed to have vanished into thin air.

How could this be? Lucy wondered.

"May I help you with something, miss?"

It was a Washington City policeman, looking at her with genuine concern.

"No, thank you, officer. I was just looking for someone. I thought we were supposed to meet here, but I guess I was mistaken."

"Well, miss," cautioned the officer, "I think it would be best for your own safety if you were to move out of the center of the street."

"Yes, yes I shall. Thank you."

Lucy returned to her carriage and touched the seat that only minutes ago Alex had occupied. With great sorrow, Lucy climbed aboard and turned the horse toward home.

APRIL 15TH – PRESENT-DAY

Sunlight streamed through the curtains framing the window. A beam fell upon Alex's face and he opened his eyes. He had no immediate idea of where he might be. The last thing he recalled was sitting next to Lucy in the carriage and losing his balance. Then all went blank.

He awoke to find his head resting on a pillow and the bedcovers pulled up to his chin. This was the way he always slept. He scanned the room. The first thing he saw was a flat-screen television set atop a dresser. On the nightstand to his left were a telephone and a lamp. The sound of an air-conditioner hummed in the background.

Oh, my, he thought. *That was some dream I had!*

Alex usually did not remember his dreams with any detail, but this one was different. This dream he remembered from start to finish, all that he did and the people that he had met. Then he thought about Lucy and a smile crossed his lips.

"Well," he said aloud, "at least in my dream I was able to save the life of Abraham Lincoln. Funny how real it all felt."

He glanced at the clock sitting upon the night table to his right. Underneath the time of day was the day of the week and the date. It was the morning of Saturday, April 15th. He had to get up and catch a noon plane back to Los Angeles.

Alex flung off the covers and froze, half in shock and half in amazement. His clothes! He was dressed in a tan shirt made of heavy cloth, pants also constructed of a heavy material adorned with two buttons at the waist and a rope belt. Lying at the foot of the bed were a topcoat and a hat that were clearly straight out of the 19th century. On the floor, he saw his tennis shoes side by side.

"Oh, my God!" Alex exclaimed. "It wasn't a dream! It must have all really happened. I—I—I saved the life of Abraham Lincoln?" The last words came out as more of a question than a statement of fact.

He dashed from his bed to the laptop lying open on the desk. But when he pressed the button to turn it on, nothing happened. It was dead and needed to be recharged. He was just about to plug it in, when he again realized that he had to get to Reagan Airport within the hour to have sufficient time to clear security and catch his flight.

Alex took a fast shower and dressed in clean clothes. Then he pulled out his suitcase, tossed in his present-day clothes and then methodically packed away the clothes Crook had supplied to him. On a small side table he found, neatly folded, the modern-day clothes that he had changed out of at the Soldiers' Home, along with his wallet, car keys, watch and cellphone. He had no idea how they came to be there, but he had no time to try and figure it out. He attempted to turn on his phone, but it was also out of power. He finished packing, stuffed the personal items into his pants pocket, left his room and took the elevator down to the front desk.

"Checking out of room 403," he announced as he strode up to the desk clerk.

"Haven't seen much of you lately. Where'd you disappear to?" the clerk inquired.

"What do you mean?" asked Alex, somewhat bewildered.

"Well, sir," the clerk responded, "you checked in Wednesday evening, headed out Thursday morning and we didn't see hide nor hair of you again until just now."

"Oh, um, well, I had a few things to do and they kept me busier than I had anticipated."

"Too bad," replied the clerk. "If you'd been here last night, you could have experienced the special dinner that the restaurant next door puts on. You see, once a year the owner of the restaurant pulls out dozens of antiques that he normally keeps in storage and dresses up the place like it used to look in 1865. He even puts up a specially made sign to rename the place for one evening, the same name as the restaurant that occupied the spot back then—Chambers' House and Grille. Used to be run by a well-known Washington City woman. What was her name? Leslie, Laurie—something like that." The clerk returned to the business of assisting Alex in checking out. "Anyhow, you're all set. Here's your receipt. Have a pleasant trip home."

Alex was momentarily dumbfounded. He thanked the clerk and looked at his watch. He had a couple of minutes to spare before he had to head to the airport, so he walked next door to the adjoining restaurant.

I'll just step inside for a quick peek and then I will be on my way, he thought to himself. But when he got to the door, a posted sign indicated the restaurant did not open until five. He cupped his hands around his eyes and peered through the window. Of course, the interior looked nothing like it had when he had dined there and met Lucy. But there, still hanging on the wall above the bar, was the photograph of a man and his daughter from a bygone age. Alex flashed back to that brief period in time when he and Lucy had shared their fleeting moments and sighed. Then he made his way to the taxi stand to catch a cab to the airport.

At the terminal, Alex picked up his boarding pass and proceeded through security. Arriving at the gate, he heard the announcement that boarding was about to begin. The process went smoothly and the plane took off right on time. Alex settled back into his seat and looked for an outlet to plug in his laptop, but the older plane he was travelling on had not been updated with this technology. With nothing else to do for the next six hours, Alex began to rerun in his mind the events of the past two days. He still could not totally fathom that he had actually been transported back in time and was able to achieve the unimaginable—to keep John Wilkes Booth from murdering Abraham Lincoln.

Now, all he could think about was getting home, firing up his computer and learning what became of the post-Civil War United States, with President Lincoln still at the helm. How different Reconstruction must have been. And what did Lincoln do after he completed his second term? He had always talked about a desire to visit the Holy City of Jerusalem and also to see California. Had he and Mary traveled to these locations?

Then Alex had an eerie thought. Everyone but he knew that, instead of being assassinated that night at Ford's Theatre, Lincoln had finished out his second term. They also knew to what age he lived and how he eventually died. Alex would now have to learn all this. He could hardly wait to explore anew the closing chapters of Lincoln's life.

As he settled back in his seat, he thought about all he experienced in 1865 Washington and the time spent with Lucy. Before long, he drifted off to sleep. The next thing he knew, a voice over the intercom was announcing their final approach into Los Angeles International Airport. Soon, he was looking out the window at the Fabulous Forum, the old Hollywood Park Racetrack and the 405 Freeway passing below. Seconds later, the plane touched down and taxied to the gate.

Alex retrieved his carry-on from the overhead compartment and made his way off the plane. He walked through the terminal, took the escalator to the ground level, exited and walked to the shuttle stop to await the van and the ride to the lot where his car was parked. Since departing the hotel earlier that morning, he had been bursting at the seams to tell someone, anyone, about his experiences in 19th-century Washington City. But how could he? For whoever he told would surely think he was nuts. Now though, his mind contemplated more than ever what he might find when he got home, accessed his computer and Googled "Abraham Lincoln."

The van dropped Alex off at the stall where his car was parked. He maneuvered out of the lot onto Century Boulevard and then into the heavy traffic on the San Diego Freeway north. The ride home was interminable, but he finally pulled into his driveway. Removing his suitcase and laptop case from the trunk, he hastened inside. Alex could not get to his computer fast enough. There was a note on the entryway table: "Hello dear. Welcome home. I am out running errands and will be home soon. Love, S."

Alex made a beeline for the den, sat down in his desk chair and turned on his computer. While waiting for the screen to come to life, he leaned back in his chair and tilted his head as well. In so doing he inadvertently looked up at the shelf above his desk where he kept the books he had collected about

Abraham Lincoln. He then spotted something incredibly odd. There were gaps between books that never before existed.

He got up and took a closer look at the empty spaces which were once occupied by books. Suddenly he realized that the titles that were now absent included the seminal work *The Day Lincoln Was Shot* by Jim Bishop, as well as *American Brutus: John Wilkes Booth and the Lincoln Conspiracies* by Michael Kauffman and *Blood on the Moon* by Edward Steers, Jr.

Alex smiled broadly. "If these books do not exist," he said aloud, "then Mr. Lincoln was never assassinated. And if he was never assassinated, then I really did it! I saved the life of the greatest American president!"

Alex went back to the computer. Seeking confirmation that his task was successfully completed, he typed into the Google search engine: "Assassination of Abraham Lincoln." His finger hovered above the "enter" key. A feeling of raw excitement flashed through his body. Taking a deep breath, he pushed down on the key. The screen went blank for a moment and then a list of web sites popped up. References to "Abraham Lincoln— Wikipedia," "Life of Abraham Lincoln" and "Abraham and Mary Lincoln" appeared, but no reference to the assassination of Lincoln. There were no websites regarding the assassination.

"I just can't believe it," Alex whispered.

He decided not to click on any of these offerings. He had another idea. He went back to the Google search box. Alex recalled reading the edition of the *Washington Evening Star* while seated at the table in Lucy's restaurant. He typed in, "Washington Evening Star, April 15, 1865." He again paused with his index finger hovering over the enter key and after drawing a breath, pressed it. There on the screen in front of him was the

Saturday, April 15, 1865, edition of the *Evening Star*. It was the headline in the left upper-most column of the front page that took him completely aback. There in bold print were the words, "EXTRA—NATION MOURNS THE DEATH OF THE PRESIDENT."

Alex rubbed his eyes, as if they were playing tricks on him and reread the headline. It did not change.

"How can this be?" Alex felt a lump rising in his throat. "How could the newspaper report Mr. Lincoln's death if I had prevented it?"

He moved in closer and began to read the account as reported in the tabloid.

April 14, 1865
Abraham Lincoln

Aftermath

The interloper had run through the stage set, closely followed by John Wilkes Booth. The audience stood in amazement. No one said a word. Even the Lincolns, Major Rathbone and Miss Harris were silent, stunned by what had just occurred. Then Laura Keene, the consummate actress, stamped her foot as if the interruption was part of the performance and delivered the next line. The other actors immediately picked up her cue and the play resumed as if there had been no disruption whatsoever. The audience remained standing, seeming unsure of what to do. Miss Keene, breaking character, stepped to the footlights and called out:

"Don't you all want to know what happens?"

Some in the audience responded with a resounding, "Yes," while others simply applauded. Then, everyone took a seat and the show continued. In the box above the stage, Mary Lincoln placed a shawl over the president's shoulders, sat back down and again placed her left hand on her husband's right arm. Lincoln responded by covering her gloved hand with his own bare hand, and both settled in to watch the actors as they moved toward the theatrical conclusion.

In less than fifteen minutes, the actors on stage were taking their post-production bows. Laura Keene was the last cast member to be welcomed by her fellow performers and the result was a standing ovation by the audience members. Miss Keene took several bows, and then, taking a couple steps forward, turned and pointed to the presidential box. She waved to Mr. Lincoln and directed her own applause in his direction. The audience turned and warmly acknowledged the president. Smiling, Lincoln waved in return. Mary beamed at the attention being paid to her husband by both the show's star and the assemblage. Miss Keene then took three steps back and the curtain was lowered.

An audible hum could be heard from below the box as the patrons began gathering up their personal belongings. Everyone was in good spirits. Some chatter focused on the event that had caused the play to come to a sudden stop, while others were commenting on the show itself.

The four occupants of the presidential box got up and they too collected their things.

"Mr. Lincoln," Mary said, "you must put your gloves back on before we leave."

The president sighed and reached into his coat pocket for the kid gloves. As he pulled them on, Mary reached behind her seat and removed her coat. Major Rathbone politely held it for her, then turned and provided similar assistance to Miss Harris. Lincoln positioned his stovepipe hat upon his head and prepared to leave the box.

Ordinarily, the president would have allowed the ladies and Major Rathbone to exit the box ahead of him, but, suspecting that a throng of people would be waiting at the end of the staircase for a glimpse of him, he led the way. Lincoln moved behind the rocking chair and took one long stride with his left foot toward the closed door. In the manner of his usual gait, the entirety of the bottom of his foot made simultaneous contact with the floor. He reached out, turned the knob and slowly pulled the door open.

Lincoln took his second step with his right foot, crossing the threshold and again landed flat-footed. Mary was directly behind him, followed by Miss Harris and the major. The president was now three strides from the top of the descending stairs. One more step with his left foot placed him completely within the dimly lit landing. Many in the crowd below remained near their seats, looking up in hopes of seeing the president before he left the theater.

As the President lifted his right foot to continue, Mary Lincoln took hold of his forearm affectionately. "Oh, Father," she whispered. "They love you so."

As Lincoln looked at her over his right shoulder, he took another step forward. Seeing that he was looking in their direction, Miss Harris audibly thanked the president for kindly inviting her and her fiancé to be their guests that evening. As the president was about to respond, he continued his methodical walk, bent slightly at the waist, his right foot now rising, moving forward and descending toward the carpeted floor.

Unbeknownst to him, or anyone else, when John Parker had forcefully shut the door to the box when leaving his post earlier that evening, the dowel that Booth had concealed behind the door tumbled to the floor and rolled under the door clearance. It came to rest less than a foot from the top of the stairs. Then disaster struck.

The president's right foot came down squarely on the dowel, causing it to roll backward under his foot and propel his body forward. He was suddenly launched over the descending stairs. His head was still turned so that he was looking over his shoulder at Mrs. Lincoln. Instinctively, he tried to reach out for something to steady himself, but there was nothing. In an instant, he was airborne and falling uncontrollably downward. The left side of his head struck the edge of a step and a sickening snap could clearly be heard.

"Mr. Lincoln! Mr. Lincoln!" Mary screamed. "Are you all right?"

Lincoln's body lay motionless. Blood was seeping out of his left ear. Mary, Miss Harris and the major rushed to his side. Mary, the first to reach her husband, shook him, first gently and then a little more forcefully.

"Please, Father," she implored hysterically. "Say something to me! Look at me!"

The president did not respond. Sensing the seriousness of the injury, Rathbone instructed Clara to assist Mrs. Lincoln and then, in almost the same breath, he shouted, "There has been an accident. We need a doctor here at once. Please, somebody help us!"

Mary sat on the step and cradled the president's head in her lap. Miss Harris removed a handkerchief from her purse and held it against his bleeding ear.

A young U.S. Army surgeon, Charles Leale, had been sitting in the orchestra level. Hearing the frantic cries for help, he rushed up the stairs, followed by Laura Keene. Mrs. Lincoln was beside herself with grief and despair. She placed her face near that of her husband and continued to call his name, hoping desperately for some type of response. Miss Keene whispered something to Miss Harris, who bent down and took Mary's

elbow, coaxing her gently away her from her husband. Miss
Keene took Mary's place and began stroking the president's forehead, which was now resting on her lap.

Dr. Leale assumed control. He knew immediately from the
grotesque angle of the president's head and neck that the injury
was very serious. Lincoln was unconscious and his breathing
was uneven. Blood continued to flow from his ear. Dr. Leale
asked Miss Keene for her sash and she untied it and handed it
to him. Leale wrapped it carefully around the president's head,
in an effort to apply pressure and stem the bleeding. He opened
one of Lincoln's eyes and found the pupil to be fully dilated.

Dr. Leale was convinced that the president had suffered a
catastrophic injury and was about to announce this to the gathered crowd when he saw Mrs. Lincoln looking at him. She had
calmed down considerably and was searching his face with eyes
full of hope.

"Oh, doctor," she implored, reaching out toward him. "Will
my husband be all right? Is it serious? Please, tell me what you
think."

Dr. Leale could not bring himself to tell her that it was
unlikely her husband would ever regain consciousness. "It is
a bit too early to know," he replied, as convincingly as he could.
"Our immediate concern is to make him as comfortable as
possible."

Dr. Leale knew that his patient would not survive a bumpy
carriage ride back to the White House. The president had to be
moved to a location where he could be tended and Leale asked
Major Rathbone to go downstairs and find some men to assist
them.

Rathbone ran down the stairs and returned with four men.

One of them was John Parker, who had been waiting below for the president so that he could accompany the Lincolns back to the White House.

"There has been a terrible accident," Leale told them. "We need to lift the president slowly and carefully and take him to the nearest house, where I can tend to his injuries."

The men lifted the stricken president and began to negotiate the staircase down to the lobby of the theater. Dr. Leale proceeded ahead of the men, clearing the way. Miss Harris and Miss Keene followed behind with Mary, doing their best to assure the grief-stricken wife that her husband would be fine, although none of them truly believed in their hearts that such would be the case.

A young man named Henry Safford happened to be standing on the outside stoop of the Petersen House, a boarding house directly across the street from the theater. Seeing a group of men carrying someone who was obviously injured, he called, "Bring him over here!"

Dr. Leale waved to the men carrying the president to follow him and they crossed the street toward where Safford was standing. As they conveyed their charge up the stairs, Safford saw for the first time that the injured man was the President of the United States.

"Oh my God," he exclaimed. "What happened?"

"No time for that now," responded Leale in a curt manner. "We need to get the president to a bed."

"Follow me," said Safford.

Walking through the front parlor, they carried the president to a back room that, although being rented to William T. Clark, was vacant at the moment. As they began to lay Lincoln on the bed, Leale quickly saw that Lincoln was too tall to be positioned normally, so he instructed the men to set him down so that he was lying diagonally. Leale partially unbuttoned the president's shirt and loosened his belt in an effort to make him as comfortable as possible.

Mary Lincoln entered the room and immediately bent over her husband, alternating between crying and calling him by endearing names. She begged him to respond, but her pleas were met with silence. Dr. Leale, along with several other doctors who had followed them across the street, began to examine the president, while Laura Keene gently escorted Mary to the front parlor so the doctors could attend to him.

Shortly thereafter, the Lincolns' family physician, Robert K. Stone, arrived on the scene. Although he surrendered control of the situation to Dr. Stone, Leale never left the president's room. He pulled up a chair and sat next the bed, almost constantly holding the president's hand. Both he and Dr. Stone continued to monitor their patient.

Word soon spread that the president had been involved in a horrible accident. Tad Lincoln, their youngest son, had been at nearby Grover's Theatre watching a production of *Aladdin! Or His Wonderful Lamp*. At its conclusion, he was informed of the tragedy and, wanting to see his father at once, was told the president was in good hands and it would be best if Tad returned to the White House.

Robert Lincoln was in his room at the White House when Tad arrived and told him what had happened. After attempting to reassure his younger brother that their father would be all right, Robert went directly to the Petersen House and spent the evening there, alternating between sitting at his father's side and trying to console his mother, who was anxiously waiting in the parlor.

Throughout the night, there was a steady stream of visitors to the room where the president lay. Many of Washington's prominent doctors stopped by to see if they could render aid, but were advised that there was little they could do. Members of the Cabinet, most notably Secretary of War Stanton, came as soon as word reached them. Occasionally, during the ordeal, after promising Robert that she would retain her composure, Mary entered the room where her husband lay motionless. But she soon began to shriek with anguish and was escorted back to the front parlor.

As the night wore on, the president's condition worsened. The wound began to bleed again and his breathing became much more labored. In the early morning hours, a steady rain began to fall outside. At around 7 a.m., Mary was once again permitted to join in what was now a death watch. There were long pauses between Lincoln's breaths, an indication that his demise was imminent.

Mary looked down upon the face of her husband, the man she had loved and supported for over 25 years and said, "Love, live but one moment to speak to me once—to speak to our children." Then she let out an earth-shattering cry and nearly fainted. It was at this point that Secretary Stanton, who had never gotten along with Mrs. Lincoln, said, "Get that woman out and do not let her in again!" Mary was once more ushered to the front parlor and was never again to be in the presence of her beloved husband.

At 7:22 a.m., on April 15, 1865, Abraham Lincoln drew his last breath. Dr. Leale had a firm grasp of the president's hand when he died. Later, Leale explained that sometimes recognition returns just before death, and he wanted the president to know that he was not alone. Stanton looked upon the face of the man he had grown to love and admire, and intoned, "Now he belongs to the ages."

Mary Lincoln, still sobbing in the parlor, was informed, "It is all over. The president is no more." She was escorted to a carriage waiting to take her back to the White House. Approaching the coach, she looked across the street at Ford's Theatre and repeatedly exclaimed, "That dreadful house—that dreadful house! This awful place!" She was then compassionately assisted into the carriage for the slow, mournful ride back to the White House.

HOME

When Alex finished reading the account of President Lincoln's accidental death as it was reported in the *Washington Evening Star*, he sat stock-still in his chair, dumbfounded at the newspaper report. He harked back to the 36 hours he had spent in 19th-century Washington City and the opportunity that had been afforded to him. Yet for all of his efforts, he, in actuality, changed nothing. As before, the president never left Ford's Theatre under his own power. Alex did not spare Mary the loss of her beloved husband. Robert and little Tad both still became fatherless. And, perhaps most monumental of all, the nation was deprived of the one man who would have been able to guide it through the crucial period of Reconstruction.

Mr. Lincoln expressed it himself, in his written message to Congress on December 1, 1862: "Fellow citizens, we cannot escape history." Little could he have imagined at the time that he was penning this fatalistic sentiment about his own mortality.

As Alex contemplated his experiences in the Washington of April 1865 and the unfortunate end met by Lincoln in Ford's Theatre, a tear came to his eye. Why, he wondered, would an opportunity such as this be presented to me with so little hope of success? Then came another thought: Was there something he missed? Something he should have done, or someone's assistance he should have solicited? Could there have been some way to ensure that at the end of the evening of April 14, 1865, the

Lincolns would have exited the theater arm in arm and ridden happily in their carriage back to the White House? Then he realized that he could go on and on like this but never find the answer. In his heart, he knew that he had done the best he could. But perhaps, in the end, Mr. Lincoln was right. We cannot escape history.

And then there was Lucy. Having met her as he did was like once again being single and trying to make an impression on a member of the opposite sex. He had rather enjoyed that long-forgotten feeling of butterflies in the stomach that a man experiences in the presence of an attractive woman. Lucy had probably saved his life, not just once, but twice. Alex wondered if, as the years passed, Lucy had ever thought about the brief time they had spent together. And, especially, what could possibly have gone through her mind when he flew out of her carriage and simply disappeared? Thinking about her, he hoped that Lucy had found happiness in her life.

Suddenly, Alex heard the front door open. "Honey, I'm home," Sarah called out. It was a welcome voice indeed. He got up from his chair and went to meet her. She threw her arms around him in a warm and loving embrace and he returned the hug so enthusiastically she let out a squeal. Sarah gave Alex a kiss, took a step back and said with a laugh, "My, it's like you haven't seen me in more than a hundred years!"

She guided him toward the living room. "Come and sit down and tell me all about your trip." Then, seeing the wound above his ear, she asked, "Hey! What happened to your head?" He smiled at her. Where to begin?

EPILOGUE

The fact that the plans of the conspirators had been changed dramatically resulted in their own lives being forever altered. While the attack upon Secretary of State William Seward did, unfortunately, still occur, Alex's interruption of Booth's intended action caused the lives of all the other participants to be significantly modified. The following provides a brief description of how these differing events affected each of them.

JOHN WILKES BOOTH

After the foiled assassination plot, Booth returned to his hotel room. In the hours before learning of the accident that took the life of Lincoln, he began to formulate in his mind how he might once again make an attempt upon the president's life. He knew that Lincoln did not shy away from public appearances and thus was certain another opportunity would present itself. This was what he was thinking about when he drifted off to sleep.

The next morning when he went down for breakfast, he heard about the fateful fall the president had taken the night before and that he had died just hours earlier. He received this news with mixed emotions. Even though the ultimate result had been achieved, Booth had hoped that he would have been the instrument of Lincoln's demise. He honestly thought that this act would solidify his status as a hero throughout the South.

Booth spent the next several days roaming about the city. He had read the April 15, 1865 edition of the *Washington Evening Star*, reporting on the death of the president, as well as the attack upon Secretary of State Seward and the arrest of Lewis Powell. However, Booth never made any attempt to contact Powell, whether directly or through an intermediary. And he never sought to communicate with any of his band of co-conspirators. Since the president was no more, he had no further use for them.

One evening, about a week after the event at Ford's Theatre, Booth was found in an extremely compromising position by the jealous husband of Booth's current paramour. Enraged by what he had witnessed, but chivalrous to a fault and all the while blaming Booth completely for his wife's transgression, the man challenged Booth to a duel. Booth readily accepted the challenge and plans were made for the two men to meet and "seek satisfaction."

It was decided that the duel would take place two days hence, just after sunrise. Since dueling within the city limits of Washington was illegal, a spot had to be chosen so as to avoid detection by the authorities. Ironically, this location was a remote field outside the city that had been part of the Bull Run battlefield, where the initial military conflict of the Civil War between the Union Army and the Southern Army had taken place.

At the appointed time, both men arrived with their customary seconds. For his, Booth had decided to contact David Herold, knowing that Herold could be trusted to maintain his silence about the duel. Although to the very end Herold had tried to talk Booth out of the duel, the latter had steadfastly refused. Not only was his honor at stake, but Booth was of the egotistical opinion that the various stage roles he had played, where a duel was part of the production, had adequately prepared him for this very moment. Unfortunately, he underestimated the proficiency of his opponent.

The two men faced one another and single-shot pistols were given to each. They stood back to back, paced off twenty steps and then turned and fired their weapons. Booth fired first. The ball glanced off the left arm of his challenger, who returned fire, striking Booth squarely in the chest, the mini-ball shattering his sternum and lodging in his spine.

Booth crumpled to the ground, unable to move. Blood gushed from the wound. Herold rushed over and knelt down next to his comrade. He knew right away that Booth had been mortally wounded. With labored breathing, Booth asked Herold to hold up the hands that had so often been integral to his stage performances. Looking at his hands, John Wilkes Booth muttered, "Useless, useless," and he died.

LEWIS POWELL

There was no intervention that prevented Lewis Powell from attacking Secretary of State Seward. Just as he had been instructed to do by Booth, Powell appeared at the Seward home, seeking entry upon the pretense of delivering medicine for Seward, who had recently been badly injured in a carriage accident. When the housekeeper who answered the door told Powell he could give him the package instead, Powell forced his way inside. As he rushed up the steps, he was met by Seward's son, Frederick, who attempted to intercept the intruder. Powell hit him in the head, fracturing his skull, and continued up the stairs to the secretary's room. Seeing Seward lying helplessly in bed, Powell struck at the man several times with his knife. Convinced he had completed his task, he retreated from the house.

Fortunately, William Seward was wearing a metal jaw brace due to the injuries received in the carriage mishap and this blocked the fatal blows to his throat. While he did receive a significant wound to the face, it was not fatal. His son, too, recovered from his injuries.

Lewis Powell was captured the next day based upon a description provided by Seward's daughter, Frances, who was a witness to her father's attack. At the time of his arrest, Powell learned that Seward was still alive. In his subsequent trial for the attempted murder, he continually professed he had been put up to this deed by John Wilkes Booth. No one believed this story. He was convicted and sentenced to 25 years in prison. Lewis Powell died during the course of his incarceration.

MARY SURRATT

Although Booth and the other conspirators had held meetings at the boarding house owned and run by Mary Surratt, there was never any inkling that she was somehow involved in the plot to kill Lincoln. When she learned that the president had died, but not at the hands of Booth, and that William Seward had survived the attack by Powell, Mary Surratt decided that it would be best for her to leave Washington for good. She sold the boarding house, which she and her late husband, John, had built in 1852 on H Street and permanently relocated to her country tavern in Surrattsville in Prince Georges County, Maryland. She remained there, providing lodging and meals for travelers, for many years until her death in 1887. Never once during her remaining years did she ever talk about the meetings at her Washington boarding house during the spring of 1865.

DAVID HEROLD

David Herold had been given the job of escorting Booth in his escape through the Maryland countryside and into Virginia. Herold was very familiar with this part of the country and assured Booth that he could navigate an escape route for the two of them. With the assassination plot foiled, this service was never required. Herold never expected to hear from Booth again, so he was stunned at being contacted with a request to act as his second in a duel.

After Booth was killed in the duel, his body was placed in a buckboard wagon that had been brought to the site for just such a purpose. Herold drove the remains back to Washington and left them with a friend of his who operated a funeral parlor. The proprietor assured Herold that he would contact Booth's family for the purpose of taking care of the final arrangements. Leaving Booth's body there, Herold disappeared into anonymity.

George Atzerodt

Booth had assigned George Atzerodt the job of murdering Vice President Andrew Johnson. While he apparently agreed to do so, it is unclear whether he was ever truly committed to the task. Early on the morning of April 14, 1865, Atzerodt rented a room at the Kirkwood House directly above the room occupied by the vice president. He went so far as to inquire of the Kirkwood House's bartender the customs and habits of Vice President Johnson, ostensibly to plan the time and place of the attack.

Atzerodt was to kill Johnson at the same time that Booth and Powell were to murder Lincoln and Seward. But Atzerodt could not go through with the plan and instead got drunk at the Kirkwood House bar, after which he spent the rest of the night wandering aimlessly around the city.

The next day, he learned that Booth had not killed Lincoln and that Powell had been unsuccessful in his attempt upon the life of Secretary Seward. Atzerodt decided to maintain a low profile and wait to see if he was contacted by Booth. However, several days later, word reached him that Booth had been shot to death in a duel.

Atzerodt had originally emigrated from Germany and had opened a carriage repair business in Maryland. However, that business had soon failed. After the aborted events surrounding the conspiracy, he decided that it was best for him if he left Washington for good. His last known whereabouts were in eastern Pennsylvania where he had gotten a job in a blacksmith shop.

DR. SAMUEL MUDD

Samuel Mudd was a physician who resided and practiced in southern Maryland. He had met John Wilkes Booth in a church in Bryantown, Maryland and it was rumored that the meeting was for the purpose of soliciting Mudd's help in what was then a plot to kidnap President Lincoln. Of course, nothing ever came of this scheme.

Since the assassination plot did not proceed as planned, there was never any further interaction between Booth and Mudd. The doctor continued to practice medicine in Maryland until his death from pneumonia in 1883.

And, the term "Your name is Mud," has no current association whatsoever with the doctor in American lexicon. Rather, its usage dates back to a book published in England in 1823, when the term referred to one's name being "as dirty as mud" in connection with the performance of an unsavory act.

THE SECRET SERVICE

Since Abraham Lincoln had not been killed at the hands of another, the Secret Service continued to concentrate its efforts on investigating the passing of counterfeit money. It did not take on the role of protector of presidents until 1881, with the assassination of President James A. Garfield. Ever since then and up to the present day, this organization has been trusted with ensuring the safety of the President of the United States and his family, the vice president and immediate family, as well as other high-ranking public officials. In addition, its agents are still empowered with the obligation of investigating financial crimes such as counterfeiting, forgery, credit card fraud or theft of federal securities.

William H. Crook

William H. Crook had a long and distinguished career at the White House. After serving in the Civil War and attaining the rank of Colonel, Crook joined the Washington Police Force. In January 1865, he was appointed one of four men to act as bodyguard to President Lincoln. He and Lincoln developed such a close rapport that the president referred to him as "My man Crook."

After Lincoln's death, Crook continued to serve at the White House. And in 1870, President Grant, a longtime friend, gave him the title of Executive Clerk of the President of the United States. In 1877, Grant made him the disbursing agent of the White House, a position that Crook held through the succeeding ten administrations.

William H. Crook died of pneumonia in March 1915. At the time of his death, he was performing his duties for President Woodrow Wilson. Ever since his passing, and fueled by self-imposed though unwarranted guilt, the ethereal spirit of William Crook has been keeping vigil near a large sycamore tree located in the center of a lawn adjacent to the Soldiers' Home, just outside the city of Washington. Although the most recent time traveler had been able to prevent Lincoln's assassination, his efforts did not alter the fact that the handiwork of John Wilkes Booth continued to be the primary instrumentality in the death of the president.

Thus, Crook's spirit continues to patiently await the arrival of the next dazed, unsuspecting individual, mysteriously transported back to April 1865, to whom Crook will carefully and gently explain that he has 36 hours to save the president.

Acknowledgments

I want to thank my own Great-Aunt Rosamond Becker, who really did give me *The Prairie Years and the War Years,* my first Abraham Lincoln book. This is what started me on the path toward an appreciation and fondness for the great man.

I wish to thank all of the wonderful authors, some whom I have mentioned by name in the preceding pages, who, over the years, have entertained and educated me about the life and times of Abraham Lincoln.

My sincere appreciation goes out to Gregory, Meghan and Jeffrey who were kind enough to painstakingly read through the manuscript and make welcome suggestions as to substance and style. I also want to thank Bryan and Kristen for their support during the writing of this book.

And finally, I would be sorely remiss were I not to express my gratitude to my wonderful and caring wife, Sue, who has carefully read every page of this book innumerable times, while making suggestions on its content, some of which were gladly accepted, and others gently declined.

Through his years of working with youth, ☑ **S0-AAA-459**
shows his unique ability to relate to today's youth in this remarkably
practical book. In a very readable way, he explains the whys behind
God's desire for people to wait until marriage for sex. And how to make
that desire a reality! This is a must read for youth, youth workers, and
parents. You won't be disappointed.

Judge Chuck Simmons
Youth advisor and national speaker, FamilyLife

Sex is for marriage only. Greg Specks does an excellent job of re-
enforcing this truth by talking about all the issues surrounding teens
today. It is obvious the benefits of waiting far outweigh the tragedies
of sex before marriage. A must read for teens and their parents.

Dennis Rainey
President, FamilyLife

Greg Speck is a man of enormous passion and integrity and one of
the funniest human beings I have ever met. And what he brings to
an enormously serious and important issue is passion, integrity,
humor, and the fundamental promise that as we listen to the plan of
God we inevitably find the compelling heart of God. His labor will
help many parents and their children wrestle with sexuality in light
of God's love of sex and his deep passion for us. This is a must read
for any person who longs to know the wisdom of God for their body.

Dan B. Allender, Ph.D.
President, Mars Hill Graduate School
Author of *The Wounded Heart, To be Told,* and
Leading with a Limp

Greg Speck does a great job covering a wide variety of sexual issues
impacting adolescents today. This book is direct, thorough, and uses
an appropriate dose of humor. Greg uses his wide experience of working with students to bring real life stories and personal letters into the
book, giving even greater credibility to his words of warning. The book
also gives great hope to those who have crossed lines or have been victims of abuse. Greg has provided a great resource for youth pastors,
parents, adolescents, and anyone who works with them.

Dr. Bob MacRae
Professor of Youth Ministry, Moody Bible Institute

GREG SPECK

SEX:

IT'S

WORTH

WAITING

FOR

MOODY PUBLISHERS
CHICAGO

All Scripture quotations are taken from the *Holy Bible, New International Version®*. NIV®. Copyright © 1973, 1978, 1984 by International Bible Society. Used by permission of Zondervan. All rights reserved.

ISBN: 0-8024-7704-6
ISBN-13: 978-0-8024-7704-0

Editors: Ali Diaz and Randall J. Payleitner
Interior Design: LeftCoast Design
Cover Design: Bill Chiaravalle, DaAnna Pierce (www.brandnavigation.com)
Cover Image: PixelWorks Studio
Getty Images

Library of Congress Cataloging-in-Publication Data

Speck, Greg.
    Sex: it's worth waiting for / by Greg Speck.
        p. cm..
    Summary: From a Christian perspective, discusses the ethical aspects of such sexual questions as masturbation, pregnancy, premarital sex, and homosexuality.
        ISBN: 0-8024-7704-6
        1. Sex instrustion for youth—Religious aspects—Christianity. [1. Sex—Religious aspects—Christianity. 2. Sexual ethics. 3. Christian life.] I. Title.

HQ35.S624   1989
306,7'07—dc20   89-36571

We hope you enjoy this book from Moody Publishers. Our goal is to provide high-quality, thought-provoking books and products that connect truth to your real needs and challenges. For more information on other books and products written and produced from a biblical perspective, go to www.moodypublishers.com or write to:

Moody Publishers
820 N. LaSalle Boulevard
Chicago, IL 60610

1 3 5 7 9 10 8 6 4 2

Printed in the United States of America

To Bonnie, my friend, lover and wife.
Other than my Lord, there is no one
I love more. Being married to Bonnie
was worth waiting for.

Special thanks are due to the following individuals for their help with this book. Thank you for your time. Thank you for your effort. Most of all, thank you for your friendship.

Stephen A. Bly	Ralph Gustafson
Dave Busby	Doug Houck
Gary Chapman	Marvin Jacobo
Fritz Dale	Mel Johnson
Joe Donaldson	Marty Larsen
Brian Farka	Kevin Leman
Brian Float	Scott Pederson
Steve French	Julie Pederson
Gail Groenink	Scott Peterson

Dann Spader

And to Tom Ives and Dave Childers, for their hospitality in London so that I could work on this book.

Contents

1. **I Know That!** *(Sex Is More Than a Single Act)*   9

2. **How Far Can I Go?** *(Intercourse, Touching, Kissing)*   23

3. **What Does God Have to Do with Sex?**   33
   (The Positives of Sexuality)

4. **Reasons for Waiting** *(Besides What the Bible Says)*   51

5. **What Other Teens Say** *(A Word from Your Peers)*   77

6. **What God Can Do** *(Should I Tell My Parents?)*   89

7. **It Can't Be Happening to Me**   99
   (Pregnancy—and What to Do Now)

8. **Incest** *(What to Do and Understand if You Are an Incest Survivor)*   115

9. **Rape** *(Why it Happens and What to Do)*   131

10. **What Is the Virtue in Virtual Sex?** *(Pornography Is Addictive)*   141

11. **Masturbation** *(Why Doesn't Anybody Talk about It?)*   157

12. **Homosexuality** *(Is There Hope?)*   171

13. **For Girls Only** *(A Single Guy's View on Women)*   193

14. **For Guys Only** *(A Single Woman's View on Guys)*   209

15. **But I've Already Gone Too Far** *(Your Options)*   221

16. **Purity** *(How to Regain It/How to Maintain It)*   237

17. **Life That's Worth Living** *(How to Belong to Jesus Christ)*   249

1

I Know That!

(SEX IS MORE THAN A SINGLE ACT)

Let's be real. We all have questions.

Couples have come to me in tears saying, "Greg, we don't know what happened. We wanted to wait until marriage, but we were just sitting there kissing and touching—and then it happened!"

It's like saying, "Something jumped up and bit us."

I had just finished speaking to a group of about eight hundred teens about sex. Hanging around in the back of the crowd was a beautiful tall blonde—bright blue eyes, tanned, and stylish. She waited till most of the other teens had left. Then she came up and asked if we could talk in private.

We walked over to the side of the room and she said, "This is really embarrassing, but I need to ask you a question."

She wasn't making eye contact with me, and I could tell she was uncomfortable. But I assured her she could ask any question, and I'd give her an honest answer.

After taking a deep breath she said, "Well, my boyfriend says that if we have sex standing up then I can't get pregnant. Is that true?"

I felt like crying and laughing at the same time. Here was this beautiful seventeen-year-old being manipulated by her boyfriend because she was basically ignorant about sex.

I told her that what her boyfriend had told her was not true. She could become just as pregnant standing up as lying down. We then had the chance to discuss some other areas she was confused about as well. At the end I had the privilege to pray with her as she decided to take a stand for purity.

These days we're a part of the sexually enlightened generation. We're supposed to know all there is to know about sex. Ask the wrong question in sex education class, and the room erupts in laughter. The guy in front of you turns around and says, "Didn't you know that?"

> *"We should never be ashamed to talk about what God was not ashamed to create."*
>
> **—Howard Hendricks**

With that kind of pressure, we would rather just sit and smirk and say, "I knew that!"

But let's be real. We all have questions. We don't know it all. So let me talk with you about two areas basic to the understanding of sexuality: (1) What is sex? and (2) How does the opposite sex respond?

WHAT IS SEX?

What is sex? Now all of us ought to know the answer to that question, but let me tell you what I usually hear. A couple will come to see me. We will talk, and after awhile the guy will say something like this:

Guy: *"Greg, we have decided not to have sex until we get married."*

Greg: *"Great! That's fantastic. But let me ask you a question. What is sex?"*

Guy: *"Huh?"*

Greg: *"What is sex?"*

Guy: *"Don't you know?"*

Greg: *"Yes, but I want to hear what you think it is."*

Guy: *"Well . . . uh . . . it's a . . . you see . . . we could . . . I mean, we wouldn't . . . not now . . . later . . . I mean, after . . . after we're married! . . . It's only . . . because . . . well, I . . . Could you repeat the question, please?"*

Greg: *"What is sex?"*

Guy: *"Oh, yeah . . . well . . . um . . . you see, sex is intercourse, and we're not going to have intercourse until we get married!"*

Now what is he saying? He is saying that sex is just the act of intercourse. And that is absolutely wrong! Sex isn't just a single act. Sex is a progression. Sex begins with kissing and then goes to French kissing. After that we begin to touch with our clothes on, and then the clothes come off, and the end result is often intercourse.

The couple that does everything up to intercourse but stops short of intercourse itself is doing something unnatural to both bodies.

Here's what happens. You stop the car in this isolated, romantic spot overlooking the dump. Then you talk for at least thirty to forty seconds. All of a sudden your lips touch.

You begin to softly kiss, and your body says, *This is nice!*

Then you move to French kissing and your body says, *I think I'm getting excited!*

You move into touching over or under her or his clothes, and your body says, *I know I'm excited!*

Then your clothes come off, and your body says, *"This is better than cookie-dough ice cream!"*

All of a sudden you say, "Stop!"

To which your body replies, *"Aaugh!"*

At that point, what happens between you and your body?

You feel: *Anxiety.*

Your body says: *I can't take this kind of abuse anymore. What if I never get a chance to experience intercourse? What if I die tomorrow? What if she dies tomorrow? What if our parents find out? We'll both die tomorrow!*

You feel: *Frustration.*

Your body says: *I never have any fun. You've got me on a diet. You make me run every morning. You never change your socks. And now this!*

You feel: *Pressure.*

Your body says: *You don't understand what this is doing to me. I can't take it anymore. You don't get me enough sleep. I can't hear anything because of those headphones. I haven't even seen a vegetable in six months. I can't remember my locker combination. And this date isn't turning out the way I wanted it to. I'm warning you—I think I'm going to blow up, or if not that, at least I'll throw up.*

You feel: *Anger.*

Your body says: *If you ever do this to me again I'll give you hoof-and-mouth disease!*

You see, our bodies were never meant to build to that point and then stop. That's why we feel all those emotions. And usually what those emotions do is to encourage us to put pressure on the other person. So we begin to give out some stupid line. Let me give you an example of some common lines and some possible answers:

Line: *"If you love me, you'll let me!"*
You: *"If you love me, you won't."*

Line: *"I can't believe you said no."*
You: *"I can't believe that you even asked."*

Line: *"Don't you love me?"*
You: *"Don't you respect me?"*

Line: *"I'll just call someone else."*
You: *"Here; you can use my cell phone."*

Line: *"It's no big deal."*
You: *"It's a big deal to God, and it's a big deal to me!"*

Line: *"But I just want to express my love to you."*
You: *"The best way to do that is to stop pressuring me."*

Line: *"I already told everybody that we did it."*
You: *"Fine; we don't have to do it a second time."*

Line: *"I won't tell anyone."*
You: *"That's because there will be nothing to tell."*

Line: *"Either we do it now, or we'll break up."*
You: *"Bye."*

Line: *"You know I could force you if I wanted to."*
You: *"Either drive me home or to the nearest police station, now!"
(If need be, leave the car, and call someone to come pick
you up.)*

Line: *"You tell me you love me, but you don't mean it."*
You: *"Does that mean that you think I'm a liar? If you can't believe
what I say, then you can't possibly trust me."*

Line: *"I've never wanted anyone as much as I want you."*
You: *"Let's keep praying that God will bless this relationship."*

Line: *"What's the matter? Are you scared (or gay, or diseased)?"*
You: *"Listen, anytime I choose to I can lose my virginity, and it's sure
not going to be to someone who stoops to name-calling."*

Line: *"Nobody is going to care."*
You: *"A lot of people would care—our families, our youth group
friends, and God."*

Line: *"But I need to have sex."*
You: *"Sex is a drive that can be controlled. Needs for you would
be food, water, oxygen, and a cold shower."*

Line: *"I'm leaving tomorrow, and who knows when we'll see each
other again?"*
You: *"Wow! Well, then, let's be sure to keep in touch."*

Line: *"OK. Let's take off our clothes and just be together. We
don't have to touch or anything."*
You: *"That sounds like torture, not fun."*

Line: *"Everybody is doing it!"*
You: *"That's not true. I'm not doing it, and tonight neither are you!"
(smile).*

Line: *"Someday we'll get married. I promise."*

You: *"And I promise you that it will be worth waiting for."*

It's so important that you do not allow others to manipulate and pressure you to give in.

Ladies and gentlemen: there are some people who will say whatever they need to say to get you to take your clothes off. You've got to get a lot tougher. When someone is pressuring you, you don't have to be kind! Tell them in a straight-forward manner. Don't beat around the bush. If you want a person to respect you, then you need to demand respect for yourself. You will not get that respect if you allow someone to put their hands all over your body.

Anyone who pressures you to take off your clothes doesn't respect you.

Listen to one young woman's experience:

> I was going out with a seventeen-year-old last year for two months. I was fifteen. He broke the relationship off, and I took a lot of things into consideration and came to the conclusion that he dumped me because I would not "make love." Breaking up hurt a lot, and I grieved for quite some time.
>
> A year went by, and he came around again and wanted me to go back out with him. Like a stupid fool I went back to him. From the first day we started going out, he told me he loved me every chance he got. I fell head over heels in love with him, and after going out for

How long do you think it took this guy to get this girl to take off her clothes?

> After going out for three days, we made love. We made love almost every chance we got. I figured by doing this I would keep him. I never did anything to hurt him or get him upset. Everything seemed perfect.
>
> After going out for two months, he just up and decided he didn't want to go out with me anymore. Well, I am very hurt and feel like all

his "I love yous" were a bunch of lies. I have been used, and the hurt has now turned into bitter hate.

Do you think that if this girl had a chance to do it over again she would do things differently? Yes! So don't you make the same mistake. When someone pressures you for sex, remember that you don't have to be kind—be tough!

Where are the men of character and integrity? You need to be the one who is loving—not lusting after—women. If there is one person the girl should be able to count on to protect and care for her, it is the guy taking her out on a date. There is an old adage that says, "Men play love to get sex, and women give sex to get love." Both are wrong and destructive to you and the person you are going out with. To be a man of character means that you want what is best for the woman, and you seek purity in the relationship with her. You should be able to say to her, "You can trust me because I would never take advantage of you."

Women can be just as sexually aggressive as any man. Guys have been laughed at, teased, ridiculed, sworn at, threatened, and gossiped about because they were not aggressive enough sexually on dates. Guys have told me that girls have accused them of being gay because they didn't want to have intercourse. Being a woman of character means that you seek sexual purity, have high standards, and you never force a man to compromise his standards.

Some guys get involved sexually not because they want to but because they have been pressured by the girl, or they think this is what is expected of them.

Men, how do we deal with this situation? The answers are not easy, but let me suggest some things you need to be aware of.

➤ Don't date a woman who has a reputation for aggressiveness and sleeping around.

Imagine being on a date where the woman takes off her clothes and attempts to undress you! You don't need to be strong to withstand that sort of temptation—you need to be comatose!

➤ Date only women who are Christians.

Now this doesn't necessarily solve the problem. Some women who say they are Christians are sexually active. Even Christians can yield to temptation.

But let's say you go out with a woman, and you didn't realize what she thought about sex and purity. You've been studying so hard that you haven't had time to even think about women (sure!). But you're on the date, and suddenly this woman begins to make moves on you. What do you do?

First, try to understand her. This is a pattern she has fallen into. It is something she has learned men like. She may feel this sort of behavior is expected of her on a date. Besides, it's a fast and easy way to feel close to someone.

But let's also understand that this woman needs help. Someone must help her break the pattern. The longer she continues, the more wounded she will become and the more problems she will cause for herself.

What can you do to help her?

Why not be radical? Why not kindly say, "Wait a second! I like you; you're great looking, but I want to get to know you as a person. I don't want to do this now!" Perhaps quite a few guys know this woman's body, but you are saying, "I want to know you as someone, not as just a body."

What if she laughs? She might because she is so shocked. But deep down she is looking for a man who will respect and care about her.

So you can use her and be one in a line of guys, or you can care about her and make an impression she won't forget. I'm betting she is looking for a guy who is willing to try to understand her. Even if she doesn't respond positively, believe me, when she matures she will look back and realize that you were one of those few who really cared about her. That's what you want to be remembered for—not as one in a long line of lovers. You have the opportunity to give her hope. Now some tips for both genders:

> Don't isolate yourself.

  Chances are someone's not going to make moves on you in a public place like a fast-food restaurant. Don't put yourself in a spot where they have the chance to do so.

> Think about the Lord.

  He is right there, watching you. Pray to Him. Ask the Holy Spirit to give you special courage and wisdom, the right words to say and the right actions to take.

> Remember that outside of rape, a person can't make you become involved sexually.

  You can be a person of character. If they start undressing in the car, then leave or drive to a lighted public area. If you're at a party, then go somewhere else.

So what happens if the person later says terrible things about you? That you're gay, scared, or a freak?

I guess my response is, "So what?" Your friends are your friends. They aren't going to believe them. Your enemies don't like you anyway, whether you went to bed with someone or not. And other people aren't as dumb as you may think. They know who is more likely to be telling the truth. Believe it or not, most people could care less what went on between you.

If people ask, "How come you didn't sleep with them?" you can say, "Because I didn't want to. Because I'm worth more than a one-night stand. Because I don't want to be manipulated into having sex with anyone. And it's pretty egotistical on their part to think that if I don't want sex then I must be some freak."

You'll find a lot of individuals agreeing with you, and you will gain respect in the eyes of many. There are whole groups of people who will be very attracted to a person with that kind of character. This will open the door for you to tell them the most important reason you didn't get involved—because you love Jesus.

For you who are reading this and are sexually involved right now, do you want to find out if this person really loves you or not? Try this. Go to him or her and say, "I love you so much. But I want us to work on other areas of our relationship, so I want to stop having sex."

You'll discover really quickly whether the person loves you. Some of you know right now what would happen if you said that. That person would be out the door. Now if you know that and continue to be involved with the guy or girl sexually, you aren't valuing your whole person—which has spiritual, emotional, intellectual, and physical dimensions. If you want respect, then demand it! If someone tries to touch you where you don't want to be touched, say, "This is my body. This is not your body. Please stop."

Talk with your friends or parents. Make a deal that if you are ever in a situation where you are being pressured, you can call them and they will come and get you, no matter where you are or what time it is.

So, number one, remember that sex is a progression. When we move into touching each other's bodies, breasts, and genitals, one of four things usually occurs:

1. You end up having intercourse, or you bring each other to an orgasm through oral sex or mutual masturbation.
2. You break up, often influenced by all the pressure and problems that result.
3. You get married just in time.
4. By God's grace you are able to pull back on your physical affection and set new standards.

Don't start the progression, and you won't have to worry about where it's all going to end.

HOW DOES THE
OPPOSITE SEX RESPOND?

How does the opposite sex respond? Women, do you understand how males respond? Men, do you understand about women?

Researchers brought a group of men into a room. They wired up whatever needed to be wired up to measure their emotional responses and then began to flash pictures upon a screen. They flashed the picture of a . . .

Why do you go out with people: love or lust?

Flower. Yawn. Not much reaction.
Hot car. Mmm. The needle began to move.
Baby. Oops. Very little needle movement.
Naked woman. Wow! All of a sudden there were lights, bells, and buzzers. The needle moved off the page!

Women, you need to understand that a man, generally speaking, is visually oriented. That means by just looking at you he can become sexually excited. He doesn't even have to touch you.

Now some women say to me, "Oh, come on, I don't believe that. That's stupid."

If you women would walk down to a gas station or quick-stop market, you would see a section of pornographic magazines. Now if you picked up these magazines—and I highly recommend you don't do this—you would discover that all of them have one thing in common. They are filled with pictures of naked women.

Pornographic Web sites get more hits than any other type of Web site. I am sorry to say that the pornographic business is a multibillion dollar business in the US alone. Millions go to these Web sites every day. It's not just men; some women are also attracted to porn. Whether you are male or female, it is very destructive spiritually and emotionally to look at this stuff.

Now why do you think pornographic magazines, videos, and Web sites are so popular? Because a man can buy, rent, or surf; and just by looking at the pictures he can become sexually excited.

Matthew 5:28 tells us that it is wrong to look lustfully at a woman. Men, we need to practice eye control. When a woman bends over in front of us, we need to look away. When an attractive woman walks by in a little bathing suit, we need to look away. You can't help seeing something, but you can help staring. We need to see women as people—not objects to be gawked at. When we lust after women we are showing them disrespect and treating them like they are objects. This is all about you making good choices. Decide that you will look away when you are faced with temptation. But, women, you can do a lot to help your Christian brothers not to lust. How? By what you wear!

For example, what does your swimsuit look like? If your suit is somewhat revealing—and you know better than anyone else if it's revealing—what do you think the guys are looking at? If you think it's your pretty little eyes, then you are wrong. In many cases they are checking out your body and lusting after you.

Women, how did you dress the last time you went out with a guy?

Women have said to me, "Oh, I just love it when guys lust after me. It's so exciting!"

If that's your reaction, then you don't understand what goes on in the mind of a man. When a man lusts after you, you become a piece of meat! He could care less that you have hopes, needs, dreams, and desires. All he wants to do is get his hands on your body. *Lusting* is not a complimentary term. Sometimes a guy will see you, get turned on, and that evening you will become the object of his masturbation. I believe you are worth far more than that; and, remember, if you want men to respect you, then you must demand respect. What you dress like on the outside communicates to men what you must be like on the inside—whether it is true or not.

Women, I know some guys would lust after you if you wore a bathing suit with long sleeves, pant legs, and a turtleneck. That's not your fault. That's the fault of the guys. What I am saying is, look good, be stylish, but don't become an object.

Stay away from tight clothes, revealing clothes, short skirts, low-cut tops, as well as running around braless, etc. Listen to your mother when it comes to the question, "Will this turn a guy on or not?" Dad also ought to be able to give you some insights. Men think much differently than women do, and your dad will be able to give you insight into the mind of a guy.

Put on your outfit, stand in front of the mirror, and ask yourself, "What am I trying to emphasize and draw attention to?" If it's just your curves, then in many cases you're going to be treated like an object. Doesn't it make sense that if you seek to emphasize certain parts of your body, then you will attract men who are primarily interested in those parts of your body?

Guys, there is something that really bugs women. When you talk with a woman it's important that you make eye contact with her. *Stop staring at her chest.* You don't think she notices, but she does.

Again, males tend to be visually oriented, but I am speaking in generalities. You could say, "Well, that isn't true of my Uncle Joe!" OK, bless Uncle Joe's heart. But generally men are attracted by what they see.

Understand also that the male usually reaches his sexual peak—when the sexual drive is strongest—sometime between the ages of fifteen and twenty-five. But in most cases a woman does not reach her sexual peak until she's between twenty-five and forty-five. For that reason there may be a big difference in the way men and women act. For the woman, the sexual drive may not be strong during her teen years, but for the guy it may be powerful. If you are not aware of these basics, you will find yourself in trouble.

Guys ask me, "How come we reach our sexual peak so early when we can't do anything about it?" It is because God wants to develop character in your life. He wants you to be a man with self-control. Remember that the Lord is always more interested in your character than He is in your comfort. I know it is hard to wait, but it is good for you and will help you in the future. You honor God by waiting and show Him that you are a man that He can trust.

Stay away from alcohol. Drinking can set you up so that you are more easily seduced. When you've been drinking, it's much easier for someone to get you to take your clothes off.

Now what about those researchers and the women? They wired up the women and began to show them pictures of a . . .

Flower. Nice. Needle moved a little.
Hot car. Huh? Not much movement.
Naked man. Hardly any movement. What a blow to the male ego!

Do you know what got the biggest reaction from the women? The cute little cuddly baby. (One guy came to me after I shared this and said, "Boy, from now on I'm carrying around baby pictures." Obviously he got a lot out of my talk.) Not all women feel this way about babies, but the difference is notable.

The woman, generally speaking, is touch oriented. It is usually not until the touching stage, when her body is being caressed, that she gets turned on.

That's why people have said, "Women, it's your responsibility to handle the physical part of the relationship. If things get carried away, it's your fault." Now I say that's garbage! Men, we need to take responsibility in that area and seek to love a woman, which means not to use or abuse her.

But the reason people have said this to women is this: If you allow the relationship to get to the place where he is touching you all over your body and you lose control, chances are that the guy's lost control a mile down the road. If you don't say no, then he won't say no, and you'll end up having intercourse.

So understand these two basics—(1) sex is a progression, and (2) men and women respond differently. Apply them to your dating relationships, and you will be saved a lot of trouble.

Questions to ask yourself:
1. How have I dressed around the opposite sex?
2. How would I define sex now?
3. Honestly, how much of a temptation is sex to me right now?

2

How Far Can I Go?

(INTERCOURSE, TOUCHING, KISSING)

*"We really love each other and have been dating for a long time,
and I want to know how far we can go."*

Recently I spoke at a Christian high school's spiritual emphasis
week. They had an optional meeting one night, when the students
could write down any questions they wanted to ask me.

Not everyone turned in a question (they couldn't think of one,
couldn't write, they know everything already, etc.). But of the fifty
or so questions I received, at least twelve asked this kind of question: "We really love each other and have been dating for a long time
[at least two weeks], and I want to know how far we can go."

That's the big question I am always getting. I think by asking
that question we are saying, "I'm curious; it feels good, so I want to
go as far as I can while still being a Christian." It's natural to be curious, and curiosity ought to raise questions. Ask them! We ought to
be able to deal with sex in a straightforward manner within the
body of Christ.

You're also right. It does feel good. It should. God made it to
feel good! But the question you ask is dangerous and flawed. We
want to know how far we can push it—how close we can get to the
fire without actually getting burned.

If sex is so great (and it is!)—if sex is so wonderful (and it is!)—
if sex is so exciting (and it is!)—then I shouldn't be asking how

close I can get to destroying that good thing. I should be asking, rather, "What do I need to do so I can eventually experience God's very best?"

What if I took you and your friends with me to Switzerland for an all-expense-paid vacation? What if I took you up the Jungfräu where there was a sheer drop of several thousand feet? How many would ask, "Oh, boy, how close can I get?" Would you run to the edge and hang your toes over? "Oh, boy, look at me. . . . Whoa . . . Oh, no . . . ahhhhhhhh . . . !" *Splat!* As they say, "The fall never kills you—it's that sudden stop at the bottom."

God is not out to get us. He gives us commands because He loves us and wants the best for our lives.

But some of us are trying to get as close as we can to the edge. We want to see how physical we can get, and we're about to take a major fall.

So what are some guidelines? Ephesians 5:3 says there shouldn't even be a "hint of sexual immorality." God isn't even talking about your actually being involved sexually. He just says there shouldn't be the slightest hint.

That is to say, what you do in public suggests what you do in private. People are going to jump to that conclusion whether you're sexually involved or not. So don't give them any cause to think that way.

Men, we should always seek to protect the reputation of any woman we are with. We don't want anyone to think less of a woman because she is out with us.

You've seen the couples at your school that make out between classes. We look at that, and there is the tendency to think, *If they do this in the hallway, what must they do in private?* This cheapens them in the eyes of other people. So in your relationship there shouldn't be even a hint of sexual immorality.

How far can I go? If you want some thoughts, here they are:

WHAT ABOUT INTERCOURSE?

What about premarital intercourse? God says it's wrong. No rationalizing will change that fact. You can make a lot of excuses, but never ever say that God approves. He doesn't. *Fornication* is a premarital sexual relationship, and God tells us not to do that. First Thessalonians 4:3 says, "It is God's will that you should be sanctified [set apart for God's use]: that you should avoid sexual immorality."

People try to come up with all kinds of excuses for having intercourse.

"It's OK because we really love each other." They are saying that love makes premarital sex OK and cancels God's command against it. That is stupid!

"It's OK because it feels so right." Feelings do not tend to be a good indicator of the difference between right and wrong. It might feel right to lie, shoplift, gossip, or disobey your parents. You may feel deprived. But moving toward maturity is doing what is right (at school, at home, at work, in relationships) even when it feels difficult. If God wanted us to act just on how we feel, He wouldn't have given us the Bible—specific to our conversation, He wouldn't have told us to refrain from sexual immorality.

"One day we are going to get married so it is OK to have intercourse now." Wrong. The fact is that you are being disobedient to the Lord right now. Marrying the person doesn't mean premarital sex is not sin.

"We are having intercourse so it is like we are already married." Cleaving to someone in marriage implies commitment that isn't supposed to be broken. Until you make that commitment in a marriage covenant, God doesn't want you to give your body to anyone. And marriage is a lot more than having intercourse. It is bills, pressure, jobs, conflict, dirty diapers, the flu, commitments, and responsibility.

"Some of my friends are doing it." That doesn't mean it is the right thing to do. Just because your friends are making bad decisions doesn't mean you should follow in their footsteps. You have to know what is right and true, and then live according to the truth.

Remember also that your personal happiness is not the most important concern. The most important concern when you date should be God and others! We exercise discipline over ourselves and our relationships. We ask ourselves the question, "What is best for the person I'm dating? How can I help this person develop?"

WHAT ABOUT ORAL SEX OR MUTUAL MASTURBATION?

Oral sex is when you use your mouth on your partner's genitals to stimulate them. Mutual masturbation is where you use your hands on your partner's genitals. Oral sex and mutual masturbation are similar to intercourse in their attempts to bring another person to an orgasm. More and more teenagers tell me that they are turning to oral sex to maintain their virginity, protect against pregnancy, and avoid sexually transmitted diseases.

We should be asking ourselves, How I can bless this other person?

You may stay a virgin physically but not emotionally, and still go much further than God intended you to go outside of marriage. Read Ephesians 5:3 again: oral sex and mutual masturbation go way beyond "hinting of sexual immorality." Those actions are sexually immoral. Not to mention that you can catch a sexually transmitted disease through oral sex just like you can through intercourse. Oral sex does not protect against most STDs. Oral sex and mutual masturbation have no place in a dating relationship.

Let me ask you a question. Are STDs a curse from God to those who are being disobedient to Him? No, they are a consequence of being disobedient. God's desire is that you won't have to worry about STDs. My wife and I don't have to worry about them because we remain faithful to each other. You too can make the choice to stay sexually pure, and later to remain faithful to your spouse.

WHAT ABOUT JUST
TOUCHING EACH OTHER?

It used to be called petting. It's the fondling and caressing of each other's bodies, especially the breasts and genitals (the erogenous zones) with our hands. In marriage we would call this foreplay, because it prepares us for intercourse by getting each other sexually excited.

I have heard this great excuse: "We want to wait until we get married to have intercourse, but sometimes we've touched each other because it releases our sexual tension, thus protecting our virginity."

Now that sounds pretty good at face value. But when you look closer you discover that it's a terrible excuse. Why? Because touching each other does not stop further desire; it does just the opposite. It sexually excites you and reduces your self-control.

It's dumb for a couple to rationalize that because engaging in intercourse is a temptation to them, their best protection is to fool around in other ways. They are only drawing closer and closer to intercourse. Foreplay was not designed to satisfy but to excite!

Remember that touching each other is subject to the moral law of diminishing returns. That means the more you do something, the less exciting it is. So in order to keep it exciting, and to gain satisfaction, the amount and intensity of it must continue to increase. The problem is that touching each other without a climax cannot indefinitely increase in intensity.

So the person involved in fooling around and sexual touching can go through four stages:

1. This is great! I feel so close to you. The more I'm involved, the more exciting it is, and I just want to be with you all the time.
2. I've seen everything there is to see. I've touched everything there is to touch, and I'm getting kind of bored. I'm getting less satisfaction from this.
3. The satisfaction isn't even worth the effort. We both feel used and frustrated.

4. We break up, usually finding another partner and starting this pattern all over again.

How do we keep getting into this mess over and over again?

Well, we are really attracted to the opposite sex. Sometimes we even call it love. We go out together, but when a date is unplanned, we have a lot of time on our hands. We rationalize that getting physical is a way of expressing our love to each other. Besides, it feels good! It relieves the boredom and requires no intelligence or conversation.

But more and more, fooling around begins to control us. We want to go further and further. First we touch each other. Then our hands go under the clothes. Then the clothes come off, and there we are—two naked bodies seeking to satisfy our desires.

Soon many of our relationships begin to deteriorate. We ignore our friends and families. Our relationship with God goes down the tubes. And instead of going out on a date to get to know each other, we are stuck in the same old rut, two people sharing their least common denominator—their bodies.

The well-known Kinsey report on sex and sexual behavior says this: "Petting [that] does not proceed to a climax may seriously disturb a person, possibly leaving one or both individuals in a state of nervous tension, a tension that may produce hypersensitivity and an increased irritability, all of which in time will strain the relationship of the couple and possibly prevent the development of love and the desire for marriage."

Dr. Kinsey is saying that it is better to pet to a climax or not to pet at all. But as Christians we must face the fact that petting to a climax is morally little different from intercourse itself.

However, if we don't bring each other to a climax we can add psychological problems to our relationship. Plus, remember Ephesians 5:3? Touching each other's erogenous zones screams of sexual immorality.

What does 1 Corinthians 6:18 talk about? Listen to what God is saying to you. "Flee from sexual immorality. All other sins a man commits are outside his body, but he who sins sexually sins against his own body." We tend to focus on the "flee" part, but I want to direct you to the part that says, "He who sins sexually sins against his own body." God sees sins the same, and one sin is not greater than another, but how sin affects us can be totally different. The sexual sin is different because it targets our body in a way that other sins don't.

When you allow someone to begin to touch you sexually, you allow them to begin to engrave themselves on you. Their touch is beginning to program you. You learn to respond to a certain type of touch and kiss. How they hold you, caress you, kiss you is all programming you to become turned on. That would be great if it were your spouse on your honeymoon, but it is bad when it is only a boyfriend or girlfriend.

After you break up and get together with someone else, their touch is different and they kiss you a different way. Sometimes it is better and more enjoyable, but sometimes it may not feel as good. Pretty soon you have allowed all these people to place their marks on you.

After you marry, it can become confusing and sexually frustrating. In your long list of lovers there will be someone who touched and kissed you better then your spouse, and you will have flashbacks about these past relationships. Other people's sexual imprint in your life will cause frustration in your marriage. How many people do you want to sexually program your spouse? Do you want to allow someone to program you sexually whom you are not going to spend the rest of your life with?

Another problem with premarital sexual activity is how it affects the excitement of sex in marriage. The fleshly urge that comes with the "forbiddenness" of certain acts is not there in marriage. That premarital urge can be described by thoughts in your mind like, *We aren't supposed to do this, but we just can't help it; let's just do it really fast so we don't have to talk or think about it.* That's not there in marriage since it is the intended and blessed arena for sex.

It is obvious that premarital sexual experiences are not to be a part of Christians' dating relationships. Now you who have crossed the line may find my position impossible. But don't give up. Check out chapter 15.

WHAT ABOUT KISSING?

Well, then, what about kissing? What about "making out" for an hour and a half until our lips bleed?

Kissing ought to be a giving experience. "Because I love you I want to give you this kiss." But let's face it; it can become a taking experience that causes us to want more and more. You'll begin to want to go further by unbuttoning, unzipping, unsnapping, untying, unVelcroing, ungluing, unbolting—unbelievable!

Your kisses ought to be valuable. You shouldn't just hand them out like handshakes, because if you really end up liking the person, what are you going to give next—a kiss? No, you've already given that.

People say to me, "Are you saying that kissing is a sin? Then I've sinned millions of times!" No, I am not saying that kissing is a sin, but where does the Bible say that to have a healthy relationship you must be involved physically? Nowhere. As a matter of fact, some of the *unhealthiest* relationships I've seen were primarily physical.

After you have been dating for a while, I see nothing wrong with a good-night kiss, or a kiss of appreciation, or a kiss to say "You're really special." But remember, ladies, you don't owe any guy a kiss. Maybe a guy says to you, "Hey, I took you out to a nice place to eat. Don't I deserve a kiss?!"

You say to him, "I don't owe you a kiss because you had the pleasure of taking me out." If he doesn't take you out anymore because you wouldn't kiss him, then he really doesn't like you. He is just attracted to your luscious lips.

I am hearing from more and more teenagers who are saying, "We have decided not to even kiss a member of the opposite sex until they say, 'I now pronounce you husband and wife.'" I think that is awesome, and I support you 100 percent. If you say to me, "That is stupid and I am not going to do that," fine, but what *are* you going to do? Where are your boundaries? You can reset them even today.

If you wait until the car stops on a dark road to decide what you will and will not do, it's too late. What should your standard be? Well, let me ask you this, "What turns you on?" Now take a giant step back from there, and be tough on yourself! Some of you will need to set your standard at holding hands or good-night hugs because the sexual temptation is a struggle for you.

The world ought to see a difference in the relationships of Christians. We need to stand out as light in a darkening world. "You are the light of the world. . . . Let your light shine before men, that they may see your good deeds and praise your Father in heaven" (Matthew 5:14, 16).

As you are setting your standards please keep in mind Colossians 3:17: "And whatever you do, whether in word or deed, do it all in the name of the Lord Jesus, giving thanks to God the Father through him." If it doesn't glorify Jesus Christ, then don't do it. If you took that seriously, what would your standards be?

Our standards should be so high that the world and our friends notice a distinct difference. Then when they question us, we can tell them about Jesus and how He has made a difference in our lives.

Talk with your parents. Ask them about their sexual involvement before marriage. Do they have any regrets? If they dated now, what would their standards be? Were they insecure? How did they get out of potentially sexual situations?

I also realize that some parents are really messed up. I had a girl come to me at a retreat and say, "My mother wants me to bring guys home to have sex with, so that I will be more popular. She is providing me with birth control and condoms. What do you think?" I told her that her mom was wrong. So no matter what people say, the bottom line is that you are seeking to glorify Jesus Christ. Your final authority for life and living is the Word of God. If anyone contradicts the Word of God then they are wrong!

I know it won't be easy, but be tough and wait. It's worth it.

Questions to ask yourself:

1. What would God want your standards to be?
2. Your yesterdays do not determine your tomorrows. What does that mean to you?
3. Have you been a giver or a taker in your past relationships with the opposite sex?

3

What Does God Have to Do with Sex?

(THE POSITIVES OF SEXUALITY)

*It's time we look at sex and sexual
relationships from God's point of view.*

Sex is great. It's wonderful, tremendous, exciting, spectacular, and awesome! And sex has a lot to do with God because He is the One who made it.

God made Adam and Eve "male and female" (Genesis 1:27–31; 2:25). He made them sexual beings, and they stood before Him naked. What was God's reaction to them? Did He say . . .

"Gross Me out—put something on! Here, take this designer leaf!"

No.

Or, "Well, I guess these bodies will have to do."

No.

God looked at them and said, "They are *very* good!"

You are a sexual being, and sex is very good. There is nothing gross, dirty, or terrible about it. Only God could have thought of something as wonderful as sex.

It's time we look at sex and sexual relationships from His point of view.

God is not against sex. Since He made it, it would seem reasonable to assume He ought to know how we can experience sex at its very best.

Popular culture has given us a perverted outlook on sex that has really cheapened it. Where did you learn about sex? Here is where teenagers receive their information:

> 1% credit their parents.
> 9% say that sex education classes at school were helpful.
> 90% say their sex information came from peers, TV, movies, music videos, and pornographic Web sites! (Many teens admit that they and their friends have talked about things they really had no clue about.)

Because we are so bombarded by sex we tend to lose our perspective. What is the purpose of sex?

SEX IS GOD'S CREATION

Sex is wonderful, but I want you to know that it was created for marriage relationships where spouses have first committed themselves to one another spiritually, emotionally, and intellectually. When we take sex out of the proper place God has created it for and put it in the backseat of a car, or at a party when the parents are gone, it can make us feel guilty. But God never planned it that way.

A young woman once told me, "Greg, I have a boyfriend, and I want you to know that we are having sex. Do you know what I do first thing after coming home from a date? I take a shower, because I feel so dirty that I want to wash it all away!"

How sad. God never meant us to experience guilt with sex. But this is what happens when we compromise God's plan for our lives.

Get your Bible and underline 1 Thessalonians 4:1–8. What is this passage saying to you? Let's go through it and see what the Lord is trying to teach us.

"Finally, brothers, we instructed you how to live in order to please God, as in fact you are living. Now we ask you and urge you in the Lord Jesus to do this more and more. For you know what instructions we gave you by the authority of the Lord Jesus" (verses 1–2).

Do you want to live a life that pleases God? You are about to find out what you need to do. Who are the instructions coming from? They aren't coming from man; they are given by the authority of the Lord Jesus Christ.

"It is God's will that you should be sanctified: that you should avoid sexual immorality; that each of you should learn to control his own body in a way that is holy and honorable, not in passionate lust like the heathen, who do not know God" (verse 3–5).

Do you want to know God's will for your life? Teenagers ask me all the time, "What is God's will for my life?" Here is God revealing His will for you.

First He wants you to be sanctified. What does it mean to be sanctified? It means to be set aside for God to use. That means you are living in such a way that you are available for God to work in and through you.

Next He wants you to avoid sexual immorality. It means to stay away from any sexual sin.

Then we control our bodies in a way that is holy and honorable. Is what you do with someone behind closed doors holy? Is it honorable to undress each other or touch each other in sexual ways? The answer is no, and you can see that spelled out in Scripture right before your eyes.

Imagine Jesus joining you on your next date. What would you do and what wouldn't you do? Guess what? He is right there with you— so start using your bodies in ways that are honorable and holy.

"And that in this matter no one should wrong his brother or take advantage of him. The Lord will punish men for all such sins, as we have already told you and warned you" (verse 6).

You should never take advantage of someone you are going out with, someone you meet at a party, or just someone you find attractive. You are taking advantage of someone when you are sexually involved with them. Whether you realize it or not, you are hurting them and robbing them of their future. You are cheating their future spouse, and you are robbing them of purity, peace with God, healthy self-esteem, a clear conscience, and on and on we could go. You call what you are doing *love*; but it is *lust*, and you are using them to meet the wants and passions in your life. Then add to that the hurt you are causing yourself and your future spouse.

Here's a truth we don't want to believe. There will be consequences if you take advantage of someone sexually. Maybe you didn't know that before, but you know now. The consequences might be physical or they could be emotional. Have you been having a lot of problems lately? Have you ever considered that God might be trying to tell you something? That premarital sexual activity will hurt you? Why does He allow consequences? He wants you to repent and come back to Him. Does this sound serious? It is.

You see, sex affects you more than just physically. It affects you emotionally, relationally, and spiritually. Your sexual life now shapes your heart and your personality and who you will become. Will you be close to God and discern a good path for your life? Will you have a healthy personality, self-image, and identity in Christ? How will sexual activity with someone who is not your spouse affect you? How will you know, and when will you know, how it has affected you? Will you trust God in this matter and believe the counsel of others who have been there? More important than the question, "Why would Greg (or pastor, or so-and-so) lie to me?" is, "Why would God lie to me about this?"

"For God did not call us to be impure, but to live a holy life. Therefore, he who rejects this instruction does not reject man but God, who gives you his Holy Spirit" (verses 7–8).

He didn't call you to be impure; that is not part of His will for you! If you choose to reject this and become sexually involved, you are not rejecting Greg Speck, you are rejecting God!

Stop trying to rationalize your behavior by saying that one day you will be getting married or that you really love each other. This isn't about your love for someone of the opposite sex; this is about your love for Jesus Christ. It is a sin for you to live with a member of the opposite sex and be sexually involved.

Again, God is not against sex. He created it. He wants us to enjoy this wonderful gift. We do not stay away from premarital sex because something is wrong with sex. We stay away from premarital sex because:

> ➤ It keeps us from God's best and it is not God's will for our lives.
> ➤ In the long run it will cause far more emotional and spiritual pain than it will ever give physical pleasure; being right with God and emotionally healthy is better.
> ➤ It tells God that we are rejecting Him.
> ➤ It's contrary to God's purpose for our lives.

We experience sex at its ultimate when we participate in it the way God intended—within a marriage relationship.

"But I want to be free! What has happened to freedom?"

If you are a Christian, you are free. Look at John 8:36: "If the Son sets you free, you will be free indeed."

"Yeah, well, then, how come I'm limited and can't have sex right now?"

It's important that we realize there are limitations in all of God's creation. For example, take a cute little sparrow. Isn't it a shame that this bird is limited to sky and land only? Three-fourths of the earth's surface is covered by water. It isn't fair—this sparrow should be able to go underwater.

So let's take the sparrow down to sixty feet, where all the beautiful coral formations are, and set it free.

"Swim, little sparrow, swim!—you're not swimming. As a matter of fact, you're not even moving! Uh-oh."

Or take a big, beautiful rainbow trout. It's not fair that this fish should be limited to the water. There is so much to do and see on land. Let's take the trout to downtown Chicago and let it go.

"Now you can check out the John Hancock Building, do some shopping at Water Tower Place, and visit the famous Moody Bible Institute—come on, all you're doing is flopping around. You can get a great underwater watch. What's wrong? Maybe you want something to eat. This place has a great fish fry with—oops—I mean, how about pizza? How come you don't want to eat? How come you don't want to buy anything? How come you don't want to see anything? How come you've stopped flopping around?"

Finally take a kitten, a tiny fur ball. Would you say, "It isn't fair that this kitten is limited to the ground—it should have the opportunity to fly"?

So we take the kitten to the top of the Sears Tower and throw it off. "You're free! Fly, fly, fly! . . . Wow, little kitty is now a big mess."

This was not freedom for the sparrow, the trout, or the kitten; because their freedom is found within the limitations of what God has created them to be and to become.

We are free to be all that God has created us to be, but there are limitations. I hope it has become obvious to you that God's limitations are not to stifle you but are there for your good.

Yes, we're free within limitations, and you will discover that these limitations will actually heighten your joy and give you life that is really satisfying. God desires what is best for us.

That is why He gave us the law. It gives us boundaries and keeps us from getting hurt and in trouble. The best sex education is teaching the truth of God's Word. Leviticus 20:10–21 says that incest, adultery, bestiality (having sex with animals), and homosexuality are acts of wickedness. In that era, those acts were punishable by death. That means God sees it as very serious. Just because we don't kill someone now for breaking God's moral law doesn't mean He no longer holds us accountable. We will reap what we sow, for good or for evil.

Sin will manipulate, bind, control, and eventually kill you. Jesus Christ wants to set you free. He wants you to experience life that will last forever. Romans 6:23 says, "The wages of sin is death, but the gift of God is eternal life in Christ Jesus our Lord."

Freedom will never be found in doing something contrary to the very purpose for which God created the human body. "The body is not meant for sexual immorality, but for the Lord, and the Lord for the body" (1 Corinthians 6:13). The body is not meant for premarital sex. And God ought to know, because He created sex.

SEX IS WONDERFUL
IN A MARRIAGE RELATIONSHIP

"May your fountain be blessed, and may you rejoice in the wife of your youth. A loving doe, a graceful deer—may her breasts satisfy you always, may you ever be captivated by her love" (Proverbs 5:18–19).

Sex has always been wonderful, and the place to enjoy it is in a marriage relationship. The sexual relationship with your husband or wife is a time for rejoicing, laughter, encouragement, enjoyment, and becoming one.

First Corinthians 7:9 indicates that there are many men and women who have a deep desire for sexual relationships: "If they cannot control themselves, they should marry, for it is better to marry than to burn with passion." Marriage gives us an opportunity to fulfill those desires, free of guilt, in a way that is pleasing and honoring to God.

Solomon is admiring his wife in Song of Songs 7:1–9. "How beautiful your sandaled feet, O prince's daughter! Your graceful legs are like jewels, the work of a craftsman's hands. Your navel is a rounded goblet that never lacks blended wine. Your waist is a mound of wheat encircled by lilies. Your breasts are like two fawns, twins of a gazelle. Your neck is like an ivory tower. Your eyes are the pools of Heshbon by the gate of Bath Rabbim. Your nose is like the tower of Lebanon looking toward Damascus. Your head crowns you like Mount Carmel. Your hair is like royal tapestry; the king is held captive by its tresses. How beautiful you are and how pleasing, O love, with your delights! Your stature is like that of the palm, and your breasts like clusters of fruit. I said, 'I will climb the palm tree; I will take hold of its fruit.' May your breasts be like the clusters of the vine, the fragrance of your breath like apples, and your mouth like the best wine."

It is good and exciting to admire one another sexually after we are married. Modesty is a really good thing in public, but it is not needed in the bedroom between husband and wife. We are free to look at and enjoy each other's body. Enjoying sex in a marriage relationship pleases the Lord. He wants you to enjoy it and have fun. He wants it to feel good and wants you to desire sex.

Remember how excited you were about Christmas when you were little? Remember how much you looked forward to it and how the anticipation would grow day by day. God wants you to experience that same excitement and anticipation as you look forward to your honeymoon.

We often don't take time to enjoy each season of our lives. Satan lies to us and tells us that we are missing out, and what we don't have is better than what we do have. So instead of enjoying life and being content with our current season of life, we seek the forbidden.

Adam and Eve could go anywhere and do anything except eat from one tree in the garden. So what did they do? Were they content with all that God gave them? No, they reached for the one thing they were told not to touch.

King David had wives and concubines enough to satisfy any man. Was he content with what he had? No, he reached out for a married woman.

God has given you wonderful gifts, talents, and abilities. Are you content with these? Are you happy with this season of your life and being unmarried? Or are you reaching out for sex even though God has told you not to touch it?

Will you learn from the mistakes of others, or do you need to make the same mistakes?

It should be enough for us that God, our loving heavenly Father, has said, "Don't commit adultery and don't get involved in premarital sex." We see the consequences and how they affected Adam, Eve, and David. If they could do it over again, they would all obey God because they now understand that the commands were for their own good.

SEX MAKES YOU ONE WITH THAT OTHER PERSON

Sexual relationships are so important God set out some steps: "For this reason a man will leave his father and mother and be united to his wife, and they will become one flesh" (Genesis 2:24).

We are first to leave and then to be united. The result of that leaving and uniting is becoming "one flesh."

These steps are so important that Jesus Christ puts His stamp of approval on them in Matthew 19:5–6 and Mark 10:7–9.

Let's look at the two steps and their result in more detail.

LEAVE

Simply stated, this means to become married. You are leaving your home and your parents to begin a new life with another individual.

Marriage is a huge step and one that is often taken much too lightly. In this millennium it's not unusual to live to be seventy. If you marry at twenty, then you are saying that you will live with this other person for more than fifty years. That is twice as long as you have already lived.

The decision to marry is one that should not be made on the basis of our emotions. It's a commitment you make to that other person "till death do you part." God remains your number one priority, but your number two priority becomes your spouse. Divorce is *not* an option. That is why it is so important that you are sure, and your parents and godly friends are supportive, before you take this step.

There are some people you will fall in love with that you should never date or marry. Just because you love someone doesn't mean it is a good relationship or you should be hanging out with them. Someone says to me, "But God brought them into my life." How do you know it was God? Satan can bring someone into your life just as easily as God can. If people who love you and know you say the relationship is bad, why won't you listen to them? You may say, "They don't know the other person like I know them." Exactly— you are too subjectively involved—love *is* blind. Someone on the outside can see objectively, and God promises there is wisdom in the counsel of many (Proverbs 15:22). So listen to your parents and other godly men and women.

Be sure that you are open and honest with each other. You don't want to have any secrets. Make sure that the person you are going to marry knows the good, bad, and ugly about you and you know those things about them. Do they struggle with pornography; do they have any food issues; are they depressed, etc.? I recommend you both reach spiritual and emotional health before you get married.

It is better to break an engagement than it is to break a marriage.

People say to me, "What's the big deal about getting married and signing a piece of paper? Is it that important?" Yes, for two reasons.

1. God ordained marriage, and we set ourselves up for a lot of pain when we try to skirt what God has already established as good and right. Obviously you can't expect God to bless your disobedience.
2. You are publicly declaring unconditional love and commitment for one another. You are vowing to love that person "for richer, for poorer, in sickness and in health, for better or for worse"—(believe me, there will be some worse)—"till death do you part," and you are doing it before witnesses.

If you unconditionally love and are committed to each other, there is no reason you wouldn't want to be publicly married. If you're not ready to take that step, then you aren't ready for sex. Sex at its very ultimate, the way God intended it, is found only in a relationship of total commitment—marriage.

Women have said to me, "My boyfriend is afraid of marriage because of all the pain and problems it can cause. We love each other, and he says he wants to save me from that pain, so he thinks we should live together. What do you think?"

My response to that is, "Don't be stupid! When you live with him you are giving him all the benefits of a marriage relationship without any of the responsibilities." When there is no commitment, anytime someone wants to leave they can. Cleaving to someone sexually is intended to be a union that is unseverable, just like friendship, loyalty, servanthood, and unconditional love in marriage are to last forever. It's a package deal, sex being *one* great part of it.

Don't live together. People have said to me, "To live apart would cost us so much more money." That isn't what's most important. What really matters is your character and God's honor. No one has given anything up that God doesn't eventually repay. The Lord will take care of you financially if you will honor Him.

In marriage there will be some pain and hard times, because these are a part of love, marriage, and commitment. All sunshine and no rain make a desert. It is through some of the hard times that couples grow closer. You can't take two unique creations of God with different personalities, likes, gifts, dislikes, talents, and abilities, put them in a marriage relationship and not have conflict. Conflict is not bad; through it issues can be resolved, and couples will grow in their communication. Those people who say they never have conflict don't impress me because that means one or both of them get walked on. That doesn't honor God.

Conflict is not bad, but how you handle conflict can be bad. Instead of yelling, screaming, and slamming doors, couples learn to sit down, calm down, and talk it out. Then conflict encourages understanding and growth in the relationship.

UNITE

How do we become united? We are united by our mutual commitment, made visible through the marriage ceremony, and by the unseen union God creates. One aspect of this union is sexual intercourse. This uniting is meant to form a lasting relationship to be broken only by death.

For example, take two pieces of paper and glue them together. Let them sit for twenty-four hours, and then attempt to separate them. Try as you might, you'll end up tearing, ripping, and destroying the paper. Some parts of the paper are inseparable.

The same is true in a relationship where there has been intercourse. Separation causes tremendous pain, problems, and destruction.

You are never, ever meant to part from the person you have had intercourse with. The sex relationship is not supposed to be a cheap

thrill but rather the uniting of two individuals within the boundaries of marriage.

Too many teenagers have turned these steps around. Instead of
leaving and uniting, they are uniting and then leaving. God's desire
is that you find a person who can be your best friend "till death do
you part." Someone you can laugh with, listen to, play with, explore
life with, and love until death parts you. God created humans with
hearts to yearn for this—don't settle for anything less.

When considering marriage, you need to ask yourself and your
significant other, "Is divorce an option?" If the answer is yes . . . then
don't marry that person! Years ago, when my kids were little, I
brought them into the dinning room on Valentine's Day and said to
them, "I will never leave or divorce your mother." You may say to
that, "Greg, you can't say that because you don't know what will
happen next week, month, or year." No, my love for Bonnie is not
based on my feelings. Love is a commitment, and I am committed
to Bonnie no matter what happens until death separates us.

ONE FLESH

Here is the result of doing it God's way: You leave your family
and unite in marriage and then you become one flesh. The problem
is if you sleep with someone after the party on Friday night—you
still become one flesh. This is not God's best for you.

It makes you one flesh with that person but it doesn't make you
married to them. Because you have chosen to have sex with someone doesn't mean you should marry that person. Marrying someone
doesn't make premarital sex okay. Your future husband or wife
needs to be a godly man or woman; don't settle for anything less
than that.

Casual sex degrades God's gift. It's like being presented the magnificent Michelangelo sculpture *David* as a gift, then taking it and
hitting it with a hammer. You have abused it, and it will never be
the same again. Some of us seek after cheap thrills and think they
have no lasting impact on our lives. But they do. Every time you
sleep with someone you leave a little part of yourself with him or

her. You give something to someone that belongs to your future spouse. You end up cheating your future spouse and yourself.

Take a stand for purity now before you go deeper into sin. It is never too late. God is ready, willing, and able to forgive you and give you a brand-new beginning. But start making good choices now. Break off bad relationships and decide that you will no longer compromise.

SEX AS GOD INTENDED
IT IS A GIVING EXPERIENCE

"The husband should fulfill his marital duty to his wife, and likewise the wife to her husband. The wife's body does not belong to her alone but also to her husband. In the same way, the husband's body does not belong to him alone but also to his wife. Do not deprive each other except by mutual consent and for a time, so that you may devote yourselves to prayer. Then come together again so that Satan will not tempt you because of your lack of self-control" (1 Corinthians 7:3–5).

In the marriage relationship my desire is to please my wife sexually and to give her satisfaction. I want what is best for her. The same is true of my wife; she wants to please me. So in a marriage relationship we have two individuals who are seeking to give to and please the other person.

In a dating relationship we are often seeking self-gratification. We want to feel good. We want to be excited. We want all we can get, so we pressure the other person. We are seeking to please ourselves.

Do you love the person you are dating? Let me ask you three questions:

1. Is the relationship morally pure?
2. Because the other person has dated you, does he/she have a better self-image?
3. Because of going out with you, is the other person closer to Christ?

If the answer is yes, then you probably love the other person. If the answer is no, then it's probably lust.

SEX IS A WONDERFUL WAY TO GET TO KNOW YOUR HUSBAND OR WIFE

Go through the Bible and look at all the times that the word *know* is substituted for sexual intercourse.

Sex causes you to be vulnerable. You see, before marriage you need to become open—naked—with that other person emotionally, intellectually, and spiritually. The better he or she gets to know you, the more vulnerable you become. Then the final step is the honeymoon, when you become naked and vulnerable before your partner physically.

The sexual relationship in marriage is a great way to keep the lines of communication open. Sex is meant to develop oneness, a wonderful closeness, and the desire to be emotionally open and vulnerable.

I am sure that you know a lot of different people in a lot of different ways and at many different levels. But sexual knowing is special, meant for just you and your spouse.

Remember that though sex is sharing, it is just a part of what is shared in marriage. You also share bills, tears, the flu, laughter, cooking, cleaning, shopping, dirty diapers, praying, worshiping, and reaching out to others. These things are all part of the total commitment you make to each other. Marriage is the haven where sex can become better and better, because spouses grow together in all areas —physically, spiritually, emotionally, intellectually, and beyond.

SEX IS FUN

Proverbs 5:18 says, "May your fountain be blessed, and may you rejoice in the wife of your youth." Sexual involvement with your spouse is something to look forward to, something fun to do. Being involved sexually the way God planned is a happy, wonderful experience. But then it ought to be. God, who created the whole universe, also made sex.

Women, you have something called the clitoris, and it is there for no other reason than sexual pleasure. How great is God to design you with the clitoris? He wants sex to be a celebration between a husband and wife. A time when you please each other, have fun and do something that feels really, really good! There is nothing better than experiencing sex the way God created you to experience it—without guilt, regret, or sadness!

God created sex to feel really good.

A good book to read in the Bible is Song of Solomon or Song of Songs. It tells of a man and woman's courtship, marriage, and celebration of the wonderful gift of sex.

What a great gift! Save it. Experience the joy and the fun. Please don't settle for any imitation of God's best.

SEX ENJOYED THE RIGHT WAY IS PLEASING TO GOD

First Timothy 6:17 says, "Command those who are rich in this present world not to be arrogant nor to put their hope in wealth, which is so uncertain, but to put their hope in God, who richly provides us with everything for our enjoyment."

Suppose you buy a child what you consider to be the perfect Christmas present. If the child opens it, gives a shout of glee, and tells you, "Thanks a lot," and begins to play with it, are you upset?

Do you say, "Stop playing with that toy. Sit here next to me and stop enjoying yourself"? Of course not. You are pleased the child is enjoying the good gift you gave him.

As a matter of fact you would be pretty upset if he didn't enjoy and use this toy.

When we enjoy the sexual relationship with our spouse in a loving, tender, and giving way, this is pleasing to God.

SEX IS FOR REPRODUCTION

"God blessed them and said to them, 'Be fruitful and increase in number'" (Genesis 1:28).

To have children is a reason to be involved sexually. Children are an awesome responsibility, but they are truly a blessing from God.

Bonnie and I have four wonderful children, and we could not imagine life without them. They are a delight and a joy to us. Is it always easy? No, sometimes our children drive us crazy, and sometimes we drive them crazy. That is all part of being a family.

God could have made sticking each other with sharp pins the method for reproduction. (If this were the case, we wouldn't have a lot of premarital pin-sticking going on.) But our God, in His great wisdom, linked together the possibility of having children with something as exciting and beautiful as intercourse!

SEX IS WORTH WAITING FOR
(I GUARANTEE IT)

If you decide to wait—and I really hope you do—then I'm sure if I were to call the morning after your first night together you would say, "I'm so glad we waited!"

So why didn't God just make us so we wouldn't want premarital sex? If He did that we wouldn't be sexual beings, and we wouldn't want sex within marriage either. Also, to do that would take away our ability to choose, making us like robots. God wants to build our character. Restraining from sex teaches us things. It teaches us discipline, self-control, identity, and delayed gratification—all of which we need to successfully navigate our lives. You'll need virtue to say no to a lot of things that are sinful. But the flip side is that you'll say yes to a lot of things that are good and best for your life.

He wants us to make right choices now so we get into the habit of following His leading. If you want God to use you in great ways later on, then be faithful in the little areas now.

Our question shouldn't be, "OK, what do I *have* to do?" but rather, "How much do I love Jesus?" If I truly love someone then I want to please him, and doing that isn't a burden; it's a pleasure.

Nobody sets out to make mistakes, but it happens, many times because of bad choices based on how good we thought we would feel. God never called you to feel a certain way; He called you to be obedient whether you feel like obeying or not. You may not see results right away, and at times you will probably feel deprived.

Let's understand something else. Sex is not a need! Food is a need. *I need food or I'll starve to death.* Water is a need. *I need water or I'll perish.* Is sex a need? *I need sex or I'll blow up.* Nope—sex is not a need; it is a drive, and it requires direction. You must drive your sexual desires and not allow your sexual desires to drive you. Is it better for an adult or a six-year-old to drive a car? If you put the six-year-old behind the wheel, you are moments away from a crash. You must be the adult, because your sex drive will play the part of the six-year-old—not caring what happens or what the consequences are—just wanting to drive. If your sex drive is out of control you are heading for a spiritual crash.

Sexuality is deeply a part of who you are, and it is normal to feel curious. I mean, if you've never been turned on by a member of the opposite sex, then you'd better check the obituaries, because I think you're dead. No matter how spiritual you may be, you will be tempted by the lust of the flesh at one time or another.

It's part of living to feel sexually stimulated and at the same time to control one's desires. We need to learn to live with unfulfilled desires. Don't condemn yourself because you are tempted. Be upset when you yield to the temptation.

Your body doesn't even belong to you. You were bought and paid for by Christ on the cross. "Do you not know that your body is a temple of the Holy Spirit, who is in you, whom you have received from God? You are not your own; you were bought at a price. Therefore honor God with your body" (1 Corinthians 6:19–20).

Sex can be compared to a fire. Build a fire in the fireplace on a cold winter evening, and it becomes warm, cozy, inviting, and romantic.

But build the fire in your lap, and suddenly it becomes frightening, destructive, and painful.

"Can a man scoop fire into his lap without his clothes being burned?" Proverbs 6:27–29 says. "Can a man walk on hot coals without his feet being scorched? So is he who sleeps with another man's wife; no one who touches her will go unpunished."

I can't make you do what's right. You've got to decide. You've got to purpose in your heart to be strong, courageous, and morally pure.

But remember, ultimate victory will not occur because you follow all the steps Greg Speck lays out in this book. Your dependency must be upon the Holy Spirit. He is the One who will give you strength, courage, and wisdom to do what is right, even when it's hard.

Your own willpower is likely not enough to stay pure. We need to ask God (sometimes several times a day) to give us the strength and patience to *wait* and trust Him that He knew what He was doing when He created sex for marriage. In the same way, friends who have the same goal of purity should pray for each other and encourage one another in love. They should be a safe place to empathize and talk when it becomes difficult to not get physical. Here the body of Christ can help each other be accountable and keep growing according to God's continued work and power in us.

Each day, decide to surrender to the control of the Holy Spirit. Pray something like this for yourself and your friends, "Holy Spirit, we now surrender our lives to You. I ask that You fill and control us. We give You our feelings, wants, needs, and sexual desires. We want to honor You today with our lives. Lead us and we will follow. We need You and we love You. Thank You that Your power is strong enough to sustain us. In Jesus' name, amen."

Questions to ask yourself:
1. Am I controlling my sex drive or is it controlling me?
2. Am I surrendered to the Holy Spirit?
3. Am I content with this season of my life?

4

Reasons for Waiting

(BESIDES WHAT THE BIBLE SAYS)

*I believe that teenagers today, empowered by the Holy
Spirit, can do whatever they set their minds to.*

Have you noticed that many sex education courses, sex "experts," Planned Parenthood, and so on, stress making wise decisions as to when you are emotionally ready for sex?

They take the approach that says, "Teens are going to be sexually involved anyway, so let's at least try to stop unwanted babies either before or after conception." But the answer is not birth control, and it's not abortion. You and I both know that. Instead of valuing purity, society is valuing "safe sex."

Why do people assume that teenagers will not respond to a positive approach that says self-discipline is what we want to strive for?

These so-called experts insult you by speaking to you like you were a bunch of animals. I believe that teenagers today, empowered by the Holy Spirit, can do whatever they set their minds to. They can turn the tide by saying, "Sex is so great that it's worth waiting for." The turnabout can start with you.

I speak in quite a few public high school assemblies. Obviously I can't talk about God, Christianity, and the Bible there, but still students want to know, Why shouldn't I get involved sexually?

OK, here are some reasons—apart from what the Bible says—for not getting involved sexually.

YOU WANT TO GIVE YOUR BEST

Someday you will probably get married. Now if I asked, "Are you going to love the person you marry?" you would say, "What a stupid question. Sure, I'll love them." You'd probably say you'll love that person more than you've ever loved anyone.

Then I would ask, "Do you want to give them your very best?" And you would say, "Of course!" I would say, "Great. Then how come that applies to every area but sexuality?"

A woman may mess around with John, Jimmy, and Jason, and her husband-to-be is at the end of the line. A man may play around with Julie, Joanna, and Jen, and his wife is at the bottom of the list.

Your husband or wife should have first place. Your spouse should get your very best. How sad to say on the honeymoon, "Well, here I am, sweetheart, all the leftovers just for you. All these other people have been involved with me, and now here you are at the very bottom of the list."

Let me ask you this: Do you want someone sleeping with your future husband or wife tonight? Then don't you sleep with someone else's spouse.

Teens say to me, "But what happens if I get on the honeymoon and I don't really know what I'm doing? I mean, I don't have any experience, and I don't read so well. What happens then?"

I say you'll have fun practicing! You have a whole lifetime to-gether. It's not supposed to be professionals coming together. It's supposed to be two novices who love each other. Good sex is not primarily the result of experience, positions, or technique. Good sex is primarily the result of a loving, committed relationship, and you don't need any experience for that to happen.

We are in an instant society. We have instant messaging, instant breakfast, instant replays, so it's natural to want instant relation-ships. It's natural to say, "I want to feel good, and I want to feel good *now!*" We must learn to give up instant gratification for the much deeper satisfaction of developing a healthy person. That's where self-control comes in.

In the past, adults have tried to control teenage sexual urges by laying on tremendous feelings of guilt. That's stupid and ineffective. Guilt does not prevent sexual stimulation. Guilt does not give you positive steps to deal with it, and it usually leads to a poor self-image. Instead we need to stress self-control, which is a positive way of waiting for sex at its very best—in a marriage relationship. You are not an animal or something that merely reacts out of instinct; you are somebody. You have a will and you can practice self-control. You can choose to do what respects others and builds yourself. You should be insulted when someone stands before you and assumes that you will have sex before you are married because you are only a teenager. That is a person who doesn't believe in you, but I know it is possible to abstain.

People love to ask, "What if we aren't sexually compatible? Shouldn't we sleep together to discover that?" It sounds like we are mechanics here. This isn't like trying to fit a Cadillac engine into a Honda Civic. The wonderful thing is that all the parts fit. If you're worried about this, you can go to a doctor, and he can examine both of you. But unless there is some major physical deformity, you don't have to worry.

Right now, for good or for bad, you are making memories.

Remember, the quality of sex is not dependent on positions, size, or technique but on the quality of the relationship. Good sex comes out of strong, committed marriage relationships!

PREMARITAL SEX WILL CAUSE COMPARISON PROBLEMS

You never forget past lovers. The sexual relationship is such an intimate, binding experience that you'll never, ever forget them. Once you are married you can have flashbacks and start to compare your spouse with past lovers.

Then there is the worry of whether or not your spouse is thinking about someone else while making love to you—and the concern as to whether you are as good as all the rest.

You better be real careful if you decide to marry someone who has had sexual partners in the past. Are you ready to deal with their memories of someone else? If they say, "I never think of or remember past lovers," they are lying to you.

There isn't supposed to be a comparison. If your relationship isn't as great as you would like it to be, then you work at it to make it better.

Plus, a person you are considering marrying better have shown some self-control. If they couldn't control themselves before, how will they control themselves after they are married?

YOU GIVE AWAY
YOUR VIRGINITY ONE TIME

Popular culture has made a big joke of virginity. It will say, "Are you a virgin? What's the matter with you? You must have some major problem. Come on and lose it!"

Do you know why people do this? Because they've already lost their virginity. They can't tell you virginity is important, because then they would feel guilty. So because misery loves company, they put pressure on you.

Listen to me. Your virginity is not something to be ashamed of but rather something to be proud of. For you to give your virginity to another is to give your greatest gift. If you are still a virgin, that is a badge of honor.

Individuals have said to me, "Intercourse is a sign of maturity. When you finally grow up, then you have sex. That's the sign of maturity; it means you are a real man or a real woman."

That's a bunch of garbage. However, in a subtle way, that is exactly what you hear in your sex education classes. "You've got to be emotionally ready; you need to be mature." Well, everybody wants to think he or she is emotionally mature, so we try to prove it by having intercourse.

Give me a break. Think about it; two hippos can have intercourse. On second thought, don't think about that! Two warthogs can have intercourse. You don't walk up to your pet warthog and say, "What a man! You must be very mature."

Having intercourse isn't a sign of maturity, but I'll tell you what is, and that is being able to say *No*! It takes courage, self-discipline, and strength to wait, and that is the sign of a real man or a real woman who will be able to handle the myriad of vocational, social, intellectual, and emotional challenges of life.

It's OK and good and right to say no. Having high moral standards doesn't make you weird. And you'll find that your real friends will stick with you, because they will allow you to be you.

As you say no to premarital sex, and stick by that conviction, people will respect you. But let's be honest. Some individuals may laugh at you and turn away. Realize, however, that they aren't actually rejecting you. They just feel bad about themselves.

When you stand for what is right and get your life together, people begin to compare themselves with you—and they don't look so good. They have two choices: get their lives together (that would be hard and take a lot of work), or they can try to tear you down (which is much easier).

Say no. Stand for what is right. Being a virgin is something to be proud of. You've got everything to gain, and all you lose is fake friends and dates from people who are only after your body.

YOU MAY DEVELOP
A TASTE FOR VARIETY

If you have had sexual experience—or if the person you marry has—what makes you think that you or your partner will now be interested in only one sexual partner till death do you part? Research has shown there's a correlation between those who were involved in premarital sex and those who are now involved in adultery.

A person can develop a taste for variety. New experiences, different bodies, exciting conquests can, in time, lure a person away from an otherwise good marriage. In many cases, the individual wishes he or she would not yield to temptation, but the urge is so strong and the past so vivid they are pulled into it.

Also remember that a virgin can imagine what it would be like to be involved sexually with a person, but once a person has been involved, imagining is no longer necessary. They have been there! So the temptation becomes even stronger for someone who has been sexually active.

Involvement in premarital sex can cause you to see sex as trivial. You'll find yourself saying, "It's no big deal." You have really robbed yourself, because sex is one of the most exciting experiences in life.

YOU LOSE AN OBJECTIVE VIEW OF THE RELATIONSHIP

When you go out with a person, you get to know him or her spiritually, emotionally, and intellectually. You begin to develop open communication.

HOW WELL YOU KNOW EACH OTHER

```
        1   2   3   4   5   6   7   8 . . .
Spiritual      ───────▶
Emotional      ─────────────▶
Intellectual   ──────────▶
Communication  ─────────────────────▶
```

Then you ask, "Do you love me?"

"Well, I love you."

So you decide to sleep together. Now suddenly you know each other very well physically:

HOW WELL YOU KNOW EACH OTHER

```
        1   2   3   4   5   6   7   8 . . .
Physical       ──────────────────────────▶
```

All of a sudden you say, "I feel we are so close. I feel we know each other so well." But this is a false feeling, because there is a gap between where you feel you are and where you really are. Sex has distorted the relationship.

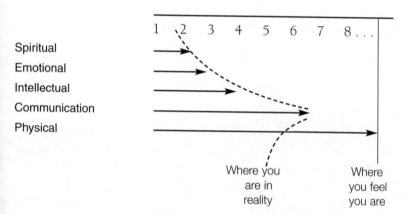

HOW WELL YOU KNOW EACH OTHER

What are some indications this is happening?

1. *There is a lot of conflict in our relationship.* "Greg, I feel we should be so close, but we fight a lot and have stupid arguments. If we aren't having sex, then we are having a hard time getting along."
2. *We don't really talk on a deeper level.* "Most of our conversations seem so surface level. We don't really talk about important stuff."
3. *We should feel better.* "If this is so good, how come I feel guilty and bad?"
4. *The longer we are together, the less close I feel to them.* "It seems like we are drifting apart more and more as time goes by."
5. *I don't feel secure in the relationship.* "Instead of feeling at peace and being content, I am worried that they are going to leave me."

All of this indicates that you have fooled yourself and settled for an imitation of intimacy.

When you become sexually involved, suddenly you can lose an objective view of the relationship. You may become very subjective, or feeling-oriented. You begin to do things that you never would have dreamed of doing a few months before. You become rebellious. You won't listen to anyone who has anything negative to say about that other person. You lie. You sneak behind people's backs. You deceive. And what is your excuse? "I'm in love."

Stop to think a moment. Is that what real love causes you to do? The answer is no, and if this is what is happening to you, then you need help! Listen to your parents and others around you, because they can see the situation more objectively. Get away from the relationship for a while. Stop having sex. All these things will help you to see the relationship more realistically.

If this relationship is corrupting you, then it is a bad relationship. I know you don't want to hear this, but you need to end bad relationships. Bad company corrupts good character.

PREMARITAL SEX PREVENTS YOUR DEVELOPING IN OTHER IMPORTANT AREAS

Premarital sex has a tendency to block the very thing it was meant to promote in a marriage relationship. Things like making you feel better about yourself, giving you a sense of peace and contentment, deepening your communication skills, and making you emotionally and physically one with that other person. At first you both may think, "This is great. It has really pulled us together." But in many cases, after awhile things begin to change.

➤ The emotional area.

I've already explained the gap between where we feel we are and where we are in reality. Emotionally we are on a roller coaster that goes from extreme highs (where we are so much in love), to ultimate lows (where we are depressed and hate the relationship).

➤ The intellectual area.

Usually we are not much interested in pursuing the intellectual area. Finding out what a person thinks, where they stand, and what they believe in is often overlooked. Because we are attracted to the physical, it is much easier to be physically involved than to get to know what the other person thinks.

Develop the intellectual dimension of your relationship. For example, read something together and then talk about what you've read. How do you feel about what you've read? Do you agree? Disagree? Talk about current events, discuss what you are learning in school, and ask each other questions.

Decide that you will come up with three questions you can ask to get to know the person better. Do something that will help you get to know the person intellectually each time you get together. This will deepen your relationship, develop your communication skills, and give you insight into their lives. Be fun and creative. It's not as easy as making out, but now you have a chance to really get to know the person.

➤ The area of communication.

"We just don't talk like we used to. When we do talk it ends up in an argument." Why? Because we have substituted sex for communication.

What happens is that the whole relationship begins to center on sex. We go to a ball game: "Come on, get over, and please don't go into overtime! Great, let's get out of here." Then we have to go out and eat a little something. "Hurry, shovel the hamburger in! Suck down the fries! Good. Now at the same time drink your Pepsi. Finally we're done. Now we can go park and have sex."

It is easy for there to be loss of respect. We lose respect for ourselves. We lose respect for the other person. We become unhappy. We want to stop, but we feel trapped on this physical merry-go-round. The relationship begins to fall apart. Eventually we feel used instead of loved, and finally we break up. If we could only start over.

"But, Greg, I never know what to talk about!"

Remember that everyone's favorite subject is himself or herself. Find out what your date is interested in, and ask questions about that.

Or ask each other this: "What are three things that happened to you today, and how did you feel about them?"

The lifeblood of a relationship is communication. A lack of communication is a lack of love because you naturally communicate with someone you love. Communication is something you learn through practice. It's like riding a bike; at first it is awkward and uncomfortable, but the more you do it, the better you become at it. All of a sudden it becomes really easy because you have worked on it. Communication will become easy if you work on it.

PREMARITAL SEX KILLS CREATIVITY IN EXPRESSING LOVE

Once we get involved sexually, we tend to rely on sex as a way of expressing our love for the other person. But there are many other ways of showing love. Gary Chapman has written a number of books on the love languages. Love languages for men, women, couples, young people, and so on. He has identified five major love languages, and you can appropriately show them all in a dating relationship. Here are some examples of creative ways we can love each other:

1. Use words of affirmation.

   With your words you bring life, or with your words you bring death. You either build up or tear down. Think about this past week. How many times have you built someone up, complimented someone, or expressed your love? Now how many times have you been sarcastic? I am the king of sarcasm, and sometimes it is funny, but sometimes it becomes a mask we hide behind so we don't have to be vulnerable. Words are an important way to express love.

Tell them how much you care for them. Share some things that you appreciate about them. Notice when they dress nice, smell great, and try to look good for you. Compliment them. Build their self-worth. Tell them what a fine athlete they are. Phone them just to say you care.

Don't just talk about how good-looking they are on the outside but talk about how beautiful they are on the inside. Compliment them on their courage, trustworthiness, care, servant's heart, being a listener, their joy, or patience.

2. Spend time together.

Take a walk. Play tennis. Go out to eat. Go shopping. Listen to music. Ski together. Do a service project. Go horseback riding. Play mini golf. Go to a concert. You can think of 101 other things you could do. This way, you can truly get to know the other person because of the time that is spent together in various settings. Movies are not always the best ways to get to know each other, because you are both just staring at the screen. Talk and listen to each other.

3. Give gifts.

For no special reason, give something the person would enjoy. It's not Christmas, Valentine's Day, anyone's birthday, or Groundhog Day, but here's a little gift to say I care about you; you're special. You can make a gift. You can give flowers, candy, a key chain, a stuffed animal, a can of tennis balls. Write poems, send fun cards and love letters, sing a song. You can say, "Here, I picked this poison ivy for you." (That would actually be a bad gift.) When you give a gift you are saying to that person, "I have been thinking about you even when we are not together."

4. Be helpful.

Help them with homework by explaining how to do it. Help with housework, gardening, mowing the lawn, delivering papers. Help with some work, or even do it, so that the person can make a special appointment. This is saying, "I care about you!" You are looking to serve them and to make their load lighter.

5. Appropriately touch the person.

I am neither talking about painful touch, like slugging them, nor sexual touch. I am talking about touching them in the purest sense of the word, giving them a hug, holding their hand, or putting your arm around them. Touching someone is a wonderful way to communicate love. But be careful where you touch and how much you touch. A woman can tell the difference between a touch done in love and one done in lust.

Sex is separate from the love languages shown in a dating relationship. It is a wonderful way to say "I love you" in a marriage. I am encouraging you to wait to have sex until marriage for a lot of good reasons and concentrate on the other five ways to love this special person. It will allow you to be creative and romantic—which are both good things.

> *Love is all about serving the other person and seeking what is best for them.*

Keep in mind that everyone has a primary love language. That means in one or two of the areas I mentioned above, they feel the most loved. We usually love others in our primary love language, but that isn't always their main love language. So find out the person's primary love language (you can ask them) and concentrate on that area.

SEXUALLY TRANSMITTED
DISEASES (STDs)

"To use a condom is to practice safe sex." Have you heard this one before? It's a lie! Wearing a condom is to practice safer sex but not safe sex. Is it safer to have sex with a condom? Absolutely, yes. Is it safe to have sex with a condom? Absolutely not! Listen to some doctors who know a lot more about this area than you or me.

"Saying that the use of condoms is safe sex is in fact playing Russian roulette. A lot of people will die in this dangerous game," said Dr. Teresa Crenshaw, member of the U.S. Presidential AIDS Commission and past president of the American Association of Sex Educators.

"Relying on condoms for protection can mean lifelong disease, suffering, and even death for you or for someone you love," says Dr. Andre Lafrance, Canadian physician and researcher.

Years ago there were only two types of sexually transmitted diseases: syphilis and gonorrhea. Today there are over twenty STDs. Did you know that STDs are tiny organisms that are smaller than sperm? For example, the HIV virus is so small that two million of the disease-causing organisms could fit on the period at the end of this sentence. Condoms have tiny holes called "voids" that are small enough to stop the sperm from getting through but not the AIDS virus.

Plus, there is a condom failure rate that is anywhere between 10 percent to 36 percent, depending on which survey you read. So let's pick something in the middle and say that 20 percent of all condoms fail. So if you have intercourse ten times the condom might fail twice. That greatly increases your chance of getting pregnant or catching a disease. Take a gun that has five chambers and take out four bullets so that 20 percent of the chambers are filled with bullets. Now is this a safe gun? No, one bullet can kill you just as fast as the five can. Is it a safer gun? Yes, but it is not a safe gun. A young lady, who in the past was sexually active with several different partners, said, "The days of casual sex are over, if you value your life at all!" Notice that in many cases the person you are going to have sex with doesn't even know they have a STD because they have not experienced any symptoms. A majority of the time STD carriers will have no symptoms at all. So if you ask them, "Do you have any kind of STD?" they can honestly answer, "No!" But the reality is that they do, and if you have sex with them (and that includes oral sex), there is the possibility that they will pass it on to you. Is it worth the risk? Over sixty million people in the US with an STD would say *no*, but what about you? If you catch HIV, herpes, or HPV there is no cure, and you will have it for the rest of your life.

Here are some of the common STDs that you expose yourself to if you become sexually involved.

CHLAMYDIA

This is one of the most common sexually transmitted diseases. It lives in vaginal fluid and semen and is passed through vaginal and anal intercourse and can be passed through oral sex. It can also be passed by hand-to-eye contact, but this is much less common.

This is called the silent disease because 75 percent of women and 50 percent of men have no symptoms. If there are symptoms it will usually be a discharge of mucus or pus, and it can be painful when you urinate. Other symptoms for women could be abdominal pain, a slight fever, pain during intercourse, and a need to urinate more often. For men it could be inflammation of the rectum and swelling or pain in the testicles.

If it's not treated, it can move farther into the body; and in women it can affect the cervix, fallopian tubes, and urine canal and can lead to pelvic inflammatory disease (PID). PID can increase your risk of infertility. Do you realize this means you may never be able to have a baby? For men you can find yourself with an inflammation in the testicle area that could lead to sterility (again, no children). It can also lead to infections of the throat after oral sex. The overall infection can be cleared up, but any damage that has been done prior to treatment can't be undone.

SYPHILIS

The majority of syphilis sufferers are male. The syphilis bacteria are easily spread from the ulcers of the infected person to the linings of the mouth, genitals, and anus of their sexual partner through oral, vaginal, and anal sex.

The symptoms occur in stages. The first stage is painless sores called "chancres," which usually appear on the genitals but can also appear on the lips, tongue, and other body parts. They will disappear in a few weeks, but if you don't get treatment then you will move to stage two. This begins with the syphilis rash, which is brown and usually appears on the bottom of the feet and the palms of the hands. There can also be fever, sore throat, swollen glands, and hair loss. The third stage can last for several years and can cause heart problems, joint and bone damage, blindness, numbness in the extremities, and even death. Syphilis can also increase the chances of your catching the HIV virus.

GONORRHEA

Women who are fifteen to nineteen and men who are twenty to twenty-four are the most at risk of becoming infected. You can get gonorrhea through vaginal, anal, and oral sex. It is passed through semen and vaginal fluid.

Symptoms can take between two and ten days to show up. For women it can include bleeding after sex, pain or burning sensation when urinating, a need to urinate more frequently, a vaginal discharge that is either yellow or bloody, cramps, nausea or vomiting, and fever. In men the symptoms can include a yellow or green discharge from the penis that will be painful, a burning sensation when urinating, and swollen testicles.

It is very common for people to be infected with gonorrhea and chlamydia at the same time. Treatment will clear up the infection but it cannot undo any damage that gonorrhea has done to the reproductive system prior to treatment. If you don't treat gonorrhea, it can lead to infertility in both men and women and can cause joint inflammation, as well as infect the heart valves and brain.

HUMAN PAPILLOMA VIRUS (HPV)

There are more than one hundred different types of HPV and about thirty different strains are considered to be sexually transmitted. This is the most common STD today. It is spread through vaginal, anal, and oral sex.

You may not develop any symptoms or you may have genital warts. They may appear a few weeks or months after being exposed to the virus. The genital warts look like very small cauliflowers and are usually flesh-colored, soft, and moist. Women will usually see them appear on the vulva, cervix, or in and around the vagina. Men may develop warts on the scrotum or penis. But both sexes can see them appear on the anus, thighs, buttocks, and throat.

There is no cure for HPV and no treatment for it. In most cases you won't even know that you have it, and your body's immune system will fight it.

If you develop the warts, then you will want to have those treated through medication or burning the warts off.

There is high-risk and low-risk HPV. If you have high risk then you have significantly increased chances of developing cervical cancer, vulvar cancer, anal cancer, or cancer of the penis. There is evidence that says condoms are not very reliable in offering protection against the virus, because it is also present on dry skin on the surrounding abdomen, not just the genitals. It can be passed by rubbing against each other, and then the virus can move to the genital area.

HERPES SIMPLEX (HSV)

There are two types of the virus, HSV-1 and HSV-2. Usually Herpes Simplex Virus 1 is associated with oral herpes that produces cold sores around the mouth. While HSV-2 is thought to be the cause of genital herpes, it has also been discovered that HSV-1 can be the cause of genital herpes. It is passed through direct skin-to-skin contact with the infected area during vaginal, anal, or oral sex.

It can take between two and ten days for the symptoms to appear, which can include a burning or itching sensation and pain around the infected area. There can also be painful lesions in the vagina, on the penis, around the genital area or anus, or on the thighs and butt.

But the big problem is that most people do not even know that they have herpes because most people have no apparent symptoms.

There is no cure for herpes, but you can get medication that will help with the discomfort during the outbreaks and make the outbreaks less frequent. During an outbreak of herpes, your risk for HIV infection is greatly increased because it is easy for the virus to enter your body through the lesions.

TRICHOMONIASIS

This is one of the most prevalent STDs and is transmitted through unprotected sexual intercourse, either penis-to-vagina or vulva-to-vulva. Women can be infected by both men and women, while men are usually only infected by women.

For women the infected spot that is most common is the vagina and for men it is the urinary tract.

The bacteria can live outside the body for up to forty-five minutes, so it is possible to come into contact with it through infected towels, bedding, and bathing suits; but it is very rare to contract the infection in this way.

Ten to 50 percent of all men show no symptoms when they have this bacteria. If there are any symptoms for the men it can be irritation of the penis, a burning sensation when having an orgasm or urinating, and a thin, whitish discharge from the penis. Women are much more likely to show symptoms that can include a yellow-green discharge from the vagina, itchy genitals and thighs, and pain during intercourse or urination. Women may also suffer from "strawberry cervix," which are lesions that form on the cervix and vaginal walls and gives the appearance of redness. If trichomoniasis is not treated, you can become up to five times more likely to be infected with the HIV virus that causes AIDS.

HEPATITIS B (HBV)

This is potentially very serious and attacks your liver and can cause ongoing sickness and even death.

About 10 percent of those who are infected will develop chronic hepatitis B, which means the virus can stay for years. Fifteen or more percent of those with chronic hepatitis B will die from liver disease.

It is passed on through the exchange of bodily fluids during vaginal, anal, or oral sex. You can also be infected with contaminated drug, tattoo, or piercing needles.

About 30 percent of those infected have no symptoms. Those with symptoms may experience a yellowing of the skin or the eyes, fatigue, loss of appetite, nausea and vomiting, abdominal pain, fever and chills, dark tea-colored urine, and grey or clay-colored bowel movements.

It typically takes anytime from nine to twenty-one weeks for the symptoms to show up. There is no cure, but most infections will clear up within a few months.

HUMAN IMMUNODEFICIENCY VIRUS (HIV)

This is the virus that gives you AIDS. It is transmitted through vaginal and anal sex, and you may be able to be infected by performing oral sex on someone who is infected.

Initial symptoms of HIV are very similar to the flu and include fever, swollen lymph glands, headaches, muscle aches, and fatigue. But, once again, there are many people who don't perceive any symptoms.

There is no cure for HIV and AIDS. This STD can end up killing you. The HIV robs the body of its abilities to fight off disease and eventually develops into AIDS, which breaks down the immune system and makes you more susceptible to death from a wide variety of ailments.

The U.S. Centers for Disease Control and Prevention says, "Open-mouth kissing is considered a very low-risk activity for the transmission of HIV. However, prolonged open-mouth kissing could damage the mouth or lips and allow HIV to pass from an infected person to a partner and then enter the body through cuts or sores in the mouth. Because of this possible risk, the CDC recommends against open-mouth kissing with an infected partner. One case suggests that a woman became infected with HIV from her sex partner through exposure to contaminated blood during open-mouth kissing."[1]

PUBIC LICE

This is also called "crabs" because of their pincers. This is a parasite that can attach to coarse body hair on the arms, legs, armpits, eyebrows, eyelashes, and the genital area. Genital crabs are one of the most common STDs.

Crabs are easily transmitted between sexual partners. If your sexual partner is infected, there is a 95 percent chance that you will become infected.

Symptoms include itching and irritation in the genital area. The crabs live off of your blood, so you may see bluish spots where the crabs have been feeding. Dark spots may be visible on your skin or underwear—these are their feces. You may be able to see the crabs crawling around in your pubic area, and the eggs may also be visible. It is common to run a slight fever and feel irritable and run-down. Crabs are easily treated and do not pose a major health threat.

We talk a lot about safe sex. What is safe sex? It is abstaining from sex before you are married and then remaining faithful to your spouse afterward. The scary truth is that one in four teens will contract an STD this year; and, remember, in some cases they won't even know they have it. If you remain sexually active, you need to realize that by age twenty-five one in two people who are sexually active will have contracted an STD.

Do you want to live a healthy life and be able to marry someone STD-free? If the answer is yes, then you need to make good choices today. The choices you make right now are going to seriously affect your future, and that includes your marriage.

PREMARITAL SEX
CAN WRECK YOUR HONEYMOON

Your honeymoon is meant to be a wonderful and exciting time when you come to know each other sexually. Hopefully you have developed your relationship emotionally, spiritually, intellectually, and conversationally, so all that is left is the physical. If you have already been involved sexually, you have removed a lot of the magic of the honeymoon. You will not be doing anything you haven't done before.

This may surprise you, but very few individuals come to me and say, "I wish I would have messed around more when I was in high school and college. I just wish I had had more experience going into this marriage." As a matter of fact, I've never heard that, but I do hear a lot of, "Greg, if only I hadn't been so stupid! Why didn't I wait? I wish I could do it over again, because I would do it so much differently."

Premarital sex can cause sexual dysfunctions after you are married. Let's suppose that as a woman you believed strongly that you shouldn't climax with anyone until after you were married. However, you were involved sexually. You just made sure that you stopped before climaxing . . . or maybe you would do everything except have intercourse.

Now you get married, and you're on your honeymoon. You begin to move toward intercourse and climax that first night, and then all of a sudden your body turns off. Why? Because you've programmed it to do just that. You become frustrated; he becomes frustrated, and now you have a problem that didn't have to be if you had waited.

People usually suffer through this type of situation for a while, hoping it will clear up on its own. However, the stress and tensions build, making it even harder to respond. Now you're stuck in this vicious cycle, and if counseling is not started soon, the relationship is at risk of breaking up.

Your honeymoon should be wonderful, exciting, and something

brand new. Don't spoil it by lacking self-control. I have heard of couples who broke down and had sex the week of their wedding. How stupid is that after waiting for so long?

PREMARITAL SEX DOESN'T LEAD TO EMOTIONAL STABILITY

Our culture forces us to grow up much too fast. We are bombarded by sex on TV, on radio, in magazines, in movies, and on Web sites. All you have to do is look at the covers of men and women's magazines (and I am not even talking about pornographic ones) to see how obsessed we are with sex. So many articles are about sex. Why? Because sex sells! So we are drawn into this sex craze! Intellectually we understand the sexual act and the mechanics involved, so we think we are ready. Socially we are advanced, and we certainly have the possibility of willing partners, so we think we are ready. Physically we're developed, and our bodies can function sexually, so we think we are ready. Our parents work; we have access to a car. There are always parties going on, so a place is really no problem, so we think we are ready. I guess I'm ready, right? Wrong!

Showing sexual self-control is a sign of spiritual and emotional maturity.

We forget one crucial area, and that is our emotional side. Most teenagers like to think of themselves as mature. When I ask a teen, "Are you mature emotionally?" I have very few who say, "Nope, I'm pretty squirrelly."

Now I know this will tick some of you off, but I feel I need to speak the truth in love and tell you that as a teenager you're just not ready for sex emotionally. Emotional maturity only comes with time and growing up. You aren't as mature at seventeen as you will be at twenty-five or as you will be at forty-five. With emotional maturity comes better judgment and understanding.

Your teen years are an emotional roller-coaster ride. Just look at the number of your friends who are unhappy, depressed, suicidal, and moody. Premarital sex doesn't lead to emotional stability. Often it does just the opposite. It causes emotional chaos. Even if you love each other very much, have known each other a long time, and have sat down and talked about sex and decided you both want it, you still aren't ready emotionally.

Ask a twenty-five-year-old if there is any difference in his emotional maturity now compared to when he was a teenager. You'll find there are some big changes. If there haven't been changes, then that person is in trouble because he isn't growing.

Emotional maturity will happen as you grow older, so wait, please. Don't give away something now that later on you're going to regret having given away.

I can hear it already: "But we're different. We are very emotionally mature, and we truly love each other. This isn't infatuation."

Almost every couple I meet feels this way. But try for a moment to be objective. If that was really true, then you could wait. If you really had emotional maturity, then you would be more interested in your future than the moment. Emotional maturity looks for creative ways to love the other person. Emotional maturity says no to lust in a dating relationship and says yes to sex in a marriage relationship. One way you truly show that you are emotionally mature is by saying no to premarital sex.

Look around you, and tell me how many teen relationships are lasting for years. Few of us would think—or want to admit—that our relationships are purely physical. I have heard it said that the average American falls in love seven times, and I read that in a United Airlines magazine so you know it has to be true.

Now some of you will fall in love only two or three times. Others of you are going to seek to establish a new entry for the *Guinness Book of World Records.* Are you going to sleep with every one of those individuals? How can you be sure that this is the one? You wait until marriage!

Now I know that even in marriage there is no guarantee there won't be divorce or adultery, but that is because we don't really understand what love and marriage ought to be.

Love is not just a feeling; it is a commitment. It is something you do whether you feel like it or not. The same should be true of marriage—it is a commitment till death do you part, not till feelings begin to fade.

So we ought to hold off on sex until we commit ourselves to someone for the rest of our lives. That happens in marriage, not in a dating relationship. Feelings change. A commitment does not.

Let me tell you a little secret. I don't always feel that I love my wife, Bonnie. And Bonnie doesn't always feel that she loves me because we get angry with each other. But regardless of those occasional feelings, we are committed to one another for better or worse, in sickness and health, for richer, for poorer, till death do us part! *That* is love.

TRUST IS BROKEN

Trust becomes broken with the loss of self-control. If your partner can't be trusted to control themselves before marriage, can he or she be trusted to do what's right after marriage? You may say, "But we won't have to show self-control after we are married because we will be making love five times a day!" Welcome to Fantasy Island! During marriage you will have the flu, be traveling for business, not be in the mood, have your period, etc. If you can't show self-control before you are married, why should it be expected in a marriage?

Can you trust the person you are dating? Keep this in mind: if the person you are dating will lie to their parents, then they will probably lie to you. We are talking about a character flaw of lying here. Love is unconditional, but trust is earned. Can you really trust this person? If they lied to you before, how do you know you aren't being lied to now? All of a sudden there is suspicion, which can quickly lead to possessiveness and jealousy. Never date or marry someone you can't trust; and if someone lies to you, that means you can't trust them!

PREMARITAL SEX CAN
LEAD TO PREGNANCY

I won't spend much time here on the subject of pregnancy. A whole chapter on the topic is coming up. But don't let anyone tell you that with birth control you can't get pregnant—that is a lie. The only sure way of not getting pregnant is using self-control.

After the birth of our third child Bonnie and I were using birth control, and guess what? Bonnie became pregnant with Garrett, which is a good thing, but at the time it was a major shock to both of us!

You say to me, "If we get pregnant then we will get married." That is one of the hardest ways to start off a marriage. You want to have time for just the two of you before children come into the picture. Getting married when you are pregnant will just add to your stress level.

THE BOTTOM LINE

Don't let your future spouse be in the back of a long line of others. When "friends" say to you, "Hey, how come you're not sleeping around? What's the matter? You weird? Scared? Gay? Come on, I do it because everybody else is doing it (which, by the way, is a total lie —statistics are saying more and more teens *aren't* doing it). Can you give me one good reason why you aren't?" tell them, "No, I don't have one good reason. I have twelve!"

Here we'll return to the best reason of all to wait, and it is not secular. God says wait and He knows what is very best for you. We haven't talked about the spiritual part of your relationship, but that should be the most important part. When you are having sex you are telling Jesus to, "Kiss off." The spiritual area started down the tubes as soon as you started messing around. Within marriage a good sex life is pleasing to God and helps our spiritual development. But for a dating couple, sex has just the opposite effect. It kills the spiritual dimension of the relationship. *You can't tell God you love Him and then continually, willfully disobey Him.*

Major changes can occur in this country in the area of sexuality. I believe those changes can begin with teenagers, and I would like to see them start with you.

But you've got to decide. You need to start making decisions with your head and not with your hormones. Your parents, teachers, pastors, and friends can't make those decisions for you.

Yes, I believe that you, controlled by the Holy Spirit, can do whatever is right.

Questions to ask yourself:
1. What are some reasons why you would wait till marriage to have sex?
2. Is it possible for me to fall in love with someone I shouldn't date?
3. What is my primary love language?

Note
1. http://www.redcross.org/servces/hss/tips/openkiss.html.

5

What Other Teens Say

(A WORD FROM YOUR PEERS)

"After a month he invited me to his house;
his parents were gone."

Premarital sex will cause you far more emotional and spiritual pain than it will ever give you physical pleasure. And the Word of God is specific about some of the problems that go along with it. Let's take a look at four Scripture passages. Notice the importance of what the Bible says, and learn from some of your peers who have written about their experiences.

"Dear friends, I urge you, as aliens and strangers in the world, to abstain from sinful desires, which war against your soul" (1 Peter 2:11).

Premarital sex will rob you of peace. Put another way, what feels good now can make you miserable later.

Guilt, confusion, and anxiety often arise from saying you love Jesus Christ while you ignore Him at the same time. You become two-faced, acting one way around your Christian friends and parents, and another way around your partner.

Look at Psalm 51:3. It says, "My sin is always before me." That's true, isn't it? Even though we rationalize and try to come up with good excuses, it's still there before us. We know it's wrong, and it slowly eats away at us from the inside out. *That is, until we get rid of it.*

John 10:10 tells us that Jesus came so we could experience life in its fullness. We often miss out on that exciting, abundant life because we are compromising, and being robbed in return.

Listen to what seven of your peers have to say:

➤ "I loved him so much that it just felt right to have sex. But after we broke up, I felt so guilty. He doesn't even know this, but I was pregnant when we broke it off. I was so depressed. I tried to kill myself. The next day I had a miscarriage. Oh, Greg, I killed my baby. For so long, I have cried, and I feel this pain deep down in my heart. I expect I always will."

➤ "At camp I met this guy, and we spent the whole week together. Toward the end of the week we got a chance to be alone, and we started out with just kissing. Then his hands began to wander. We never went all the way, but we got involved in heavy petting. He said he loved me, but the next day we had to leave, and he didn't even say good-bye. After I got home I called him, and he was very cold and short with me. It seemed so beautiful at the time, but now I feel awful."

➤ "What's wrong with me? People told me not to have sex, but I did anyway. Now I find that I just let guys use me and treat me really badly. No one understands why I do that, and I'm not too sure I can really understand it either. It seems to me that guys look at me like I'm an object. Whenever I'm out with my friends or the youth group, there is always at least one guy who will try to pick me up."

➤ "Awhile back I had sex with a girl. Not because I loved her or because she loved me, but because it was something to do, and it felt good. Afterward I felt so guilty. I was miserable on the inside, and it affected my relationships with others. I was angry and rude toward others. I began to give in to lust, which only depressed me more. I finally talked with some-one, and I'm on my way back. I want to be a missionary and really serve God. This was a terrible mistake that I'll never make again."

➤ "I met this guy at a roller skating rink. We were too young to date, but I would see him once a week at the rink. After a month he invited me to his house. . . . His parents were gone, and he wanted to have sex with me. I really wanted to say no, but I was afraid of losing him, so I said yes. A week later we started to fight, and we broke up.

"I feel so crushed! The love turned to lust, and the lust to nothing. I feel so empty inside. I want a guy who will love me the person, not the body. I want someone I can love and someone to respect me. Am I asking too much?"

➤ "Please tell people to wait to have sex, because the pleasure is not worth the pain. We were going to be different. We loved each other. We were mature. We even used birth control. She got pregnant, and now we're married, and I'm only seventeen.

"I'm working, trying to get my GED, be a husband, and be a father. How can I be a father? I still want to be a kid. I don't even think I love her, and now it's for the rest of my life. I sometimes wonder what God could have done with my life."

➤ "'I love you!' That's what he told me. We spent all our time together, but it wasn't great. Twice we thought I was pregnant. We had sex for two months—we were too young. Then he left, and now I feel like he never really cared. I am still so hurt. Even after four months I still cry because it's so painful. I've been used, and he lied to me to get something he wanted.

"In two days it will be our six-month anniversary. Does he even remember? I cry and wish I were still a virgin. I wish I had never done it. I've lost something I will never get back again. Only after it's too late did I know the value of virginity."

"Your iniquities have separated you from your God; your sins have hidden his face from you, so that he will not hear" (Isaiah 59:2).

Premarital sex will damage your relationship with God. After coming home from a date where you have sought each other's body, it can feel like there is a wall that keeps you from seeking God. You're more interested in pleasing man than in pleasing God.

Can you learn from other people's mistakes, or do you need to learn the hard way?

Listen to these five teenagers:

➤ "Everyone said what a great Christian I was and how God was going to use me. Then I met this girl, and soon my interest in God became less and less, and she became more and more important. We started having sex, and now she is pregnant. Do I marry her? If I could only start over again. I want to be used by God. That's when I was the happiest."

➤ "Although I know God has forgiven me, I can't seem to shake the guilt. I regret this ever happened. All I want to do is get rid of this guilt and start over with the Lord. Why can't I do this? It seems as if my relationship with the Lord is totally shattered."

➤ "My girlfriend and I knew it wasn't going to work. We'd talked the friendship-turned-relationship to death. I wanted to marry a Christian, so I could no longer date someone who didn't see Jesus as Savior and Lord. We decided to go our separate ways.

"No sooner had we come to that decision than we started making out. And though I can hardly believe it, we ended up having sex for the first and only time. In the moment, it seemed to relieve the stress. It was the opposite of being apart, being together that way.

"But afterward, much deeper panic hit. It ended up that we still needed to break up. I became cold and withdrawn from my Christian friends. With sex came guilt and a painful good-bye."

➤ "Greg, I was thinking about what you said about wishing to go back in time and be able to do things differently —nothing would make me happier. I have made so many mistakes. Over and over I ask God to forgive me, and you say He forgives and forgets. But I can't forget.

"I feel terrible about myself—things I've done and how I am. I'm so far away from God, and I'm going to have to live with my past until I die and maybe even after that. I am so depressed because I am about as low as they come. I've lost track of the number of guys I've made love to. I'm spoiled rotten. I'm obnoxious, and, worst of all, I killed my baby.

"I thought only of myself when I had the abortion. Only myself. How can God forgive me? How can I forgive myself? I've thought of jumping off the nearest bridge. I'm so confused. Please help me if you can."

➤ "I can't even believe that I'm writing to you about this, because I never thought it would happen to me. My boyfriend and I have been dating for two years now. At first everything was great, and he really loved the Lord. We had made plans to get married, and I loved him so much that I couldn't imagine being without him.

"But after a year, things started to change. We started doing a little petting, but I kept stopping it, and he would get frustrated and angry. He decided to break off the relationship. Our physical relationship had interfered with our relationship with God. We were both confused and depressed, and we felt even further away from God.

"We decided to get back together again, but our relationship is so different now. We never talk about God anymore. I needed him so much that I let him touch me wherever he wanted. When we were together I didn't care what we did. I loved him and wanted to show him how much I loved him, so one evening we made love. Since then we have been making love a lot.

"I have completely drawn away from Jesus, and I haven't been to church in a long time. I guess I have a new god—sex! But, Greg, I know he is going to break up with me soon. I can't handle it, and I'm scared I'll do something stupid. I have no one to talk to because I gave up all my friends for him.

"Please help me, Greg. I never would have dreamed that I would ever be in this mess. How could I have done this? Oh, God, I'm going crazy."

EPHESIANS 4:19

"Having lost all sensitivity, they have given themselves over to sensuality so as to indulge in every kind of impurity, with a continual lust for more."

Sexual immorality causes us to lose sensitivity to the Holy Spirit. How do I know that? Because we begin to rationalize that what we are doing really is OK—we are "different from everybody else." When we continue in sin the conscience is seared and spiritual sensitivity wanes.

If you don't deal with the sin in your life it will only get worse.

If you get caught up in this trap, wrong will begin to seem right. You'll lie to your parents, get involved in other sins, reject your friends, become rebellious, and all this will seem right to you.

Premarital sex never really satisfies, even though it feels good for the moment. The desire becomes insatiable. The more you get, the more you want. You always want to go farther and farther. The pain becomes deeper and deeper.

➤ "It's hard to believe I'm only seventeen. My friends and I started talking a lot about sex, and it sounded pretty fun to me. Last year I started going out with this non-Christian guy even though I knew it was wrong.

"I started thinking about having intercourse with him. I'm

a Christian, but the more physical we got, the further away God seemed. We finally had sex and continued to have it for two months.

"After we broke up I started dating other guys, but I can't control myself physically. Now I sleep with everyone I go out with. Every time I come home I make these promises to stop, but I never do. My reputation is so bad, and guys just date me now because they want sex. How can I stop? I'm so scared!"

➤ "I'm enjoying myself. Sure there are problems, but then again that's nothing new. Drinking and sex are fun. Actually the biggest reason I go to dances is to find someone I can have sex with, and that's not too hard.

"I've been involved with five different girls in the past five weekends. Yes, I'm disgusting, I know."

➤ "A friend of mine set me up with an old boyfriend of hers. We hit it right off in the beginning. At first I stuck by my standards—no sex before marriage. Well, one day I dropped them. I didn't care. It wasn't long before I regretted that decision. All we did was have intercourse. That's all he wanted to do.

"I tried to deceive myself and convince myself it was OK. I lied to other people and myself. I started to believe that what I was doing wasn't wrong, because we were going to get married. We never set a date, but it was part of our future plans. Well, he just decided he wanted to break up and told me he had cheated on me. What did I do?"

➤ "I'm supposed to be this really good Christian girl. I go to a Christian high school where I'm a cheerleader and a member of the Honor Society. I'm even an officer in my youth group, but it's all a joke. I started going out with this Christian guy, and we both fell deeply in love.

"My parents weren't thrilled, because he was five years older than me. My parents wanted us to just be friends, but pretty soon my whole life began to center around him.

"I convinced myself that my parents didn't really understand me or the situation, so it was OK to lie to them. We talked about how much we loved each other and sex. We both agreed that we wanted to wait till marriage to have intercourse, but our relationship was different. We were so close and such good friends that it was like we were married, and we got along better than our parents.

"So one night I lied about staying at a friend's house and went to his house. His parents were gone. We decided that sex was OK because we would get married someday. We really loved each other, and both of us were virgins. It was wonderful, and I didn't feel bad or guilty. I was ecstatic, and I had never been happier in my whole life. Now we were married in God's eyes.

"We started making love a lot, but each time it became less and less perfect. It began to feel cold, and each time was faster than the other. I told him that I was feeling used, and this upset him a lot. We began to fight, and he decided we needed to be apart for a while.

"Now he's dating another girl, and it turns out that he had had sex with three girls before me."

➤ "We were such good friends that it didn't matter that he wasn't a Christian. My mother was against the relationship, and that made me so mad. He told me everything, and we trusted each other completely.

"After a month, one night he said that he didn't want to have sex but he just wanted to feel close to me, so he wanted to lie on his bed with me with our clothes off. I don't know what I was thinking or if I was thinking, but we did that and nothing happened.

"A week later we went back to his room, and this time we

had sex. It was like I was so blind that I couldn't listen to my parents or my friends. He broke up with me and told the basketball team everything we had done."

GALATIANS 5:19

"The acts of the sinful nature are obvious: sexual immorality, impurity and debauchery." One sin tends to lead to another.

➤ "My boyfriend and I were really sexually attracted to each other. My parents told me to stay away from him, but I snuck around and lied to them so I could see him. He was older and could get drugs. We spent most of our time in his bedroom. Then to make things worse, I got pregnant. He said he would pay for an abortion, and it seemed like the best way out at the time. He soon broke up with me. I guess we never really loved each other anyway. I've never told my parents. They would have hit the roof."

➤ "I have sex with men but only after I am drunk, because it's easier that way. I'm nineteen years old, and I want a good relationship. But I don't know how to start or what to do. Please help me."

➤ "I'm married now, but before I was engaged my husband and I started having intercourse. He loved me, but I wasn't sure I loved him. We were having sex every night, and this really hurt and confused our relationship. But that was the only way we could show our love for each other, because we couldn't communicate.

"But instead of getting closer we were fighting all the time. There was also the fear of getting pregnant. It was terrible, and we finally decided to either stop or break up. We stopped, and two months later we got married.

"Our wedding night wasn't anything that I had ever dreamed of. It wasn't like it was supposed to be, because we had already wrecked it. If there is anyone else in this situation, I would say wait. If I had to do it over again, I would have waited to have sex until after marriage.

"Some girls think if you don't give, then he'll dump you. But I think if he really loves you, he'll understand. Well, Greg, I hope this will help someone."

➤ "I remember you saying that there is a war going on inside your life between your old and new natures. And the nature that wins out is the one you feed the most. Well, I've been feeding my old nature, and I'm really in trouble.

"When I was fifteen my parents brought this girl into our house who was an unwed mother. She was nineteen. After the baby was born she gave it up for adoption but continued to live with us, because her parents wouldn't let her back in. We became good friends, and one afternoon when my parents were gone she came into my room, and we had intercourse.

"This was my first time, and we made love for one year, and I thought I loved her and wanted to get married. My parents had no idea what was going on. After a year she moved in with two other guys and left me.

"I was really mad. I forgot about God and got really into pornography. At seventeen I met this fifteen-year-old girl, and we made love for six months. I never really loved her, but she wanted to marry me. Now I'm involved with another girl, and all I really care about is her body.

"I know this is wrong, but I feel like I'm out of control and my old nature is leading me. I know I need Jesus. I want to stop. Please help me, because I'm so scared that I've permanently messed up my life."

➤ "I've lived a wild life when my parents and people from church and school weren't around. I've hated myself and attempted suicide several times. I have even considered prostitution.

"I see now that I have to let go of the past and let Christ change my life. Thanks for talking with me. I came to the conference seriously considering ending my life, but now I have a reason to live."

These peers would tell you the pleasure is not worth the price. Do you want to go through what they've gone through? You don't have to learn the hard way. Listen to them, and don't make the same mistakes.

Read that last letter again. Maybe you think it's too late for you. But that's not true. There is hope and a fresh start waiting for you, if you'll turn over your life to Jesus Christ. He's the One who gives us a reason to live.

Questions to ask yourself:
1. Do I want to live my life with big regrets? (No one has *no* regrets.)
2. Am I seeking sexual purity?
3. What did you learn from reading these letters from your peers?

6

What God Can Do

(SHOULD I TELL MY PARENTS?)

*Her mother saw the business envelope
and thought it was junk mail. . . . !*

I love to watch the wonderful ways in which God works.

God desires to work in and through our families. On the whole, we do not appreciate our parents enough. We don't think they will understand what we are going through.

But parents have tremendous wisdom, and in the majority of cases they love us very much. That means we ought to be going to our parents more often with our needs and problems.

Here is a letter I received from a teenager. She had not told her parents what was happening in her life. She wanted to work through it herself, but God had a better idea!

LETTER A

Dear Greg Speck:

If you cannot help me, I think I will go utterly out of my mind. My precious walk with Jesus is constantly being axed down by the number one weakness in my life, and if I don't gain victory over it soon, I really believe my insides will be so screwed up that I may even turn my back totally on Jesus out of mere frustration and confusion!

My impossible weakness is sex. By sex I mean from heavy kissing all the way up to that precious gift God gave us of making love.

I want to quit so much. I want to live for my Lord so bad! But my stupid desires keep tripping me up. And I am sick of it. Yet I cannot give them up. I've prayed, oh, so earnestly. Yet I keep selfishly taking back what I give. . . . I really wanted to talk to you, but I was afraid. . . .

The talks you gave on sex were so meaningful to me. And one thing that has remained in my mind and heart was when you said, "Once you've started touching each other's bodies, once you've gone so far, it's so hard to go back again."

Well, I think I disagreed with that then, since my boyfriend and I had gone a few steps too many. I was out to prove you wrong (subconsciously). Yet, looking back, everywhere I turned, everything we tried, failed.

I am 18, and my boyfriend is 20. We've been dating on and off for about 3 years, and up until a few months ago we had done everything (physically) except go all the way. Never once did he pressure me. Never once did he even nudge me, but over all those months, my once strong-willed ability to say no weakened and weakened.

Now, we've done it 3 times. Special? I don't know. I don't see us getting married, because he is not a spiritual leader, and Christ has never really been number one for him. But, Greg, I still hang on to him. Why? I love being with him. I love him as a person, and I care so much for him, and I pray and hope that someday he can be a spiritual leader and be on fire for Christ! But I am not in love with him.

Oh, we've broken up and had cooling-off periods, but I always let us come together again.

In fact, we're in a cooling-off situation now. But it isn't working. I know what I have to do. But I can't do it.

Greg, I really don't know what I'm asking from you. You must have so many burdens and problems to deal with that I'm just another one of those in the sex category. That's understandable, but to me this is the most devastating thing that has ever happened to me in my life. I'm me, and I thank God for making me the way He did. But look what I've done and keep on doing.

I am so disappointed in myself. I never, ever thought I would make love before I was married. I promised myself. I was secure in that. And I believe I am a strong-willed person.

But now I may have caused bad memories for my boyfriend and hurt feelings in his future wife. And the same goes for me. When I'd hear of other girls doing it, it was so distant from my understanding. Now I'm dealing with it. And I hate it.

I am such a dirtbag, sleazy, slimy, dirty-minded sinner.

And, Greg, I am a leader in my youth group and looked up to by kids as well as by adults!

If they only knew me! I am on fire for Jesus except when my desires come around. They always take over.

I know I am forgiven, but how can I really stop? How can I get away from my boyfriend and hold to it? Please don't say trust in Jesus, 'cuz I have. It just seems to dwindle.

I am so weak here!

A struggling sister

Well, I wrote back sharing some steps she could begin to take to reestablish purity. (Check out chapter 13 for what I said.)

Now I sent my reply to her home address, but in the meantime she had left for college. Her mother saw the business envelope and thought it was junk mail. She was about to throw it out but decided to open it, just in case it was something important. She started to read and . . . well, listen to the mother. She can do a much better job of explaining than I can.

> *Sin will keep you from others, or others can help keep you from sin.*

Here is the letter the mom wrote to her daughter:

LETTER B

Dear _____

[Two letters came in the mail for you today.] And I didn't really pay too much attention to them, figuring they were just ads or more requests for money, etc. At first I was just going to throw them both away, but decided I'd better check them out first just to be sure they

weren't important, or if maybe I should keep them for you until you came home again.

I honestly wish now that I hadn't opened the one, but I couldn't un-open it, especially since I just ripped it open, and once I had read it far enough to figure out if it was important, there was no use trying to pretend I didn't understand what it was all about.

Please believe me, I never intended to "snoop" or read something that personal. Even if I had stopped reading after the first page, it was too late. And with the envelope ripped so badly, there was just no way to pretend I didn't understand what Greg Speck was writing about.

I did read the whole letter. My heart was beating so fast. I kept hoping that I had misunderstood and that if I kept reading I'd find out the guilt you wrote him about was for sinful thoughts or desires, and when I finished reading it, I guess I just felt numb. I think I still do.

There is so much I wish I could say to you, and of course I can understand why you couldn't come to me. But I feel so bad knowing that you carried this guilt around and finally had to write to someone you respected and could trust with your secret.

I don't know when this happened, and it isn't important for me to know. . . . I guess you've been carrying this guilt for quite a while. . . .

The advice he gives you seems very good, and I hope, since you asked for advice, that you will really consider and pray about what he wrote. It's definitely not easy advice, and the toughest part about it is that he's asking you to honestly face what happened and why. That means you may have to relive the guilt at a time when you had hoped to put those feelings behind you.

I guess I am also going to have to say some things you may not want to hear either.

When you were home last weekend, I guess I was disappointed to come home and find you lying on the couch with [him]. This is something I have mentioned to you before (many times). I have always felt this is not a good habit to get into with any boy. . . . I understand that it sounds silly to call it dangerous, but . . . one step just naturally leads to another, and guys can't handle that much intimacy very long. Neither can girls.

After reading the letter from Greg S., I guess I'm really trying to understand why you even allowed yourself to get on the couch with him this past weekend. . . . I know that God promises He will "not allow anyone to be tempted beyond what he is able to bear, but will with the temptation provide an escape," but, honey, God expects you to use your sense and not give Satan a chance to tempt you. . . .

Decide once and for all that whether you are with [him] or some other guy, you simply will not do anything that you would be ashamed [of]. . . .

Finally, honey, I want you to know that I love you very much, and my feelings of respect for you have not changed. You made a mistake, and I know you are really disappointed with yourself and probably even feel your relationship with God can never be quite the same again.

But now is when you have to really place all your . . . trust in the promises in the Bible, [which] you know are true. "If [when] you confess your sin, He is faithful and just to forgive you your sin and cleanse you from all unrighteousness." God promises that He will forgive and forget, and you need to say, "Thank You, Lord" and get up and start all over brand new.

I'd like to tell you that if God forgets it, then you need to forget it too—but that's not going to happen. You do need to forget it as far as not dwelling on it [is concerned] and doing everything in your power to push it out of your mind whenever it comes back. Satan would love it if you kept dwelling on your guilt and trying to analyze how and why it happened. If he can keep you feeling guilty it will also keep you from reestablishing your relationship with God.

And eventually a person who refuses to forgive himself will try to find ways to excuse . . . or justify [himself]. It may take years before you find you can get through even one single day without remembering your sin, but it will happen. Do I sound like a person who has gone through a little guilt in my life? I am!

One more thing, and then I promise I will be done. I think I can understand now why going to [school] and getting away was so important and why you were so convinced that this was also God's will for you. When the guilt comes back, think about how faithful God was to provide that escape. He really did work a miracle for you.

Be sure that you don't fool yourself into thinking that just seeing [him] "less often" will solve everything.

God has given you the chance to really put step 3 in Greg's letter into practice. . . . You've only been gone for three weeks, and yet you have been home once with [him]—and this weekend [he] will be there visiting you. If God has provided a way of escape . . . you can't keep opening the door of temptation. You seem to be still trying to handle this in your own wisdom.

Don't you see that Greg is right—you need to make a complete break for at least six months to give God a chance to help both [of you]. In your heart . . . you know that [he] is spiritually weak, and I'm sure you've convinced yourself that maybe you're not so spiritually strong yourself.

And maybe you aren't as strong as you thought you were. But two spiritually weak people will never make one spiritually strong person. You can't give [him] the strength he needs. Only God can do that. You can't do that for [him] any more than I can do it for you. All I can do is remind you of what you already know.

If Satan hasn't already tried, he will try to convince you that you have spoiled any chance of waiting for God's best. Or he will try to convince you that [this boy] is God's best.

You know Satan is a liar, and God still wants His very best for you. Maybe it will be [him], or maybe it will be a minister, but you have to let go of [him] and open the doors again for God to work in your life. I don't care what's happened in the past with [him]. You don't owe [him] anything, but you owe God everything.

Please keep in contact with Greg Speck. Just having someone to write to about your struggles and doubts is going to help a lot. Greg could be the other escape God is offering. When you are really serious about only accepting God's best, God will keep offering help; and He'll send people into your life to keep encouraging you.

I love you, honey.

Mom

Shortly after her mom wrote that letter, I received another note from the college girl. And she was ecstatic! Why? Because she is seeing God work in her life through her family.

As you read this letter, I pray that God will soften your heart toward your own parents.

LETTER C

Dear Greg,

I want to thank you so much for writing back when you did. The timing was all in the Lord's will, and you could not even begin to realize how your one letter has been used this weekend.

I wish so much I could talk to you face-to-face and just give you the biggest hug and cry with you in joy!

Let me try to give you the whole picture because this truly is a miracle!

I'm going to college [and when your letter came], my mom opened it thinking it was more mail from other ministries, wondering whether she should send it to me or not. She read your whole letter, Greg, and my secret I'd ached with for so long crept into her, and she found out about it all.

In the meantime, [my boyfriend] was going to come up for the weekend so we could spend some time together (obviously we hadn't totally given each other up to the Lord yet). My mom gave him an envelope to give to me. In it was a letter to me and one to him. . . .

Greg, I cannot believe this happened. After reading my mom's letter, I was so relieved, so relieved, that she finally knew. The horror and pain was finally beginning to lift. My mom and I are very close, and I tell her everything but could not come to her with this problem.

I hope I'm not hogging your time by writing so much, but this is so beautiful the way it happened! I cannot thank you enough, Greg. [My boyfriend] and I thought a lot this weekend. We avoided the topic at first but then really had a good talk. We are going to take your advice, Greg. We are going to cut off our relationship. No letters, no phone calls, no seeing each other when I come home—for six months at least.

Greg, this is what I've been waiting for! I've heard the Lord telling me to break up and serve Him fully for so long! But I didn't obey. I didn't obey! And now, through all this hurt and pain, the terrible pain I've caused my mom, the awful hurt of really letting go [of him] and knowing I won't see him for so long, all of this hurts so bad, but God finally got through. I finally said, "Okay, Lord, it's Yours. Take it."

He had to pound me over the head. But I finally yielded, Greg! And it is wonderful. All my burdens are off of me. My horrible sin is gone! It doesn't haunt me anymore!

Greg, this is the most traumatic thing that's ever happened to me. I've never cried so much as I have this weekend. But I've never felt so happy and relieved either. This is really a big stepping-stone in my relationship to God—and I am so excited. I know it's going to be so hard, but I'm leaning on Him.

I prayed that He would hold me up by both of my armpits, 'cause I don't think I can do it any other way. I know I can't. I need all of my Lord's strength. . . .

Oh, and you asked about using parts of my letter for your book. Please use whatever you want. My heart goes out to so many girls, and I want them to make the right decision and to remain pure and to not make the mistake I did! If anything could be helpful, I want you to use. it . . .

I have the best mom in the whole world, and I love her so much. I'm rejoicing in Him too! In Christ's wonderful love . . .

God so desires to work in your life as well. Read the last part of her letter again. She doesn't want you to go through what she has gone through, and neither do I.

So go have a love affair with Jesus Christ. The pleasure you will get from being with, being used by, and being loved by the King of Kings and Lord of Lords will far surpass any love affair with another person.

Even if you're involved sexually now, it's not too late. Remember renewed virginity, which says, "Yes, I've done it, but from now on I'm seeking to glorify Christ with my body."

It's never too late, but why go through another day of pain when you could be free?

Fall in love with Jesus! He is Someone you can be with every moment of every day. He will listen to you. He loves you. And He won't dump you!

Questions to ask yourself:
1. Have you talked to your parents about sex?
2. What do they think your standards should be?
3. Why wouldn't you want your parents' advice?

7

It Can't Be
Happening to Me

(PREGNANCY—AND WHAT TO DO NOW)

What am I going to do?

"The test was positive. This can't be happening to me. Other people get pregnant, but I never thought I would. What am I going to do? What will Bill think? Will he still love me? How am I ever going to tell my parents? If I could only turn back the clock and do things differently! I don't want to have a kid—I just want to be a kid."

What should she do?

What would you do?

What have you done?

Before I relate some steps this girl can take to get help, let me first say what shouldn't be done. *Don't get an abortion.*

Immediately the girl may think, *How can I get out of this as fast as possible with the least amount of embarrassment?* Of course, the quick fix is abortion. In many cases there is a sense of relief immediately following the procedure. But women are now coming forward five to ten years later with tremendous emotional pain from their decision.

It's hard to believe that we actually murder children. And why? Mostly for convenience' sake. We don't want to be bothered by emotional trauma or physical discomfort or public humiliation.

Look at some children around you today. This is who you are killing when you get an abortion—not things, not even masses of tissue with potential. We are talking about lives with souls.

Did you know that at about:

18 days – the mouth begins to open
24 days – arms and legs are beginning to take shape
42 days – fingers are forming on the hand
67 days – hair is now growing
75 days – the baby is seeing

If a miracle is growing inside you, how could killing it even be an option? Do you know what I wish? I wish people had a little window to the womb. If people could only see babies in the womb, babies that are connected to their mothers, they wouldn't so quickly take life away from them.

An unborn baby is counting on your protection, love, and care.

The abortion clinic makes it sound so easy. No hassles. Well, it is easy for the doctor, and she or he is making good money. Some doctors specialize in abortion. They took an oath to save lives, but they're getting rich murdering babies. Abortion clinics are exploiting women, and you need to know some of the facts.

First, understand that abortion is a surgical procedure where there is the risk of complications. Here are some of the physical problems that women are experiencing as a result of abortions:

➤ Damage to the cervix
➤ Increased possibility of future miscarriages
➤ Premature births
➤ Tubal pregnancies
➤ Painful perforation of the uterus
➤ Inability to have children
➤ Infections

HOW AN ABORTION HAPPENS

At least 50 percent of all individuals who go into an abortion clinic never come out alive. They say it's a safe procedure for mothers, but it's deadly for your baby.

Would you like to know what your child goes through if it is aborted? Well, here's some info, but I warn you that this isn't pretty, and reading about these methods could cause some emotional trauma, especially if you or someone you know has already had an abortion.

RU-486

This is a drug that produces an abortion. It is taken the morning after having intercourse or after the mother misses her period. It is used up until the second month of pregnancy. It blocks a crucial hormone that causes the uterine lining to no longer provide food, fluid, and oxygen to the baby. Without this hormone the baby can't survive. Then a second drug is given that causes the uterus to contract, and the baby is expelled. There can be sickness, cramping, throwing up, and bleeding. When the abortion is complete the mother will see a tiny blob of tissue—her baby.

DILATATION AND CURETTAGE

In the dilatation and curettage method, several shots are given at the mouth of the womb to deaden the area so that the pain and discomfort are relieved—but not for the baby.

They have to dilate the cervix with a variety of instruments. Then they will take the curette, a long instrument shaped like a spoon, and push it into the uterus. The baby is then mashed and smashed into pieces and scraped from the wall of the uterus.

Now are you ready for this? The assisting nurse must put the parts together again to make sure they got everything so the mother doesn't get infected. At this point the baby doesn't have to worry about infection. As you can imagine, there is usually a lot of bleeding.

VACUUM OR SUCTION ASPIRATION

In vacuum aspiration, once again they need to dilate the cervix. But this time they insert a tube into the uterus. You may think this is better, but it isn't.

This instrument is like a vacuum cleaner in that it sucks the baby out of the uterus—but not in one piece. The suction is so strong that the child is ripped to pieces and deposited in a jar.

It's pretty difficult for the nurse to get all the pieces, because they are torn and don't have clean cuts. But after enough time the vacuum usually does a complete job.

SALINE INJECTION

This procedure has been largely replaced by the other methods for abortion. If this procedure happens it is usually done after four months. Why? Because a certain amount of fluid needs to have built up in the sac around the baby. A long needle is thrust through the abdomen into the sac. The abortionist will suck out some of the fluid and then inject a salt solution. The baby will swallow this.

The child starts to jerk and kick, suffering severely because they are literally being burned alive by the solution inside the womb. If there ever ought to be a safe, protected place, it should be the womb. I wish both parents had to watch this procedure.

It will take the child more than an hour to die. If the woman has been pregnant for five months or longer, she will feel the baby fighting and kicking to live.

Usually within twenty-four hours, she will go into labor and deliver this tortured baby, dead, with skin burned away.

But there is another problem. After all that suffering, the baby may still be born alive. Imagine wanting to live that much. The doctor or nurse will sometimes take this poor burned baby and place it in a corner to die. This will be somewhere out of sight, so no one has to watch.

Many times they will place a towel over the baby's face to induce suffocation. I think in other situations we would call this murder.

If the doctor wants to, she or he could try to save the baby, and it could be put up for adoption. But this rarely happens.

DILATATION AND EVACUATION

The dilatation and evacuation procedure is usually performed later in a pregnancy, usually after the third month. Plain and simple, they will take what resembles a pair of pliers and cut the baby piece by piece. The tough part is the head, which is usually the largest part and needs to be crushed to get it out. Although the discomfort may be minimal for the mother, it isn't for the baby.

PROSTAGLANDIN ABORTION

This is a hormone that induces labor. The baby usually dies from the trauma of the delivery. The baby can be born alive if old enough. To prevent this, some abortionists use ultrasound to inject a lethal drug into the baby's heart. Then they give the woman the hormone, and the baby is born dead.

DILATION AND EXTRACTION

This abortion is used when the woman is four to nine months pregnant. The abortionist inserts forceps and grabs one of the baby's legs, and the baby is pulled out of the birth canal except for the head. The baby is alive, and the abortionist hooks his fingers over the baby's shoulders and jams a blunt-tipped surgical scissor into the base of the skull and spreads the tips apart to enlarge the wound. A suction catheter is inserted into the baby's skull and the brain is sucked out. The head collapses and passes easily out of the woman.

I hope you see how sick and wrong it is to abort your baby. This is like medieval torture. Notice that I do not call these people that perform abortions *doctors*, because a doctor takes a pledge to protect life, and these people make a living off of killing babies.

We treat mass murderers better than babies who are being aborted. We execute people in kinder ways than we kill our babies. I don't get it; this is not a choice issue because the one who is really affected, the baby, isn't being consulted at all. I can understand how a teenager might want the baby's life ended out of convenience. A teenager is young, scared, and emotionally immature. But I have no idea how a medical professional could ever perform or justify abortions. How do these people sleep at night? I can tell you one thing: they are definitely counting on there being no God, heaven, or hell. One day they will be accountable for every baby who died at their hands. That includes nurses, receptionists, and everybody else who helped to maintain the abortion clinic.

EVERYONE IS HURT BY ABORTION

Here is a poem by a young woman who had an abortion:

> The tables they turned so quickly,
>   I was left with no time for thought.
> I'm not sure why I did it,
>   For regret is all it brought.
>
> I gave in for their reasons
>   Because I had none for myself.
> I heard the life inside me
>   Would be gone with nothing left.
>
> Me and the baby entered together,
>   Left alone once we were inside.
> I asked for this last time together
>   Before the baby of mine would die.
>
> I wondered if the baby could hear me
>   And knew this choice wasn't really mine.
> Then just as I whispered, "I'm sorry,"
>   I heard a knock and knew it was time.
>
> The pain I felt had made me scream
>   It was more than I could take
> But nothing could prepare me
>   For the emptiness that took its place.

If I have hurt your feelings, I'm sorry, but that hurt is nothing compared to the hurt caused to a child who is aborted.

We are outraged at the clubbing to death of baby seals, and we are crying out to save the whales. As noble as these two causes are, let's start with saving the babies.

We need teenagers like you who will be willing to speak out against abortion. Let's face it, we wouldn't dream of treating our dog or cat the way some of us have treated our own flesh and blood.

On a car I saw two bumper stickers: Save the whales and abortion on demand.

God speaks of the child growing in the womb as someone, not just some*thing*. Please get a Bible and read these verses. Then write down what the Bible says about that unborn child.

Psalm 139:13–16

Jeremiah 1:5

Luke 1:41–44

Isaiah 49:1

Proverbs 24:11–12

LAME EXCUSES

Even with all this spelled out, many still try to rationalize it. Here's what teens have said to me:

➤ *"What right do you have you to tell me this? It's my body!"*

No, it isn't. Look at 1 Corinthians 6:19–20: "Do you not know that your body is a temple of the Holy Spirit, who is in you, whom you have received from God? You are not your own; you were bought at a price. Therefore honor God with your body."

➤ *"What if my parents or pastor tell me to get an abortion?"*

We are to obey our parents unless what they say contradicts the Word of God. You cannot obey your parents if that entails murdering your child. But at the same time, don't be rude. Try to explain as kindly as possible what God is leading you to do. Remember that your parents are in crisis now too. They have what is called parental ego, and they are concerned about how their friends might react. They may be embarrassed also. As for a pastor who advises abortion, I'm saddened, but he is totally off and wrong in his advice if he recommends abortion. Regardless of what your parents or pastor say, you need to refuse to get an abortion. If they threaten to kick you out of the house, then contact me and I will find a family you can stay with.

➤ *"It's better to have an abortion than to have an unloved and unwanted child."*

Well, maybe unwanted and unloved by you. But there are hundreds and hundreds of couples who want to adopt a child and pour on their love. Get some counseling, love, and support. Allow others to serve you during the time of pregnancy. It is worth nine months of pregnancy in order for your baby to have life and a loving family.

➤ *"Even if abortions were illegal, women would get them anyway, and then their lives would be in danger. So it's better to have abortions in a safe, sterile environment."*

Let me give you another scenario. A mother wants to kill her three-year-old son, but to do that she has to go into a bad neighborhood where there is a chance that she will get hurt. So what's the solution? Pass a law so that she can kill her three-year-old son in a safe, clean environment.

I hope you'll think that's stupid too. But that is the rationale people are using for abortions. We want to make it safe for a mother to kill her child.

IF YOU'VE HAD AN ABORTION

Others have said completely different things to me. They express remorse.

"Greg, I made the worst mistake of my life. I had an abortion when I was a teenager, and now it is killing me. What do I do?"

For you who have already gotten an abortion, I want to share some thoughts with you.

1. *God loves YOU!* You made a mistake, and what you did was wrong, but that hasn't affected God's love for you. He has not rejected you, and I won't reject you.

2. *Face the fact that what you did was wrong and stop trying to make excuses.* Just because something is legal doesn't mean it is right. Face the fact that it is having an impact on your life and relationships in a negative way. A woman who has had an abortion never forgets. At best you cover it up for short periods of time. If you are going to be healed, then you need to remember and admit it was wrong.

3. *Come to God and repent.* Tell Him how sorry you are and agree with Him that what you did was a sin. He will forgive you and remove your sin from you, as far as the east is from the west.

4. *Forgive yourself.* For that you may need some help. You are no longer your own; God has bought you with a price. If He forgives you, who are you to hang on to the sin? Pray out loud and say, "God, thank You that I am forgiven, and right now I choose to forgive myself."

5. *Forgive others.* A boyfriend who didn't care about anything except having sex with you and who wanted the convenience of an abortion . . . people who encouraged you to get the abortion . . . the person who performed the abortion . . . the nurse(s) who assisted—forgive everyone the Lord brings to your mind.

6. *Get some help and counseling.* You can start with a trusted

friend, but then you need to open up to someone who has the skills to help you deal with everything you are feeling. Open the lid on your emotions and share everything you remember. Bring it all out into the light so that you can receive healing and freedom. It is good to cry and be broken before the Lord and others. Weeping can open the door to comfort. And it's better to cry with someone than to cry alone.

7. *Give your baby to Jesus.* Jesus loved children and He said in Luke 18:16, "Let the little children come to me, and do not hinder them, for the kingdom of God belongs to such as these." Maybe that means saying a prayer, or perhaps you will want to have a memorial service. Invite family and some friends, and have a youth pastor or senior pastor conduct the service. Or maybe you'll want to do something symbolic. You could play some worship music, sit in a chair, and picture yourself holding your baby. Then take your baby and lift it up to God and picture Him taking your child in His arms.

WHAT PREGNANT COUPLES CAN DO

If you are considering an abortion, I beg you on behalf of that life developing within you, *please* don't get the abortion. If your womb only had that window, I know you would be amazed and overwhelmed at what a miracle new life really is.

You say to me, "OK, Greg, then help me. What are the options?" Well, as I see it you really have three options:

> ➤ *Keep the child as a single parent.* To keep the child is a huge commitment, whether you are the father or the mother. More often than not, this needs to be a whole family decision because, realistically, your parents will take on a lot of responsibility.

> ➤ *Get married and have the baby.* Now let me be honest and tell you that the odds are really against you. More than 70 percent

of teen marriages end in divorce. The younger you are, the harder it is. Then add the pressure of a new baby, and it will be very tough.

But if you're ready to stick to your vow "till death do us part," marriage could work for you. If you're twenty now (remember, it's not unusual to live to be seventy), that means being married to the same person for fifty years. If you're still determined, then get as much help and support from your families as possible. If your parents are against the marriage, then don't get married. I believe that God works through our parents for our good, whether they are Christians or not.

Then get yourself some good marriage counseling. The couples who ask me to marry them must meet with me about eight times for two hours per session. In addition, they have outside work to do. I also recommend Family Life marriage conferences. They offer excellent preparation for marriage. See www.familylife.org.

➤ *Let the child be adopted.* Many wonderful, godly couples can't have children and are praying for the chance to adopt. This would be a tremendous sacrifice, I know, but you would be thinking of the baby's well-being above your own. Abortion leads to death and depression, but adoption leads to life and hope!

You're pregnant. It was a bad choice, but it's not the end of the world. Now let's make a good choice that's positive for everyone, including the baby. What do you do?

➤ *You need to tell your parents.* "But my dad will kill me!" Are you sure? Think of other crises that have occurred and how your parents responded. You may be very surprised at how well they respond to this. When you tell your parents, you don't have to be alone. Have your pastor, youth pastor, adult friend, teacher, or friend go with you.

➤ *Get things straight with God.* He has never stopped loving you. As a prodigal son or daughter, come back home. His forgiveness is complete. There is tremendous hope for the future. Your life isn't doomed.

What were you before you became pregnant, and what did you want to become? Well, it's still possible, because you've got a great God. Just decide not to be involved sexually anymore so that the next time you're pregnant it will be with your husband.

➤ *Talk to each other and to both sets of parents.* It would be good if both families got together and talked it out. The father needs to take on responsibility and at least bear some of the financial burden.

➤ *Go to your pastor and decide what steps should be taken within the body of Christ.* It would be good to go before the church and confess. That way you have the body of Christ coming to your support, and the problem's out in the open. You'll feel 110 percent better. And that's better than trying to sneak around or away.

➤ *Be patient with yourself.* You will go through several steps: denial, anger, fear, and finally acceptance. This may take awhile, but it will happen quicker if you are open and allow others to love and support you.

When you make the right decisions, you'll never regret them. Abortion is a horribly wrong decision you will live to regret.

Let me give you a twenty-four hour crisis pregnancy counseling hotline. If you are scared, alone, confused, or pressured, call 1-800-238-4269. They will find you help, plus give you some solid answers to your questions. Tell them Greg Speck told you to call. It's toll-free.

I have a good friend named Ruth who is a teenager. Ruth made a bad choice, and she became pregnant. I asked if she would write a letter about her experience that I could put in this book.

Thank you, Ruth, for caring enough to go through the heartache of putting this all down on paper for us. I know it's your prayer and mine that this will be of help and encouragement to other teens.

Dear Greg,

This has been one of the hardest letters I've ever written. I've tried over and over to try to get things to come out right, and they just haven't. Today I called a friend and explained to her that this was really getting to me. I knew I wanted to write, but it just wouldn't come together.

She gave me good advice. She told me to write from the heart. To forget all the big words and just write it as it comes out. "Let somebody else put the big words in for you later."

Well, that's what I'm going to try. Maybe this will all just be choppy and jumbled, and at this point I don't care if you even use it for your book. I just need to get it out as part of my own healing process. I realize that now.

I'm not sure why I had sex. Maybe it was the common "I don't really like myself" problem. Maybe I was looking for love. Maybe I just wanted to please him because if I didn't, I'd lose my boyfriend, and having a boyfriend was the "in" thing.

Maybe it was just curiosity. Maybe it was rebellion because sex was forbidden. Maybe it was peer pressure. Maybe it was all of those things together.

I know that he liked me. I liked him, and it felt good to be liked by someone. I don't say "loved," because I never really loved him, and I don't know if he loved me or not. Looking back now I don't think so, but I don't know what he felt for sure.

Whatever the reason was, we did have sex, and I know it was wrong. I knew it was wrong when it happened. I knew it was wrong long before it happened. I had even decided long ago that I would never have premarital sex, but I did. The guy I was dating was not a Christian, and I got farther away from God the longer we were going

together. I let my standards drop, and I rationalized myself into think-
ing it was OK just once, and nothing would ever happen.

In the back of my mind I knew once was all it took to get preg-
nant, but I thought that would never happen to me. I don't know why
I thought I was immune. I did get pregnant, and I told him about it
after I went to a clinic to find out for sure. He was truly shocked and
said, "I thought you took care of that."

Greg, I hate it when it gets to this part, because now I know
how precious life is and what a miracle babies are, but I told him real
casually, "I will take care of it. I'll just get an abortion," like it was the
thing to do on your typical Saturday afternoon.

He said he'd pay for everything. A couple of weeks later I told
him I'd changed my mind, and I wanted to have the baby. He told
me I would ruin his life and how he couldn't be a father now
because his whole life was ahead of him, and he was finally gradu-
ating and going out into the real world. He didn't speak to me after
that.

I went through a lot of counseling, and God worked on me a lot.
I had the baby and placed her for adoption.

It's been a year now since my baby was born—her birthday was
two days ago (three days after mine). Now she's one-year-old. They
tell me she's walking and has six teeth. ("They" meaning the adop-
tive parents.) She has curly hair—that's from her father.

I miss her, Greg. I haven't cried for her in a long time, but I am
now—sorry if the pages get wet.

Sometimes I cry out of happiness. From the two letters I've
received from her adoptive parents, I can tell they love her so much.
They do things with her. They're a real family. I could never have
given her that. Her dad reads to her, and she tries to turn the pages
—she can't quite do that yet.

She calls them Mama and Daddy. I have mixed feelings about
that. At first I was so happy for them. My first prayer is for her salva-
tion; my second is for them to grow together as a strong family—
and they're doing that.

I want her to know that they are her family. They are her mom and dad, who will be there when she cuts herself or scrapes her knee or throws up all over her bedroom floor. They'll clean it up, not me. I want them to know she is their daughter.

I won't knock on their door someday and demand her back. I won't search for her and kidnap her from school, never to be heard from again. And so, I am happy that she calls them Mama and Daddy, and yet it hurts deep down where I try not to feel anything.

It doesn't hurt like it did before. I have no real regrets or bitterness about adoption. I have worked through that, and God has healed me, but it hurts in a different way to know that she'll call someone else Mom on Mother's Day. You have kids, Greg. You can understand.

By now I'm done crying—you see, I really am a lot better. I don't sob endlessly anymore because of missing her. Most of the time I remember the good times—the days in the hospital when I held her and fed her, the times when I saw her smile and sleep so peacefully, the friends I've made through my pregnancy, and the lessons I've learned. These are all good things that I remember.

This has been a really heavy-duty letter, and it's not really book material. But it sure has made me feel a lot better.

I guess the thing I hate the most is the feeling that I could tell someone my whole story, but it wouldn't mean anything unless they knew me. I mean, I read books like yours, and I was stupid enough to do it anyway.

I had to learn from my own experience instead of someone else's. My dad says that real wisdom is being able to learn from someone else's mistakes rather than having to learn by making your own.

I don't mean this to be a "downer" about your book, Greg, because there are wise people out there who can learn from other people's mistakes—even mistakes of people they don't know. And for just one of them not to have sex, I'd write a whole book to send to you. I guess to one of those people I'd say, don't have sex because . . .

Obviously you could get pregnant. *Pregnancy is not fun for an unwed, confused, teenage girl. . . .*

Well, Greg, it is midnight, and I'm gonna call it quits. I feel a lot better. Thanks for being there for me, Greg—I love you. I pray for you often—don't forget that.

> *Love and prayers,*
> *Ruth*

Questions to ask yourself:

1. What will you do if you or someone you know becomes pregnant?
2. What are you doing to save the unborn?
3. Am I choosing to do what is right or what is easy?

8

Incest

(WHAT TO DO AND UNDERSTAND
IF YOU ARE AN INCEST SURVIVOR)

*"When I walk down the street I wonder if
people can see through me like a glass."*

I want to thank Scott Harrison for his insight and help with this chapter.

Today I am thinking about you who struggle with this situation, feeling so alone, so misunderstood, so hopeless.

Not a spiritual retreat goes by that, if I mention incest, at least two or three individuals come and talk with me. Both boys and girls are incest survivors.

Then there are the letters from teens who have been suffering silently. Let me share an excerpt from one letter I recently received.

> *There are things in my life that are so confusing and so painful that I have just longed for my death, and I feel like this because I can't picture myself living life with a never-ending feeling of agony. It is so very hard for me to wake up every morning and face the day. No, I will never take my own life, but I can't help but wish that some- one would.*
>
> *Sometimes I will cry and cry, and I just feel so helpless. I don't know what to do. All I can think about is my brother and why, why would he; how could he? And, oh, it is so devastating, and I am so*

empty inside, like I've been drained and he took everything wonder-
ful that I could feel at this time in my life.

Such a feeling . . . of violation, and anguish, and so much . . .
anger. If he could step inside of me and feel the pain in my heart and
confusion in my mind, it would drive him insane, absolutely insane!

When I walk down the street I wonder if people can see through
me like a glass. It scares me. They shan't ever know. And my family
. . . I want and need so much to be held close, wrapped up as secure
as a cocoon, and [to] know that I am safe from any more pain.

Of all the feelings I have ever known, it is my loneliness and grief
and personal tragedy that hold me . . . in such a vicious grip I can
not tell you! . . .

Never before have I reached so deep into my heart and pulled
out all that makes me what I am and shared this with anyone. I do
not have to face you, or be near you, or . . . see your reaction, so
this is not hard.

I shall hope that one day the battle that lies within me . . . will
come to rest so that I may heal and become everything that God
knows I am capable of becoming and the person I so desperately
desire to be!

Thank you for being such a friend.

Did your heart break as mine did when I read that letter? I want
to reach out, give this woman a hug, and tell her there is hope. This
chapter is for her and for all of you who feel caught in the incest
trap with no way to escape.

Allow me to share some thoughts with you. First of all, I have
not gone through what you have experienced, so I can't know exactly what you are feeling. But I have talked to and listened to many
teens who are incest survivors so I have their insights.

Let me start by dealing with a series of unanswered questions—
good questions like:

➤ What exactly is incest?
➤ Am I the only one?

➤ Why did it happen in our family?
➤ Why are my feelings so confused?
➤ Why not just forget it and go on?
➤ What can be done about it now?

WHAT EXACTLY IS INCEST?

Simply stated, incest is any sexually arousing contact between family members. It may include prolonged kissing, fondling of breasts or genitals, mutual masturbation, and/or oral, vaginal, or anal sex. It makes no difference how long it went on or how innocent in nature it appeared. Any inappropriate sexual contact between family members is considered incestuous.

One way incest is often categorized is by the relationship involved. Although father-daughter incest is the most reported, it is thought that brother-sister incest happens most frequently. Few of these cases get reported, however, since many times they involve sexual experimentation between children of similar ages.

Other types include every imaginable family relationship, including a stepparent. Legally speaking, incest is a felony and can be punishable by a prison sentence.

AM I THE ONLY ONE?

No, you are not alone and you need to hear that it is not your fault. I will deal with this more later on in the chapter.

You may feel extremely alone emotionally, but there are literally millions of others who have gone through or are going through similar situations. The irony of it is that you may see each other every day and not know your common bond. They may sit next to you in class or go to your church. No doubt you have talked with them. All the while both of you are pretending that everything is OK, and in the back of your minds each is saying, "If you only knew . . ."

If you are an incest survivor the shame is not yours; the shame is on the person who abused you.

Not only are you not alone, but yours is not the only social class, economic level, race, religion, or neighborhood affected. Incest is no respecter of persons. It cuts through all such barriers, just as it has since Bible times. (Laws concerning incest go all the way back to Leviticus! You can read about it in Leviticus 18.)

You are definitely not alone. Many who are younger, many who are older, and thousands who are just your age, are experiencing the same hell that you have lived in.

WHY DID IT HAPPEN IN OUR FAMILY?

Although it is helpful to know that you are not alone, it is far more important to hear the second statement that all survivors need to know. If you forget every other word of this chapter, don't forget these four: *IT'S NOT YOUR FAULT!*

Write them down, put them over your mirror, scribble them on the back of your wallet picture, write a song about them! How can I say with such confidence that it is not your fault? Because it is impossible for incest to *ever* be the child's fault!

Let me illustrate this very important point by telling you a parable.

One day a man walked into a nice restaurant to have dinner. The menu was filled with pictures of all their finest delectables. There was only one problem. The man's doctor had forbidden him to eat desserts. But he rationalized that he could make up for it tomorrow, and besides, it had been a very stressful day. So after his meal he chose a piece of banana cream pie for dessert.

After he'd thoroughly enjoyed his first few bites, his conscience began to bother him. A second later he threw down his fork and screamed for all to hear, "It's the pie's fault!" He began to scream at the pie, complaining that the pie had caused him to blow off his diet and get in trouble with his doctor.

Do you see the point of this silly illustration? Just as it is impossible for a piece of pie to be guilty of making anyone decide to go off a diet, it is also impossible for an incest survivor to be guilty of the abuser's decision to abuse them.

No matter how you rationalize that you may have "led them on" or in any way contributed to the occurrence, it is still your abuser's responsibility to decide and act.

As one victim aptly put it, "If they [the fathers] don't commit it [the incest], it doesn't happen." May I repeat, incest is *not* and *cannot* be the child's fault.

So why did the incest happen? This simple question can only be given a complex answer.

In most cases the incest is just the final large explosion of little "land mines" that had been ready to go off for quite some time. Some of these were set during the parent's own childhood. Many abusers were abused themselves as children.

However, not all abusing parents were victims. Many of the mines were set during the parent's marriage.

Little mines commonly found in both parents are low self-image, poor communication, little or no problem-solving skills, unrealistic marital expectations, and an inability to handle change or stress.

The father's minefield often includes being very authoritarian, extremely possessive, violent, and a substance abuser, lacking impulse control, and always in need of emotional fulfillment.

This abusing father's wife (the mother) often has mines of extreme dependency, immaturity, and coldness in her relationship with her daughter. This "relational gap" is usually created through a role reversal, where the mother in effect becomes the little girl, and the little girl is expected to fill her mother's shoes. She has to clean, cook, take care of her smaller brothers and sisters. As a whole, the family tends to isolate itself from the rest of society. The family can appear to be perfect on the outside. Mom and Dad can be involved in all kinds of committees, groups, be in church leadership, and be respected by the community. There is pressure to maintain this perfect image, but on the inside there is this terrible secret of sexual abuse.

It is the combination of these many typical characteristics, or land mines, all exploding at once that blow the doors wide open for incest to occur. However, don't allow all this verbiage to cause you to forget the main point. There are reasons for why they did what they did, but there is no excuse for their actions. What they did was terrible and wrong.

Moms and dads are the ones in charge in the family, and it is their responsibility to protect and care for you. No child should ever have to put up with the horrors of incest.

In other words, *IT'S NOT YOUR FAULT!*

WHY ARE MY FEELINGS SO CONFUSED?

Because the very people who I should be able to count on to love and protect me are the ones who have hurt me, I am not sure how to react or what to do. You may have hundreds of thoughts and emotions running through you, like:

➤ You thought it was okay because your family said they cared about you.

➤ You were looking for love but were made an object of lust.

➤ You wanted protection from the outside world but instead were abused by your inner circle.

➤ You were only a child but were treated as an adult. In most cases it felt good to have emotional needs met, but not in that way.

➤ You hated the act but at times could enjoy the power that it brought.

➤ Perhaps there was the enjoyment of natural physical sensations, yet terrible guilt came with it.

➤ There may have been the disgust of knowing a "public" dad and a "private" dad.

➤ The fear of becoming pregnant, yet there was assurance that it couldn't or wouldn't happen.

➤ Wanting desperately to tell, yet facing the potential frustration and embarrassment of not being believed.

➤ Wanting to tell, yet feeling responsible for "holding the family together" by not telling.

➤ Wanting to tell, but not wanting to hurt Mom or be hurt by Dad.

➤ Hoping and praying for things to change but living with cracked hopes and broken promises.

➤ Wanting to run away but not being old enough.

➤ Begging for support from Mom but getting a cold shoulder.

➤ Wanting the incest to stop with you but not wanting it to start with your siblings.

➤ Detesting your own family and being jealous of "normal" ones.

➤ Feeling in the pit of despair yet not allowing yourself to dwell on it.

➤ Looking for a true apology but getting only a series of rationalizations.

➤ Trying hard to forget but interrupted so often by flashbacks or nightmares.

➤ Wanting to find help but not believing anything can really be done.

➤ Searching for healthy relationships but feeling unable, "already used," and unclean.

➤ Wanting to scream, but nothing coming out; to cry, but no tears to be found; to die, but your heart keeps pumping.

The bottom line is that no one can go through such a mixture of experiences and not feel mixed up emotionally. The value in knowing this is that it keeps you from thinking you are some kind of emotional freak.

What emotions are you experiencing—fear, hate, anger, confusion, guilt, shame, disgust, loyalty, sadness, apathy, jealousy, depression, love, hopelessness, concern? You probably could add more to this list. What about the feelings of pleasure? Even in the worst of situations you can sometimes feel pleasure, and there is a tendency to think, *What kind of a pervert am I to have experienced some pleasurable feelings?* This can easily lead to self-hatred. But the truth is that it isn't unusual for an incest survivor to have felt some pleasure, either emotional or physical or both. There is nothing wrong with you at all. But all these emotions need to be worked through. If you don't get help, then they will continue to haunt you.

As a matter of fact, the degree of emotional confusion can be directly related to the type of incest, the length of the incestuous period, your age at the time, and the amount of treatment you have already received.

If the reality of emotional confusion is never faced, emotional healing will never come. It is important that you don't try to work these emotions out on your own. You will need to trust someone who has the skills to help you work through all the emotions that are spinning around inside of you.

WHY NOT JUST FORGET IT AND GO ON?

There are two good reasons why you can't just forget about the incest and go on with life.

The first is probably obvious to you from your own experience. You simply can't forget. It's just not possible. It would be like trying to forget your name. It simply becomes part of who you are. Though this is difficult to accept, you must understand this truth: you will always be a survivor—a triumphant survivor is my hope and prayer.

The second reason you can't just forget and go on is that you bear what one survivor calls the "invisible scars" that become the trademark of incest victims. These scars make it impossible to forget.

No doubt the ugliest scar of all is that of a poor self-image. This is brought on by a tremendous sense of guilt for having been involved in something that was against your conscience. Even though it is false guilt (since incest is never the fault of the child), it is close enough to the real thing to become a terrible emotional weight, and it robs you of any self-worth.

So your mind sends a message to your heart: "You're no good

and you're of no use to anyone." This message can affect every part of your life if you don't get help.

Later on you might have the desire to run away or to marry at an early age. It can cause difficulty in forming intimate relationships with friends or the opposite sex. You might not care about you or your body and end up becoming a prostitute. (One study of adolescent female prostitutes found that 75 percent had been survivors of incest.) It can lead to deep depression and even suicide.

How do you numb that deep emotional pain? You may turn to excessive drinking, drug abuse, or cutting yourself. There can be sleep disturbances, sexual dysfunctions, eating disorders, and the sad possibility of passing the abuse on to the next generation.

> *One of the characteristics of being a follower of Jesus Christ is allowing others to love and serve you.*

Although the incest can never be forgotten, some victims still try to cope by "just ignoring it." Some develop creative techniques like never sitting still long enough to think, stubbornly denying it ever happened, or even focusing all their energies on solving others' problems. All are diligent exercises in futility. Sooner or later the makeup wears off, and the ugly scars are exposed.

This is why you just can't forget it and go on.

WHAT CAN BE DONE ABOUT IT NOW?

For most survivors the words, "What can be done about it now?" are not asked as a sincere question but rather as a hopeless declaration. I trust that you don't want to fit into this category, because it is this kind of attitude that keeps most "survivors" from ever becoming "triumphant survivors."

Many get caught in the trap of only thinking of the act of incest itself. They say, "It's over now, and besides, I can't change the fact that it happened." That's right; you can't change the past, but you can stop the past from ruining your present future.

There is a way out! Incest survivors are stepping out from their basements of despair and into a future of hope and promise. You may be tempted to stay where you are because this is what you are used to or comfortable with. You have all your defense mechanisms in place and you feel safe there. Stepping from the basement can feel scary and uncertain. You don't want to live through the memories of the pain. But whether you step out or not, you are still going to be dealing with the memories. The question you need to ask is, "Do I want to deal with the memories as part of a healing process or sitting alone in my emotional basement?"

With the help of someone skilled in this area I want to see you take five steps.

1. *Assign blame where blame belongs.*

Every incest survivor is confronted with two major options of where to assign blame. Is it your fault or is it the fault of the person who abused you? Initially so many want to blame themselves. "It must have been something I said or did that made this person want me sexually." But that is a lie from the pit of hell. If I brought a little girl to you who had been sexually abused by a family member, and asked you to tell her whose fault it was that this happened to her, what would you say? Would you tell her it was her fault? No, you would take her in your arms and tell her that it wasn't her fault. You must give yourself the same counsel. Right now I want you to say out loud, "It was my [brother's, father's, stepparent's, mother's or sister's] fault." That is the truth, and that is the first step to freedom. John 8:32 says, "Then you will know the truth, and the truth will set you free."

You'll know that this transfer has been accomplished when you can honestly say, "I truly believe the incest was not my fault at all." Remember the little girl who you are talking to; is it possible that any part of the abuse was her fault? *No, no, no!*

I also want you to know that God hates sexual abuse. He will punish the person who did this to you, and His punishment will be just. No one gets to walk away after sexually abusing someone without suffering emotionally, physically, spiritually, and/or financially. You may not see it but they will experience God's judgment.

Don't misunderstand me. I'm not asking you to disown your father or even to throw darts at his picture. I'm saying that your healing won't begin until you understand it is the abuser's responsibility, not yours.

2. *Know that God's plan for your life includes healing from the sexual abuse.*

Jesus deeply loves you. God has a purpose, plan, and destiny for your life, and that includes victory over sexual abuse. He can take the worst of situations and turn them around for good. I want you to rest in the arms of Jesus and know His love, comfort, and peace. "Peace I leave with you; my peace I give you. I do not give to you as the world gives. Do not let your hearts be troubled and do not be afraid" (John 14:27).

God wants to raise up for you a wonderful counselor who will help you to take the steps you need to take. He will be with you every step of the way. Hang on to Jesus.

3. *Forgive your abuser.*

The purpose of transferring the blame is not to transfer hate. You want to forgive them so that you are free to become everything Jesus Christ created you to be. You might say to me, "I will never forgive them; you don't understand what they did to me." You are right; I don't understand what they did to you, and I can't possibly know what it is like to be in your shoes. But when you refuse to forgive I want you to keep these things in mind.

Think of all the things you have done that were wrong, said that were wrong, and how sick your thought life has been at times. When have you ever come to Jesus and said, "I am so sorry. Would You please forgive me?" to hear Him answer, "Forget it!" Never! He has always forgiven you and loved you. Because you are greatly forgiven you can also forgive others.

When you refuse to forgive, it makes you cold and hard on the inside. It begins to kill you emotionally and spiritually. Your heart becomes hard and you stop caring. You don't care about others, you don't care about God, and you don't care about yourself. In the end you become a lonely, miserable individual. I heard this quote: "Refusing to forgive is like trying to hurt an enemy by drinking poison." All you end up doing is hurting yourself.

When you refuse to forgive, you allow this person to continue to manipulate you. The memories continue to haunt you and hurt you emotionally. Those memories can lead to destructive and at-risk behavior. Do not allow this person to continue to control you. They may not deserve forgiveness but you forgive them, not because they deserve it, but so you can be free. They may even deny the fact that they abused you. This is a very sick and evil person who would do this, but you need to forgive them anyway. Not for their sake necessarily, but for your sake.

> *Refusing to forgive is like trying to hurt an enemy by drinking poison.*

You'll know you've taken this step when you can say to your abuser, "I understand that what you did to me was wrong, but by the grace of God I choose to forgive you." (If your abuser is no longer living, you may simply write them a letter to this effect, sign it, and then burn it.)

4. *See yourself through the eyes of God.*

Your value comes from who you are in Christ and not what you have done or what has been done to you. You are a wonderful, special, gifted, talented, beautiful creation of God. None of this changes because someone hurt you.

What if I offered you a one-hundred-dollar bill? Would you be happy to take it? What if I stepped on it first or crumpled it in my hand or smeared it with dirt—would you still take it? Of course you would, because it is still worth one hundred dollars. You have been abused but that doesn't affect your value as a person. You are someone of great worth and value. The more you see yourself through the eyes of God, the more you will realize this. How do you discover who you are in Christ? By studying God's personal love letter to you, the Bible. All the promises are for you and all the truths apply to you. Remember God's promise we looked at earlier? If you know the truth then the truth will set you free. You are wonderful, and that is the truth!

5. *Turn open wounds into scars.*

Often wounds will remain, such as low self-esteem, non-assertiveness, sexual dysfunction, distrust of the opposite sex, poor communication skills, flashbacks, and depression. Working through these issues will enable you to deal with the everyday struggles without gaping wounds draining your energy before you can even get started.

In high school I received a very severe knee injury while playing baseball. I had to have knee surgery, and I had a huge wound. For a while all I could think about was the pain of the wound, but they kept changing the bandages and working with me until that wound became a scar. I still have the scar, though I hardly ever think about it. When I remember it, the emotional trauma is gone. It can be the same for you. Every time you are willing to get help and open up, it is like changing the bandage, and you are on the way to healing.

There are excellent godly counselors who are trained to help people heal from the wounds of incest. Get some help so you can be free. But keep this in mind: it is better to have a competent non-Christian counselor than an incompetent Christian counselor.

IN CONCLUSION

First, these steps can't be taken overnight—or in any shortcut fashion. Remember, any cost for your total healing is worth it.

Second, like I said before, you shouldn't take these steps alone. You'll need an outsider who knows how to deal specifically with incest. This toll-free number can put you in touch with people in your area who will assist you in finding help: 1-800-422-4453 or go to their Web site at www.childhelp.org, and you will find more information to help and encourage you.

I also want to add the fact that physical and emotional abuse is wrong. If your parents or boyfriend is slapping, slugging, pushing, kicking, or throwing you—that is wrong. When a person is being physically abused I ask them, "Whose fault is it that you are being abused?"

They often say, "It's my fault. If I didn't make them mad they wouldn't hit me." That is false. If you are being physically abused, you need to seek out some help. If it is a boyfriend, you need to break off the relationship. Any man that physically attacks a woman is sick.

Emotional abuse is also wrong. I had a girl come to me and say, "My mother told me that if they had it to do all over again they would have gotten an abortion." That is emotional abuse. If your parents or the person you date say things like, "Shut up," "You're an idiot," "You're worthless," "You're pathetic," or "You're stupid," that is wrong. So is swearing and other cruel language. Talk to some people and get help. If it is a person who you are dating, end the relationship.

In closing, I want to add that God loves you just the way you are. There is nothing you can do that will make Him love you any more or any less than He loves you right now. He knows what it feels like to suffer; He knows what it feels like to be all alone; He knows what it feels like to be rejected, and He knows you better than you know yourself. He is waiting and wanting to comfort and care for you.

Have you responded to His love for you? If you haven't, please check out chapter 17 and make the decision today.

Questions to ask yourself:
1. Whose fault is it that you were abused?
2. Who do you trust and respect enough to talk to about this?
3. Have I been seeing myself through the eyes of the abuser or through the eyes of Jesus Christ?

9

Rape

(WHY IT HAPPENS AND WHAT TO DO)

When you aren't prepared, then the
chances of rape greatly increase.

Ask a woman, "What's one of the worst things that could happen to you?" and more often than not, she will say rape.

Most of us don't want to talk about rape, because it is such an ugly subject. But we have to talk about it. It may happen to us or to someone we know. Each year more than 80,000 women report being raped, but it's estimated that more than 900,000 never report the attack. And this in one year! Also we are seeing an increase in the number of men being raped by other men.

If you deny that rape could ever happen to you, then you are not preparing yourself for the possibility. When you aren't prepared, then the chances of rape greatly increase.

WHO MIGHT RAPE ME?

The mental picture most of us have is of a dirty, gross individual who hides in alleys, ready to grab a victim. Yes, those people exist, but do you also realize that more than 50 percent of those raped know the person who does it?

For example, you need to be aware of date rape. Girls are being raped by the very men who are taking them out.

Certain men will feel justified in forcing you to have intercourse with them if any one of these four things has occurred:

➤ If he gets excited. (We have already learned that men tend to be visually oriented. You could have excited him by just walking to the car, having done nothing inappropriate at all.)
➤ If he feels you have been leading him on.
➤ If you have previously messed around a little.
➤ If you said yes but later changed your mind.

Understand that, from the man's point of view, he may not consider this rape. He may feel that if anyone is at fault, it's you!

But the fault is not yours—it is his! No man has a right to touch you without your permission. Only a sick man would ever force himself on a woman.

> *Do not settle for anything less than God's very best for your life.*

But these facts only solidify the truth that you had better know the person you are dating. Bonnie and I have a friend named Nancy. She says she would be insulted if a guy just called her on the phone and asked her out if she didn't really know him. Why? Because obviously he was mostly just attracted to her appearance.

Let me make some suggestions that will certainly lessen the likelihood of being attacked.

➤ Date only Christians.

I can hear it now. "But there are hardly any Christians around me, and those I do know I really don't want to go out with!" Look, you have trusted Jesus Christ with your eternity, so you can trust Him with your dating life. He knows your needs better than even you do. So don't just talk about trusting Jesus—actually trust Him.
➤ Be friends first.

Get to know a man before you go out with him. Invite him over to your house, and let him meet your parents. He is less likely to attack you if he has developed a relationship with your parents.

➤ Don't date alone.

Go out on group dates, or at least double-date. That way you'll have other individuals around. It's always better to be safe. Find a place you can get by yourselves in a crowd. Do not isolate yourself in a car or house.

WHY DO THEY WANT TO RAPE ME?

Most men do not rape for sexual reasons. They rape because . . .

➤ They want to feel important. They may have a poor self-image or feelings of inferiority, and to rape a woman makes them feel powerful and significant.

➤ They may be angry—angry at their mother or sisters. Maybe they're angry because of some embarrassment they have experienced at the hands of a woman, so they are getting even.

➤ They want to be in control. They have been dominated in the past, and this is their opportunity to dominate someone else.

➤ They want to inflict pain. There are sadistic individuals who derive pleasure from hurting someone else.

➤ They want to belong. In the case of gang rape, they can be accepted by a group. If they don't participate, they might be rejected.

When you understand some of the reasons for rape, you discover that rape is not primarily sexual; it is an act of violence. There are hardly any similarities between rape and sexual intercourse in a loving marriage relationship.

Realize that a rapist is most often looking for a woman who is weak and vulnerable. So in a dating situation, be firm. Don't try to be kind. "Well, I don't want to hurt his feelings," women tell me. Go ahead and hurt his feelings, because he is seeking to hurt more than just your feelings.

If he senses you are unsure, confused, or fearful, he may try to take advantage of you. Remember that any man who tries to rape you is certainly not in love with you.

WHERE DOES RAPE USUALLY OCCUR?

The three most likely places for rape are:

➤ Your house or apartment
➤ A car
➤ His house or apartment

You see, for a man to rape you, he needs to somehow get you isolated. So don't let that happen.

Don't park with him. Don't get caught at each other's place when nobody is home. Here are some other suggestions:

➤ Whatever you do, don't hitchhike. You don't know who is going to pick you up.
➤ When traveling alone, always check the backseat of the car before you get in.
➤ If you're outside at night, stay in lighted places. Don't take shortcuts through dark, isolated areas like alleys and parks.
➤ If you sense you are being followed, go to a public place and call the police. Don't go home if you are being followed, because then he will know where you live.
➤ In other words, be careful.

WHAT SHOULD I DO
IF I AM ATTACKED?

I wish I could tell you one thing to do that always works if you are attacked. But I can't. Each rapist is different, and each is raping for different reasons. What works for one person may not work for another. I can give you six possible options. I'm sure there are more, but at least these will give you some ideas.

Before I list these, please know that it's important for you to stay as calm as possible. Now I know that's easy for me to say, but I say it for two reasons. First, if you panic, you may excite him. You will be meeting his expectations. He knows that a weak and vulnerable woman will react that way. But if you can remain calm, that communicates strength to him.

And second, you've got to *think*, and you won't be able to do that if you're out of control. So what are some options?

> Pray out loud.

Ask God to protect you and make His presence known. Pray for your attacker and for his soul. Quote Scripture that you have memorized. The Word of God is powerful and sharper than any two-edged sword. There is a good possibility that the rape is demonically inspired. In that case prayer and the Word of God are your best weapons.

> Be personal.

Tell him some things about yourself so that he can see you as some*body* and not some*thing*. Show some concern for him. There are probably areas in his life that he is struggling with. You want him to see you as more than just an object. Calling him terrible names will just make him angrier.

> Be gross.

Stick your finger down your throat and throw up all over yourself. Pick your nose. Put the mucus on your face, or eat it. Urinate on yourself and wherever you are. Cause some concern and confusion on his part by asking him questions like, "Have you ever had herpes?" "Do you want to get AIDS?" "Does it matter to you if I have a sexually transmitted disease?" or "You want to do this if I'm having my period?" You want to seek to be disgusting and do things that will make you less attractive to him.

➤ Be bizarre.

Pretend you have snapped mentally. Act strange.

➤ Play along.

You could momentarily play along, as though this is something you enjoy and want. You are doing this so that he will relax, let down his guard, loosen his grip, and you can escape. But it's important that you have somewhere to escape to. If he has isolated you—if you're parked out in the middle of nowhere—then this won't work. (Remember that this scenario and the others require you to be an actress, and you had better be good. If he senses that you are trying to trick him, he can become even more hostile.)

➤ Counterattack.

You can try physical violence yourself. But if you decide to do this, you are going to have to really hurt him. He has got to be stunned long enough for you to get away. Again, this won't work if you have nowhere to run.

Take a sharp object—pencil, pen, key, nail file, scissors, tweezers—and jam it as hard as you can into his eye. If you are successful I guarantee this will immediately stop the rape. Or grab his testicles and squeeze hard. If you do this as hard as you can, he will experience tremendous pain. The rape attempt will stop, and you should have a few moments to get away. But it's important that you don't just lie there. Push or kick him out of the way and move quickly.

I warn you that you are taking a tremendous risk. If you fail to hurt him enough to get away, he can do terrible damage to you. Then it boils down to whoever is more violent wins, and that will usually be the man.

You stand a much better chance if you have had some training in self-defense. Even with that, it's going to be very difficult. When prisoners in jail for rape were asked what they would do if a woman fought back, about 50 percent said they would let her go. But the other 50 percent would have become more violent.

I suggest you take this step if you believe your attacker is going to kill you. At that point you really have nothing to lose.

HOW DO I KNOW IF I'VE MADE THE RIGHT CHOICE?

If you're alive, you've made the right choice. Many women never live through this ordeal.

WHAT DO I DO IF I'M RAPED?

➤ Get to a safe place.

If you're with him in the car, promise anything as long as you can leave. Go to a gas station, restaurant, market, anywhere there are people, so that you can get some protection.

➤ Get some support.

Call someone to come to be with you right away, perhaps your parents. They will certainly need to know. Or call your youth pastor, pastor, or friend. Don't go through the next several hours alone.

➤ Call the police.

They must be notified. If possible, this guy needs to be caught. You don't want him to do this to some other girl and have her go through what you're going through now.

But don't touch anything. Don't wash, comb your hair, brush your teeth, change your clothes, or try to clean yourself up. You could destroy important evidence. You'll desperately want to shower, but don't!

In the past I was one of the volunteer chaplains for the Rockford, Illinois, police department, and we were trained in this area. Police make a big effort to be sensitive and kind to someone who has gone through rape.

➤ Go to the hospital.

Go even if you don't think you need to. Most women are in shock at this point, and you really do need to be checked out. If for no other reason, they want to make sure you haven't picked up any disease or infection, and they want to gather evidence in case you want to prosecute.

➤ Get some counseling.

You're going to need some help in the days and weeks to come. You will feel so much better if there is someone who can not only weep with you but also help you sort through the emotions.

➤ Allow others to serve you.

One attitude of a servant of Christ is that of allowing others to serve you. You need to surround yourself with family and friends who will continue to just love you with unconditional love.

➤ Be patient with yourself.

It's going to take time, but, yes, you can recover. Be patient with yourself, because recovery doesn't happen overnight.

Men, never force yourself on a woman. If you do, you are a sick man and a rapist.

I want you to know that I get very angry at men who do this. In conclusion let me mention two facts for those of you who have been raped:

1. This is not your shame but rather the shame of the one who did this terrible thing to you. Even though you may have led him on, dressed seductively, teased him, and got yourself

into a bad situation, a man never has the right to force himself on you. *Never*. Rape is never justified.

2. You are still a virgin. "What? How can you say that, Greg?" Because no one can take your virginity. That is something you freely give. The same is true for an incest survivor. After being raped, you can feel like your virginity was stolen from you, so you don't care anymore. You may get the idea that sex just becomes something you do during a date. You may feel cheap and gross, but the truth is that you are wonderful and beautiful.

It is time you stop allowing others to use you and begin to take a stand for purity. God will allow you to start all over again. Many who have been in your shoes have become sexually active, but now you know the truth, so don't. Starting now, honor God with your body and refuse to compromise. You can be different because Jesus Christ gives you the power to be different.

My prayer is that none of you will ever have to experience rape, although unfortunately many already have. But at the same time I must stress the importance of being prepared. Think ahead. Be aware, so that if it does come, you'll be better able to deal with the situation. Better yet, you'll hopefully know how to avoid it altogether.

Questions to ask yourself:
1. Men, is it ever OK to force yourself on a woman?
2. Women, if a man tries to rape you, what will you do?
3. What would you say to someone who has been sexually assaulted?

10

What's the Virtue in Virtual Sex?

(PORNOGRAPHY IS ADDICTIVE)

We don't even need to search for it because it will find us.

Years ago if you were interested in pornography you would need to get into your car and drive to a bad neighborhood. You would have to park and walk down the street to the store, looking over your shoulder to see who was watching. If you were underage you couldn't get into the store. Then there was the embarrassment of being there with other men looking through the stuff. If you decided to buy something, you would have to face the embarrassment of the clerk seeing the materials that interested you. After an experience like that you would probably feel dirty and disgusting.

Today all you need to do is go into your room, shut the door, and turn on the computer. Every sick, evil, and degrading act is available for your viewing at the touch of a button. Virtual sex bombards the Internet. We don't even need to search for it because it will find us. Seemingly innocent advertisements open up to the world of sexual perversion. But the similarity remains between years ago and today—in the end you will still feel dirty and disgusting.

Sexual interest and curiosity is starting earlier and earlier. We get more sexual information at a younger age but less training in moral responsibility and good decision making in this area. Media exposes us to sex every chance it gets. How many comedies or dramas do you watch on TV that promote sexual humor or suggestions? How many advertisements do you see that use sex to sell a product? How many music videos include people in different stages of undressing and sexual involvement? How many times do you see sexual involvement portrayed in a movie?

Many people who would never consider being sexually active with a living being are caught in the trap of virtual sex. They rationalize that this is better then the real thing, and it really isn't hurting anyone. We will debunk that myth in a moment. These people live in a fantasy world of sexual adventures, trying to meet their needs through . . .

Pornography,
Soap operas,
Romance novels that are secular,
Chat rooms,
Strip clubs,
Voyeurism (peeking at other people),
900 numbers,
Exhibitionism (exposing yourself in front of other people), and
Massage parlors.

Cybersex is exploding in the United States and around the world. It is a multibillion-dollar business in the U.S. alone. There are over four million porn sites on the Internet, and every day they receive over sixty million hits. But remember Colossians 3:5–6. "Put to death, therefore, whatever belongs to your earthly nature: sexual immorality, impurity, lust, evil desires and greed, which is idolatry. Because of these, the wrath of God is coming."

Is this just a search for sexual images? I don't think so; instead I think we are all searching for intimacy with the opposite sex. We want to connect with someone and have them like us as we like them. But that is scary, and we have to risk being rejected. I was once turned down because my prospective date said she had to wash her roommate's hair. Relationships are hard and take a lot of work even if you find a good Christian to date. But we don't like things that take a lot of work; we want something that feels good—and feels good immediately—so we turn to virtual sex. It all ties in with our impatience, desire for intimacy, and the pace of our instant society. We have instant cash, instant replays, instant food, and so we want instant intimacy. You make the choice: do you only want sexual lust for tonight or sexual love for a lifetime in marriage? We give up instant gratification and learn self-control for tonight—then in marriage we can experience the greater satisfaction of purity, love, and sex.

Virtual sex might seem to be the answer because of the force of sexual desire and sexual attraction. The media puts their stamp of approval on it, and peer pressure makes it seem like everyone is getting a quick fix. So we deal with our problem by creating a bigger problem for ourselves. We think the cure for intimacy and sexual desire is to feed our sexual desire. It's like seeking a cure for the common cold by giving yourself cancer. It turns out that the cure is the killer.

Virtual sex creates a fantasy world in our minds. Everything plays out exactly the way we want it to. So every woman is interested in us and is ready to do anything, at any time, and loves doing it. Every man is good-looking with six-pack abs. They have the ability to take the women to the very heights of sexual ecstasy.

So would I rather live in reality where the opposite sex doesn't seem to respond to me, or do I retreat to my fantasy world? Each day the fantasy world looks better and better. I never have to deal with rejection or be disappointed. It looks good on the outside, but it leaves you empty on the inside. Yet we continue to retreat deeper and deeper into our fantasy world. Pretty soon we are addicted to it.

We all have sexual feelings, which are natural. When those sexual feelings become the most important part of our lives, then we become sexually addicted. You will find yourself living for the sexual high. At school you will think about it and look forward to escaping into this world. Relationships, studies, and sports all take a backseat to this addiction. The sexual feelings will begin to control you instead of you controlling the feelings.

We know men are visually oriented and women tend to be touch oriented, so we may conclude that men are the only ones seeking after porn, but this simply isn't true. More and more women are searching the Internet for pornographic images. Why are we seeing more and more women drawn to virtual sex? I think there can be a lot of reasons, like curiosity, fascination, information, peer pressure, sexual excitement, lusting, and loneliness. A woman can become just as addicted to porn as any man. They may seek it for different reasons and think about it differently, but it has the power to control them just the same.

Alcohol and heroin addicts have said that pornography is a worse addiction and harder to overcome than their drug of choice.

Do you see this all as harmless fun? Something to do to help you relax or release stress?

This is not harmless at all; it destroys you emotionally and spiritually. You might think you are in control, but just the opposite is true. You are a slave to whatever controls you.

Satan takes everything God created and seeks to distort and pervert it. God created sex to be *very* good. Satan has taken something that is very good and made it seem very evil. Christians are sometimes accused of being anti-sex, but that is just not the case. We are pro-sex but we are also anti-perversion. Virtual sex is taking what God created and robbing it of its beauty. It's like seeing a beautiful painting and then scribbling on it with a magic marker. You destroy what the master intended for his most prized possession.

Why is virtual sex so bad? Let me give you some reasons why I think it is so destructive and some incentive to stay away from it starting right *now*!

1. *It is degrading to the opposite sex.* Virtual sex causes you to see them as something rather then someone. Do you realize some of the women on those porn sites are slaves? They are forced to pose and perform for the camera. To refuse is to suffer beatings and sometimes death. What about teenage girls or those who are even younger? Do you think they are being

manipulated and used? Is this what you would want for your sister or daughter one day? Virtual sex turns people into objects who are used to satisfy your sexual desires.

2. *It kills your relationship with Jesus Christ.* How much time have you spent seeking the Lord compared to seeking virtual sex? The more you follow your sexual desires, the less you're interested in pursuing a relationship with Christ. When you are involved in virtual sex, it feels like you are building a wall between you and Jesus. You are saying yes to what God is saying no to, and that means you are going to be hurt in the long run. Your conscience will be seared, the Holy Spirit silenced, and you will slip deeper into sin.

3. *It hardens your heart.* Virtual sex leads you to begin to think, *I don't care.* I don't care that my relationship with Christ is suffering. I don't care if the people I am looking at are being manipulated and used sexually. I don't care that this is leading to lusting and masturbation. I don't care that I am becoming addicted. I don't care that this is all leading me to lie, deceive, and do things in secret.

A hardened heart and an "I don't care" attitude lead to rebellion. This rebellion is against parents, teachers, youth pastors, and those in authority, but most of all it's against God. What is the condition of your heart right now? Do you see yourself saying or thinking, "I don't care"? Have you been rebelling against those in authority over you?

4. *Virtual sex hurts our self-esteem.* Subconsciously we begin to compare ourselves with the images. Men worry their penis isn't big enough. Women wish their breasts were bigger. We are no longer happy with how God created us. We long to be someone we aren't. We are deceived into thinking that all men want women with big breasts, or the quality of sex for a woman is dependent on the size of the penis.

5. *We compare the opposite sex to the images and stories.* We are disappointed with them because they don't act or look like the people we have created in our minds. So we retreat back to our fantasy world. We become more and more isolated and less and less in touch with reality.

6. *We see sex as being performance-based.* This leads to fear and worry that we won't be good enough. We think we will fall short of what a real man or woman does as a lover. We see good sex as primarily moves, techniques, and positions. Our whole view of sex becomes unrealistic because it has become unreasonable, and it feeds two of our biggest fears: we will never really be loved, and we will never find someone we can love. We think all of this because we're afraid we won't be able to measure up in someone else's eyes.

   Sex is just part of a loving and committed relationship with your spouse. It is not about performing or meeting some virtual sex standard. You are more than how you perform. You were created in the image of God, so never define yourself only in terms of what you do and how you perform. God gave us sex as a wonderful gift, and gifts are not about comparing but about enjoying. Sex is about loving your spouse and seeking to please him or her. It is about growing together, getting to know each other better, and falling deeper in love. Sex gets better as time goes by because you come to know each other more and fall in deeper levels of love. It is not about performance but rather patience and love.

7. *Virtual sex says, "What is really exciting is what is not allowed."*
   Virtual sex is all about you being sexually involved before you are married with a variety of different partners instead of waiting for your husband or wife.

   Then after marriage it is about being involved with someone else's spouse and not your own. It is the excitement and adventure of committing adultery. Being faithful, committed, and loving is stupid; and being a liar, cheater, and untrustworthy is sophisticated.

It is being with a much younger person, and it implies that younger is better. Unless you are young—then it says you need an older lover, and older is better.

It tells you that having sex with animals, children, and the same gender is fine. It tells you that if you find this disgusting, then you are narrow-minded and something is wrong with you.

It says that torture and bondage are acceptable. It implies that girls really do like to be dominated, used, and raped. It says their fighting and resisting is just an act, and they do want you to take advantage of them.

Pornography says that what is normal, good, and right in God's eyes is boring, and what is sick and perverted is what is really exciting. Virtual sex is now a matter of personal preference and not sin. You do your thing, and I will do my thing, and there is no standard for right and wrong.

All these lies never show you the consequences up front —the pain, suffering, and crisis you put yourself and those you claim to love through. You slip deeper and deeper into darkness. Your sexual desires become more and more selfish and perverted. You lose touch with reality and what is good and right. You start to despise yourself. And you become filled with shame, guilt, and self-hate.

> Pornography is a deep pit that will drag you down and destroy you.

8. *Virtual sex is insatiable.* One of virtual sex's biggest lies is, "Next time!" Just one more video, secular romance novel, porn site, strip club, or soap opera, and *then* you will be satisfied. But it is never enough; and the more you get, the more you want. So what you don't have always seems better than what you do have. The naked image you see won't be as good as the naked image you will see on the next site. The result

is that you are never satisfied and you are always looking for the next sexual high.

9. *Sin doesn't remain static but always seeks to get worse.* Virtual sex will move you toward a living hell one step at a time.

The more you see and become involved in virtual sex, the more desensitized you become to it. The pictures and words become less and less shocking as you get deeper and deeper into it.

We may start with soap operas and sexy romance novels to stir our imaginations.

Next we look at the magazines with images of partially clad individuals.

From there we move to pornographic sites of naked people.

After awhile just seeing naked people doesn't seem that exciting, so we look for sites that are more and more perverted.

We go into chat rooms and try to meet people online who will fulfill our fantasies. We call 900 numbers and go to strip clubs.

After that we may cross a major line and begin to peek into other people's windows. We want to see people taking off their clothes or having sex. We become voyeurs, and we are breaking the law.

The final step may be to want control over people, so we force ourselves on them and become a rapist.

No one sets out to be a rapist, but it happens one step at a time. I know a girl from a missionary family who ended up being a prostitute in a massage parlor. Do you think that she came off the mission field and immediately became a prostitute? No, she took it one step at a time, moving from sin to sin until she was doing things she never would have considered in the past.

Sin is never content to stay where it is but always wants to get worse and worse. That is why the wages of sin is death. The ultimate goal of sin is to kill you emotionally, spiritually, and physically.

10. *Virtual sex is addictive.* I watched a TV program about pornography and they interviewed a man who said, "I have been addicted to drugs and smoking, but it was nothing compared to the addiction I had with sex and pornography."

Sex was meant to be a part of your life, but not your whole life. When sex becomes your whole life through thinking, searching, and desiring, it becomes your god. You will end up serving it and giving your life to it. It will control you, pervert you, and destroy you.

Most people would not swim toward a great white shark; most people would not try to play with a rattlesnake; most people would not approach a mother grizzly bear with cubs. Why? Because they all have the potential to kill you. Don't walk away from virtual sex—*run* from it! Do whatever you need to do to get away from it, because if you don't it will devour you. Look at what 2 Timothy 2:22 says: "Flee the evil desires of youth, and pursue righteousness, faith, love and peace, along with those who call on the Lord out of a pure heart."

I feel very passionate about this, and do you know why? Because I have been caught in the web of pornography; and I know how addictive, exciting, and enticing it can be for me. I have seen firsthand how it has hurt me and negatively affected my relationships. It all started when I was little and found some *Playboy* magazines that belonged to one of my friend's older brothers. What started out as innocent curiosity became a sexual obsession. The more I saw, the more I wanted to see. Now I am older and wiser, but I find the lure of virtual sex still calls to me. Lust of the flesh will be a battleground for me till my dying day.

What have I done to gain victory over virtual sex, and what can you begin to do?

1. *Face it and accept responsibility for your actions and choices.* Whose fault is it that I have struggled with pornography? It is my fault! Some of you are in denial and continually make excuses for your sin. The worst excuse is, "It isn't that bad. I can stop anytime I want." It is really bad, and if you could have stopped anytime you wanted, then you would have stopped by now. Look, if you are going to get better, you first have to admit you are sick. Maybe no one has ever told you this, but if you are involved in virtual sex then you are a sick person.

2. *Get a heart transplant.* If you have a hard heart then you just don't care what you are doing to yourself or others. Get a heart transplant so you can begin to care about God, yourself, and others.

   How do you get the heart transplant? Check out Ezekiel 36:26: "I will give you a new heart and put a new spirit in you; I will remove from you your heart of stone and give you a heart of flesh." That new heart is just a prayer away. You could pray something like this, "Dear Jesus, I know I have a hard heart, and I ask You to take my hard heart and give me a softer one so I can begin to care again. Thank You for the new heart, and I want to tell You I love You. Amen."

3. *Come back to Jesus and rest in His arms.* No one loves you like Jesus loves you, and He understands the battle you are going through. He knows how hard the temptations are and how strong the lust of the flesh is for you.

   How do I know this is true? All we need to do is read Hebrews 4:14–16. "Therefore, since we have a great high priest who has gone through the heavens, Jesus the Son of God, let us hold firmly to the faith we profess. For we do not have a high priest who is unable to sympathize with our weaknesses, but we have one who has been tempted in every way, just as we are—yet was without sin. Let us then approach the throne of grace with confidence, so that we may receive mercy and find grace to help us in our time of need."

This passage says we need to hold on to our faith and our relationship with Jesus Christ. He understands the struggle because He was tempted with lust of the flesh. He sympathizes with us and invites us to approach Him. What will we receive when we do this? Do we receive condemnation and anger? No, we receive mercy, grace, and help during our time of need. Jesus deeply cares about you and the battle you are facing. The question is: when are you going to start caring?

4. *Seek after the Lord.* Matthew 6:33 says, "But seek first his kingdom and his righteousness, and all these things will be given to you as well." As you spend time worshiping, studying the Word, praying, listening, and getting back in touch with God, you will discover your relationship with Christ strengthening and the chains of virtual sex loosening. The Holy Spirit will give you the power to do what you need to do—the strength to resist what is evil and the desire to seek what is good.

5. *Realize you are in the middle of a battle between good and evil, light and darkness, demons and angels, Satan and God.* If this is a weakness for you, the Enemy is going to hit you in this area as hard as he can. Satan is a master of lies and deception. At first he says, "Here is the virtual sex: taste and enjoy." After you have tasted he says, "You are sick and disgusting." He encourages and then accuses—he keeps you on the merry-go-round of cheap thrills and deep regret.

Stop listening to his lies. Here are some other things he wants to whisper in your ear, like, "You are a terrible and disgraceful person." Wrong—you are a wonderful and special creation of God, but you have made some bad choices.

Or, "If people knew what I was doing, they would reject me." Do you see what this lie does? It keeps you isolated and keeps you from getting help. We are all in the same boat. Many of us struggle with lust of the flesh. If someone really loves Jesus they are not going to reject you, and in most cases they will be able to identify with what you are going through because they have gone through the same stuff.

How 'bout this one: "I need to change if anyone is going to love me." This also keeps you isolated from the very people who could help you. Jesus Christ loves you just as you are and wants to make something beautiful out of your life. You come to Jesus just like you are. He will love you and give you the power to be different. And also come to others just as you are so they can love and encourage you.

What do you need to do? Put on the full armor of God, as it's listed in Ephesians 6:10–18. What solider would ever go into battle without being fully equipped? Every day you need to pray and clothe yourself in God's protection. As you get dressed in the morning, be sure that you are also dressing spiritually.

James 4:7 says, "Submit yourselves, then, to God. Resist the devil, and he will flee from you." In other words, commit your life to Jesus Christ and depend on Him and then resist the Enemy. You do that by prayer (and it is important that you even pray out loud). Command the forces of evil to be quiet and leave your presence in Jesus' name.

When you look at porn, you open the door for demons to enter your room and attack you. Even when you end that time, the demons may stay to scare, harass, and attack you. To seek after virtual sex is to seek after Satan and his demons. Does that sound bad to you? Don't do it!

6. *Remember the blessing and promise in the battle.* I am only a moment away from making a bad choice, so I must stay close to the cross and dependent on God. Admit your weakness and you will receive God's strength and power. Second Corinthians 12:9–10 says, "But he said to me, 'My grace is suf-

ficient for you, for my power is made perfect in weakness.' Therefore I will boast all the more gladly about my weaknesses, so that Christ's power may rest on me. That is why, for Christ's sake, I delight in weaknesses, in insults, in hardships, in persecutions, in difficulties. For when I am weak, then I am strong." God is ready to deliver you from evil, but He doesn't remove evil from the world. We are all susceptible to sexual temptation. The day you stop being tempted is the day you die. So focus on God and know He is still in control. God is all powerful; the forces of evil are not. You are strong when you are waiting, depending, needing, and desiring the Lord's presence in your life. Knowing your sickness and being aware of your sin causes you to stay close to Jesus.

7. *Watch what you take into your life.* Your lifestyle choices will either make it easier or harder to be pure. Remember what you take into your life is what comes out of your life (Matthew 12:33–35). Put garbage in and garbage will come out. Put purity in and purity will come out. What kind of person do you want to be now and become in the future? This is not rocket science; what you are doing today is what you are becoming tomorrow.

8. *Make yourself accountable.* "As iron sharpens iron, so one man sharpens another" (Proverbs 27:17). You need someone in your life with whom you can share openly. He needs to know all the bad and ugly so he can keep you accountable. Knowing that once a week you are going to have someone ask you about pornography will help the good choices to be made.

Get your computer in a high-traffic area and out of your room or basement. Your computer needs to be somewhere people can walk by at any moment. Put some guards on your computer that will protect you from the porn sites. Ask your parents or accountability partner to put in a code that will not allow you to get onto porn sites. Sign up for a service that will monitor where you go on the computer. So if you go to a bad site it will send a warning to your accountability partner. Tell your parents about the struggle you are having so they can help you out. Some parents want to trust you, but by doing so they have set you up to fail. Do what you need to do to protect yourself and God's reputation from evil.

9. *Think about it objectively.* Realize what an incredible waste of time this has become for you. Think about how much time you spend seeking after virtual sex. God has a purpose, plan, and destiny for your life. Do you think this plan includes seeking after evil? No! So starting now, refuse to settle for anything less than God's very best for your life. You can be different because God will give you the power to be different. "For God did not call us to be impure, but to live a holy life" (1 Thessalonians 4:7).

10. *Be honest and realize you may need to get involved in some professional counseling to help you deal with what is happening inside.* The virtual sex can be an indication you are struggling with other things too. If you can get to the root causes, then the virtual sex will begin to lose its grip on your life. More and more churches are having sexual addiction groups available for those struggling in this area.

We started the chapter by asking this question, "What is the virtue in virtual sex?" The answer is that there is no virtue, no redeeming value, and nothing that should give us any excuse for spending time chasing after virtual sex.

Let me close this chapter with Psalm 51:1–17, and I want you to make this your prayer to God from your heart.

"Have mercy on me, O God, according to your unfailing love; according to your great compassion blot out my transgressions. Wash away all my iniquity and cleanse me from my sin. For I know my transgressions, and my sin is always before me. Against you, you only, have I sinned and done what is evil in your sight, so that you are proved right when you speak and justified when you judge. Surely I was sinful at birth, sinful from the time my mother conceived me. Surely you desire truth in the inner parts; you teach me wisdom in the inmost place. Cleanse me with hyssop, and I will be clean; wash me, and I will be whiter than snow. Let me hear joy and gladness; let the bones you have crushed rejoice. Hide your face from my sins and blot out all my iniquity. Create in me a pure heart, O God, and renew a steadfast spirit within me. Do not cast me from your presence or take your Holy Spirit from me. Restore to me the joy of your salvation and grant me a willing spirit, to sustain me. Then I will teach transgressors your ways, and sinners will turn back to you. Save me from bloodguilt, O God, the God who saves me, and my tongue will sing of your righteousness. O Lord, open my lips, and my mouth will declare your praise. You do not delight in sacrifice, or I would bring it; you do not take pleasure in burnt offerings. The sacrifices of God are a broken spirit; a broken and contrite heart, O God, you will not despise."

Questions to ask yourself:

1. Are you addicted to virtual sex? Why do you seek out pornography?
2. Have you told anyone the struggle that you are having?
3. Do your parents know the battle that you are having?

11

Masturbation

(WHY DOESN'T ANYBODY TALK ABOUT IT?)

*Many of us have listened to Satan's lies and
actually don't believe we can ever have self-control
in this area. This is just not true.*

Certain things strike fear into our individual hearts. For a swimmer it's the word *shark*. For a dieter it's, "Hey, anyone here want a hot fudge sundae?" For a student it's, "Clear your desk for a surprise quiz." For you who are going out on your very first date, it's a zit! And for the Christian seeking to lead a pure life, it's the word *masturbation*.

The word itself causes a variety of reactions: embarrassment, anger, guilt, shock, disgust. Why is it that masturbation causes such a stir among Christians?

I believe masturbation evokes such responses because the problem is so personal and it affects so many of us.

Now you can find statistics to support just about anything you want to talk about. But conservative statistics today would say that over 90 percent of males and 70 percent of females have participated in masturbation. That means that most of your fathers, mothers, and even pastors have struggled with masturbation while growing up. To be perfectly honest, some of them continue to struggle with it.

You see, it's very difficult for people to talk about masturbation because so many of us have participated in it. But I believe we need to discuss it openly and honestly, and that we should view it from a Christian perspective.

What is masturbation? It is stimulating one's own genital organs to bring about orgasm, or sexual climax.

You will find a wide range of opinions concerning masturbation. Some people will tell you it is God's gift and you should enjoy it. Others say masturbation is absolutely a sin and an abomination in God's sight.

One reason for such diversity of opinion is that God's Word is silent on the matter. Certain verses relate somewhat to masturbation, but there is no place where God specifically mentions it. As a result, everybody formulates their own opinion.

I agree with Dr. James Dobson that masturbation can be very harmful if it is followed by feelings of extreme guilt. But I see it as sinful if any one of the following develops:

> If the masturbation occurs in groups. This can easily lead to homosexual involvement.
> If the masturbation continues after marriage. You then are cheating your spouse. Instead of focusing your sexual energy on your wife or husband, you focus on yourself and your private fantasies. In addition, many times the person you imagine yourself to be with sexually is not your spouse.
> If the masturbation is done in conjunction with lusting and/or pornographic material. Colossians 3:17 says, "Whatever you do, whether in word or deed, do it all in the name of the Lord Jesus, giving thanks to God the Father through him." Jesus tells us that if we look at a woman lustfully we have already committed adultery with her in our hearts.
> If the masturbation begins to control you, rather than you controlling it.

    And that can happen. Masturbation can become a habit. We may use it to release stress, to fall asleep at night, as a reward for accomplishments, or as an escape from loneliness. The lust of the flesh takes control.

Look at these two Bible verses, and see how they tie into what I've just said:

> ➤ "They promise them freedom, while they themselves are slaves of depravity—for a man is a slave to whatever has mastered him" (2 Peter 2:19).
> ➤ "It is God's will that you should be sanctified [set aside for God's use]: that you should avoid sexual immorality; that each of you should learn to control his own body in a way that is holy and honorable, not in passionate lust like the heathen, who do not know God" (1 Thessalonians 4:3–5).

People tell me they masturbate to relieve sexual tension. The sad fact is that masturbation usually does not relieve sexual tension. In the long run it causes even more tension. You see, the more you masturbate, the more you want to masturbate. Then masturbation becomes an obsession. It grips you with such force that you lose all control.

Many of us have listened to Satan's lies and actually don't believe we can ever have self-control in this area. This is just not true. Too many of us interpret 1 Corinthians 10:13 this way: "No temptation has seized you except what is common to man. And God is faithful; he will not let you be tempted beyond what you can bear [except when it comes to masturbation]. But when you are tempted, he will also provide a way out so that you can stand up under it [except for masturbation]."

We spend more time thinking about masturbation than we do thinking about Jesus. And when we take our eyes off the person of Jesus Christ in the midst of testing, that's when we get into trouble.

Look at Peter. He was sitting in a boat, safe and secure, when he saw Jesus Christ walking on the water. Peter, who suffered from a terminal case of athlete's mouth, opened it again, removed his left foot, and put in his right foot by saying, "Well, if it is You, Jesus, tell me to get out of the boat and come to You." So Jesus said, "Come along, Peter."

Peter stepped out of the boat and began to walk. He kept his eyes right on Jesus Christ, and he said to himself, *Oh, boy, I'm walking on water. Oh, boy, I'm walking on water!—I'm walking . . . hold on . . . What am I doing out here walking on water?*

And then he made a serious mistake. Peter took his eyes off Jesus and began to focus on the situation around him—the waves, the stormy clouds, the raging wind—and now began to say to himself, *Hey, listen, nobody ought to be out here just walking on the water!*

And what happened to Peter? He began to sink. Then one of the most sincere prayers ever uttered by any individual was said. As that cold, cold water began to creep up Peter's body, he focused back on the person of Jesus Christ and cried, "Help!" Jesus lifted him up and put him back in the boat.

Too many of us have taken our eyes off Jesus Christ. We have focused on the masturbation. We have failed so often we say to ourselves, "There is no hope—I can never have self-control." As a result we have sunk into all of the garbage, the rubbish, and the lies Satan feeds us.

Instead, let's turn our focus back to Jesus Christ. Let's call out for help. Let's allow Him to lift us above our circumstances and empower us to deal with this problem.

Face the fact that masturbation never really satisfies. It's important to understand one of the purposes of sex is to end loneliness. In the marriage relationship, sex between two people is a form of communication. Masturbation is lust directed toward ourselves rather than love directed toward another person.

Down through the years, people have thought the best way to counsel a young person about masturbation is to frighten him. Here are some of the things people used to say would happen if you masturbated.

> You will grow hair on your palms.
> You will eventually become impotent.
> You will go insane.
> You will develop warts.

> You will lose your sex organ.
> You will become blind.
> You will become gay.
> You will develop acne.
> Your growth will be stunted.
> Dark circles will form around your eyes.

None of these things will occur if you masturbate, and the answer is found not in frightening someone but in giving wise advice. (If you try to frighten someone, the usual result is that the person will hide his habit instead of dealing with it.)

If you are caught in the cycle of mastur-bation, you need to know there are individu-als who have gained victory over this prob-lem. *Have confidence that God can also give you victory.*

Masturbation begins to control you instead of you controlling it.

Let me give you some suggestions about what you can to do gain victory over masturbation.

FACE IT

Stop avoiding or rationalizing the problem. Some of us try to pretend the problem isn't there. We think that by ignoring it some-how it will just go away. But that isn't true, and you've already dis-covered that, so let's stop playing those games.

All too often we merely seek what feels good. We would rather masturbate, and gain pleasure for the moment, than serve Jesus Christ and gain a much greater satisfaction in the long run. Romans 13:14 says, "Rather, clothe yourselves with the Lord Jesus Christ, and do not think about how to gratify the desires of the sinful nature."

It's important to deal with masturbation now. Some have thought as soon as they get married they will never again be tempted to masturbate. These people are in for a big surprise. After the new-ness of marriage has worn off, if you have masturbated or fantasized in the past, there is a strong possibility you will continue after marriage. And you will probably be fantasizing about someone other than your husband or wife.

PRAY SPECIFICALLY

Go to God, and ask Him for strength to begin to practice self-control.

Name the problem. Don't beat around the bush. God knows what you are struggling with, so tell Him you need His help in the area of masturbation. But don't make promises you can't keep!

Here is what we will typically do. We'll say to God, "Oh, God, I'm so sorry, but if You'll just forgive me one more time I promise I will never do it again."

Well, what do you think happens? We do it again. Then what happens? We've made a promise to God, and guilt sets in. Satan laughs at us, and we feel totally out of fellowship with Him. Some people give up on their relationship with Christ altogether because they cannot gain victory over this habit. Don't make promises you can't keep!

EVALUATE WHAT YOU ARE TAKING INTO YOUR MIND

What kind of magazines, books, music, television, and movies are you reading, listening to, and watching? All these things affect you.

If you are struggling with masturbation and continue to watch sex on TV, you are only adding to your problem. Your standard for anything you take into your life ought to be Philippians 4:8: "Finally, brothers, whatever is true, whatever is noble, whatever is right, whatever is pure, whatever is lovely, whatever is admirable—if anything is excellent or praiseworthy—think about such things."

Let me tell you openly and honestly that one of the worst things you can take into your mind is music videos. I know this is not going to endear me to many of you, but if you watch music videos on a regular basis, take pen and paper and list three categories: sex, violence, and spirit occult-type activities.

Then, as you watch, write down the name of each video and the name of the performer. If you see any sexual content, or violence, or spirit occult activity, put a check by the proper category. Do you know what you are going to discover? You are going to see that music videos are full of all three of these—especially sex.

FILL YOUR MIND
WITH WHAT IS POSITIVE

We should want to be pleasing, acceptable, and pure in God's sight.

> ➤ Romans 12:1: "Therefore, I urge you, brothers, in view of God's mercy, to offer your bodies as living sacrifices, holy and pleasing to God—this is your spiritual act of worship."

There's no getting around it. You need to spend time in the Word of God. The Bible is to your spiritual growth what food is to your physical growth. If you do not eat for a while you are not going to feel too good. If you do not eat spiritually for a while, you're not going to feel very good spiritually.

You also need to be on your knees in prayer. A lack of communication indicates a lack of love, because when you love someone you communicate with him or her. When's the last time you and God have done some real communicating?

The Bible, prayer, and Jesus Christ will keep you from sin, or sin will keep you from Bible study, prayer, and Jesus.

Begin to listen to Christian music. There is excellent contemporary Christian music out today. Take advantage of entertainment that doesn't drag your mind through the gutter.

Be careful about the friends you hang around with, because they are going to have an impact on your life. Remember 1 Corinthians 15:33: "Do not be misled: 'Bad company corrupts good character.'"

Memorize Scripture. Fill your mind with what is good and what is positive, and guess what? That's exactly what is going to come out of your life. Galatians 5:16 says, "So I say, live by the Spirit, and you will not gratify the desires of the sinful nature."

NOTE YOUR MASTURBATION PATTERN AND BREAK IT

Masturbation often has a pattern. For example, your alarm goes off at 6:30 in the morning, but you don't have to get up until 7:00. So what happens? You lie there, and fantasize, and eventually masturbate.

Or you come home from school, and the first thing you do is go into the bathroom (you've been waiting to go to the bathroom since third hour, so it's a priority). While looking through the magazines, you find pictures that excite you or stimulate your imagination, and that's when you masturbate.

Remember, masturbation becomes sinful when it is performed in conjunction with pornographic material. An example is found in Matthew 5:28, which warns against looking on a woman and lusting after her. When you do that, Jesus says, you commit adultery.

Or it happens before you fall asleep at night.

Notice when it usually occurs, and try to break the pattern.

That means setting your alarm for 7:00 a.m. When it goes off, get up and get ready for school. Or when you come home from school, don't grab a magazine and go to the bathroom—grab your Bible and read it when you are in the bathroom. Or if you find it difficult to fall asleep at night, do a little reading. Do some praying, and really ask God to be in control of your thought life at that time. Meditate on Scripture. Begin to break out of the pattern of controlling masturbation.

You may also notice an emotional pattern. You may find it happens when you are under a lot of pressure. You masturbate to gain a pleasurable release. You need to come up with some creative substitutes to cope with pressure. Get involved with people and activities that generate joy for you.

Second Timothy 2:22 says, "Flee the evil desires of youth, and pursue righteousness, faith, love and peace, along with those who call on the Lord out of a pure heart."

PUT YOUR INTELLECT BACK IN CONTROL

When you masturbate, your emotions are in control of your intellect, and that is not good.

If you are a smoker, you know that smoking is not necessary, and there are two ways you can try to quit smoking. One is to quit cold turkey. Now some people can do that and be successful, but not everybody. The second way is to cut down the number of cigarettes you smoke until you eventually get down to where you are smoking so few cigarettes it's much easier to stop.

Yes, some of us will be able to stop cold turkey. God will give these people victory immediately, and they will never have to masturbate again. But others of us are going to need to cut back on the frequency of the habit, doing it less and less, until we will eventually find it is much easier to stop.

What I want us to begin to do is let our intellect control our emotions. Next time you are tempted to masturbate, I want you to ask yourself, "Is this necessary?" If the answer is no, then don't do it! The frequency of the masturbation will be cut back almost immediately.

You don't have to masturbate. You have a choice. If you don't masturbate, nothing terrible is going to happen to you. You're not going to blow up or turn green. Neither your toes nor any other body parts will fall off. And as you see some victory in this area, as you see the frequency of the masturbation being cut back, you will have the encouragement and the courage—along with Christ's power—to eventually stop altogether.

GET A NEW PERSPECTIVE
ON THE OPPOSITE SEX

Realize that men and women are creations of God. Each is, or at least potentially is, your brother or sister in Christ. Not only is it unhealthy for you to lust after another and masturbate, but it is also unhealthy for the other person. When you masturbate, you are not looking at the person as *somebody*. You are merely looking at him or her as *something*.

Now I understand when a woman masturbates she is not always thinking about a sexual encounter. A woman may just be thinking of being held or cared about. But, again, I do not believe that masturbation is the best thing we can be doing with our bodies.

Men, let's remember Job 31:1: "I made a covenant with my eyes not to look lustfully at a girl." I mentioned this earlier, but let me remind you again—when you are talking to a woman, always make eye contact with her. Women have told me how degrading it feels when they talk to a man and his eyes are moving up and down their bodies.

Let's begin to see the opposite sex not as objects of our desire but as our brothers or sisters in Christ, to be respected, protected, and loved.

WE ARE IN A BATTLE

Let's get in the fight. The following is an effective way to combat Satan and his attacks in the area of masturbation. We need to arm ourselves (Ephesians 6:13–18) with the . . .

➢ Belt of truth.

This holds all the armor together. You need to be a man or woman of integrity. You must know and speak the truth. Have a clear conscience. If your word doesn't mean anything, then you don't mean anything, because you are your word.

➤ Breastplate of righteousness.

Live a godly life by the power of the Holy Spirit. The life we live either fortifies us against Satan's attacks or makes it easier for us to be defeated. There is a war going on inside between our old and new natures. Whichever one you feed the most is the one that will win.

➤ Shoes of the gospel.

Take the initiative. Talk about Jesus Christ in the power of the Holy Spirit and then leave the results to God. By our actions we are either drawing people closer to Christ or pushing them further away.

➤ Shield of faith.

Trust in the power and promises of Christ. When Satan attacks, claim those promises and resist him (1 Peter 5:9).

➤ Helmet of salvation.

Let your mind be controlled by God. Study and know the Word of God.

➤ Sword of the Spirit.

Use the Word of God to rebuke Satan in the name of the Lord Jesus Christ. It's important that we memorize Scripture. Otherwise, if Satan attacks when we have no Bible handy, we could be in big trouble. Don't be caught in the middle of an ambush without your weapon.

Now that's as far as people usually go when talking about putting on the full armor of God. Then I heard about a seventh piece! It works. I know, because I've tried it. It is . . .

➤ Prayer in the Spirit.

"Pray in the Spirit," Ephesians 6:18 says. We are to use prayer as an offensive weapon every time we feel tempted by Satan. This is what you can do:

1. Think of one non-Christian who could do tremendous damage to Satan if he became a Christian.

2. Think of one Christian who is apathetic spiritually but who, if he came alive, would be a blow to the Devil's kingdom.

3. Think of some leaders in government.

Now, anytime you are tempted to masturbate, or are tempted in any area, I want you to pray for these individuals. You will discover the temptation will weaken or stop altogether.

Why?

Because now you are advancing into Satan's very territory by praying for individuals he is controlling. He will feel that attack, and he will flee from you. Again, why? Because of the tremendous power there is in prayer. Satan doesn't want to risk losing any of the people he controls. Satan can tolerate a lot of things that Christians do, but he hates our praying. Pray without ceasing, and let's attack him at his very heart. The war is already won. We are just fighting some closing battles, so let's stop acting like losers.

TALK WITH SOMEONE

Talking with someone else about your problem is perhaps one of the most difficult steps to take. But find somebody whom you respect and whom you can trust. Men need to go to men, and women need to go to women. Find somebody who is older and wiser than yourself. Sit down with this person and tell about the struggle you are having.

The more we withdraw and hide, the more likely we are to masturbate. Everything seems to be bigger and worse and more terrifying when it's hidden in the dark. After we see it in the light of day, it really isn't as bad as it seemed. Confide with somebody openly and honestly, and get the help, support, and care you need to begin to deal with it.

You'll have somebody who will be praying with you and for you that God will grant you victory. And, second, you'll have someone to whom you can be accountable. Periodically he can come up to you and say, "How are you doing? How's the battle going?" And you'll always know that someone is going to be checking up on you. This will be an encouragement not to give up but to hang in there and do battle.

Remember the statistics: more than 90 percent of men and more than 70 percent of women masturbate. A lot of us have been involved in masturbation. We'll be able to identify with you and the struggle you are going through.

GET INVOLVED IN SERVICE AGAIN

Get involved in service again. Too often we do desire to follow Jesus Christ, but because we are struggling with masturbation we don't think He can use us. So we take 90 percent of our energy and concentrate it on this one struggle. We stop growing, we become ineffective, and we no longer serve the Lord. How stupid is that? If we couldn't serve Jesus Christ until we were perfect, guess what? None of us would be serving Him, because we all struggle.

If you could be perfect, Christ would never have had to die for you. So put your eyes back on Jesus, and allow Him to fill you with His Spirit.

First Timothy 4:12 says, "Don't let anyone look down on you because you are young, but set an example for the believers in speech, in life, in love, in faith and in purity."

In spite of the fact that you are struggling in the area of masturbation, God can and will use you. Let Him.

BE PATIENT WITH YOURSELF

God is patient with you. You need to be patient with yourself.

In dealing with masturbation, it's really important that you relax. Many of you are so uptight that your tension just adds to the problem. Relax. Don't make the problem bigger or worse than it really is. When you fail, don't give up; don't toss in the towel. Get back up and keep going. It took you some time to get involved in masturbation. It will probably take you some time to gain victory over it.

Don't heap condemnation on yourself. Most of us are tougher on ourselves than anyone else would be on us. But we do have our priorities messed up if we spend more time lusting and masturbating than we do worshiping and serving Jesus Christ. Be patient; work on your priorities, and don't give up!

Jesus is near to you when you make good choices or bad choices. Be more conscious of God's personal presence in your life.

As you begin to take these simple steps, you will find masturbation having less and less and less of a grip on your life. One day you may wake up in the morning and think, *Wow! I haven't masturbated in weeks!* And really, you haven't even had a desire to do so. Jesus wants to give you victory, but you need to be willing to work on it.

Is it wrong to have strong sexual feelings? Absolutely not! God has made us sexual beings. It is normal to feel strong sexual desires. Instead of ignoring those feelings or pretending they don't exist or trying to run away from them, why not, instead, thank God for them?

Thank Him also for His power so you can be in control of this area of your life.

"So I strive always to keep my conscience clear before God and man" (Acts 24:16).

Questions to ask yourself:

1. Do you struggle with masturbation?
2. What is the next step that you need to take to begin to gain victory?
3. What have you been looking at and thinking about?

12

Homosexuality

(IS THERE HOPE?)

*Homosexuality is more a matter of what you choose
to do than it is a matter of what you are.*

"Am I gay? 'Cause I'm sure not happy!"

I am running into more and more teenagers who are being faced
with the question of homosexuality. Some are afraid they may be
gay. Others have been approached by strangers, or sometimes even
friends, asking them to become involved sexually.

In this chapter I would like to answer five questions that will
help us better understand and cope with the issue of homosexuality.

WHO IS A HOMOSEXUAL?

What are we talking about? Who is a homosexual? Well, *homo*
means "same." A homosexual, then, is someone who is attracted to
and excited by members of the same sex, which leads to involvement sexually with partners of the same sex. Female homosexuals
are called *lesbians*.

It's really important that we don't confuse homosexuality with
love for members of the same sex. It's important and good and proper
to have close, loving relationships with members of the same sex.
Look at 1 Samuel 18:1–3:

After David had finished talking with Saul, Jonathan became one in spirit with David, and he loved him as himself. From that day Saul kept David with him and did not let him return to his father's house. And Jonathan made a covenant with David because he loved him as himself.

David and Jonathan deeply loved each other and were not afraid to show their love. They loved each other in the purest sense of the word. There was no sexual involvement whatsoever.

Let's never let the world so intimidate us that we are afraid to show affection for or have close friendships with the same sex. Don't be afraid to show your love to close friends by giving them a hug. That's good and right, and only a strong person can be open with his or her love like that.

IS HOMOSEXUALITY WRONG?

Is homosexuality wrong? Yes. But when I say that, society becomes extremely angry with me. They call me homophobic because I don't agree with them. They say that I am intolerant and politically incorrect. Why?

Society, to a large extent, has rejected absolute truth and a personal, all-knowing, all-powerful God who reveals truth to us and thus gives us a basis for determining right and wrong.

Today we have right-and-wrong morality that is being decided by the media and certain groups of people. Now if a group of people, based on their personal opinions, can determine what is right or wrong, then truth becomes situational. So what was sinful fifteen years ago may be acceptable today because this group of people is making the decision.

On what does this group base its decisions? Usually upon their feelings, opinions, and thoughts as to what they believe is true and right.

I hope you can see how absurd and dangerous this is. A group now advocates sex with children as a good way to develop closeness between adult and child and to give the child a sense of security. This group's motto is "Sex by eight or it's too late!" Now if a group of "experts" begins to say this is OK, then are incest and sexual relationships with children suddenly right? I hope you are shouting "No!"

You say to me, "It will never happen, Greg."

And I would say to you, "That's what they used to say about homosexuality."

We must take a stand and clearly say there is a God who has communicated absolute truth to us; this truth is found in the Bible, and the Bible is our basis for making decisions about morality. Today we need teenagers who are unashamed to lovingly communicate the truth of God's Word.

I want to speak the truth in love and tell you that homosexuality is not merely an alternative lifestyle. It is sin. No amount of legislating, campaigning, advertising, literature, media coverage, or acceptance will make it any less a sin.

How do you determine what is right and what is wrong? What do you base your standards on?

This also includes bad theology. There are some who might try to throw out certain passages in the Old Testament that speak against homosexuality and reinterpret New Testament passages to fit into their pro-homosexual belief. That is an incorrect interpretation of the Scriptures. Do not allow these people to confuse, trap, or lead you astray. Remember 2 Timothy 4:2–4, "Preach the Word; be prepared in season and out of season; correct, rebuke and encourage—with great patience and careful instruction. For the time will come when men will not put up with sound doctrine. Instead, to suit their own desires, they will gather around them a great number of teachers to say what their itching ears want to hear. They will turn their ears away from the truth and turn aside to myths."

Nowhere in the Bible does God approve of homosexuality. Let's look at four examples:

➤ Leviticus 18:4, 22: "You must obey my laws and be careful to follow my decrees. I am the LORD your God. . . . Do not lie with a man as one lies with a woman; that is detestable."

➤ Leviticus 20:13: "If a man lies with a man as one lies with a woman, both of them have done what is detestable. They must be put to death; their blood will be on their own heads."

➤ Romans 1:24–27: Therefore God gave them over in the sinful desires of their hearts to sexual impurity for the degrading of their bodies with one another. They exchanged the truth of God for a lie, and worshiped and served created things rather than the Creator—who is forever praised. Amen.

Because of this, God gave them over to shameful lusts. Even their women exchanged natural relations for unnatural ones. In the same way the men also abandoned natural relations with women and were inflamed with lust for one another. Men committed indecent acts with other men, and received in themselves the due penalty for their perversion.

Some people have tried to water down this passage by saying, "It's only talking about those who are promiscuous. If you have a gay relationship where you are committed to one person, then it's OK."

But that's not what this passage says at all. It says that homosexuality is a perversion, the degrading of your body, shameful, unnatural, and indecent. God isn't being vague here. Homosexual acts in all situations are wrong.

➤ 1 Corinthians 6:9–10: Do you not know that the wicked will not inherit the kingdom of God? Do not be deceived: Neither the sexually immoral nor idolaters nor adulterers nor male prostitutes nor homosexual offenders . . . will inherit the kingdom of God.

That passage says if you continue in the homosexual lifestyle, you will not inherit the kingdom of God. This is a serious repercussion and ought to cause you to stop and think. Don't throw an eternity with God away in order to live in disobedience for one short lifetime.

But notice that this verse also lists the sexually immoral, idolaters, adulterers, and male prostitutes. We want to concentrate on the homosexual offender, but what about you? Are you sexually immoral in other ways? Do not live in that lifestyle. The point is that while homosexuality is a sin, it is not the ultimate sin.

We all sin and struggle in different areas; we all need God's grace and mercy. There is no place for thinking you are any better than anyone else; calling a gay person by some rude name or showing prejudice against them is not OK. We are instructed to love others with a real love, not one that is conditional on the way they live. I long for a church where people can come and openly admit their struggles with pornography, homosexuality, substance abuse, eating disorders, cutting themselves, etc., and find love, understanding, and encouragement.

It is still important to realize that homosexuality is *not* normal. Civilization down through the ages cries out that homosexuality is abnormal. Our race would be extinct if homosexuality were the norm.

Look back to the beginning of God's creation in Genesis 2:18–25. God said, "It is not good for the man to be alone." So who did He create? Another man? No, He created a woman. The whole idea of homosexuality just doesn't make sense in the context of God's creation.

Homosexuals will say to me, "It's none of your business what I do, so leave me alone. It's a private act between two consenting adults."

I respond in two ways to that. First, it isn't merely private. It has become public. Because of this private act, we have a public disease known as AIDS that has brought tremendous suffering upon society — emotionally, physically, and financially.

Second, the homosexual act is not only carried out between consenting adults. Many, many children are molested, leaving scars that will last a lifetime. (Let me make clear that heterosexuals also use children sexually, and that is also wrong and sinful.)

The homosexual community would also have us believe that most homosexuals are involved with just one partner. But in reality this seems the exception rather than the rule. Statistics bear that out, and the counseling I have done would confirm that the average homosexual is involved with multiple partners.

I talked with an older gentleman who has led a gay lifestyle. He has had more than five hundred different partners, and he knew other men who had been with more than a thousand partners. What I said to him, and what I would say to you if you're heading in this direction, was, "You deserve better than one-night stands or quick encounters in public bathrooms. People aren't things. We're not merely pieces of meat. You are somebody special, and God has a better plan for your life than that."

Homosexuality becomes damaging to a person's self-worth. The homosexual loses all self-respect. His conscience becomes seared, but the emptiness and pain remain. He tries to escape by having more sexual encounters, thinking: *This next one will be different. This encounter will make me happy. Now I'll be fulfilled.*

But he isn't. The gay lifestyle can only lead to more destructive behaviors that will be used to soften the emotional pain.

There can be a lot of excitement and good feelings in a homosexual relationship. (If it didn't feel good, no one would do it.) But the pleasure is temporary and never really satisfies, because the mental, emotional, spiritual, and physical pain outweigh that single moment of pleasure.

Homosexuality is wrong. It is a sin, but not greater than other sins. My purpose is not to condemn or destroy you. I want to offer you hope.

> ➤ 1 John 1:7: If we walk in the light, as he is in the light, we have fellowship with one another, and the blood of Jesus, his Son, purifies us from all sin.

Jesus Christ is ready, willing, and able to forgive you and give you a brand-new beginning. There is tremendous hope for you if you've been involved in the homosexual lifestyle.

> 1 Corinthians 6:9–11: Homosexual offenders . . . [will not] inherit the kingdom of God. And that is what some of you were. But you were washed, you were sanctified, you were justified in the name of the Lord Jesus Christ and by the Spirit of our God.

It's not too late. Even though you have been caught up in the homosexual lifestyle, you can be washed and cleansed by the Lord Jesus Christ.

AM I GAY?

Am I gay? Why do teenagers ask me this question? A lot go through what I call homosexual panic. They have had some feelings along this line—perhaps even some experience—so now they are scared to death they are gay. I tell them, "Relax. Just because you've had certain feelings or even experiences doesn't mean you are homosexual. As a matter of fact, a lot of individuals go through this when they are young. These are some of the typical things I hear."

> *"I saw this pornographic Web site with gay individuals, and I got turned on."*

Especially for the male, the visual can be very sexually stimulating. Pornographic Web sites take "beautiful people," put them in interesting places, and pose them in exciting positions. Their whole goal is to sexually excite you.

Seeing naked people involved sexually can be stimulating no matter what your sex may be, so being excited by some pictures does not mean you are gay.

Realize also that, if this is one of your first exposures to sex, you are attracted to it not because you are homosexual, but because of the initial sexual arousal it caused inside you.

You need to stay away from both homosexual pornography and heterosexual pornography.

➤ *"I feel this strong attraction to members of the same sex."*

There is a big difference between being attracted to someone and being involved with that person sexually. The first is temptation; the other is sin. Many individuals at some time in their lives have been attracted to members of the same sex. It is not necessarily a sin to have homosexual feelings. The sin comes when you act on those feelings and become sexually involved.

➤ *"I actually had a sexual experience with a member of the same sex when I was young, and it excited me."*

God made sex, so it is no surprise that sex is enjoyable. And in the worst of situations there can still be excitement and pleasure. The fact that homosexual sex excited you doesn't make you gay, even though you continue to think about it. You see, we tend to be attracted to and fantasize about experiences we have had. Today some teenage girls are getting involved in what is called recreational lesbianism. They become sexually involved with other girls because it is very sophisticated to be able to say, "I am bisexual." They do it because it becomes a turn-on for guys, and it allows the girls to be in a certain group they perceive as a step up in popularity.

➤ *"I've been rejected by a member [or members] of the opposite sex, so I guess I was meant to be with members of my own sex."*

We have all been rejected by members of the opposite sex—even me! (How come my wife just rolled her eyes?) It's a fact of life that some people we fall in love with don't love us back. That certainly doesn't make us gay.

➤ *"I actually had sex with a member of the opposite sex, and I didn't enjoy it that much. So I must be gay."*

Wrong! The media have given us such an unrealistic view of sex and sexual relationships that we feel tremendous pressure. We worry about not measuring up to all the standards of a real man or a real woman. With all these high expectations, it's easy to become disappointed.

Sex can initially be embarrassing, uncomfortable, or even painful for many different reasons. Engaging in it before marriage can add guilt, fear, and confusion, which together can make for something quite a bit less than the pure ecstasy you were led to believe you would immediately experience.

Yet another good reason to wait to have sex until you're older and married!

➤ *"I was physically, emotionally, and/or sexually used and abused by members of the opposite sex."*

I'm sorry for the pain you have gone through. It is understandable that you might be attracted to members of your own sex. But I want you to know that's a wrong choice, and you can't let people from your past manipulate you into making a bad decision today.

You can't judge an entire sex because of the bad actions of a few. You need to meet some members of the opposite sex who will treat you with love, kindness, and compassion.

It may be that you lack judgment as to what kind of person you should date or spend time with. My suggestion is that you make yourself accountable to your parents and/or other godly men and women. Ask them to screen possible dates and help you make good choices.

➤ *"People always told me that homosexuality was OK."*

Then I understand how and why you got involved in it, but Jesus Christ says in John 8:32, "You will know the truth, and the truth will set you free."

The truth is that homosexuality isn't OK, and you need to move away from it.

➤ *"I just don't fit the image of the 'real woman' or the 'real man.' I've just always felt a little different."*

There is no set standard for a "real woman" or a "real man." We are all unique creations of God.

You don't have to be, nor are you supposed to be, like

everyone else. You have special gifts, talents, and abilities. Physically you're supposed to look different from others. Don't let anyone say you've got to be this tall, have these measurements, this color hair, or do these certain things to be a "real" man or woman. You are a real man; you are a real woman. You are a creation of God Almighty, and that makes you everything you need to be.

Be careful not to fall into another trap. Perhaps people begin to call us names or hint that we may be homosexual. Lies and gossip might be going around. What do we do? Well, we want to prove to others—and in some cases to ourselves—that we aren't homosexual, so we begin to get involved sexually with someone of the opposite sex.

In an effort to take care of our problem, we have only caused another problem for ourselves.

You don't have to prove anything to anybody. The bottom line is that your friends are going to believe you, and those who aren't will find something else to gossip about even if you disprove the homosexuality. So ignore them, be with your friends, and trust God to take care of your reputation. And that leads us to the question . . .

WHAT CAUSES HOMOSEXUALITY?

What causes homosexuality? Well, I hear four theories over and over again.

➤ You inherit these tendencies.

The gay rights movement would like you to believe this. You are born gay, and this is what you will be for the rest of your life. It's part of your makeup. You've got blond hair, blue eyes. You're right-handed, homosexual, and five feet five inches tall. There is little scientific evidence for this.

➤ There's a hormonal imbalance.

Since each of us has male and female hormones, this

could be a possibility. But, again, the results of this research are at best inconclusive.

➤ There's a spiritual problem.

If you would just commit your life to Jesus Christ, then you wouldn't have these temptations. The ultimate answer to the needs of man is a personal relationship with Jesus Christ, but I also see man needing help with problems even after he has come to know and love Jesus Christ. Just think of all the problems and temptations you are still facing in different areas of your life!

➤ An overwhelming amount of evidence points to the conclusion that homosexuality is a learned behavior.

What factors would lead us toward an attraction to members of the same sex or even to a homosexual lifestyle? There are many, but let me suggest ten.

➤ First experiences

A first homosexual experience or sexual excitement can lay a foundation for the future. In time, our bodies can be programmed to respond and react to certain stimuli. However, if we have taught our bodies to respond one way, then we can *reteach* them another way over time.

➤ Feelings of rejection

Members of the opposite sex have rejected you. You're down, depressed, and you feel "there must be something different about me." Right now you have become very vulnerable to anyone who will appear to love, understand, accept, and reach out to you. If a member of the same sex begins to express interest, it's easy to see how you would respond.

➤ Unforgiveness

You've been abused in the past: raped, beaten up, torn down emotionally, are a survivor of incest, or worse. You are unwilling to let go of this hatred and anger by choosing to forgive the offender.

However, the hatred you have toward that person doesn't affect him at all. It just continues to kill you on the inside. By not forgiving, you are allowing the offending person to continue to abuse and manipulate you emotionally and spiritually.

Your hatred will soon turn to bitterness, which will harden your heart. You will then lose your sensitivity to God and His Holy Spirit, which in turn will lead you toward sin. One such sin is hatred toward members of the opposite sex; another would be homosexual relationships. Recovered homosexuals look back and see the releasing of anger and the offering of forgiveness as the beginning of their healing process.

It is not wrong to want our needs met, but how we seek to get them met can be wrong.

➤ Fear

What if I fail? Fear of failure is widespread today. Many feel fear in relationships with the opposite sex. What if I don't meet their expectations? What if I make mistakes? What if I don't perform as well as others? What if I really try my hardest but fail anyway? What if I'm not appealing to them? What if they laugh about me? What if they gossip to their friends about me?

We desperately want to be loved, to belong, to achieve, and then to be recognized for those achievements. So we will turn to those who are meeting those basic needs. The truth is that in the homosexual lifestyle almost everyone is accepted. The "failure rate" is low.

So stop a moment and think. When you find yourself fantasizing about members of the same sex, usually you are not looking for sexual fulfillment at all, but rather for someone to meet your basic need to be loved, to belong, to be accepted, to achieve, and to be recognized. (Want to know a secret? Jesus Christ would like to meet all those needs in your life!)

➤ Poor sex education or no sex education

If you have been kept in the dark about sex and sexual relationships, you become very vulnerable to an individual or individuals who would lead you toward a homosexual lifestyle.

Some sex education programs teach homosexuality as merely an alternative sexual preference. They say they aren't making any moral judgments. But let's be realistic. We both know if we are teaching homosexuality as an option, then we are putting our stamp of approval on it. Are they teaching sex with children or sex with animals as an option? No. Why? Because they think that is sick behavior, and it is! But you can be sure that if we don't take some stands now, we are going to find our society headed in the direction of one day teaching adult-child and human-animal sex as two other alternatives.

➤ Excessive self-pity

We fall into a pit of despair. "Nobody really understands me. Nobody really cares. Nobody has had the kind of trauma, pain, and problems I have had. This is just who I am, so I'll give up and give in to homosexuality."

A person like this usually seeks out others who are like-minded, and you find a lot of this mind-set in the gay movement. We concentrate on the pain of our past, but don't seek to deal with it. Focusing on our pain helps us to rationalize our own sinful behavior now and justifies our continuing sin in the future.

➤ Satan

Just as there is a real God who wants to forgive, love, and set you free, there is also a real Devil who wants to bind, use, and destroy you. Satan always seeks to pervert God's good and perfect creation. We are involved in a spiritual warfare, and our real battle is not against flesh and blood. We are fighting Satan and his demons.

Don't look at temptation as just an isolated incident. Think of it as an attack, and start fighting back.

➤ Not really understanding the opposite sex

We are unsure about how the opposite sex thinks, feels,

acts, and reacts. We are uncomfortable around them, and we may say or do stupid things that make us feel awkward. Not really understanding the opposite sex and having had some early bad experiences can push us toward homosexuality.

➤ Poor parental role models

For example, the opposite-sex parent who is abusive physically, emotionally, or sexually can drive the child toward homosexuality. Rejection will do this: "I never wanted you." "I wish you were never born." "Why couldn't you have been a boy?" "Why couldn't you have been a girl?"

Attacking one's sexual identity can lead to homosexuality: "You're not a real man." "You're not a real woman." "Men wouldn't act like that." "You don't act like a woman. No man would ever want you." "What girl is going to go out with you?" For a man, having a very domineering mother and/or a very weak father can cause anger and fear toward women in general, coupled with a loss of self-respect.

It's interesting and sad to note that very few homosexuals have had good relationships with their fathers.

➤ No personal relationship with Jesus Christ

Without Jesus you really lack the power to do what you know is right. Within the person of Jesus Christ, however, is forgiveness for the past, power for right now, and hope for the future.

With Jesus the best is always yet to come. He is waiting, and you don't have to be good enough. You just need to be humble enough to say, "Dear Jesus, please help me, come into my life, forgive my sin, and empower me to live a life that is pleasing to You. I thought I could make it on my own, but I can't."

Without Jesus Christ you really have no strong moral foundation from which to develop your beliefs. But with Christ not only will you discover right and wrong, but you will have new strength through the Holy Spirit to do what is right even when it is difficult.

SO WHAT DO I DO?

So you say to me, "OK, Greg, I understand that homosexuality's not right, and it's not good. So what do I do?" Let me suggest some things.

➤ See it as sin.

Stop making excuses; stop rationalizing; stop trying to justify it. Just admit to yourself and God, "You're right. I have been sinning."

Once we are willing to face that, we are not to continue in sin. "What shall we say, then? Shall we go on sinning so that grace may increase? By no means!" (Romans 6:1–2).

You see, homosexuality is rebellion against God. Your sin is first and foremost against Him. "Against you, you only, have I sinned and done what is evil in your sight" (Psalm 51:4).

But at the same time, you are no worse than anyone else. Each of us struggles with sins in a variety of different areas. Those who would look down at you are either intimidated by you and don't really know how to help, or they are hiding some sin themselves.

The fact is, if they had been in your shoes, and had gone through all that you have gone through, they would probably be exactly where you are right now. Ignore them. They, thank the Lord, are in the minority.

In the past you tried to deceive yourself, and you traded God's truth for a lie. But now you're back on the right track.

➤ Come to Jesus Christ.

The hope for you as a homosexual is Christ. Nobody understands as well as Christ does what you've been through, what you're going through, and what you're going to face.

Hebrews 4:15–16 says: "For we do not have a high priest who is unable to sympathize with our weaknesses, but we have one who has been tempted in every way, just as we are—yet was without sin. Let us then approach the throne of grace with confidence, so that we may receive mercy and find grace to help us in our time of need."

Jesus Christ wants to forgive and strengthen you. Some of you have been running a long time, and now you need to come on home.

Our Lord would love to put His arms around you and say, "Welcome home. I've missed you so much."

➤ Each day ask the Holy Spirit to be in control of your life.

In the past you have sought after sin; you have sought to please yourself and others. Now actively seek to please the Lord. The Holy Spirit will give you all the power you need.

Then just take it one day at a time. Wise old Chinese philosopher say, "Trip of one thousand miles begin with first step." The idea is that we live one day at a time, and we don't rely on our own abilities to do what's right. We rest on the Holy Spirit.

You say, "But, Greg, right now I am so weak." And my answer is, "Great. Look at 2 Corinthians 12:9–10: 'But he said to me, "My grace is sufficient for you, for my power is made perfect in weakness." Therefore I will boast all the more gladly about my weaknesses, so that Christ's power may rest on me. That is why, for Christ's sake, I delight in weaknesses, in insults, in hardships, in persecutions, in difficulties. For when I am weak, then I am strong.'"

➤ Seek the Lord.

Matthew 6:33 says: "But seek first his kingdom and his righteousness, and all these things will be given to you as well."

How do you seek God?

- *Read and study His Word daily.* It will teach, train, rebuke, and correct you to be thoroughly equipped for every good work (2 Timothy 3:16–17).
- *Pray.* That is, talk to God. If you're going to have a friendship and love relationship with Christ, be sure

you spend time talking with Him daily.

- *Memorize God's Word.* "I have hidden your word in my heart that I might not sin against you" (Psalm 119:11). The Word of God is powerful. The more you memorize, the more tools you give God for working in your life to build and develop you.

➤ Desire to change.

Ask yourself, "Do I want to change?" The question is not, "*Can* I have victory in my life?" but, "Do I *want* to have victory in my life, and am I willing to take the steps necessary, even though it's difficult?"

➤ Get some counseling.

Find or let someone help you find a Christian counselor. Remember, we talked about some of the causes of homosexuality. A good counselor will be able to open your eyes to some of the reasons you are in the shape you're in. You need to look beyond the fact that you are attracted to a member of your own sex to the reasons for that attraction. Please, please, please get some help and counsel. You'll feel so much better, and so will I.

Here is the contact information of a good organization to get in touch with:

Exodus International
PO Box 540119
Orlando, FL 32854
888-264-0877 or 407-599-6872
www.exodus-international.org

They will be able to help you.

➤ Seek your parents' support.

Your parents can make great friends, and in most cases nobody (other than God) loves you more than they do. Maybe you're messed up now because you didn't listen to them. So go back and say, "I'm sorry for the way I've been, and right now I really need your love, support, encouragement, and wisdom."

Yes, your parents made mistakes, but if you're sharp enough to see all the dumb things they did, then be mature enough to forgive them.

➤ Be vulnerable but cautious.

Ask God to give you the name of one godly man or woman —other than your counselor—to confide in. You need a friend to rejoice with and weep with. The encouragement of a friend will be helpful, and it will remove a lot of pressure from you.

You're not looking for another counselor but rather someone who will listen and love you unconditionally. It's important to talk about and let out all the fears, worries, anger, confusion, and questions that you have.

I'm not asking you to tell the whole youth group. Just pick a friend. It will probably be better if he or she is several years older than you are. An adult would be good.

➤ Get rid of the garbage.

You know the things that draw you toward a homosexual lifestyle. You need to get away from these. What might they be?

- Videos
- Magazines
- Parties
- Pictures
- Books
- Letters
- Places
- Friends

This last one is probably the hardest to deal with, but if you're going to make it, you're going to have to sever some relationships. "Do not be misled: 'Bad company corrupts good character'" (1 Corinthians 15:33). It's true, and you have seen it happen.

This will be difficult because for a while you may find yourself alone as you seek a new lifestyle. But God will honor you and help you to gain far more than you ever gave up.

➤ Be encouraged.

The victory is yours. Find hope in the fact that others have gone before you and Christ has set them free.

Second Corinthians 5:17 says: "Therefore, if anyone is in Christ, he is a new creation; the old has gone, the new has come!" The homosexual person has passed away. No more do you have to listen to Satan's lies or live in sin.

➤ Be patient with yourself.

Usually no one is harder on us than ourselves. Overcoming will take time. There will still be temptation and maybe even some failure, but don't give up.

You may even find that for a while the temptations will get stronger and sin will be unusually available. Why? Because you're in a battle, and Satan is trying to pull you back down before you get stronger.

If things get harder than ever, take courage, you're on the right track. Satan will do everything he can to stop you because he knows how valuable and special you are. Otherwise, he wouldn't bother. So remember 1 John 4:4: "You, dear children, are from God and have overcome them, because the one who is in you is greater than the one who is in the world," and don't give up.

➤ Develop healthy same-sex friendships.

It's good to continue close relationships with members of the same sex, but the key word is *healthy*. Up to this point the relationships have been sexual in nature and therefore unhealthy. You need to discover that you can have a fulfilling, close relationship without sexual involvement.

➤ Right thinking is important.

A process is going on in your life. Whatever you take into your mind goes into your heart, and it is out of the overflow of your heart that you act and speak.

For example, the gay movement would tell you that one out of every ten people is homosexual. You begin to think about that. It starts filling your mind. And then you ask yourself the question: *Could I be homosexual?*

Doubt, fear, and confusion flood your mind. The more you think about it, the more you convince yourself you must be gay.

Then one day your heart overflows with this garbage, and you experiment a little. Suddenly you discover you can be turned on by a member of the same sex. So that settles it, and you immediately jump to the conclusion, "I am gay." Now you are at least temporarily trapped, and it all goes back to faulty thinking.

So what should you be taking into my mind and dwelling on? "Finally, brothers, whatever is true, whatever is noble, whatever is right, whatever is pure, whatever is lovely, whatever is admirable—if anything is excellent or praiseworthy—think about such things" (Philippians 4:8).

Should we then dwell on homosexuality? Let's find out by asking some questions:

- Is it true? No.
- Is it noble? No.
- Is it right? No.
- Is it pure? No.
- Is it lovely? No.
- Is it admirable? No.
- Is it excellent? No.
- Is it praiseworthy? No.

Should we be taking thoughts of homosexuality into our minds? No. Instead of spending all this time thinking about homosexuality, spend more time thinking about Jesus Christ. Who is He? What is He like? What has He done for you? How can you get closer to Him?

➤ Practice self-control.

Homosexuality is more a matter of what you choose to do than it is a matter of what you are. All of us have to learn to control our sexuality. When you're single, you have to practice self-control and wait to be involved sexually until after you're married. When you're married, you still have to practice self control. You're not to commit adultery. Sexual relationships are reserved for your spouse only.

You might say, "I'll never be able to fulfill my desires for the same sex." That is true, but remember that those who never marry are not able to fulfill their desires for the opposite sex. So, it is not impossible. It is possible for you to control those homosexual desires. It's possible for you to develop desires for the opposite sex. "I can do everything through him who gives me strength" (Philippians 4:13).

I am asking you to give up the instant gratification that comes from homosexual encounters—a gratification that never lasts—for the much deeper satisfaction of pleasing the Lord. Giving up a homosexual lifestyle opens the door for God to pour out His blessings upon your life.

You can do it. I know you can! How do I know that? Because of what Jude 24 says: "To him who is able to keep you from falling and to present you before his glorious presence without fault and with great joy . . ."

Because God is able!

Questions to ask yourself:
1. In God's eyes is the homosexual act right or wrong?
2. Are you facing temptations toward members of the same sex?
3. What is the next step you need to take to get help?

13

For Girls Only

(A SINGLE GUY'S VIEW ON WOMEN)

By Matt Roop: Matt is a young man who deeply loves Jesus Christ. He is a graduate of Moody Bible Institute with a major in youth ministry and an emphasis in sports ministry. He is currently living in Naples, Florida, and working as a golf professional. His desire is to use golf as a way to sharing Jesus Christ with others.

As a female, have you ever had trouble understanding a guy? Have you ever been speechless? Surprised? Confused? Well, take comfort in the fact that as a guy I have often been confused myself! Guys are complex beings. It should come as no surprise that guys operate differently than you do. We act differently. We think differently. Our longings and desires are different from yours. We process life differently than you do. We have been innately created and wired differently than you have—even when it comes to relationships and sex! This probably does not come as much of a surprise to you.

Have you ever felt clueless? About guys, I mean . . . I know I have felt clueless about girls. Many girls have told me, "If I only knew what he was thinking . . . I don't understand why he . . . ," and so on. One girl said it like this, "I wish I could get inside a guy's head. Actually, I probably don't wish I could. I know I'll never be able to understand them, but I want to, in a way!" Another girl said, "I want to know how guys function. I honestly want to know the first thing they think about when they see me." Another girl said, "I want to know why certain things that don't even faze us [girls] cause a guy to stumble."

If you're a girl, I am sure you have many questions. Many unanswered questions. I hope to be able to answer some of those questions for you in this chapter. At the same time, I am sure you are well aware that this subject of "understanding a guy" is wide and deep. It is a subject that will be discussed and written about as long as guys are around. Because the subject is so wide and deep, I obviously will not attempt to tackle everything in this chapter. But for your own sake and the questions you may have, I have decided to briefly address three extremely important and relevant issues: *the essence of every man, the battle of every man,* and *the desired woman of every man.* Whereas the first two issues are explanations of every guy's heart, the last issue is an expression of every guy's heart toward you.

THE ESSENCE OF EVERY MAN

If we read the Genesis account of God creating humanity, we quickly learn that God created both men and women *in His image.* Genesis 1:27 tells us, "So God created man in his own image, in the image of God he created him; male and female he created them." We are all created in God's image either *as men* or *as women.* It is very important this is understood. God did not create us all as one gender. Because God does not have a body, the uniqueness between men and women exists far beyond our physical differences. The differences between men and women also exist within our hearts.

Have you ever listened to your heart? I imagine every one of you desires *to be loved.* No, I'm not just talking about hearing the simple words *I—love—you.* It's much deeper than that. . . . I'm talking about real love. To be *cherished.* To be seen as *beautiful.* To be *wanted.* To be loved for who you truly are. Have you ever desired *to be loved*? It's who you were created to be. It's part of how you were designed. You can't get away from it. Nobody can take it away from you. To deny this desire means to deny a part of who you know yourself to be. *To be loved* is definitely part of what it means to be a woman. It is a quality of your *essence*.

Men's desires, their deep heart longings, are much different than yours. God distinctly created the masculine heart separate from the feminine heart. This is revealed and confirmed in the differences between men's desires and women's desires.

One of your basic needs is to be loved!

Many individuals have tried to pinpoint the exact desires of every man's heart. Certainly one man cannot speak on behalf of all men. Nor can I speak on their behalf. But if we look at all men throughout history, we see four qualities or desires rise to the surface. Stu Weber, pastor and author of *Tender Warrior: God's Intention for a Man*, calls these four desires "the four unshakable pillars of masculinity." Weber claims these four "pillars," or deep desires, are rooted in the heart of every male child. These four desires are simply: *King, Warrior, Mentor,* and *Friend.* Weber explains them in the following way:

> The heart of the *King* is a provisionary heart. The king looks ahead, watches over, and provides order, mercy, and justice. He is authority. He is leader. The king in a man is "under orders" from a higher Authority.
>
> The heart of the *Warrior* is a protective heart. The warrior shields, defends, stands between, and guards. Whether he's stepping on intruding bugs or checking out the sounds that go "bump" in the night. Whether he's confronting a habitually abusive Little League coach or shining a flashlight into a spooky basement. Whether he is shoveling snow or helping women and children into the last lifeboat on the *Titanic. Men stand tallest when they are protecting and defending.* . . . A warrior is one who possesses high moral standards, and holds to high principles. He is willing to live by them, *stand* for them, *spend* himself in them, and if necessary die for them. . . . Maybe these are some of the reasons why the most humiliating thing you can call a man is "coward."

The heart of the *Mentor* is a teaching heart. The mentor knows. He wants others to know. He models, explains, and trains. . . . A man is supposed to know things. . . . Men are supposed to know how things work. And what to do next. And where to go from wherever you are. Men are supposed to be able to teach life.

The heart of the *Friend* [or Lover] is a loving heart. It is a care-giving heart. Passionate, yes. But more. Compassionate ("I will be with you"). The friend in a man is a commitment-maker.[1]

You may have seen some of these qualities displayed in the lives of guys you know. Your dad? Your brother? How about your cousin? Your guy friends at school? Your boyfriend? How about a young boy? Have you ever watched a young boy play? When young boys play, the qualities of *king* and *warrior* shine!

More likely than not, the young boy you may be thinking of likes toy guns. I loved toy guns when I was younger. I couldn't get enough of them! I loved pulling all my toy guns out and playing war with my friends. We would split up into two teams and figure out where our "army bases" were. Once we had our bases determined, it was all-out war from there. I loved shouting out commands to my friends. After all, I knew how to defend and protect our base, and I wasn't going to let it go down. I loved devising "war plans" of how we would conquer our enemies.

When my friends had to go home, I loved spending time shooting at targets. I don't think my parents loved it as much as I did. . . . Usually my parents let me know they didn't like finding darts stuck to the windows, the TV, or the china cabinet in the dining room. When I got tired of nonmoving targets, I would go after bugs and flies. When I got tired of trying to nab flies, I would camp out and wait for my parents or brother to come down the steps or around the corner. As soon as they were in sight, I would nail them in the stomach or the forehead, laughing my head off. My parents' least favorite "target practice" memory would have to be the day I shattered the glass patio door with a stone launched from my slingshot.

Believe me, if a little boy doesn't have a toy gun, he'll find one—whether it be a crooked stick or even his finger.

Every guy out there desires and longs to be *king, warrior, mentor,* and *friend.* Every guy is designed, and as a result, desires, to look ahead, watch over, provide order, lead, protect, defend, stand between, guard, conquer, teach, explain, cherish, and love. But you may be thinking, *What is this guy talking about? Not my dad! Not my brother! Not my friend! Why can't I seem to find a guy who will look ahead for, watch over, provide order for, lead, protect, defend, stand between, guard, teach, explain things to, cherish, and love* me? For some of you these qualities don't describe any of the guys you know. You may wonder if the guys you know actually even desire the things I have just mentioned. Please, don't lose heart. Keep reading. . . .

One thing you must come to grips with and understand about most guys is that they struggle with thoughts of feeling like an *imposter.* What do I mean? I mean that most guys are hiding a deep uncertainty about themselves. It is this deep inner uncertainty that leaves the most confident-looking guy dreading the moment when he will be exposed as the imposter he believes himself to be. In his book *Wild at Heart* John Eldredge explains what these "complex" guys have, by saying:

> This is every man's deepest fear: to be exposed, to be found out, to be discovered as an imposter, and not really a man . . . if there is one thing a man does know, he knows he is made to come through. Yet he wonders . . . *Can I? Will I?*

Are you catching this? Do you catch the confusion that exists within the life of every guy? Let's take a quick step back and look at the whole picture. . . .

Every guy has the desire to live as *king, warrior, mentor,* and *friend.* Every guy's heart is calling him to these things. This is what he was designed and created for. Yet every guy also has his own mind working against him, telling him he is an imposter. Every guy questions whether he can actually "come through." "Do I have what it takes?"

In effect, every guy desires and wants to "conquer the world," but knows that he will have to risk humiliation along the way.

Guys, generally speaking, will begin to live one of two ways. First is the one who lets his questioning and hesitation overpower his ability to live from the depths of his calling. This is the guy who abuses his desires, denying himself the ability to live the way he knows he was created to live. This is the guy who looks for the "personally safe" way of filling his heart's desire. This involves no risk. Even though he desires to be king, warrior, mentor, and friend, he picks only the battles he is sure to win. He lives his life participating in the things that won't require vulnerability or potential exposure of weaknesses. He fears rejection so he doesn't reach out to make friends. This is the guy who only does the things he knows he is good at. This is the guy who desires love, but instead wraps himself up in pornography. Even though his heart's deep desire is to be friend and lover, he doesn't want to risk exposing his passionate side to find her or win her. So, instead, he turns to the imitation. If a man is not encouraged to live for the things his heart was made for, he will go elsewhere to find them—in cheap imitations, requiring no risk or vulnerability.

Second is the guy who is honest with himself and the desires of his heart. He actively pursues life the way he knows he was meant to live it. For this guy, it is not even an option to deny what his heart is made for. This is the guy who knows in his own mind he is taking a great deal of personal risk. But the risk is well worth it. This is the guy who knows failure and personal risk are always a possibility, but he won't let the possibility overshadow his desire to live for what his heart deeply desires. This is the guy who surrenders to his Creator, saying, "God, I doubt whether I can actually live to be king, warrior, mentor, and friend. Everything around me tells me I shouldn't. My mind tells me I can't, but I need to. My heart is calling me. This is what You have created me for. Help me. Guide me. Direct me. Empower me, Lord."

You know just as well as any guy that surrender is not easy. When someone truly surrenders, he recognizes the fact that he doesn't have the ability in himself to do what he should. *Surrender* takes great *personal risk*. Are you connecting the dots? If a guy is truly going to live the life he knows he was meant to live, he is going to listen to Christ and be fully reliant upon God, his Creator. Isn't this the kind of guy you desire?

Don't you want someone who loves Jesus Christ more than he loves you?

Isn't this the kind of person your heart is attracted to? The good, honest, real man, whose strength makes your heart flourish? Did you know you have the ability to encourage guys to be this kind of man? Please don't misunderstand me. I'm not saying it is in your control. What I am saying is that you can encourage and help a guy in this process to become the man he was created to be.

"What can I possibly do?" Most guys are actually very vulnerable and insecure underneath their confident exteriors and personalities. They are constantly trying to prove themselves to themselves and those around them. They often wonder if they have what it takes to be the man they were created to be. A man wants to know you respect, love, and believe in him. Your words of affirmation or criticism will either bring life or death to him. You have the ability to build up or tear down a man.

This is not at all how most women think and process the issues of *love* and *respect*. I imagine all of you would look at *love* and *respect* as two separate things. But remember, God created women different from men, and men different from women. Whereas most women look at *love* and *respect* as two separate things, most guys see them as one and the same. If you don't respect a man he will not feel like you love him. What does this mean for you? What it means is this: if you want to encourage and help guys in the process of becoming the men they were created to be, *they need your respect.*

Your respect is extremely important. How important? Consider it this way. The guy you desire, the guy your heart desires, is the one who would love you unconditionally for who you truly are, right?

Well, the same is true for guys when it comes to respect. He wants and needs you to show and demonstrate your respect for him regardless of the circumstances. A guy wants and needs your respect even when he is not meeting your expectations.

If you aren't respecting a man, then you aren't loving him.

I am sure you appreciate it when you hear the words, "I love you." But isn't it even better when those around you (or your boyfriend) actually show they love you? Isn't it the best when they actually demonstrate their love for you? Well, the same is true about guys when talking about *respect*. Just as you desire the love of those around you, guys desire the respect of those around them. And even though they love hearing the words, "I respect you," they like it even more when respect is demonstrated or when they hear the words, "I trust you. I am so proud of you." Guys have been created and "wired" for respect.

As a woman, you must understand the incredible power you have. You have the ability to encourage, help, and build up men. But you also have the ability to tear them apart. Respect from the women in a man's life encourages him to strive to be the man he knows he was created to be. Just as you may be touched to hear the words, "I love you," a guy's heart is deeply touched when hearing the words, "I am so proud of you." Such words and demonstrated respect will contribute to the men in your life becoming king, warrior, mentor, and friend.

THE BATTLE OF EVERY MAN

Some of you may have a basic understanding of male sexuality. I'm sure you have heard various things from parents, siblings, friends, sex education class, etc. But I would imagine most of you still have plenty of questions. Male sexuality is a deep, large issue—something I won't be able to adequately cover in this chapter. But there are a few things I would like to share with you, hopefully answering some of the questions you may have.

I'm sure some of you grew up hearing the phrase, "Men are

visual." But do you actually know what this phrase means? I would bet most of you don't. If you did understand, I would think it would dramatically affect the way you present yourself to guys and interact with them. Allow me to explain this common yet vague phrase with a little more detail.

The idea that *men are visual* simply results from this truth about male sexuality: *most guys are sexually stimulated through their eyes.* What does that actually mean? It means that men are aroused, turned on, "set and ready" for sexual intercourse just by looking at you. Whereas girls are generally stimulated sexually through *relationship* and *touch*—the stroking of an inner thigh or rubbing of a breast—guys are stimulated through the sight of *nudity*.

There is no question that God created the gift of sex (including foreplay) for the marriage relationship. In Ezekiel 23:3, God portrays the disobedience of His chosen people, using the picture of virgins in lustful, passionate sin (foreplay): "In that land their breasts were fondled and their virgin bosoms caressed." More than just foreplay, God clearly calls His people to a higher standard in regards to sexuality. Hebrews 13:4 clearly states that sexual intercourse is meant for marriage only: "Marriage should be honored by all, and the marriage bed kept pure, for God will judge the adulterer and all the sexually immoral." Ephesians 5:3 tells that among us "there must not be even a hint of sexual immorality, or any kind of impurity." First Thessalonians 4:3–5, 7 (italics added) sums up God's stance pretty clearly:

> It is God's will that you should be sanctified: that you should avoid *sexual immorality*; that each of you should learn to control his own body in such a way that is holy and honorable, not in passionate lust like the heathen, who do not know God. . . . For God did not call us to be impure, but to live a holy life.

God never intended for His gift to be abused and taken outside the marriage relationship. But just as Adam and Eve disobeyed God's clear command, the rest of humanity continues to disobey God's commands as well, abusing the gift of sex God has given us.

Rather than sex being something private between a husband and wife, sex is readily available everywhere. You don't have to go out of your way to find sex anymore. Just turn on the TV, go to the movie theater, see it on billboards, and in newspaper ads. You can find it anywhere and everywhere on the Internet. American companies and organizations know that sex sells. So what do they do? They use sex to market and sell their products. Our sexually driven culture does not help in any way with the battle every guy is up against.

What exactly is this battle? The battle every guy faces is the constant struggle to resist feeding himself sexual images and thoughts. Because guys are wired to draw sexual gratification through their eyes, they will inevitably come across a sexual image at some point in their lives. The image can be different for every guy. Regardless, the image becomes sexually stimulating. Very few guys, if any, are prepared for what they will experience because they don't yet understand how they have been created sexually. As a result, very few guys know how to process the feelings they experience. At some point in every man's life, he will begin to experience chemical highs (or rushes) that feel really good. Nothing else has ever felt this good. It's beyond good. It's truly stimulating. He has no idea how to process these feelings. All he knows is he feels more like a man than ever before.

Where did this chemical high come from? It resulted from entertaining a sexual image. This sexual image could be a tightly clothed girl jogging down the street. It could be a woman in a bikini at the beach. It could be a naked image on the Internet, or even a romantic interlude of kissing with a girlfriend. Regardless of what it was, this guy received sexual gratification from what he saw. What this guy does not yet know but will soon come to understand is: *for the rest of his life, he will continually be drawn to that same pleasure high he experienced as a result of the image he entertained in his mind.*

All guys receive a chemical high from sexual images when a hormone called epinephrine is secreted into the bloodstream. This locks into memory whatever stimulus is present at the time of the emotional excitement. As a result, the mind of every guy can cause the same chemical high through fantasy. This guy no longer needs a tangible image. The one he allowed his eyes to entertain has now been stored in his mental library of sexual images. This newfound ability to fantasize, coupled with the fact that guys naturally desire a sexual release about every seventy-two hours, pushes him to experiment with masturbation.

Are you beginning to get a better understanding of the battle that exists? Without any guidance or direction, any man can easily slip into a sexual stimulation routine that slowly but surely ends up controlling him. Once a guy has gone in this deep—regularly entertaining sexual images, eventually leading to regular sexual release—it becomes difficult for his body to stop what it has been "trained" to do. This is where the battle lies.

Even though every guy is constantly faced with this sexual battle, don't think for a second he doesn't have any control over what takes place. *Guys can control whether they will entertain the sexual images and thoughts, or whether they will dismiss them.* As soon as a guy comes across a sexual image or thought, he can let it linger and play with it, or get rid of it. This choice is where the distinction between *temptation* and *sin* lies.

The very fact that you are wired differently than a guy could leave you viewing this visual aspect of male sexuality as dirty and shallow. But I challenge you to not look at male sexuality through your lens of female sexuality. I challenge you to think differently. I challenge you to think openly. I challenge you to understand the struggle and battle that exists for every guy. Do not allow yourself to forget this is the way *all* guys have been created. Don't forget all men have been created in the image of their Creator. A proper understanding of male sexuality and the battle every guy experiences is something you must be aware of if you desire to encourage and help guys become all they were created to be.

Believe it or not, there are numerous things that you, as females, could be doing to help and encourage guys in the battle they fight. First, I encourage you to *become supportive*. Rather than standing at arm's length, judging, or allowing yourself to look at men as dirty and shallow, show them you truly care about who they are. Let them know you are willing to help them in any way you can to stay pure. Allow yourself the opportunity to understand his battle, from his point of view.

How you dress will either help or hurt a guy in his battle with sexual temptation.

Second, I encourage you to *strive for modesty in yourself and others*. Because you are not visually wired like men, you may not understand how your desire *to get his attention or be seen as cute* does him a world of harm. Spend your time helping guys fight these temptations, rather than contributing to them.

Third and lastly, *pray for the men in your life, as well as yourself.* Now that you have a better understanding of how real and deep this battle is, pray that the Lord would encourage the hearts of men. Pray that guys would seek after Him. Pray that men would look to the Lord, rather than themselves when they are tempted.

THE DESIRED WOMAN OF EVERY MAN

Even though the issues I have shared with you are extremely important for you to know, I consider these final paragraphs to be the most important. What I want to share with you is a conversation I try to make a point of having regularly with my girlfriend. It is a conversation I will someday make a point of having regularly with my wife. It is a conversation I will have someday with my daughter, if I am so fortunate. It is as simple as this: *God wants you to be comfortable with and confident in who you are!*

Believe me—I'm sure you have heard this before. I'm sure you have thought about this before. But I want you to think about it again. I want you to be able to take this phrase to heart. You need to know this is truly the desired woman of every man—a woman who is comfortable with and confident in who she is.

I would like to think that every single one of you reading this book has the desire to have a deep, intimate, passionate, connected, fulfilling relationship with a man someday. Because you are human, because you were created *as female*, in God's image, you long to be recognized, loved, and cherished for who you truly are and to be romanced by a guy, to be valued by him, and to be seen as beautiful by him. Most likely, your desire is to be loved for who you are.

Do you ever go to school, church, or various activities throughout your week trying to find that one guy who will love you like this? Do you think if you could find this one person, your desires for true intimacy, passion, connectedness, and fulfillment would be met? Don't you think you would be more comfortable with and confident in who you are if you knew someone loved you for who you truly are? Wouldn't there be great freedom, comfort, and security in such a relationship? If you answered yes to any of these questions, ask yourself the question that is most appropriate:

Why have you settled for less?
Why are you settling for less?
Why should you settle for less?

The very fact that you are human tells me you have a mental picture of who you see yourself to be. Some would refer to this as self-image. Every one of us bases our self-image on something— whether it be how popular we are, how much attention we get, how much we are loved, you name it. . . . The foundation of our self-image begins the moment we are born. It is when we begin relating to our parents, other members of our family, and the world around us. When we are able to understand words, a whole new avenue of understanding ourselves develops: *verbal communication*.

We then begin to perceive ourselves based upon what we are told about ourselves. As we "grow up" and develop as individuals, we come to see ourselves as others see us. Based upon the reaction we get from those around us, we learn what our individual qualities are. Among many other things, we learn what we do well and what we do poorly. We learn how intelligent we are, how acceptable we are, how attractive we are, and how lovable we are. You see, as a result of living and growing up in this world, we are instinctively taught: *we can be comfortable with and confident in who we are only when those around us confirm our worth.*

You may be asking, "Why do we look to someone else for our worth and value, when they are only looking to someone else for theirs?" Let's look at the bigger picture. To base our worth in the opinions and views of another is inconclusive, because no standard exists when trying to determine our worth and value. Why should we let others tell us who we are, how great we are, how attractive we are, or how worthwhile we are, when they are only looking to someone else to answer the same question? If you're thinking in your mind or shouting out loud, "We shouldn't! We cannot. It doesn't make sense to do that. It's inconclusive!" you are absolutely right.

But what about last week when you saw the hottest guy in your class at his locker and you flirted with him as you passed by, hoping for a response so you could feel good about yourself? How about that tight, revealing shirt you wear with the short skirt that sits really, really low on your hips? Didn't you want at least one guy to look at you and think you were cute, hot, or sexy, so his attention would confirm your beauty? How about the time you gave in to your boyfriend and had sex because your heart longed for deep connection and love? Why should we look to someone around us to confirm our worth when he or she is also looking to everyone else to confirm his or her worth? We shouldn't. We cannot. It is inconclusive.

What is really important is not who you are but whose you are!

If we are truly looking to be comfortable with and confident in who we are, shouldn't we look to our Creator, the One who designed us and created us in His image? Wouldn't He be the One who can answer this question of worth? For the One who created us surely knows who we are. Learning to be comfortable with and confident in who you are cannot be found in the people around you. It can only be found in the One who created and designed us, the One who truly knows us inside and out. This is the only way our worth is conclusive. You can be comfortable with and confident in who you are when you look to the true source of your self-image: Jesus Christ.

In Christ, we have great worth. We all were created in God's image to ultimately find our fulfillment in Him. This God-given potential is the foundation for our self-esteem. David, one of Israel's kings, expressed God's foundation for our sense of value, significance, and worth, saying:

> For you created my inmost being; you knit me together in my mother's womb. I praise you because I am fearfully and wonderfully made; your works are wonderful, I know that full well. My frame was not hidden from you when I was made in the secret place. When I was woven together in the depths of the earth, your eyes saw my unformed body. All the days ordained for me were written in your book before one of them came to be (Psalm 139:13–16).

In Christ, we are deeply loved. Jesus' disciple, John, tells us that, "God so loved the world that he gave his only Son" (John 3:16). Paul also writes in Ephesians 1:4–5 that God "chose us in him before the creation of the world to be holy and blameless in his sight. In love he predestined us to be adopted as his sons through Jesus Christ, in accordance with his pleasure and will."

In Christ, we can have confidence. God created all of us as gifted beings with great potential. In Romans 12:6–8, Paul tells us about the variety of gifts and abilities God has given to each of us: "We have different gifts, according to the grace given us." We all have a huge range of abilities, gifts, qualities, attributes, and potential. While each of us has a varying arrangement of gifts, qualities, attributes, and potential, the uniqueness of our arrangement forms the individual God intended and designed us to be.

In Christ, we can have security. The Bible is very clear on this point: God will never leave us nor forsake us (Hebrews 13:5); God promises to be with us always, to the very end of the age (Matthew 28:20); even little children have angels watching over them

(Matthew 18:10); and nothing will be able to separate us from His love (Romans 8:38–39).

You can be comfortable with and confident in who you are when you see yourself through the eyes of Christ. He knows you. He created you. He gave you your strengths and abilities. He knows your weaknesses and faults. He knows you for who you are, and He loves you dearly!

So you are free to be yourself, and you don't have to worry about boys anymore. If you have trusted Jesus Christ with your eternity, then you can trust Him to meet your needs when it comes to the opposite sex. Why not have a love affair with Jesus and wait for Him to provide you with a guy who loves Him and you?

Questions to ask yourself:
1. What did I learn about guys?
2. Do I help or hurt guys in their struggle with lust?
3. Am I showing guys respect?

Note
1. Stu Weber, *Tender Warrior: God's Intention for a Man* (Sisters, OR: Multnomah, 1999).

14

For Guys Only

(A SINGLE WOMAN'S VIEW ON GUYS)

By Erin Vesta: Erin is a twenty-four-year-old single woman living in Illinois. She graduated from Moody Bible Institute and works at First Evangelical Free Church as the Student Ministries Discipleship Coordinator. She works with both junior and senior high students. I have seen in Erin a passion for Jesus Christ and teenagers.

I love pictures! Now, I realize that pictures may not be a big hit with most of you guys. The few pictures you do have are usually given to you by the ladies in your life with little notes written on the back. But bear with me for a few minutes and step into the mind and passions of a girl.

I think it's the ability to capture the moments of life that I enjoy so much. I love the story a snapshot tells. If you were to walk into my office right now you would see many snapshots with various stories lining my walls. I have pictures of family and friends from all different phases in life. For girls, life is a series of snapshots. Each moment and interaction is a chance for connectedness.

Snapshots tell stories about the people and places that are in them. They allow you to capture emotion, friendship, love, laughter, and all the moments along the way. A girl's heart is like a snapshot. It carries many stories, both of joy and brokenness, and each girl's heart has a story it is' longing to tell. Each girl's heart is so unique, and every interaction you have with her gives you a snapshot into the young woman God created her to be.

I want to give you a snapshot into a girl's heart. Whether you are dating a girl right now or just have girls as friends, there are probably some things you have never explored about how we, as girls, think and feel. You may not even know how we are affected by you. I think the most important thing about getting to know a girl is to look at her as an individual.

On Kodak.com it says that if you want to take a good snapshot you have to, "Look the subject in the eye, and move in close." If you were attempting to capture a picture of the beach or mountains on film, you would have to move in close. This is exactly how to treat a young woman. If you get nothing else out of this, remember that each girl is an individual and she really wants you to notice *her*. Move in close to her and really look her in the eye. What she wants most of all is to be seen and known.

Let's explore the snapshots that make up a girl's heart!

SNAPSHOT 1:
HOW DO GIRLS THINK?

Allow me to let you in on a little secret. God created every girl unique from one another and very different from you as a guy! Each girl has her own thought process about life. Each one will respond differently. You will discover, as you get older, that girls think similarly about some things, but never completely the same.

We may all be different, but every girl thinks about life as a series of connections. Every interaction is a point at which to build a relationship. You need to shoot straight with us girls. If you say you'll call, we'll wait by the phone. If you buy us dinner, we think you're possibly interested in a relationship. If you pay special attention to us, we will begin to think you are interested in a more intimate relationship. We aren't usually good at reading the signs. We are told that guys are fairly easy to read, but love is blind. When we are interested in you, you can do no wrong. So, for our sakes, please shoot straight with us and always be a man of integrity, letting us honestly know where your heart is at.

Ever since we were little, we have been told wonderful stories about Prince Charming and how one day he will come and sweep us off our feet, and we'll ride into the sunset. We know, deep down, it won't really happen but that doesn't mean we can't dream about it and sometimes convince ourselves this reality does exist out there. There is a reason all those cheesy chick flicks you hate getting dragged to keep appearing in

Men, you always need to speak the truth in love.

the box office and actually do pretty well. There are people out there —girls—who will actually watch these movies, because they are attracted to the story and the "what-if" in their own lives.

Let's say for a moment you are able to bug a room where a group of girls are having a sleepover. I can almost guarantee much of the conversation would revolve around guys and the girls' futures. We love to think about whom we will end up with, what he will do for a living, how many kids we will have, where we will live, and even what kinds of vacations we will take. Actually, if you listen a little longer, the girls would start talking about staying friends forever; living in the same towns, having their husbands become best friends, and their kids growing up together. A life where they live happily ever after! You are probably thinking girls are crazy. We aren't crazy; we are girls! Dreaming is what we do.

Women are a mystery. We think and respond so differently than guys. I can remember times when people asked me, "Erin, what's wrong? You aren't acting like yourself." Often I would simply have to say, "I don't know." Guys, there are many times when we as girls don't even know what we are thinking and feeling. We can be filled with unexplainable emotions. This should make you feel better. We can't even figure ourselves out sometimes.

One thing I can tell you about girls is they have a deep desire to be loved. Girls want to feel cherished, honored, protected, and looked out for. I know that for a guy it is so different. You want to be respected. You need to know we are proud of you, we trust you, and we honor you. Girls also need to know they are respected and that someone is proud of them, but that means nothing if we feel unloved. We need to know we are special to you. It may mean staying up late on the phone with her one night, buying her flowers, or even calling her from work. Good communication is a great place to start and very important to a girl. Being a gentleman is something we like a lot. Opening doors, pulling out chairs, and seeking to serve us makes us feel very special.

If you really want to know how a certain girl thinks, you will have to discover that on an individual basis. God created each of us distinct and has given us all different experiences in life. Look at each girl as a unique person. Treat her as someone special and unlike any other. God created her to be different than anyone else. Celebrate and enjoy discovering those differences!

SNAPSHOT 2:
HOW SHOULD YOU TALK TO A GIRL?

Many of you are probably nervous to talk to girls. When a girl walks in the room, your palms get all sweaty, your voice starts cracking, you try and make a joke: "Knock, knock . . . dang it." If this is what happens to you, don't worry about it. As a girl, I understand it's hard for you to approach us. You have to make the first move, and that terrifies some of you.

Speaking from a girl's point of view, it is hard for us too! Many times we want to talk to you, but we are not sure how to do it. We don't know if we should approach you, or if you will think we are too pushy and forward.

When you take a girl out, we love it when you have things to talk about with us. Don't just come into a date thinking, *Well, we can just drive around and find something to do.* Trust me, if you don't have anything planned, that date will go downhill fast. A girl loves it when you seem excited to spend time with her, have planned things out, and desire to make conversation. We are impressed if you ask us questions. And let's face it—everyone's favorite topic is themselves.

You can never go wrong getting a girl to talk about herself. When you ask us questions and create conversation with us, it shows us that you want to get to know us. That is very attractive.

You might be thinking, *Erin, you have no idea how hard it is to be a guy. We have to take the risk of being rejected by the girl we like.* You are right. I don't know what it's like to be a guy. I can only tell you that from a girl's perspective, it is nice to have a man be honest and up front and take the initiative. We appreciate someone who is straightforward with us. Today's culture tries to confuse us by saying that "traditional" values have changed. It isn't really the guy's role to make the call or pay the bill anymore. This can cause some anxiety and confusion, so if you want to impress us, step up boldly and take the initiative.

> *Talking to a girl and asking her questions says that you see her as somebody and not just something.*

SNAPSHOT 3:
HOW SHOULD YOU TREAT A GIRL?

The answer to this question is simple. Please! Please! Please! Treat the girls you hang out with like your mom. (I bet that grossed you out!) OK, not quite, but treat them with great respect and dignity. Many of the girls in your life come across as being very independent and self-sufficient, right? Our society has trained us to put up our defenses. However, inside each girl's heart, there is a place that longs to be treated with the utmost respect. We want you to know we need you and we want you in our lives. I know a lot of times we come across like we could care less if you call or if you even talk to us, but we really do care. God created guys and girls to complement each other and make each other's lives more enjoyable.

SNAPSHOT 4:
WHAT DO GIRLS LOOK FOR IN GUYS?

Hmm . . . What do we look for? Many girls have very long lists of what they are looking for. I know several junior high girls who have their lists narrowed down, even as detailed as the guy's hair color!

Many of my girlfriends are married or are engaged to be married. I have asked all of them this question, "What is the one character trait about your fiancé/husband you could not live without?" They all had different answers, but a few qualities rang true across the board. These are responses from godly women.

The first thing is a man who loves God. I am not just talking about making an appearance at church once a week, but a guy who is sold out for Christ. A guy who is not self-directed but God directed. A guy who is willing to make some hard decisions to serve Christ. A guy who implements his faith into everything he does and every decision he makes. I know that being a godly young man is not always as popular as being the star football player, but trust me: the girls notice who makes godly decisions.

Next, she is looking for a man with character. That means a guy who holds unswervingly to the faith he has in God. A man who holds to the truth even when it is tough! Women want a guy who will stand up for his faith in Biology class when evolution is taught as truth. They want a guy who will hold the door open for the handicapped kid in a wheelchair. A guy with character would look for opportunities to see his faith lived out. They want a man who knows the truth and, more importantly, lives the truth.

Many of these women are coming into dating relationships from broken homes where they question their own father's love for them. They want to choose a guy who has character and understanding of her situation at home. It can be hard for these girls to trust the men in their lives. Many of the young women I talk with have been burned by men. Girls need to know they can trust you. You will have to prove you are trustworthy in the way you handle their very precious heart.

The girls I talk with want a guy who is a man of his word. We want a man with integrity. If you make a statement to us about something you are going to do, please follow through. This is so important in showing us we can trust you. When you say you will call, follow through and call. When you say we will go out, don't say it unless you mean it.

I am convinced you could talk to *every* girl you know, and she will desire her man to be a pursuer. As a girl, we want to be pursued and sought after. It is innate within us. We want to know we are desirable to you. It shows you are *Love is unconditional, but trust is earned by consistent behavior over a period of time.* willing to take the lead and be the man in a relationship. I have been told that men love the challenge of pursuing.

I have talked to so many girls who want to know they are desired, and yet they are still calling the guys and chasing after them. They tell me in their hearts they long for the old-fashioned way, but when a guy is not pursuing, and they still like him, they feel they need to take matters into their own hands.

We also look for confidence. A man who knows what he wants out of life, and is seeking after the dreams God has placed in his heart. The confidence I am referring to can only come from the Lord.

Men who have a sense of direction are incredibly attractive to a girl. You may be feeling really self-conscious about your body, your voice, even your sense of style. As girls, there are many things we are self-conscious about as well. We want to fit in and make a difference too! We want to be noticed, just like you do. I know that for me, when a guy is confident in who God made him to be, it turns my head to take a second look at him. I love to see guys living out the passions God has put in their hearts, regardless of what they look like or how their voice sounds.

Life is funny. You have to admit it. People say some pretty hysterical things. When a guy can laugh at life, and even more importantly at himself, a girl will like that. A sense of humor is important, although never at the cost of other people. Every girl I know thinks it is important to have a similar sense of humor as the guy they're dating. Enjoy your life. Any guy who can really laugh, without necessarily being a comedian, is attractive to a girl. When a girl is looking for a guy, she just wants someone who enjoys life and makes the most out of it.

SNAPSHOT 5:
HOW DOES A PHYSICAL RELATIONSHIP AFFECT A GIRL WHEN THE GUY MOVES ON?

When I was in high school I was invited to a school dance with a great guy. He went to a different high school and was a few years older, so we weren't friends before we dated. Because of this, my parents did not know him well and wanted to talk to him before the night of the big dance.

I remember the day so well. I am going to call the guy, Luke. Luke had met my parents before, but he was a little nervous to have this talk with them. My dad is great, but he can certainly be intimidating when he wants to be, and he wanted this guy to know he meant business.

Luke walked in the house and we all sat around the kitchen table (not so bad). My dad then started talking about how precious I am to him as a daughter and how much I mean to him and my mom. (Thanks, Dad!) He then proceeded to pull out a Barbie doll and a Ken doll from under the table. He told Luke that Barbie represented me and Ken represented Luke. My dad then put Barbie and Ken on the kitchen table and had them hold hands. He said, "Luke, if Ken wants to hold Barbie's hand on the way into the dance, Barbie's dad has no problem with that." Luke was smiling at this point.

My dad kept going. "Barbie's dad understands that when Barbie and Ken go to a school dance, they are going to have to put their arms around each other. Barbie's dad has no problem with that." Luke was still smiling.

My dad then took Ken's hands and moved them to Barbie's butt while they were dancing. My dad looked at Luke and said, "Barbie's dad should never hear that Ken touches Barbie like that!" My dad then placed Barbie gently on the table, grabbed the Ken doll, ripped his poor head off, and threw it across the room. I thought I was going to die. I was so embarrassed! Luke turned bright red, and did not even hold my hand until we had dated for a year. But through it all I knew my dad cared about my purity and cared about the guys I dated. He also sent the message loud and clear to the guys I dated that my purity is a precious gift, and they had better treat me respectfully. Or else!

Not every father could pull that stunt off. Fortunately, my dad could. Even if the father of the girl you are dating doesn't speak directly to you about it, you need to know that a girl's purity is of great worth and value. That is especially true in God's eyes, and it is not something you can take lightly.

So many girls have given themselves physically to a guy and are now regretting it. I am not just talking about having sex with them. If you do anything inappropriate with her, it will affect her deeply. When we trust you enough to give our bodies to you, you'd better believe it will hurt us if you walk away!

Young women are such emotional beings. It is so important that we know we are loved. When you take advantage of those feelings, you have no idea what this does to a girl. When a girl gives herself physically to a guy, she starts to question her relationship with God, her looks, her sense of belonging, and even her self-worth. Young women put so much into the young men they are dating. They want it to work out for the best, and when it doesn't they are crushed. We analyze the whole thing; we play it out in our minds, every conversation and every look. We even begin to wonder if there is something wrong with us.

As the man in the relationship, please take a girl's purity seriously. Lead your relationship with integrity. Not every relationship was made to work out, but if you walk away leaving a girl with the regret of giving herself to you, she will be devastated. I am assuming if you are dating someone, you care about them. Care enough for her that if you have to walk away for some reason, you can do that without any regrets.

Don't ever use a girl just to fool around with. If you choose to do this, you will never receive any respect. I have never met a girl who says, "Erin, I wish I could just meet a nice guy who would use my body and walk away. I would love to just have a one-night play date, no worry of intimacy or connection. Why is this kind of guy so hard to find?" NO WAY.

A girl should be closer to Jesus Christ and have a better self-image because she went out with you.

I hear just the opposite. They say to me, "Erin, why is it that all the guys I meet just want to use me for my body? Why can't I just meet a nice, godly man who loves me for my heart?" Girls want and need you to love them and treat them well. As a guy, you know when you are crossing the line with us. Don't go there! Please, train yourself to think about girls in a healthy way.

The flip side of treating us with purity is awesome. It means your dating relationship will be healthy, rewarding, and most importantly, God-honoring. God will bless you if you lead your relationship with a girl in a pure way. He can't help but honor you when you honor Him. You will also respect yourself, and the girl you are dating will too. She will trust you and be even more excited to date you. You will get to know each other on so many great levels and will have the ability to develop a relationship that means something.

JUST ONE MORE THING

I want you to remember that every girl is an individual and totally unique. God created her with passions, desires, interests, and a personality that only belongs to her. Whether you are dating one girl seriously, or you have a lot of girlfriends, you need to remember that.

God created you to be an individual too. If you are confident in who God created you to be, and are comfortable with it, the right girl will notice you at the right time. God has given you gifts and passions He wants you to use for His glory. God has a blueprint for what your life is going to look like. God will allow the right girl to walk in your life at the right time. When she does, pursue her with abandon. Learn to love her in a pure way. Buy her a rose. Follow through on what you tell her you will do. Always be honest with her. Pull out her chair. And *always* remember to see her for who God created her to be.

Questions to ask yourself:

1. Are you being a gentleman?
2. Do you love the girls you are with or merely lust after them?
3. Can girls trust you?

15

But I've Already
Gone Too Far

(YOUR OPTIONS)

*"If most of the people around me knew what I've been
into, they would just be appalled."*

Do you realize that at this very moment some of you are being robbed?

If you came home from a trip to find someone walking out with your TV, how would you react? Would you say, "Hey—channels three and four don't work too good, but five comes in real well. OK, enjoy the TV set." No way! You would stop him.

If somebody reached into your pocket to steal your wallet, what would you do? Would you say, "Hey, that's the wrong pocket. It's over in this one. There you go. The credit cards aren't any good, but there is plenty of cash. Good-bye." You'd probably stop him, am I right?

Well, some of you are being robbed of the joy, vitality, and abundance that are yours in Jesus Christ.

Now you may ask, "Who's doing the robbing?" In John 10:10 Jesus says, "I have come that they may have life, and have it to the full." Jesus Christ desires that we experience a full life. It is Satan who seeks to rob us of our joy.

"Why does he want to rob us of our joy?" you might ask. Because what kind of witnesses do we make for Jesus Christ if we approach the world like this: "Hi, I'm a Christian, and I want you to know that it's really depressing. There are so many problems, so many hurts, so many trials. Boy, I can't wait till I die. It would be great to just be dead! Oh, by the way, would you like to become a Christian?"

And what does the world say? "No, thanks. I've got enough problems. I don't need this too."

And finally, you might ask, "How does he rob us of our joy?" I believe one of Satan's most successful tactics is persuading us to zero in on our failures. He helps us focus on how we daily fall short of what we should be. He knows when we dwell on our failures, our view of ourselves and our view of God are drastically affected. We begin to see Him as One who is disappointed in us and can't help but reject us because of our sin.

We've been trained to think this way by the world. If you make a mistake on the job, you expect your boss to be displeased with you. If you make a mistake in the classroom, you expect a disapproving glare from your teacher. If you blunder socially, you expect to be rejected. Because of our experience in the world, we think that God must work the same way. He must reject us when we sin. Right? Wrong. That's not true at all! It's time we see sin, failure, and guilt from God's perspective, not the world's.

In Colossians 1:22 we read, "But now he has reconciled you by Christ's physical body through death to present you holy in his sight, without blemish and free from accusation."

We are deeply and unconditionally loved by Jesus Christ.

When do you become holy, blameless, and beyond reproach? The minute you accept Jesus Christ as Savior and Lord of your life. The price Jesus Christ paid for you on the cross cleanses you from all sin.

We blow it, sin, fall down, and make all kinds of mistakes—we are really good at messing up. But our acceptance by God is not based on how well or how poorly we do. Rather, we are in Christ, and since God accepts Him perfectly, we too are accepted perfectly.

You need to acknowledge the sins you commit, but there is no need to let them bind you, control you, totally take you out of service. Let me give you a silly illustration.

You have just been shopping at the mall. Walking across the parking lot to your car, you trip and fall flat on your face! How do you react? Do you just lie there and say, "Forget it. If I can't walk across the parking lot without falling down, then I quit!" Cars back out and leave, running over you in the process, but there you lie through winter, spring, summer, and fall. You finally shrivel up, and someone comes along and shovels you into a Dumpster.

You should be saying, "Greg, that's the stupidest thing I have ever heard! If someone falls down in the parking lot, he gets back up." You are absolutely right. Not only would the person get up; he'd probably get up fast to make sure nobody saw him.

Some of you have been to retreats, spiritual-emphasis weeks, on mission trips, and gotten all fired up. You've said, "This time I'm going to be God's man, God's woman. I'm going to follow Him and really allow Him to make a difference in my life." But what happened? You went home and sinned again, right?

You did the very things you promised God you would never do again. And how did you react? Some of you said, "Forget it. If I can't be a perfect, godly man or woman, then I quit!" Now how stupid is that? When you fall, get back up. Believe 1 John 1:9: "If we confess our sins, he is faithful and just and will forgive us our sins and purify us from all unrighteousness." Confess, focus your attention back on the person of Jesus Christ, and keep going.

I am tired of walking down the road of life and having to step over my brothers and sisters who have fallen down on the way and have given up. I don't care what your past has been. It's time to get up. Get up! Get up! Don't just lie there anymore—you look ridiculous.

I remember an experience from my college days. In the spring, some of the not-so-smooth guys would pick a patch of lawn and turn it into a mudhole. Then these guys would grab some unsuspecting woman on her way to class, carry her over to that mudhole, and drop her in.

I never, ever saw a woman hit that mud and lie in it, saying, "I just love mud." As a matter of fact, they would all immediately crawl out, fighting, scratching, biting, doing whatever was necessary to get out. Nobody ever just sat there in the mud, except on one occasion.

The guys dropped a certain young lady in the mudhole. She tried to get out, but her boyfriend (after this experience, her ex-boyfriend) pushed her back in. She tried to get out a second time, and he pushed her back in. She started to get up a third time, and a guy dumped a wastebasket full of mud over her head. At that point she sat back down in the mudhole and did not move for quite awhile.

This story pretty accurately describes our experience with sin. At first, when we have a good relationship with Jesus Christ, we react to sin in the same way we would to that mudhole. We fight; we do whatever we can to get out. But if we allow Satan to push us back in and keep pushing us back in, we can eventually sink back into that sin hole and give up. We say to ourselves, "Oh, well, I've already gone this far; it doesn't matter anymore." We give up on ourselves, and we give up on God.

We've got to get out of the mud. We've got to get back on our feet. We've got to allow Christ to forgive us. We've got to step out and be a servant for Him. We are created to live in million-dollar mansions, but most of us are wallowing with the pigs.

"Wait a second, Greg. You don't understand what I have been involved in. We're not talking about little tiny sins. I mean, I have done some really despicable things. I've been incredibly immoral. If most of the people around me knew what I've been into, they would just be appalled. You mean to tell me that God can forgive me?"

And I say to you, "Absolutely! Without a doubt! Yes!" How do I know that? I know it for two good reasons.

➤ Number one, God has done it for me.

There are things I have done in my past that have been terrible, but Christ's forgiveness is complete. Even though I fail miserably, He forgives me totally.

➤ Number two, He's done it for a famous Bible character.

Remember King David? Do you know what God said of King David? "There is a man after My own heart!" (See 1 Samuel 13:14.) God dearly loved David. Imagine Jesus Christ appearing in your youth group and picking out one of the guys and saying, "There is a man after My own heart." All of us would be amazed and think, *That must be someone special.* And David was someone very, very special. But did David know anything about sin? Oh, a little.

We are going to take a close look at this man after God's own heart. We'll learn from his mistakes so that we don't have to do the same thing and find out what happened in the end. We will start in 2 Samuel 11:1–27 and notice how David adds one sin on top of the other.

"In the spring, at the time when kings go off to war, David sent Joab out with the king's men and the whole Israelite army. They destroyed the Ammonites and besieged Rabbah. But David remained in Jerusalem" (verse 1).

This is a time when kings go off to war and where is David? He is still back in Jerusalem. He may have a lot of great reasons, but I want to suggest that we get ourselves in trouble when we don't do what we are supposed to do and don't go where we are supposed to go. David would not have faced what he is about to face if he had been on the battlefield where he belonged.

"One evening David got up from his bed and walked around on the roof of the palace. From the roof he saw a woman bathing. The woman was very beautiful" (verse 2).

For some reason David can't sleep, so he decides to wander on the roof of the palace. He sees a woman taking a bath and he looks at her long enough to figure out she is very beautiful. He finds himself attracted to this woman and probably is lusting, since she is naked. Does this man after God's own heart walk away, make himself accountable, and make some kind of law about bathing inside? Nope. He stood there, watched the woman take a bath, and said to himself, *Self, I'd like to get to know that woman a whole lot better.*

"And David sent someone to find out about her. The man said, 'Isn't this Bathsheba, the daughter of Eliam and the wife of Uriah the Hittite?'" (verse 3).

David finds out this woman is married. Surely this man after God's own heart will back off and forget about her. Have you ever seen or met someone you just can't forget? You are so attracted to him or her that you end up doing or saying something stupid? That is where David is right now. He is very turned on by this woman.

There were probably danger bells going off in his head at this point. He needed to get some wise counsel and avoid this woman. He was the king of Israel so he knew the law. He knew it was forbidden to sleep with another man's wife. He was burning with passion, but he could have done something about those sexual feelings and desires. All he would have had to do is call for one of his wives, and he could have satisfied his sexual desire. But he believed that what he didn't have was better than what he did have. He is about to make the biggest mistake of his life, and it would cost him big-time. Are you about to make some huge mistake? Learn from David and turn from it.

Do you think this could be part of Satan's plan to set David up to fail? How is Satan planning to set you up to fail?

"*Then David sent messengers to get her. She came to him, and he slept with her. (She had purified herself from her uncleanness.) Then she went back home*" (verse 4).

We are tempted to scream, "You idiot!" But aren't we doing some of the same stuff? Let's recap how David got himself in this mess.

➤ He wasn't where he was supposed to be, so he ended up where he shouldn't have been.
➤ He looked at a naked woman and desired her.
➤ He didn't make himself accountable or seek any wise counsel.
➤ He didn't care that she was married.
➤ He ignored God's law, which he knew and understood.
➤ He didn't seek sexual fulfillment from his own wife.

Don't even try to blame this on Bathsheba. Back in those days, if the king wanted to see you, you went! You didn't make excuses and say, "You know, I'd love to come, but I've got a cake in the oven. I just can't." You went! So she was obedient.

Now he takes her and they have sex. The passion has outweighed everything in his mind. Nothing matters except having sex with this woman. Our feelings can and often do lead us in the opposite direction of where we should be going. The quick affair is over and she is home. Everything can get back to normal and no one knows what happened. David is in the clear, right?

"The woman conceived and sent word to David, saying 'I am pregnant'" (verse 5).

Oops, Houston, we have a problem. How long did it take back then for a woman to realize she was pregnant? It would have taken weeks, and David had probably moved on with his life. But all of a sudden his sin comes crashing down on his head. Even if she wasn't pregnant, God still knew of his sin. David was deceived in thinking he had gotten away with something. If you think you are getting away with your sin, then you are deceived.

"So David sent this word to Joab: 'Send me Uriah the Hittite.' And Joab sent him to David" (verse 6).

Does this man after God's own heart confess his sin? No, he calls for her husband to come back from the battlefield and wants to get him to have sexual intercourse with his wife so they could blame the pregnancy on him. David is going to let them sleep together, blame the pregnancy on him, and then just walk away? What kind of a man allows the woman to bear all the burden of the sin? She would have to live with the knowledge that this wasn't her husband's child and constantly be reminded of her sin with David. Men, if you have gotten a woman pregnant, it is not her responsibility to bear alone; you need to step up and take responsibility. It will cost you money, time, commitment, and a lot of hard work. If you're not ready to step up to the plate, then don't play the game.

At this point all David is doing is thinking about his own interests. He doesn't care about anyone but himself. Sin can do these things even to a man after God's own heart. Sin will make you self-centered and selfish. You can read about everything he does in verses

7–13. David never counted on the fact that Uriah was a man of character. He is the hero in this whole story. He chooses to do what was right even in the face of the king. He refused to enjoy the pleasures of his wife while his friends were suffering on the battlefield.

"In the morning David wrote a letter to Joab and sent it with Uriah. In it he wrote, 'Put Uriah in the front line where the fighting is fiercest. Then withdraw from him so he will be struck down and die'" (verses 14–15).

Sin will sear your conscience and destroy your character. How can a man after God's own heart sentence an innocent man to death? Because David allowed sin to own him, he lost perspective of right versus wrong. He had rationalized the whole thing in his mind.

Uriah loved God and he loved David, but he had a beautiful wife who was pregnant with someone else's child and he is about to die. Does this make you mad? It makes me furious. Are you beginning to understand why God hates sin so much? Sin is sick, disgusting, perverted, and has the power to destroy even the most committed people. Flee from sin and avoid it at all costs. To check what happens next read verses 16–23.

A messenger is sent to David to tell him what happened. Here is the end of his report and David's response. *"'Then the archers shot arrows at your servants from the wall, and some of the king's men died. Moreover, your servant Uriah the Hittite is dead.' David told the messenger, 'Say this to Joab: "Don't let this upset you; the sword devours one as well as another. Press the attack against the city and destroy it." Say this to encourage Joab.'"* (verses 24–25).

David wants to encourage Joab? Are you kidding me? What a total hypocrite. He sounds so understanding and kind, but he just had a man murdered. He needed to show kindness to Bathsheba, he needed to show kindness to Uriah, and he needed to show respect toward God. But instead he shows Joab kindness because he made sure that an innocent man was killed.

"When Uriah's wife heard that her husband was dead, she mourned for him. After the time of mourning was over, David had her brought to

his house, and she became his wife and bore him a son. But the thing David had done displeased the LORD" (verses 26–27).

It was all better now. Uriah was dead and David married the pregnant woman. All would be forgotten in time, right? No, Bathsheba would never forget, God doesn't forget, and David is about to learn that he will never forget. You never get away with your sin; God hates it. Read the last part of verse twenty-seven again. Those are ominous and scary words. "But the thing David had done displeased the LORD." What are you doing, does it displease the Lord, and do you think you are getting away with it?

Nathan, the prophet, confronts David in a very creative way and traps him in his sin in 2 Samuel 12:1–10. David breaks down and confesses his sin, but there are terrible consequences to David's sin.

The child of Bathsheba and David becomes sick and dies.

David's son Amnon rapes David's daughter, Amnon's half sister, Tamar.

David's son Absalom kills Amnon for what he did to Tamar.

Absalom fights against David for the kingdom and has sex with David's wives.

All of this was the result of one night of passion. Do you think David thought it was worth it? Do you think if he could do it over again he would do the same thing? Next time you are tempted to get involved sexually, remember the consequences are not worth whatever pleasure you will gain from this person. If you refuse to turn from your sexual sin, be warned by these verses.

Your hormones will lead you in the wrong direction. Instead you must know the truth, live the truth, and the truth will set you free.

First Corinthians 6:9–10 says, "Do you not know that the wicked will not inherit the kingdom of God? Do not be deceived: Neither the sexually immoral nor idolaters nor adulterers nor male prostitutes nor homosexual offenders nor thieves nor the greedy nor drunkards nor slanderers nor swindlers will inherit the kingdom of God."

Ephesians 5:5–6 warns, "For of this you can be sure: No immoral, impure or greedy person-such a man is an idolater—has any inheritance in the kingdom of Christ and of God. Let no one deceive you with empty words, for because of such things God's wrath comes on those who are disobedient."

Revelation 21:8 says, "But the cowardly, the unbelieving, the vile, the murderers, the sexually immoral, those who practice magic arts, the idolaters and all liars—their place will be in the fiery lake of burning sulfur. This is the second death."

This is serious and it's a warning for those who refuse to repent and turn from their sins. Everyone who has committed one or more of the above sins can and will be forgiven if they turn to Jesus Christ and ask for His forgiveness.

With David, notice how one lie led to another lie, and one sin led to another sin. That's what happens to us, isn't it? We commit a sin, and try to cover it by telling a lie, which causes us to commit another sin, which means we have to cover our tracks in that area, which causes us to sin again. On and on and on we go until finally we come to repentance.

How much easier it would have been on David, and how much easier it would be on you and me, if we would just admit our sin and repent at the very beginning instead of having to go through the whole miserable process.

Did David spend the rest of his life out of fellowship with God? Listen to what Nathan says to David in 2 Samuel 12:13. "Then David said to Nathan, 'I have sinned against the LORD.' Nathan replied, 'The LORD has taken away your sin. You are not going to die.'"

In spite of David's gross sins, He found forgiveness. Remember that the consequences of David's sin followed him for the rest of his life, but God forgave him of his sins. What sin have you committed that God cannot or will not forgive? Psalm 130:3–4 says this: "If you, O LORD, kept a record of sins, O Lord, who could stand? But with you there is forgiveness; therefore you are feared."

Jesus Christ took upon Himself all of your sins and my sins. He was willing to die upon a cross so we could be made right with God. His body was broken so we could be made whole.

"God made him who had no sin to be sin for us" (2 Corinthians 5:21).

Too many of us try to die for our own sins. When we make mistakes or fail, we think by punishing ourselves we will somehow become worthy of Christ's forgiveness.

Understand this: when you try to punish yourself and attempt to pay for your own sin, you really make a mockery of Christ's death. What you are saying is that Christ's death on the cross is really not sufficient to take care of your sins. You are adding something to it. That is sheer folly and one of Satan's most vicious lies.

The price Christ paid for you on that cross is completely sufficient! Nothing needs to be added to it. You can't be good enough to achieve God's acceptance. You can't earn it; you just need to receive it.

We think the issue is whether or not God will forgive us. But that's not the issue at all. The issue is whether or not we will accept His forgiveness and trust Him for the strength and courage to stop sinning.

Jesus Christ has called us to repent of our sins, and repentance does not mean, "O God, forgive me so I can go ahead and do it again Friday night." Repentance is being truly sorry for what we've done, agreeing with God that it's wrong, asking Him for the power to live as He has called us to live, and turning from the pattern of sin.

How did Jesus Christ deal with the woman who was caught in adultery? He said to her, "I don't condemn you. I've come to set you free." But at the same time He didn't say to her, "Now go on back to your adulterous relationship." He said just the opposite. "Go now, and leave your life of sin."

That is what Jesus is saying to us: "I died to set you free. Now go, and leave your life of sin. I've got so many better things in store for you."

Please don't get me wrong. God's forgiveness does not give you license to sin. What I am saying is that in Christ we are free to live, to love Him, and to realize that His love for us is unconditional—it is not dependent upon our good performance. This is difficult to grasp because it is so unlike the way we often forgive each other.

My beautiful, wonderful wife, Bonnie, is from Southern California. Now it doesn't snow a whole lot in Southern California. I married Bonnie and brought her to Rockford, Illinois. On occasion it does snow here.

One winter day shortly after we got married, I came home to discover Bonnie had parked her car on the street. So I drove up the driveway (which was covered by about a quarter of an inch of snow) and into our garage. I went into the house and said, "Hi, honey. How come the car is parked out on the street?"

She said to me, "Well, I was afraid that if I pulled it into the driveway it would get stuck in the snow."

I said to myself, *How cute.* "Listen," I told her, "you don't have to worry. If it snows, just back the car up a little bit, give it some gas, and you'll go right up into the garage."

Some time later Bonnie drove home after our first blizzard. The snow was knee deep in our driveway. Bonnie pulled up to the driveway, looked at it, and said to herself, "Well, Greg said all I have to do is to back the car up, give it some gas, and I'll go right up into the garage."

So my wife backed up our brand-new Honda Civic and gave it a little gas (I take that back—she gave it a lot of gas!). As a matter of fact, she probably got going twenty to twenty-five miles per hour and hit that snowdrift. The now-airborne Honda Civic landed on a snow pile where it teeter-tottered like Noah's ark on Mount Ararat.

I came home that evening and could not believe my eyes. It looked like some giant had grabbed our car and thrown it up onto this snowdrift. And there was Bonnie, snow shovel in hand, digging as fast and as frantically as she could. I got out of the car and said, "What happened?"

Bonnie, half hysterical, said, "Well, you told me all I had to do is back up the car, so I backed up the car and went; and I flew, and I'm there, and I don't know what to do!"

Now, if my love for Bonnie was dependent on the way she acted, I would have said to her, "What is wrong with you? Can't you tell the difference between a quarter-inch of snow and four feet of snow? That's it. It's over. I want a divorce." But even though my wife may do some silly things, I still love her.

Now the only way I could possibly get this book past my wife to get it published is if I also tell a story about myself. I took Bonnie to see the *Nutcracker Suite*. It was close to Christmas and very cold. I waited in line to buy the tickets while she stood in the lobby with all the other women watching their husbands freeze to death.

Well, I finally got my turn. I bought the tickets and stepped in front of the door. Now, understand this lobby is all glass, and there are probably a hundred women staring out in my general direction. I put my money back in my wallet, looked up, and (I have absolutely no idea why I did this) stepped over to the side, and walked full blast into one of the plate-glass windows. I mean, I just smashed my face into this window. All one hundred women immediately broke into laughter, saying to themselves, "That's the biggest bird I have ever seen!"

Now, if my wife's love for me was dependent on the way I acted, I would have walked up to her saying, "Hi, honey," and she would have said, "Who's he calling honey? I've never seen him before." But in spite of the fact that I do silly things, my wife loves me.

And you see, in spite of the fact that you and I fail, sin, and do foolish things, God still loves us. For He loves Christ, and as believers we are "in Christ."

Now an individual may say, "Wow, that's great! That means that I can sin like crazy Monday, Tuesday, Wednesday, Thursday, Friday, and Saturday, and then come back and gain forgiveness on Sunday." If that's your reaction, I would question your relationship with Jesus Christ. Christians have a love relationship with Him. And love says I desire to do whatever is best for that other individual. I don't want to do anything to use or abuse him.

Imagine yourself out on a date with someone who is witty, charming, sophisticated, godly, kind, and incredibly good-looking. Now picture a balmy evening with a full moon. You're walking hand in hand. The person stops, and you turn and gaze at one another. There is a moment of silence, you smile, and your date says, "I love you."

Now what is your reaction to that? Do you say, "Good. From now on I will be rude, crude, ignore you, and act like a slob"? Of course not. Instead, you are so excited to be loved that you want to do everything you possibly can to please that other person.

When God looks at you and says, "I love you," your reaction probably isn't, "Good. From now on I'll ignore You, take You for granted, blaspheme Your name, and spit in Your face"? The Lord God Almighty, Creator of heaven and earth, loves you. That should motivate you to do everything you can to show your love to Him. And then when you do fail, fall, and sin, and confess humbly to God. He says to you: "I understand. I died to forgive it. Get back up and keep on following Me."

Answer these two questions for me. If you read your Bible and pray every day for the next six months, will God love you more at the end of those six months than He loves you now? If you never read your Bible and never pray, will God love you less, at the end of six months than He loves you right now? The answer to both questions is . . . *no!* So people ask me, "Then why read my Bible and pray?" This is what I say. "I don't read my Bible so that God will love me; I read my Bible because I love God. I don't pray so that God will love me; I am already confident in His love for me. I pray because I love God." You have a love relationship with Him, and His love for you isn't performance based. So read your Bible and pray and live for Him not because you have to but because you love Him!

You have to decide if you will love Jesus. This is nothing your parents or youth pastor can decide for you. It has to be your choice. Will you love Jesus with all your heart, mind, soul, and strength?

Some of you are like prodigal sons and daughters. You've left the Father, and you're wandering on your own. You've been involved in the sin, garbage, and filth of the world. Jesus Christ took care of all your sins at the cross. Your heavenly Father's waiting, and His arms are wide open. It's time you came home. Confess that sin. Turn your back on it. Allow God to wipe it out of your life. He'd like to make you squeaky clean on the inside. Isaiah 43:25—get a Bible and read that verse. Not only are you forgiven, but God doesn't even remember your sins—not because He is stupid or senile, but because He chooses to forget. That's how free you are!

It is also important that you are willing to apologize to and grant forgiveness to the person you were sexually involved with. Not only did you hurt yourself, but you hurt someone else as well. They might not realize this hurt them, but it has made an impact on them and their future spouse.

You are free to forgive them because Jesus Christ has forgiven you. That is, as long as you know Jesus Christ as your Friend, Savior, and God. Do you know Him personally? If you aren't sure, you can check out chapter 17.

Questions to ask yourself:
1. Do you have a clear conscience before God? Do you need to seek His forgiveness?
2. Have you ever thought of the possible consequences of your sin?
3. Do you spend time with Jesus because you have to or because you love Him?

16

Purity

(HOW TO GAIN IT/HOW TO MAINTAIN IT)

Give your body to God right now.

How can I maintain purity? How can I start over again? These are the kinds of questions I love to hear.

Christ says we are to honor Him with our bodies. "Do you not know that your body is a temple of the Holy Spirit, who is in you, whom you have received from God? You are not your own; you were bought at a price. Therefore honor God with your body" (1 Corinthians 6:19–20). What are some steps we can take to be sure this will happen?

STEP 1

If you have already gone too far, then you need to come to Jesus Christ and gain forgiveness. It's so important that you come to Him, agree that what you've done is wrong, and desire to honor Him with your body. God desires to separate us from our sins. Psalm 103:12 says, "As far as the east is from the west, so far has he removed our transgressions from us." The wonderful thing about being a Christian is that it's never too late.

Jesus doesn't just see things the way they are. He sees what they can be. No matter what your sin or failure, try to see what you could be if you decided to commit your life to Jesus Christ.

Up to this point you may have been incredibly immoral. You

may have slept with fifty different individuals. But Jesus Christ would like to do something beautiful in and through your life. He sees a diamond, and He wants to make you into a special, godly individual. What's the beginning step, then? Come to Christ on your knees, and repent of your sin.

"If we confess our sins, he is faithful and just and will forgive us our sins and purify us from all unrighteousness" (1 John 1:9).

Secondary virginity is your commitment to Jesus Christ to live a life of purity, and honor Him with your body.

Take upon yourselves secondary virginity. It is a very real thing because you are saying, "Starting now, I will honor God with my body, respect myself, and respect members of the opposite sex." You can start all over again. Honor God now so that He can bless you in the future and one day give you a wonderful and exciting sexual relationship in your marriage.

STEP 2

You need to go to your partner or partners and apologize.

Say how sorry you are that you compromised your relationship with Jesus Christ—that you dishonored Him by your sexual relationship. Say you're sorry for the bad example you have been and that you desire to be different in the future.

Then, you need to apologize for defrauding this other person. God created sex to be shared in a marriage relationship, and you have taken it out of where it belongs. In a dating relationship, sex causes far more damage than it does good. It is probable that because of your sexual relationships you have left scars on other individuals that will last a lifetime. So you need to apologize for any harm you have done.

STEP 3

If you are going to continue a relationship with that individual, then both of you need to agree to stop the sexual involvement. It is absolutely critical that you both recognize the sexual involvement you have had is wrong, and you both must desire to stop it.

If one says it is wrong and the other says it is OK, the relationship will never ever work. Nine times out of ten, the person who has no qualms about sex outside marriage will pull the other individual back down to where they came from.

But let me be up front with you. Once you have tasted of the fruit it is very difficult to maintain sexual purity. Before experiencing sex, you fantasize about what it might be like, but once you have begun to do it, it is no longer fantasy. When you try to stop, all those memories come flooding back at different times. You both must agree you need to stop. Otherwise, as a Christian, you have to break off the relationship.

It boils down to whom you love more. Do you desire to please God or man?

Look at Galatians 1:10. "Am I now trying to win the approval of men, or of God? Or am I trying to please men? If I were still trying to please men, I would not be a servant of Christ."

In this situation you cannot do both! Yes, it will be hard. Yes, there will be tears. But I guarantee in the long run you will be much better off. And God will bless you because of your courage and convictions.

STEP 4

If you decide to maintain your relationship, or if you are just beginning a relationship with someone else, it's important that you have talked to your parents and have set your standards ahead of time. Then sit down together and set standards as a couple. Never lower your standards for someone else. Once a dating relationship begins to get serious, it is healthy to agree on what is proper and what is improper with regard to physical affection. Make clear to each other that love does not use or abuse the one loved, and that you will not go beyond what the set standards are.

If you continue to have sex, break off the relationship. Why? Because you really are not loving one another—you are just lusting. I'm sure your initial reaction to that counsel is, "Oh, he's really being too hard here." You're right—I am! I think it's time somebody was.

It's time you said, "God, I love You so much that I don't want to hurt or disgrace You."

STEP 5

Make sure God is number one in your life. Matthew 6:33 says, "But seek first his kingdom and his righteousness, and all these things will be given to you as well."

Seek God first, and He'll take care of your relationships with the opposite sex. When God is number one and you find you aren't dating, instead of getting depressed perhaps you ought to sit back and do a little evaluating. Perhaps you are not dating because you are not ready to date.

If God brought a member of the opposite sex into your life at this point, maybe you would get involved physically, get your priorities messed up, have problems with your family—all because you have not matured spiritually. Make Jesus Christ number one, seek to be a God-pleaser, and He will take care of the rest.

Nothing is more important than your relationship with Jesus Christ — including someone you might be dating.

Communicate your desires to God. Tell Him, "Lord, I want You to become number one in my life. I want to love You more than a boyfriend, girlfriend, anyone, or anything." That commitment must then show itself through your actions.

STEP 6

Spend time in the Word and in prayer daily. If you want to have a healthy relationship with the Lord, you must work at it. If you're going to be any good at football, you must practice. If you're going to be any good musically, you must work at it. If you're going to have a life-changing relationship with Jesus Christ, it's going to take some effort on your part.

Listen to Proverbs 7:1–3, 5: "My son, keep my words and store up my commands within you. Keep my commands and you will live; guard my teachings as the apple of your eye. Bind them on your fingers; write them on the tablet of your heart. . . . They will keep you from the adulteress, from the wayward wife with her seductive words."

Being in the Word and in prayer will give you strength and sense to resist the temptations you're going to face.

I would suggest that, *once you've been dating for a while*, you spend time as a couple in the Word and in prayer.

I don't recommend praying on the first date. Let me set the stage for you. When you see or think about the other person, you get those warm fuzzies. Now you're on your first date. He suggests starting the date with prayer (sigh—how wonderful!). You pray together. And feel really good. Then you open your eyes and you look at one another. Do you hear the music building? You take those good feelings God has given you, and you shoot them toward each other instead of back to the Lord.

This experience can cause you to feel a lot closer, more emotionally involved with that individual, than you really ought to be.

So I suggest that you pray and read your Bible before your date. Prepare yourself spiritually for the date just as you prepare physically. Then, after you have dated awhile and know that person better, it's great to study the Bible and pray together. Just be sure you transfer those warm feelings the Lord gives you back to Him, not to each other.

STEP 7

Something that few teenagers do, but one that is crucial to withstanding temptation, is to memorize Scripture.

See Psalm 119:9–11: "How can a young man keep his way pure? By living according to your word. I seek you with all my heart; do not let me stray from your commands. I have hidden your word in my heart that I might not sin against you."

Are you really interested in having Jesus Christ radically transform you? If you are, then let me challenge you to memorize Scripture. When you get into really tough situations, the Holy Spirit is there and wants to encourage you. One way He can encourage you is by bringing verses to mind. However, He can't very well bring to mind verses you don't know. Memorizing Scripture will make a big difference in your life.

STEP 8

Be an example as a couple. We desperately need dating couples who are examples of what it means to love Jesus Christ and each other, couples who are morally pure.

Philippians 2:15–16: "Become blameless and pure, children of God without fault in a crooked and depraved generation, in which you shine like stars in the universe as you hold out the word of life." Jesus Christ would like to make you shine like stars in the universe! As you humble yourself before Him, He would like to display you before men and say, "Look, here are My children. See how they love Me? Be like them."

James 4:10 says, "Humble yourselves before the Lord, and He will lift you up."

Seek out ways in which the two of you can serve Christ and other people. What might you do together to be involved in service? Ask your youth pastor for suggestions. Just because you are dating does not mean you stop serving. Perhaps the best witness you could have as a couple is to be an example of moral purity for your unsaved friends.

STEP 9

Obey your parents. God works directly through parents, and your response to them is your response to God. I believe God will give your parents special insight into the individuals you are dating. You need to seek their advice. If you listen and heed their words, you will save yourself a lot of hurt.

Just in case you don't think you need to be obedient, let me list a few verses you can look up on your own: Ephesians 6:1; Colossians 3:20; Exodus 20:12; Luke 2:51.

It is important that you encourage the person you are dating to develop a good relationship with his or her parents also. Because of you, that guy or girl you are dating ought to be getting closer to his or her parents, not further away.

Develop a positive relationship with your parents. One of the key ingredients is communication. Talk with them. Listen to them. Work on your relationship with them.

Spend time as a couple with your parents. That means including them as part of your date sometimes. Perhaps you could all go out to dinner together, or to a ball game. You could go back to the house and spend some time with them. Most young people discover as they get older that parents really do make great friends. Why not develop that friendship now?

I know I am probably going to sound old-fashioned here, but, ladies, you need to be under the authority of your fathers. I believe that if a gentleman would like to take you out on date, he ought to check with your father. Now your initial reaction to that might be, "That is the stupidest thing I have ever heard!" But believe me, in the long run there is great benefit to you. Here are several reasons.

➤ You will discover whether a guy is really interested in you or not.

If you require him to check with your father first, you are going to be able to quickly distinguish between those who may only be interested in your body and those who are really interested in you as a person.

➤ It really takes the pressure off of you to make snap decisions.

There you are at your locker, reaching to get your books and run to the next class. All of a sudden you turn around, and there is Brett standing right there, and he asks, "Would you like to go out this Friday night?"

Instead of hemming and hawing under pressure because you've got to get to class, you say to Brett, "Thank you very much. I really appreciate it—but first you need to talk with my father."

Give him the number he can call. In the meantime you can chat with your father, and both of you can come to some decision about Brett. If you would really rather not date him at all, your father is a good one to protect you in that area.

➤ It shows the guy that your father cares about you a lot.

And if guys know your father is that concerned about you, it will gain you far more respect.

STEP 10

It's important to have your date planned. What typically happens is that you don't have to be in until midnight, so you go to a ball game, then out to eat, and it's still only 10:30. Oops! You've run out of things to do! When you have an hour and a half with nothing to do, it's very easy to get involved physically, right? Instead, make sure that you have the date fully planned, but if you do run out of things to do, choose one of these two options:

➤ End the date.

Say good night, and each of you go back to your respective homes.

➤ Or be alone in a crowd.

Go to some fast-food restaurant or coffee shop, buy a Coke or cup of coffee, go to a back booth, and talk. It gives you the opportunity of talking one-on-one without the temptations that accompany being totally alone.

STEP 11

Don't set yourself up to fail. Many couples say they want to be different. They want to do what's right. They want to be pure, but they put themselves in situations where they can't succeed. You just can't spend hours and hours and hours alone with a guy or girl you are very much attracted to and not expect to have temptation.

Here is what happens. You've got an hour or so before you have to be in, so you say to your date, "Hey, let's pull the car over on this dark road, and we'll just sit here and talk." Well, it sounds like a good idea, and you do talk—for about five minutes. Then you begin to kiss and touch, and soon you are exactly where you set out not to be.

Or you say, "Hey, come on over to the house. My parents are gone, and we have a chance to be alone." Then a favorite suggestion is: "Let's just lie here on the couch together, and we'll watch TV." Stay away from situations where it is so easy to fall.

STEP 12

Beware of dating someone with low moral standards.

"Do not be misled: 'Bad company corrupts good character'" (1 Corinthians 15:33).

It's true that bad company corrupts good character. If you date someone who has low moral standards, chances are he is going to pull you down, rather than your pulling him up. Don't settle for anything less than a godly man or woman. You have trusted Jesus Christ with your eternity; so you can trust Him with your dating relationships. If you will be patient, God will supply!

STEP 13

Why don't you consider a creative alternative to dating . . . friendship? A friendship will give you everything a dating relationship will give you without the pressure to get involved sexually. Boy and girlfriends come and go but a friend will last a life time. You have plenty of time to date and the dates you have in high school are typically not the relationships that are going to last. So have fun in high school, make a lot of good friends with the opposite sex, and wait tell you get older to date.

STEP 14

Don't lose your Christian friends. Too often when we start dating, we develop tunnel vision and blow off the rest of our friends. Don't do that! Balance your time with your friends and the person you are dating. *Listen* to your Christian friends as well. They can see your relationship much more objectively than you can. If they say to you, "This person's a loser," then listen to them. Don't argue. They are your friends, and my guess is that most of the time they are absolutely right.

Remember, you are not the only person struggling with purity maintenance. Hang out with and date people who have the same standards. You know where to look. It doesn't take that long to find out the intentions of a member of the opposite sex.

You'll want to be part of a gracious church where people believe you can repent and change and start over again. Consequences and mourning are real, but you are cleansed from your sins by Jesus' shed blood. God can give you the strength to live purely.

You say to me, "Oh, Greg, can I really change? Do you know of anybody who has ever had victory in this area?"

I would say to you, "Absolutely." Let me close this book by sharing with you a very special letter.

Dear Greg,

Thank you for your talk on dating and sex. Because of this, my girlfriend and I have stopped the physical stuff in time. Praise the Lord, because it is by His power that we can be self-controlled.

It's very hard, because it's not a question of what can I get away with. It's a question of how can I express my love to her in a deeper way. I'm so thankful and full of joy because of your sharing with me from God's Word how to express true love. "I want" doesn't cut it.

She is a very special girl, a true woman of God, and I do love her very much. Selfish fulfillment was tearing us apart from within. But now we have reestablished our priorities and standards. It's not easy. We still desire—for lack of a better word—each other very much, but we now have strength and power by virtue of the Holy Spirit. We will wait until that very special day when we are joined together in perfect union through our Lord Jesus Christ.

I know it won't get any easier, but there is power in prayer, and we love praying to our Father together. I am a weak man, but I have a strong God who lives in me. All praise and glory to the Father through His Son Jesus Christ for now and forevermore. Amen.

Give your body to God right now. Say, "Lord, by Your grace and strength I want to glorify You with my body." It's never too late, no matter how far you've gone.

If you have questions, comments, or needs, you can e-mail me. I promise I'll get back to you. My e-mail address is gregospeck@gmail.com

Don't settle for anything less than God's best. Wait! Why? Because sex is worth waiting for!

Questions to ask yourself:
1. Are you seeking to be sexually pure?
2. When you read the steps, what do you need to do next?
3. Are you allowing your parents to keep you accountable?

17

Life That's Worth Living

(HOW TO BELONG TO JESUS CHRIST)

A Christian is someone who has received Christ into his life.

Someone may have shoved this book into your hand and said, "Read it!" You find all this Bible and God stuff kind of strange. You know something about God, but you have never met Him personally. I would love the privilege of introducing you to my Savior, Lord, and Best Friend.

But before you can come to Jesus Christ, there are four things you need to understand.

➤ God loves you.

The Bible says, "For God so loved the world that he gave his one and only Son, that whoever believes in him shall not perish but have eternal life" (John 3:16).

Understand that God loves you more than anyone has ever loved you in your whole life. He loves you unconditionally— you don't have to be "good enough" to be loved by God. He offers you life now and forever as a free gift.

God's love for you is a gift you can't earn. You just accept it.

➤ But there is a problem.

You're aware of the problem—you have sinned. Again, the Bible says, "All have sinned and fall short of the glory of God" (Romans 3:23).

Sin is disobedience to God, and I know you are aware of your sins. I didn't get to know Christ until I was a senior in high school. But no one had to tell me I was a sinner. I knew that better than anyone else. Sin separates you from God. So what do we do?

➤ The great news is that Jesus Christ died for all of our sins.

"But God demonstrates his own love for us in this: While we were still sinners, Christ died for us" (Romans 5:8).

God saw that you were separated from Him so He sent Jesus Christ, who lived and walked this earth. They took Jesus and crucified Him. There on the cross He took your sins and mine, and He died for them. He was buried and three days later He rose from the dead, but your sins stayed buried. Because Jesus lives, you can be forgiven and have a brand-new beginning.

Christ was willing to hang on a cross for you and me so our sins could be forgiven. Jesus Christ allowed His body to be broken so that we could become whole! He has made a way for us to be free of our sins and to have close friendship with Him.

➤ It's not good enough to just understand these things.

We have to make a choice: "Yet to all who received him, to those who believed in his name, he gave the right to become children of God" (John 1:12).

Going to church, being baptized, taking Communion, being confirmed, behaving properly—none of these things makes you a Christian. A Christian is someone who believes that Jesus Christ is who He claimed to be and who has received Him into his life.

How do you do that? You ask Him through prayer. Have you received Christ into your life? If not, you can do it right now. You could pray this prayer:

"Dear Jesus, I know I've made a lot of mistakes. I've made some really poor choices. I've sinned. Thank You for dying for me on the cross. Please forgive me of my sins. Right now I ask You to come into my life. Please take control of my life. Thank You for forgiving my sins. Thank You for loving me so very much. Thank You for coming into my life. And, Jesus, I want You to know that I love You. Amen!"

If you meant that prayer, asking the Lord Jesus Christ into your life, you are now a Christian. E-mail me and let me know of the decision you made, and I will tell you some other important steps that you need to be taking.

And if you and I never, ever meet here on earth, someday we will be in heaven together, forever!

Questions to ask yourself:
1. Have you ever asked Jesus Christ to come into your life?
2. Do you know for sure that you are going to heaven after you die?
3. Why don't you pray right now?

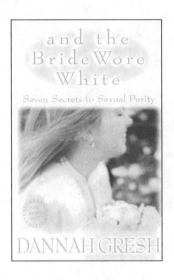

AND THE BRIDE WORE WHITE
Seven Secrets to Sexual Purity
Dannah Gresh
ISBN 0-8024-8344-5
ISBN-13 978-0-8024-8344-7

Dannah exposes our culture's lies about sex and helps prepare young women for the pressures they face in this bestseller for teens. A practical book filled with stories and personal testimonies of hurt, healing, and hope.

BELIEVING GOD FOR HIS BEST
How to Marry Contentment and Singleness
Bill Thrasher
ISBN 0-8024-5573-5
ISBN-13 978-0-8024-5573-4

A warm, wise book about trusting God for something you can't see. With anecdotal style and godly wisdom, the author tells the story of his journey through singleness toward marriage. This book will inspire singles to trust God for His best.

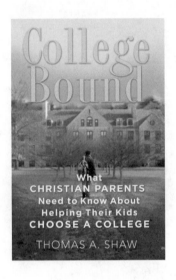

COLLEGE BOUND

What Christian Parents Need to Know About Helping Their Kids Choose a College

Thomas Shaw

ISBN 0-8024-1242-4

ISBN-13 978-0-8024-1242-3

Parents of teens in high school will appreciate this resource as they wade through detailed applications for colleges, financial aid, and admissions procedures. Tom Shaw, a parent and college administrator, helps anxious parents guide their teens to making the best choice for their college experience.